MIDNIGHT FIRE

Just go away, Chase! Go away and leave me alone—"

"What's the matter, Carly? Now that you've enticed a man to your bed, are you afraid?" He shook her again, making her long hair swirl around her face.

Tension stretched like a white-hot current between them, and Chase stared at her, fighting the unbelievable wave of desire that held him against his will. She wet her lips, and his grip on her upper arms tightened. But she didn't cry out or pull away. No longer willing to hold back, he pulled her against him until their mouths nearly touched.

"Damn you, Carly," he muttered hoarsely. Then he gave in to his thundering need, and their lips forged together, burning ... hungry ...

AVON BOOKS ◆ NEW YORK

For
Robert and Molly Ladd
Robert and Michael
and Stephanie Marie

AVON BOOKS
A division of
The Hearst Corporation
105 Madison Avenue
New York, New York 10016

Copyright © 1991 by Linda Ladd
Dragon Fire copyright © 1991 by Linda Ladd
Published by arrangement with the author
Library of Congress Catalog Card Number: 90-93390
ISBN: 0-380-75696-X

First Avon Books Printing: February 1991

AVON TRADEMARK REG. U.S. PAT. OFF. AND IN OTHER COUNTRIES, MARCA REGISTRADA, HECHO EN U.S.A.

Printed in the U.S.A.

RA 10 9 8 7 6 5 4 3 2 1

1

"Forgiveness is the broken dream which hides itself within the corner of the mind oft called forgetfulness, so that it will not bring pain to the dreamer."

—GEORGE ROEMISCH,
"FORGIVENESS"

March 1871
New Orleans, Louisiana

As the shiny black landau rumbled past a twin-galleried stucco house on the corner of Rue Royale, excitement raced through Carlisle Kincaid. Soon she and her three companions would reach the St. Charles Hotel for a gala evening in the ballroom, and she couldn't wait. Arantxa Perez, her friend from the convent school, would be there. Together they'd steal a few moments to discuss plans for Carlisle's visit to Mexico.

To conceal her agitation, Carlisle smoothed the lustrous red satin skirt of her ball gown, then laughed inwardly at the thought of how her oldest brother, Gray, would react if he knew the real purpose behind her Mexican trip. If he had even the slightest inkling that she meant to help the Perez family in their quest to topple Benito Juarez from power, he would succumb to apoplexy!

For a second Carlisle closed her eyes and imagined

what it would be like riding with the rebel forces now congregating secretly in the mountains near Saltillo.

Arantxa's family had fought with the French troops who had supported Archduke Maximilian of Austria against the followers of Benito Juarez. Both she and her twin brother, Javier, had regaled Carlisle with stories of their father's battles against the Juaristas and his close friendship with the Empress Carlota. At ten, Arantxa had learned to shoot a gun and was still an expert markswoman. Once in Mexico, she'd promised, she would teach Carlisle to handle a pistol and ride a horse—both of which Gray and her other brother, Stone, had never permitted Carlisle to do while she was growing up in Chicago.

The one time she'd seriously defied her brother and marched with Elizabeth Cady Stanton for women's suffrage, Gray had packed her off for a year's atonement in the Sacred Heart Convent, here in New Orleans. But soon she would ride with the rebels, freeing the people of Mexico from tyranny and oppression. According to Javier, the Mexican peasants suffered even more than the poor people she'd seen while doing charity work in Chicago's hospitals. He'd told her about the terrible condition in which they lived, and even worse, how President Benito Juarez was endeavoring to take their faith away from them!

In her mind Carlisle pictured herself atop a great white horse, *bandoleras* crossed over her chest in the way Javier had said the *guerrilleros* wore them. She'd be free to make her own decisions and do whatever she wanted. She could fight the injustices of the world without being punished by Gray for her actions!

In the seat across from her, Gray glanced at the woman beside him. To Carlisle's amusement, Tyler,

Gray's bride of only a few hours, coldly disregarded his presence. Gray frowned, and Carlisle knew why. He wasn't used to being ignored by women. But Carlisle really couldn't blame Tyler. The girl hadn't wanted to marry Gray, even if he was just about the most eligible bachelor in all of Chicago—and certainly the richest, along with their brother, Stone.

On the opposite seat, Tyler suddenly sighed loud enough for everyone to hear, and Carlisle vowed she'd never allow herself to be coerced into marriage against her will, as Tyler had.

The carriage rocked onward, the rolling wheels clattering against the rough cobblestone street. In the red silk-lined interior no one said a word. The leaden silence was unnerving to Carlisle, who liked friendly chatter. But after all, there was little to say. Her brother's hasty wedding earlier that afternoon had been a disaster.

Carlisle stifled a giggle as she remembered the astonished look on her brother's face when Tyler had walked down the aisle in widow's weeds to express her disenchantment with the groom. Tyler believed that Gray had stolen her family's plantation after the war, forcing her to live with her uncle Burl Lancaster, a Mississippi River confidence man. That's why she'd tried to swindle Gray out of ten thousand dollars, though Gray had discovered her scheme and contacted Chase Lancaster, Tyler's arrogant cousin from Mexico.

Chase was supposed to meet them here in New Orleans, where Gray was to have given Tyler into Chase's guardianship. But instead, he'd fallen in love with her and forced Tyler to marry him—with the help of Chase Lancaster. Carlisle bristled, just think-

ing about the two men and their high-handed ways
with women.

Against her will and after several moments of fighting the compulsion, she stole a surreptitious glance
at Chase sitting beside her, his wide shoulder pressing
intimately against her. Carlisle disliked him intensely,
but at the same time she felt a strange, immensely
annoying fascination with him, even though they'd
only met the day before, when he'd arrived to take
Tyler back to Mexico with him.

Their first encounter had been inauspicious, to say
the least, since he had caught her in a very compro-
mising position. Javier Perez had come to ask Gray's
permission for Carlisle to visit his family in Mexico
City, and she'd climbed the trellis outside her brother's window to eavesdrop on their conversation.

Chase Lancaster, the snake, had chosen that exact
moment to arrive, and had come up beneath her and
insolently peered up her skirt until she'd been forced
to climb down. He'd laughed at her and said she
looked like a monkey, but so far he hadn't told on
her. Instead, he'd been holding the threat of doing so
over her head, which was even more provoking.

With her visit to the Perezes hanging in the balance, she had little choice but to endure his constant
baiting, even when he had persuaded Gray to let him
escort her to Mexico. Thanks to his interference, Gray
had even ordered her to go to Chase's ranch near
Monterrey, instead of the Perez house in Mexico City,
as she and Arantxa had originally planned. Now she
wasn't sure when she'd make it to the capital, or
whether Arantxa and Javier would have already left
for the *guerrilleros'* camp by the time she finally arrived. Besides, the idea of staying at Chase Lancas-

ter's hacienda was hardly thrilling. Not only was he a Juavista, he was the rudest man she'd ever met—always mocking her and calling her "ma'am" in the most condescending fashion.

Chagrined, she realized Chase was leaning back against the corner, watching her. He grinned, one blond brow arching. Carlisle immediately shifted her gaze, resolutely vowing to ignore him for the remainder of the evening. He was so vain he was probably thinking she considered him handsome. She did, of course. In fact, in his black evening coat and white brocade waistcoat he looked even more attractive than usual, so tall and blond and tanned, like the big Viking warriors she'd read about in one of her brother's history books. But she'd never let him know she thought so.

Besides, Chase Lancaster knew very well how good-looking he was. The way he combed his hair straight back from his face only drew one's eyes to his high cheekbones and classically chiseled features. He was clean-shaven, which was not the fashion, but he wore rather long, neatly trimmed sideburns that accentuated his lean jaw.

And his eyes! Why, the looks Chase sometimes gave her out of his almond-shaped, dark blue eyes seemed to burn right through her clothes. Even more unsettling was the sense of latent dangerousness about him, as if he were a big sleek animal ready to devour his prey at a moment's notice—or perhaps, she thought derisively, toy with his victim for a while before he moved in for the kill.

Suddenly she shivered, imagining herself helpless in his clutches. Then she shook off the ridiculous notion, berating herself for allowing her thoughts to dwell on the disagreeable Senor Lancaster. She should just ignore him as Tyler did Gray, or better yet, she should think about Javier. He was the one she was in love with, and Arantxa said he was mad about her, too. She couldn't wait to get to Mexico, and then to the mountains where she would be with him all the time!

Carlisle was relieved when she heard their driver call out and felt the horses start to slow. She was anxious to escape the boring company inside the coach. The ball was a diplomatic affair given by the governor, and both Arantxa and Javier were probably already there. The *Mayan* would sail for Matamoros tomorrow, and though the Perezes would be aboard, they would have little opportunity to talk privately, what with Chase Lancaster hanging around her neck like a ball and chain.

Outside her window, the famous St. Charles Hotel loomed impressively, glowing with lights and bustling with activity. Groups of chattering men and women descended from their elaborate conveyances and crowded together on the steps leading to the grand lobby. Eager to join the throng, Carlisle gathered the scarlet skirts of her voluminous ball gown in one hand and reached for the door handle with the other. Chase Lancaster promptly blocked her way.

"Allow me, *por favor,* Senorita Kincaid."

Actually, he spoke impeccable English, but when he wanted to annoy her, he assumed a heavy Spanish accent. Carlisle gritted her teeth as Chase gracefully swung his large frame out the door. She looked at Gray and Tyler, but the newly wedded couple hadn't seemed to notice his sardonic tone.

Gray climbed out next and lifted his sullen-faced

wife to the ground. He led her toward the entrance as if he'd forgotten all about Carlisle. He probably had, she fumed from where she was left sitting by herself on the red velvet squabs.

Chase Lancaster looked up at Carlisle, and she had to admit he had the world's most charming smile, slow and rakish, with deeply etched dimples on each lean cheek. But she also saw the amused insolence in his eyes. She was infuriated to be stuck with him as an escort. But she decided she wouldn't let him make her angry, because she was sure he enjoyed her pique. She smiled sweetly, graciously extending her hand so he could assist her to the sidewalk. Instead, he gripped her around the waist and lifted her down beside him, keeping his hold on her just long enough to make her flush with anger.

"You can let go of me just anytime now," she said calmly, but her green eyes flashed with annoyance, and the amused look reappeared on his darkly tanned face.

"Only if you'll promise me a dance tonight, *querida.*"

He stood tall, around six feet three or four, she'd guess, and she had to tilt her head back to look up at him. She frowned. *Querida* meant "beloved," and she certainly wasn't that!

"I'm very sorry, Mr. Lancaster, but my dance card is already full."

"Full? Before you arrive? You must be very popular with the young caballeros of New Orleans. Surely you can find it in your heart to squeeze in one waltz with me?" When he smiled, his almond eyes narrowed at the corners.

"I'd rather waltz with an orangutan, Mr. Lancas-

ter,'' she told him, lowering her voice so Gray
wouldn't hear and smiling politely. ''Surely you know
that by now?''

He merely inclined his head. But to Carlisle's irritation, she had to admit that she was tempted to let
him write his name in her white silk dance book, just
to see if he moved with the same easy, masculine
grace on the dance floor.

Stay away from him, she ordered herself firmly.
Then, groaning inwardly, she realized she would have
to endure Chase, first on the short voyage to Matamoros and then for several months in Mexico. She'd
just have to arrange to join her friends at their mountain encampment as soon as possible, she decided,
even if she had to steal away in the night.

The spacious lobby of the St. Charles was magnificent, carpeted with plush crimson and black, the
walls hung with rich gold brocade. A large crowd
milled about, greeting friends and laughing, giving
the place a festive air. At the cloak attendant's desk
near the massive marble staircase leading to a beautiful, balustraded upper floor, she joined Gray and
Tyler. As she handed the maid her black silk cape,
she was delighted to catch sight of Arantxa rushing
across the marble-tiled floor, her twin brother not far
behind her.

Arantxa was just eighteen, Carlisle's own age, with
a dark olive complexion and luminous brown eyes
that nearly always sparkled with excitement. Tonight
she looked very pretty in a yellow silk taffeta gown
adorned with royal blue ribbons and matching velvet
panels down the front. Carlisle knew the two of them
made a striking pair, Arantxa's darkness a perfect foil
for Carlisle's golden-red hair and sea-green eyes. Ar-

antxa took hold of Carlisle's hands, then pressed her cheek to Carlisle's as she performed the *abrazo*— the embrace which Carlisle had learned was customary in Mexico.

"Carlita! You are very late!" she cried. "Javier was afraid you were not coming."

As Javier Perez approached, Carlisle saw his black eyes alight on her with pleasure. He was so handsome and gallant that it had been easy to fall in love with him. However, her smile faded when she felt Chase Lancaster's long fingers close around her upper arm. His proprietary gesture surprised her and she turned to stare at him. But his gaze rested speculatively on Arantxa's face, unwavering even when he spoke to Carlisle.

"I've met Senor Perez, but I haven't had the pleasure of being presented to his lovely sister," he said.

More impeccable manners to impress her friends and family, Carlisle thought. Was she the only person who saw through his civilized veneer? Down deep, under his glib charm, there lurked a dark, wild nature, she knew it! She pulled her arm out of his grasp as unobtrusively as she could, since Gray had just walked up with Tyler. She introduced Gray and Tyler to Arantxa, ignoring Chase.

"How do you do, Miss Perez?" Gray asked politely. "I've looked forward to meeting Carlisle's best friend."

"*Gracias,* Senor Kincaid, and I am very pleased you have agreed to let her visit my country. We've made many plans for her stay."

"When Carly returns to Chicago in August, you must come with her. My wife and I would like that very much."

Carlisle saw a startled look flit across Tyler's face as if she were dismayed to be reminded she was married to Gray.

"Arantxa, this is Chase Lancaster," Carlisle said. "Javier, you've already met everyone, haven't you?"

"*Sí*, I've had the pleasure," Javier answered, his white teeth flashing beneath his thin black mustache.

Arantxa curtsied before Chase, smiling up at him.

"My pleasure, Senorita Perez," Chase said, lifting her hand to his lips.

Arantxa blushed, but Carlisle noticed a certain hesitancy in her girlfriend's answer that made her realize Arantxa was nervous around Chase Lancaster.

"*Gracias*. I'm greatly honored, Senor Lancaster, to meet the foreign advisor to El Presidente. Many of our countrymen here in the city are eager to make your acquaintance."

"Indeed?" Chase answered.

Javier apparently sensed Arantxa's unease, because he answered in his sister's stead. "Senor Gonzalez represents the Mexicans living in New Orleans, Senor Lancaster. He awaits you in the receiving line. He asked me to invite you to join him there."

Chase acquiesced with a nod, then turned back to Arantxa. "I hope you'll honor me with a dance this evening, Senorita Perez?"

Arantxa held out her dance book, looking a bit flustered by Chase Lancaster's request. Carlisle frowned. Arantxa would not want to dance with a Juarista any more than Carlisle did. While Chase picked up the pencil hanging from the tiny, lace-covered book and jotted his initials on several lines, Carlisle hid her own dance card in the folds of her red skirt so Chase would not ask her again in Gray's presence, in which case she couldn't refuse.

When Chase finally moved away with Javier, Gray led Tyler to a small, secluded table where he could have her all to himself. Arantxa's gaze remained glued to Chase Lancaster's broad shoulders.

"Even if he is a Juarista, I must say Senor Lancaster is a most handsome man, *muy macho,* with those dark blue eyes."

"And he clearly knows it," Carlisle said coldly.

"Sí, his reputation is well-known in Mexico City. They call him El Gato Grande, you know."

Carlisle had been studying hard during the last few months to learn Spanish, and when it was spoken slowly, she did quite well.

"The big cat? What's that supposed to mean?" she asked, curious about Chase Lancaster's past and ready to believe anything bad that Arantxa had heard about him. But he did resemble a big, sleek cat, she thought. A lion, perhaps, with his bronzed hair and skin.

"It's whispered that he stalks the ladies, then devours them like helpless little sparrows."

Carlisle stared at Arantxa, thinking the nickname was silly until she remembered how unsettled she'd felt in the landau. She wondered how many sparrows he had consumed and how many more waited eagerly to be trapped for his next meal. Then she wondered if he considered *her* a potential snack. He'd said he found her attractive on several occasions, but he was always so sarcastic that she wasn't sure he really meant it.

Angry at herself for her continued preoccupation with Chase, she was glad when Javier arrived and took her hand.

"It's only been a day, Carlita, but I've missed you," he whispered.

A warm thrill of pleasure spread through Carlisle as the handsome young Mexican kissed each of her fingers. He was so romantic and well-mannered, and devoted to his cause. He was filled with fire and loyalty when he spoke of Santa Anna, the man the rebels wanted to bring home from exile in Cuba once they'd ousted Benito Juarez and his anti-Church supporters. According to Javier and Arantxa, Santa Anna had once been a great Mexican leader in the past, and the majority of the Mexican people really wanted him to be their president.

"Come, dance with me, Carlita," he whispered. "I've waited long to have you to myself."

Carlisle felt like a fairy-tale princess as he swept her away to join the revolving circle of dancers, swirling around the shiny oak floor. Last year, just before she'd joined the women's march and been sent to the convent, she'd had her coming-out season in Chicago, but she had not attended a dance since then. She felt gay and happy, glad to be young and alive and in the arms of a handsome man who had promised her an exciting new life of freedom and adventure.

"*Dios*, you are beautiful in that gown," Javier remarked, leaning closer than he really needed to, his dark eyes dipping to her soft white breasts.

Earlier that evening, while she had waited for Gray and Tyler to finish dressing for the ball, Chase Lancaster had come into the dining room to antagonize her. He'd regarded her with the same undisguised appreciation that Javier was displaying, except that Chase had been audacious enough to snatch the white rose she'd tucked between her breasts in the Parisian fashion. He'd placed it behind her ear instead, telling her she shouldn't hide her charms. But now just the memory of his rude boldness sent hot, angry color rising into her cheeks.

The orchestra played on, and Carlisle allowed Javier to claim every dance, feeling tireless and more carefree that she'd felt in months. In the convent, she'd grown accustomed to prayers and bells and dreary white uniforms. Music and laughter were what she'd missed most. Soon an admiring group of young men surrounded her, British naval officers and French attachés, and she flirted and accepted brimming goblets of champagne from all of them, never wanting the evening to end.

Despite her own soaring spirits, however, she did often glance toward Gray and Tyler. Sitting at their table, they both looked miserable and she hadn't seen them dance at all. Part of the reason, she knew, was Tyler's fear of the wedding night, an ordeal she must face shortly. Tyler had already confided that she had no idea what transpired between a husband and wife in bed, and unfortunately, Carlisle couldn't enlighten her. She'd certainly had no experience with men. Gray and Stone had been too strict for that.

Needless to say, Carlisle was curious. All her girlfriends referred to it as ''the thing men do to women,'' and the nuns called it ''sinful, except when submitting to one's husband.'' Tyler seemed to think it might hurt.

Tomorrow she meant to find out from Tyler exactly what did go on! She glanced at Chase Lancaster, who was dancing with Arantxa and looking deceptively like a gentleman in his impeccably tailored evening clothes. Immediately, Arantxa's story of the sparrows and big, predatory cat returned to mind.

Later in the evening Chase Lancaster stood alone near an open set of louvered doors overlooking the hotel's garden. He watched the dancers flowing in a graceful clockwise stream, then noticed Gray Kincaid escorting his cousin, Tyler, toward the door. The fact that they were leaving so early bespoke Gray's eagerness to be alone with his bride, though Tyler's expression told him that she was just as anxious to postpone it.

A twinge of guilt assailed him, and he momentarily doubted the wisdom of arranging Tyler's marriage so hastily, and without her consent. But somehow he knew he'd done the right thing. He knew that Gray would be gentle with her tonight, that he'd protect her and see that she was well provided for. Gray was an honorable, wealthy man, and he loved Tyler.

Just then, Carlisle Kincaid moved across his line of vision in a breathtaking whirl of red satin and pale coppery hair caught up in intricate coils and ringlets. She laughed up at her partner, an American officer, and the poor man looked enraptured. Unfortunately, Chase knew how he felt.

Not only was she lovely, she was all fire and spirit and perfumed white flesh—enticing in her innocent allure. She was the kind of woman who made a man incoherent, stupid, a weak-kneed fool.

Chase was no fool, but he was in the dangerous position of wanting his good friend's sister more than any other woman he'd ever seen. He and Carlisle had clashed from the moment they met, and her willingness to spar amused him. She was spoiled and pampered, but she was incredibly beautiful, and probably a lot smarter than her brothers gave her credit for. In any case, he was captivated by her and by her continued coldness to him. He liked women, and most of them liked him, too, especially when he made an effort to charm them. But Carlisle was definitely off-limits, and he'd do well to remember it. In any case, she had obviously set her sights on Javier Perez.

Letting his gaze circle the ballroom, Chase found the young Mexican among the spectators standing by the wall, his dark eyes following Carlisle's every movement. When Javier frowned suddenly, Chase looked toward Carlisle in time to see her tilt her head back and smile up at her partner. He found himself envying the dancing man along with Javier Perez. The only difference was the Mexican could probably have her if he wanted. Chase couldn't, and shouldn't even be thinking about it.

Chase had been a fool to suggest that Gray entrust Carlisle into his care while she was in Mexico. Now he'd have to act the chaperone to a red-haired, green-eyed beauty who was obviously dying to lose her virginity—and one whom he didn't dare touch without totally dishonoring himself.

Regardless, he couldn't help but want her. Most of the women in his country—at least those in his own social class—were polite, coy, boring. American women weren't quite so docile, although Carlisle Kincaid's upbringing had been strictly monitored by her two brothers. Which was most likely the reason Carlisle was so headstrong. She'd been caged up too long, and now it was apparent that she was ready to fly free. Gray would have been wise to arrange a prompt, sedate marriage for her instead of allowing her to travel to Mexico.

However, as far as Chase was concerned, Javier was not the man for Gray Kincaid's little sister. He was a known rake, and worse, the Perez family had been staunch opponents of President Juarez. They had welcomed the Austrian Archduke Maximilian with open arms, until the end, four years ago, when the emperor had been executed by a firing squad and his French supporters had sailed back to Europe. Then the Perezes had welcomed the victorious Juaristas into the capital city as long-lost brothers. Chase had no reason to trust them.

Rumors of rebel activities crept like a dank, clammy fog around the corridors of the Palacio Nacional, and Benito Juarez himself had asked Chase to look into anti-government plotting. The trip to fetch Tyler had given Chase the opportunity to inquire discreetly among the expatriates residing in New Orleans, but he'd learned little. Everyone knew about his close relationship to Benito Juarez, meaning that any traitor would remain closemouthed in his presence.

The waltz ended to a polite round of applause, and immediately a knot of admirers formed around Carlisle. When they'd first arrived, she'd kept close to Arantxa and Javier, but as the night had worn on, she'd danced with many different partners and appeared to be having the time of her life.

After a few moments Chase watched her head for Javier Perez, and suddenly he found himself eager to get her out of the hotel and safely home, as he'd promised her older brother he would. He wended his way through the crowd toward her, well aware that she wouldn't want to leave—especially if she had to do so on the arm of a man she loathed.

2

"It's beautiful outside on the terrace," Javier Perez said to Carlisle when she reached him after having waltzed with the young American officer. "Instead of dancing, shall we get some air?"

Desiring to be alone with him and hoping he might be bold enough to try to steal a kiss, Carlisle went along without further urging. The evening air was cool and refreshing after the crowded ballroom, and as she stood looking out over the balcony, a gentle wind touched her face, lifting the tiny tendrils of hair around her temples. She remembered, suddenly and without warning, the way Chase's fingers had felt when they'd brushed her breast as he withdrew the rose from her bodice. Again a slight chill swept over her bare flesh.

"I'm mad about you," Javier muttered thickly, very close to her ear.

No man had ever said such a thing to Carlisle before, probably because Gray or Stone was always guarding her like a fire-breathing dragon. She savored his compliment, feeling very wicked and deliciously adult, standing alone in the dark with a beau—something else she'd never done before. Any other time, Gray would have intercepted them before they'd even reached the balcony doors, but tonight he was much too distracted by Tyler to care. Was Javier going to kiss her? she wondered hopefully, and then her question was answered.

"Carlita, I cannot bear to stand here another moment without touching you." Javier's words were wonderfully low and tortured. Carlisle raised her face to him, closing her eyes in expectation. She'd certainly never been kissed, and her heart pounded like a drum as he drew her lightly against him. Then his mouth touched hers. To her dismay, the long-awaited experience was over in a twinkling, and though Javier certainly seemed rapturously pleased with the outcome, Carlisle felt vague disappointment.

"Dios, Carlita, do you have any idea what you do to a man?"

Javier was breathing heavily, and Carlisle wondered why on earth he was so affected.

"The thought of you traveling with Chase Lancaster fills me with anger," Javier continued, capturing all her attention. "He's notorious for his treatment of women. Every family in Mexico City hides its daughters away from him. How could your brother think to trust him with you?"

Truthfully, Carlisle had wondered the same thing. She lifted her shoulder in a slight shrug. "Gray has faith in him, I suppose. They became friends when my brother traveled in Mexico last year, and for some reason, Gray seems to think Chase is a gentleman. He's wrong, of course, but Chase puts on a good act around everyone but me. Even Tyler took his part

until he betrayed her by forcing her to marry Gray."
She glanced around, lowering her voice. "After we
land in Mexico, will you be able to come for me
soon?"

Javier hushed her with a finger to his lips. *"Silencio,* Carlita. There are many here who would expose
us."

"Do you mean Chase?"

"Sí. He is a close friend of El Presidente. You
must be careful about what you say in his presence.
He is a dangerous man. Did you know he always carries a pistol hidden in his clothes and has killed many
men with it?"

Intrigued and slightly appalled, Carlisle was entirely ready to believe the worst of Chase Lancaster.
"Who has he killed?"

"He fought with the Juaristas in our war. There
was a small village in the mountains, San Miguel,
and he was with the Juaristas who took it. They murdered everyone there, even the women and little children. That's where my brother died. They nailed his
hands to the wall of the church." Carlisle gasped
aloud, and Javier's voice changed, becoming brittle
with fury and grief. "San Miguel was an atrocity we
will never forget. We will avenge that massacre and
make them pay for their crimes."

"But how can that be, Javier? I can believe that
Chase is ruthless, but never would I have dreamed he
could murder children!"

"The war was very terrible. The Juaristas committed many horrors against those of us who fought for
the Holy Church with the French. That's why we still
fight them. And now you can help us, Carlita, more
than you know."

Carlisle's delicate eyebrows gathered in a faint frown. "I? But how?"

"Senor Lancaster is *muy importante* in Mexico. He is close to Benito Juarez and, as foreign advisor, he's privy to all that goes on in the capital. We have heard that he is eager to strengthen Mexico's friendship with the United States, but we must stop any alliance between Juarez and President Grant. Can you not see now how you can be of use? Lancaster would never suspect you to be our informer."

Carlisle stared up at him and saw that his eyes were shining with zeal.

"You want me to spy on him?" she asked incredulously, her voice a bare whisper. The notion struck her as exciting until she thought of the big, dangerous man who would be her mark.

Javier seemed to sense her sudden reluctance. "Carlita, you must know I'd never consider putting you in danger. You are much too dear to me, and to Arantxa. I wouldn't even consider it if I wasn't absolutely sure no harm will come to you. Even Chase Lancaster, with the blood of San Miguel and other villages on his hands, would not harm his friend's sister."

Carlisle didn't really think Chase would hurt her, either, not even if he discovered her anti-Juarista sentiments. But then, she didn't know him very well yet. He was unpredictable, she did know that. But if he'd done the terrible things Javier claimed, he was nothing more than an animal. Why, then, did she feel such a strong, inexplicable attraction to him?

"Carlita? I have frightened you, no?"

Carlisle shook her head. It wasn't Javier who scared her. It was her own reaction to Chase Lancaster.

"While I'm at his ranch, I'll try to learn all I can about his activities. But you must promise me that you and Arantxa will come for me as soon as you can and take me to join the *guerrilleros.*"

"*Sí,* it will be difficult to leave you in his charge. If this were not so important to us, I would steal you away from him the moment your feet touched Mexican soil."

He was close to her now. She could almost feel his breath against her cheek as he went on.

"But remember one thing, Carlita. You mustn't let on that Arantxa and I have joined the *guerrilleros* in Saltillo. Let Lancaster believe that we are awaiting your visit in the capital."

"Carlita? Where are you?"

They turned as Arantxa's low whisper drifted from the shadowy terrace. She found them a moment later, her summons urgent.

"Senor Lancaster is looking everywhere for you, Carlita! And I'm not sure, but I think he's angry. You mustn't let him find you out here alone with Javier. If he tells your brother, Gray won't let you come to Mexico! Hurry!"

The two girls quickly left Javier and reentered the ballroom by a different door. They mingled with a boisterous group of young people on the edge of the dance floor, but only a moment after they were inside, Chase appeared before Carlisle. He wore his usual charming grin, but Carlisle knew instinctively from the look in his eyes that his smile cloaked something darker.

"Senorita Kincaid, forgive me for this intrusion, but Gray has asked me to see you safely home."

For some reason, all Carlisle could think of was

how he towered over her. Suddenly she felt reluctant to be alone with him, even for the brief carriage ride home.

"It's awfully early to leave. Perhaps I could have Arantxa and Javier drop me off—"

Chase interrupted her. "I'm sorry, but I gave Gray my word that I'd see you safely home myself. And I'm afraid I'm ready to leave now."

Carlisle's anger flared when he took firm hold of her arm and bowed courteously to Arantxa.

"*Buenas noches*, Senorita Perez. I'll look forward to seeing you tomorrow aboard the *Mayan*. I hope we'll get to know each other better during the voyage. Adios."

Chase Lancaster barely gave Carlisle a chance to bid Arantxa a proper good-bye before he marched her away, still gripping her arm as if she were a rebellious child. Bristling with humiliation, she said nothing as he retrieved her cape and helped her into the waiting carriage. He paused to give instructions to the coachman, then joined her, lounging indolently beside her, though a more proper place would have been on the opposite seat. She stared coldly out the window, determined to snub him all the way home.

"Tell me, Senorita Kincaid," Chase said as the driver slapped the reins and the coach began to roll, "was your dress revealing enough to make Javier mad with desire? Wasn't that your plan when you bought it?"

His sudden sarcastic attack startled her, and as usual, she felt a dangerous surge of anger. She wanted to tell him it was none of his business, but she decided that was what he wanted. Perhaps she should try to pry information out of him now, she thought, entice him to talk about himself. He might let something slip which would be helpful to Javier.

"Why do you ask, Mr. Lancaster? Did my dress make you mad with desire?"

A low laugh was her answer. "I must say it's rather rare for me to be stricken mad with desire."

"I wouldn't think that the case, considering your reputation. Arantxa told me all about you."

Chase said nothing, but his lips curved slightly, as if he were amused. His silence made it more difficult for Carlisle to lead the conversation in the direction she wanted.

"Aren't you curious about what she said about you?"

"Not particularly. Are you?"

"I found it interesting, but I usually discount gossip unless I know it's true."

"That's very gracious of you, Senorita Kincaid."

Carlisle bit her lip, recognizing the sardonic undertone of his remark. He could make her so furious!

"You don't like me, do you, Senor Lancaster? You think I'm immature and flighty, don't you?"

"Does it matter what I think of you?"

"Why do you always answer my questions with questions?"

"Do I?"

Chase's eyes reflected the flickering glints of light filtering in from the carriage lamp swinging on its bracket outside the window, and his grin was disarming. But Carlisle was not to be put off.

"She said you're called El Gato Grande in Mexico City because you prey on women."

"Is that right?"

"Doesn't it bother you to be called such a thing?"

"One grows used to it."

"I also heard you always carry a gun, and that you're not afraid to use it."

"What are you really trying to find out, Carlisle?" Chase asked then, still sprawled carelessly beside her.

"I'm just trying to get to know you better."

"By listening to idle gossip?"

"I'm asking you about it because I don't know whether to believe it or not. Why are you being so exasperating? Can't you see I'm trying to be friendly for a change?"

"Look, Carlisle, I'm not much for playing silly word games with romantic young misses. Save it for your dandy, Javier. He's more your type."

"And what type am I?"

"Young, curious, and naive."

"You *are* despicable. You won't even let someone be civil to you."

"Why the abrupt change? You haven't seen fit to be civil before."

Had he seen through her questions already? Dismayed, she attempted a reasonable explanation. "Because you finagled your way into escorting me to Mexico and hosting me at your hacienda. Why you wanted me there, I can't imagine."

"I'm merely doing your brother a favor. He thinks you need supervision."

"Well, he's wrong. I'm more than capable of taking care of myself." She stopped, realizing the carriage had passed the corner which would take them to Gray's house on the corner of Third and Prytania streets. Surprised, she looked at Chase.

"That was our turn! Where's the driver going?"

"I ordered him to drive around town for a while."

"Why? I thought you said you wanted to go home.''

"No. I said I was ready to leave the hotel. Gray and Tyler deserve a little privacy on their wedding night, don't you think?''

"I think I'd rather spend this time at the hotel with Javier than cooped up in this carriage with you—especially since you're in such a disagreeable mood.''

"Why are you suddenly so interested in my private life?'' he asked abruptly, catching Carlisle off guard.

Trying to appear nonchalant, she lifted a shoulder in a faint shrug. "I heard rumors about you, and I was merely curious. Is that such a crime?''

"They do call me El Gato Grande, which is ridiculous, but I can't say it's ever bothered me much. And I do wear a gun, and I don't mind using it. Anything else you want to know about me?''

"Why do you feel the need to wear a gun?''

"I feel the need because there are a lot of people who feel the need to see me dead.''

Carlisle answered in the same curt, bored tone he'd used. "Tell me, Mr. Lancaster, why doesn't that surprise me?''

When he leaned back his head and laughed, Carlisle took advantage of his lighter mood.

"May I see your gun?'' she asked, leaning forward as if to slip her hand inside his coat. His fingers immediately locked tight around her wrist.

"No, you may not.''

Intrigued, she relaxed against the seat and stared at him. "Why would anyone want to kill you?''

"I made some enemies during the war. Enemies with long memories.''

"But hasn't Benito Juarez been in power for four years now?"

"*Sí*, but our government isn't as stable as yours. It'll take time to heal the wounds Maximilian and Carlota left behind them. I'm surprised Arantxa and Javier haven't explained all this to you."

Carlisle hesitated. She had to be careful. "Arantxa said her family backed the emperor, but she and Javier were very young then."

"In Mexico, even the young died at the hands of the French, Senorita Kincaid," he said, his tone low and serious. "As they did in your civil war."

"My brothers kept me in Chicago, far away from the fighting. Sometimes I feel as if I've been living in a cave all these years, a nice fancy one with velvet chairs and expensive clothes. But I don't know a thing about real life," Carlisle said, surprising herself with her candor.

"Isn't that the reason for your trip to Mexico?" Chase asked. "To try out your wings a bit without your brothers pulling you down?"

"Maybe. Is that so wrong?"

"Not if you act responsibly and don't let the wrong people influence you."

"Are you talking about Arantxa and Javier?"

"I'm saying that if you want to learn all about love, you should marry and let your husband teach you— not some inexperienced boy like Perez."

Shocked, Carlisle could only stare at him. "Sometimes you amaze me. How dare you talk that way to me?"

"Can you say you aren't interested in such things?"

Angry color flooded Carlisle's face, because she

couldn't deny it. "You're the rudest, most conceited man!"

His laugh was low, mocking. "So it's true, is it?"

His smile was totally, utterly mesmerizing, and Carlisle was so aware of his closeness that her pulse accelerated. She moistened her lips nervously. If he was such a womanizer, would he try to seduce *her?* The dark, intimate confines of the carriage were certainly conducive, and the idea was as exciting as it was dreadful. Was he thinking of grabbing her and forcing her to kiss him? Or worse?

"I've decided a duenna should accompany you on the voyage," he said, his voice disrupting her thoughts.

"A what?" Carlisle asked, rather disappointed he was obviously not considering any kind of inappropriate behavior.

"In my country young, marriageable girls such as yourself are required to have a female chaperone to accompany them everywhere they go. At least, until they're safely married and have a husband to protect them." One corner of his mouth curved into a smile. "The custom prevents unsavory scandals and assures a man that his bride is virtuous."

Carlisle was outraged. "Are you insinuating that I am . . . that I would—"

"No need to take offense, Senorita Kincaid. But I did happen to see the Perez boy kissing you out on the balcony. I'm afraid I just can't let anything like that happen again. I'd have failed miserably in my duty if I had to telegraph Gray someday and invite him to your hastily arranged wedding. So you'll just have to put up with a duenna while you're in my care."

Incredulous, Carlisle stared at him. "You were spying on us!"

"Gray told me to keep an eye on you. Otherwise I wouldn't have bothered." His smile appeared again. "Actually, by the look of Javier's kiss, I doubt if you were very much impressed, one way or another."

Carlisle's fingers curled into fists. "And what does El Gato Grande's kiss do to women? Turn them to mush?"

He laughed. "Sometimes."

Carlisle looked at his handsome face, wondering if there really was a difference in the way men kissed. Perhaps she should find out. Why not flirt a bit, sample the kiss of a man known for his philandering? It would be an intriguing experiment.

"I daresay kissing you wouldn't affect me one whit. After all, you have to like someone a little before you can enjoy kissing them."

"Shall we find out, Senorita Kincaid?"

His challenge hung between them for an instant.

"Don't get your hopes up, Senor Lancaster," she warned, but her heart skipped a beat as Chase moved toward her, his thumb and fingers gently bracketing her jaw. He held her firmly, capturing her gaze before his mouth came down on hers—soft, warm, undemanding. He began to taste her mouth, molding his lips to hers, and Carlisle was swiftly flooded with peculiar, weak, fluttery sensations in the pit of her stomach, as if dozens of canaries were trapped there. Her reeling senses settled when he paused momentarily to look into her eyes. But then he began again, more intensely, hard and insistent, compelling her to respond. When his tongue found its way to hers, she moaned and clung weakly to his shoulders. He released her then, leaning back against the squabs.

Carlisle stared at him, her fingers on her throbbing lips.

"Do you call that a kiss?" she managed shakily, determined to act as indifferent to the experience as he had.

"You mean it didn't turn you to mush?"

His description was not far from the truth, but Carlisle remained silent, striving to regain her composure.

"You're really an awful man," she finally managed to say, her voice husky. "Gray would never let you escort me to Mexico if he knew you had kissed me like that."

"True, he probably wouldn't, but we don't have to worry about him finding out, do we? Because you're not about to tell him or he'll put a stop to your little trip, and then you'd see even less of your precious Javier than you will with your duenna in tow."

His tone was so openly scornful that Carlisle was shocked.

"You're every bit as bad as they say, aren't you? You're worse than they say."

"They?" he said casually, but a different, dangerous note had crept into his voice. "Who?"

At once, Carlisle realized she'd made a mistake. Javier and Arantxa wouldn't want him to know they disliked him.

"Why, everyone, of course," she answered lightly. "Even Tyler. She thought you were wonderful until you showed up here and made her marry Gray against her will. I think it's disgraceful the way you treated her. She's your own flesh and blood."

"You seem to think your brother will be a disagreeable husband, Carlisle. Do you expect him to treat Tyler cruelly?"

"No, of course not! Gray will be good to her, but that's not the point. The point—"

"The point," he interrupted, "is that Gray is probably the best thing that ever happened to my cousin. She's lucky he even wanted to marry her after she tried to swindle ten thousand dollars out of him back in Chicago. She's behaved like a common criminal all her life, due to my own thieving father. He was nothing but a gambler and a confidence man, who taught her all his crooked games. I'd probably be as dishonest as Tyler, if my mother hadn't left him when I was young. I'm just thankful Gray's willing to take her hand."

Chase paused, his eyes pinning her. "But you, Carlisle, you're just the opposite, aren't you? You've been sheltered and pampered like a little queen by your brothers ever since you were a baby. You've gone to all the best schools, met all the right people, which probably bored you to tears. So now you're ripe to run wild and entice every man you see with those incredible big green eyes of yours."

Suddenly his voice took on an angry edge. "Unfortunately, in a moment of weakness I was thoughtless enough to offer you the hospitality of my ranch, a stupid blunder on my part, which I heartily regret but can hardly take back now. So what it all boils down to is this—whether you like it or not, you'll have a duenna to keep you in line while you're under my supervision in Mexico, because I'm already damn sick and tired of your spoiled tantrums."

Carlisle was completely taken aback. This was

hardly the first time they'd quarreled, but always before he'd shown no emotion, other than amused indifference. What had made him so furious all of a sudden?

"Actually, I'll welcome a duenna," she said quietly, slightly subdued by his attack. "If for no other reason than to protect me from any further unwelcome advances from you."

His eyes grew hooded, and she knew before he spoke that his anger would be gone, or well hidden.

"No need to worry about me, Senorita Kincaid. I only kissed you to prove a point. Now maybe you'll think twice before teasing a man you hardly know. If not, one of these days you might find yourself in a very serious predicament. All men aren't as gentlemanly as I am."

"You know," she answered furiously, "this is just what I'd expect from you—placing the blame for your own ill-mannered behavior on me!"

The coach stopped in the driveway of her brother's house on Third Street, and without replying to her denouncement, Chase climbed out, then politely lifted her to the ground.

"Sleep well, Senorita Kincaid. Our ship sails at noon."

Carlisle gritted her teeth, raised her chin, and left him where he stood. She stalked to the front door, her full skirts bunched in her hands, her whole evening ruined by his boorish behavior and unkind accusations on the ride home. How on earth was she going to stand his irritating, chafing, disagreeable presence long enough to find out the information Javier Perez needed for his revolution?

3

Carlisle hadn't slept well. She'd only had a few hours of rest, and when she awoke, she'd discovered she was still angry with Chase Lancaster, her mind awhirl with thoughts of spying on him, not to mention her breathless reaction to his kiss.

Her mood had only grown worse at breakfast. Tyler had been sitting at the table, and Carlisle had dashed into the dining parlor to find out about her wedding night, completely unaware that Chase Lancaster lurked unseen at the other end of the room.

Chase had laughed at her, and Tyler had excused herself, obviously mortified to be discussing the subject at all. Then he'd offered to explain the secrets of the marriage bed to Carlisle, if she was so eager to know!

Now, as she stood at the starboard railing of the *Mayan* several hours later, her face grew scarlet at the thought of it. Her fingers tightened around the smooth wood, and she was grateful for the winds that swept over the surface of the swirling, muddy waters of the Mississippi River, cooling her flaming cheeks. Chase

33

Lancaster always managed to make her feel so young and foolish. She was beginning to look forward to spying on him.

A quarter of an hour ago, she'd stood on the docks and said farewell to Gray and Tyler. Though she'd not expected it, she'd been very sad to leave them behind. For months she and Arantxa had planned ways to persuade Gray to allow her to go to Mexico. But when he'd hugged her and told her good-bye, she'd almost felt like crying.

And Tyler had acted strange after spending her wedding night with Gray, tired but almost content. Apparently, Gray had said or done something in their bedchamber that had left a definite impact on his unwilling bride, which only made Carlisle more curious about exactly what did go on between a man and a woman. She'd wanted to question Tyler in more detail, but since Gray and Chase hovered around constantly, a private talk with her had been impossible.

Chase Lancaster stood a few feet away from Carlisle now, deep in conversation with the dreary duenna he'd decided to inflict on her. No doubt he was giving the poor old woman all kinds of detailed orders designed expressly to make Carlisle's journey as miserable as possible.

Senora Alvarez herself, however, did not seem particularly disagreeable. The elderly woman was stout and big-boned, and appeared to be about sixty. She'd been very polite when Chase had introduced her just after they'd boarded the ship. She was a widow who wore a staid black silk dress and lace mantilla, and obviously a devout Catholic, for a heavy silver crucifix hung around her neck. The shiny metal glinted brightly in the morning sun, and Carlisle sighed and leaned against the rail.

Having a duenna would be a bore, but at least Carlisle could communicate with her. Senora Alvarez spoke the pure Castillian Spanish that both Chase and the Perez twins used, but she also knew enough English to carry on a conversation with Carlisle. Carlisle was eager to become fluent in Spanish and was making headway with Arantxa's help, but her friends had warned her that once in Mexico, she would find many different dialects used by the Indians and the mestizos, who were half Indian and half Spanish.

She glanced again at Chase and Senora Alvarez, just as the duenna nodded vigorously, in complete agreement with some remark Chase had made. He had probably suggested locking Carlisle in her cabin for the whole trip, she thought sourly. Thank goodness the voyage would last only two days. Chase saw her watching and inclined his head politely. He'd been the personification of propriety since breakfast, and he certainly looked the part of an elegant, aristocratic diplomat in his dark blue coat and gray trousers, his bronze-colored hair ruffling in the breeze.

Turning away, Carlisle relived his kiss and felt the shivers, flutters, and shudders all over again. Her breathless reaction to him made her feel foolish, and she'd asked herself a hundred times why she'd allowed it to happen. And why hadn't Javier's kiss made her feel the same way?

Angry, she scanned the waterfront. Where were Arantxa and Javier, anyway? Why didn't they come? They'd insisted she arrive on time, and now they were late! Suddenly a horrible thought struck her. What if they didn't show up? She was already stuck in a tiny,

cratelike cabin with Senora Alvarez and her big crucifix. And even worse, if the Perezes didn't come,
Chase Lancaster would be her only other traveling
companion for the entire trip. Heaven forbid!

Chase had paid her little attention since they'd bid-
den Gray and Tyler good-bye. Instead, he'd left her to
her own devices while he conversed with Jose Martinez, the captain of the steamer, a small, placid-faced
Mexican with a great head of unruly gray hair and
bushy mustachios to match. Chase also seemed well
acquainted with several other male passengers, all of
whom treated him with a great deal of respect. Somehow Carlisle just couldn't picture him as an influential
political figure. He was too young and conceited to
be the foreign advisor to the President of Mexico.

Perusing the passengers conversing around the
deck, she wondered what they'd do if they knew she
was planning to join the new revolution. She wondered what Chase would do, too. Despite the hot
noonday sun, a shudder shook her. She wasn't sure
if it was caused by fear of discovery or tingling excitement about being involved in a plot so dangerous.
She'd taken few risks, had not been allowed to. All
her life Gray had made her decisions for her.

Now Chase Lancaster would take over where Gray
had left off, and last night he'd made it clear he'd
approach the job with the same enthusiasm as her
brother. His voice had been so scornful when he'd
told her what he thought of her that she'd begun to
think she'd enjoy informing on him. He deserved no
loyalty from her. He was arrogant and insulting—and
a cold-blooded killer, if Javier was right about San
Miguel.

Carlisle's eyes sharpened as she caught sight of the

Mayan's launch pushing away from the bustling dock. She shielded her eyes against the glare off the water, watching as the longboat was rowed toward the ship. She waved when she recognized Arantxa's favorite flat-brimmed straw hat, the yellow ribbons fluttering. Javier was in the stern and he stood, hailing her with a wave of his arm, his shout echoing out over the river. Delighted, Carlisle lifted her lace-gloved hand and returned his greeting.

Moving down the starboard railing to the landing platform, she waited at the boarding gate until the small craft bumped against the hull below her. Javier grabbed hold of the rope ladder and began to climb agilely while several of the rowers helped Arantxa into the boarding chair provided for female passengers. Carlisle laughed as Javier leapt onto the deck beside her, taking both her hands and smiling into her upturned face.

"At last, Carlita, we'll be on our way—"

A stout, black-draped figure barged between them, and Carlisle found her hands quickly snatched from Javier's grasp. Senora Alvarez's usual pleasant expression was gone, replaced by a stern, forbidding glare, directed solely at Javier.

"Javier, this is Senora Alvarez," Carlisle said, a bit startled by the hostile way the widow was looking at him. "She's to be my duenna. Mr. Lancaster insisted. Senora Alvarez, this is Senor Javier Perez. We'll be visiting his family in Mexico City."

"Senora Alvarez, I am honored," Javier said, bowing with the utmost courtesy. He began a rapid discourse in Castilian, which Carlisle could not begin to follow. He ended it in English, saying, "So forgive me, *por favor*. I meant no disrespect for Senorita Kincaid. Perhaps you would be so kind as to help me chaperone my sister, Arantxa, during our voyage to Matamoros. I have promised *mi padre* to look after her, but there was no suitable duenna available."

At that, Senora Alvarez relaxed visibly. *"Sí*, Senor Perez, I will help you watch your sister. And if I may say so, it is refreshing to find a young caballero who respects the old ways."

She moved a step or two away, but Carlisle noticed that she continued to watch them closely.

"I'm sorry, Javier. This whole thing is so ridiculous. I'm a grown woman, not a child."

"I'm well used to duennas, Carlita. Arantxa has had one ever since she was a little girl. And perhaps it will be safer for you," he said as his eyes met Chase Lancaster's and the two men nodded a greeting. "I wouldn't want you to be alone in Senor Lancaster's house. He looks at you in a way that makes me want to kill him."

Until that moment, Carlisle had fully intended to tell Javier about Chase's kiss, but she heard the bitterness in his voice when he spoke Chase's name. Secretly, she was pleased he was jealous.

Strapped securely in the boarding swing suspended by ropes and pulleys to the railing, Arantxa was hoisted slowly to the deck a moment later. When she joined them, she accepted Senora Alvarez's presence with the same cheerful resignation that her brother had displayed.

"We'll find ways to escape her vigilance," she whispered conspiratorially to Carlisle. "I've done it many times with my poor Dona Consuela!"

Carlisle laughed, relieved now that her friends were aboard and they were ready to depart. Happy and excited, she stood on the top promenade deck with Javier and Arantxa, her duenna close beside them. She knew Chase was in the stern with Captain Martinez, but she ignored him as the anchor was hauled up and the ship slowly began the journey down the wide, brown Mississippi, past great plantations with magnificent pillar-supported galleries and lawns dotted by giant live oaks. Farther along, strange, gloomy bayous appeared, with tangled vines and long, gray Spanish moss waving spectrally in the wind.

Later that night, after an excellent supper of Cornish hens and rice in the large dining saloon, they retired to the adjoining lounge where small wooden tables had been bolted to the floor for card games or letter writing.

Senora Alvarez took out her sewing basket and a length of white lace she had been crocheting, then seated herself in a deep, high-backed armchair very close to Carlisle's place at a card table with the Perez twins. They pretended to enjoy monte, a Mexican gambling game Arantxa had taught Carlisle late at night in the convent after the nuns had gone to bed.

"How soon do you think I can join you in the mountains?" Carlisle whispered, furtively watching Chase, who stood with one elbow propped on the long mahogany bar at the far end of the saloon. He smoked a cheroot while listening to the group of Mexican businessmen surrounding him, but Carlisle had caught his blue gaze on her more than once during the supper hour. He glanced in her direction yet again while she watched, but she pretended she didn't notice. He was probably making sure her duenna was nearby, she decided, then gladly turned her attention back to Javier.

"We're pleased you've agreed to help us, Carlita." His voice lowered, and he continued to deal the cards as if intent on their game. "We've tried for several years to position a spy near one of Juarez's advisors, but he picks his followers well—all are devoted to him, especially Lancaster. I don't understand it. Chase Lancaster's grandfather was a great *hacendado,* Senor Juan Morelos, an aristocrat and a *gachupín,* a man of pure Spanish blood. Yet Senor Lancaster is blindly loyal to Juarez, a mere Indian lawyer from Oaxaca."

Carlisle watched him as he spoke, hearing the harsh resentment underlying each word, recognizing the look of hatred that appeared on Javier's face each time he glanced in Chase's direction. For a moment, she felt a fierce foreboding; then she remembered San Miguel and how Javier's brother had died there. No wonder Javier was so embittered.

"You must be very careful, Carlita. He must not suspect you," Arantxa said softly as she picked up her cards. "He is a very brutal man."

"I sensed he could be dangerous," Carlisle replied. "There's a look in his eyes sometimes."

"I don't want anything to happen to you," Javier insisted. "You mustn't appear too eager to become his friend. Instead you should encourage his trust in small ways, *comprendes?*"

"Yes," Carlisle answered impatiently. "But when will I be able to join you?"

"Soon, I promise. But you must go to his hacienda as if you are in no hurry to join us. You must be patient and find out all you can about him. We'll come one night when you least expect it, and then you'll fight by our side for Santa Anna's triumph.''

"Do you think there will be another war?" Carlisle asked, vividly remembering how Atlanta was burned to the ground; how many died in the War Between the States. Both her brothers had fought to preserve the Union, but even though the North had won, they had not escaped the suffering. Her brother Stone had been incarcerated in the terrible Confederate prison in Andersonville, Georgia. He hadn't been the same since he returned, and he was still driven by an awful thirst for revenge against Emerson Clan, the man who'd betrayed him.

But she intended to help him find Clan. Tyler had given her a wonderful idea. She'd said that her uncle Burl had once swindled a man by sending him notification that he had inherited a large sum of money. Carlisle was sure the same idea would work with Emerson Clan. If she could get him to go to Chicago, Stone could capture him and put him in jail where he belonged. All she had to do was work out the details, she thought, then write a legal-looking letter to Emerson Clan. She would do so while aboard the *Mayan,* and then write Tyler to let her know what she'd done. Perhaps Javier would help her. He had studied law while in New Orleans.

"*Sí,* there will be war," Javier was saying, "but many Mexicans want Santa Anna as *presidente.* They'll join us by the thousands to fight for the Holy Church once we strike against the Juarez government.''

Carlisle glanced again at Chase Lancaster. She didn't like him, but neither did she wish him any real harm. After all, he was her brother's good friend, and Tyler's cousin.

"Chase won't be harmed, will he?" she asked timidly.

"Do not feel sorry for him, *amiga*," Arantxa said coldly. "He had no compassion for those of San Miguel."

"What do you mean?"

"You remember what I told you about the massacre?" Javier answered. "About the women and children being murdered?"

"Yes, of course."

"Chase Lancaster was the one who ordered it done."

Truly horrified, Carlisle sought Chase again. War was a terrible, senseless thing, she thought, but how could he have ordered the murder of children? Surely the Juaristas didn't belong in power in Mexico if they killed the peasants and drove out the priests. Surely God was on the side of Javier and Santa Anna, because even Mother Andrea Mary at Sacred Heart had spoken against the evil of the reform laws of Benito Juarez and explained how the Juaristas had cast out whole orders of nuns and priests. Carlisle suddenly felt she was doing the right thing by spying on Chase Lancaster. Whenever she had doubts, she would remember his crimes against the people of San Miguel.

For Chase Lancaster, the short voyage across the Gulf to the port of Matamoros was uneventful. He'd spent most of his time alone or with a couple of acquaintances, government officials on their way home to the capital, and as far away from Carlisle Kincaid as he could get. She hadn't seemed to mind much, he thought as he stood near the gangplank, impatient for her to finish her farewells to the Perezes, who were sailing on to Veracruz aboard the *Mayan*.

Against his will, he turned slightly so that he would have a better view of Carlisle. Her golden-red hair shone like polished copper in the sun, and she wore a fancy white dress that was totally unsuitable for traveling. He had told her so when she'd come up on deck, but she'd ignored him. He muttered a low oath when Carlisle put her hand on Javier Perez's arm and tilted her face up to him as if for a good-bye kiss, but Senora Alvarez wasted no time in coming between them.

Chase laughed to himself, but he'd been surprised at how readily Carlisle had accepted the eagle-eyed Senora Alvarez. He'd expected her to protest loudly, but instead she'd shared her cabin and taken her meals with her elderly companion without complaint. Perhaps that was because Carlisle had managed to flirt with every male passenger aboard the *Mayan* in spite of the old lady's presence.

Chase felt anger surge inside him. Damn her green eyes! He should have kept his distance from her from the very beginning. She was trouble, the devil's temptation with the face of an angel and the soft, sensuous body of a *cortesana*, as yet unawakened and unpossessed. He wondered if she understood the power she wielded over men, if she knew how many longed to make her tremble and writhe with passion in their arms.

Scowling, Chase looked at Carlisle again, where she still fawned over Javier Perez. He thought of the night in the carriage when she'd more or less invited him to kiss her. That was when he'd become painfully aware of how much he desired her. *Dios,* he wouldn't have believed himself capable of such adolescent behavior, not in a hundred years. But he'd been as affected by that kiss as she. It galled him to think that a little slip of a virgin like her, a girl who despised him and made no bones about her feelings, had gotten to him. That's why he'd lashed out at her the way he had, why he was so angry with her now, and why he meant to make sure she kept hating him. Her contempt would make their relationship safer for both of them.

Chase had a hell of a lot more important problems than Carlisle Kincaid to occupy his mind. He sighed, running his fingers through his hair. *Dios,* would Mexico never stand strong and united like the United States now did, six years after the American War Between the States? He'd fought and killed to reinstate Juarez as the rightful, elected President of Mexico, and thought that when they'd finally driven out the French and executed the usurper, Maximilian, the turmoil would end. But it continued. Why couldn't the people see what Benito was trying to do? Why couldn't they see that the Catholic Church had held the land and wealth of Mexico in its stranglehold for too long?

He didn't want to fight anymore, not against his own people. He was tired of the blood, of the killing. He'd seen enough death to last him a lifetime.

By the rail, Carlisle and her friends still chatted gaily. Annoyed with her, he yelled curtly for her to hurry up. She glanced up, looked faintly surprised, then warmly embraced first Arantxa, then Javier, despite Senora Alvarez's frown of disapproval.

Chase looked back at the docks, eager for Esteban

to arrive. He'd not seen his *compadre* in several months, and he'd missed him. They'd been friends since childhood, and Chase felt a closer kinship with Esteban than he did with anyone in his own family. Esteban was like a brother. He would help get Carlisle Kincaid safely settled at the Hacienda de los Toros and out of Chase's hair.

Once Carlisle was at the ranch, Chase's mother could worry about her while Chase journeyed on to Mexico City and reported his findings to Benito. El Presidente would not like the rumors about increasing rebel support for Santa Anna. It had been Santa Anna who had sent Benito into exile in the early years, before the French had invaded their country.

"There was no call for you to be so rude." Carlisle's voice was furious, though she kept her tone low. "I have every right to say good-bye to my friends."

"Yes, ma'am."

Chase meant it mockingly, and she took it that way, because her green eyes narrowed with annoyance. At times he believed he argued with Carlisle just to make her angry. Enraged, she was nothing less than magnificent, with her color high and her eyes flashing. At the moment, her small chin was set at a defiant angle.

"I've decided not to let you bother me anymore, Mr. Lancaster, because I think you're actually low enough to enjoy seeing me angry," she said, uncannily exposing his own thoughts.

"Yes, ma'am, glad to hear it, ma'am. But I think we'd get along better if you could just keep that quick temper of yours in check."

"Oh, quit calling me ma'am. I don't like it. You're the most antagonizing man I've ever met."

"Please allow me to take your arm. The gangplank is steep."

"I am capable of disembarking by myself," Carlisle retorted, showing her fury despite her earlier resolution.

Waving again to Arantxa and Javier, she ignored Chase, who had rudely left her side to speak to Senora Alvarez. Then she lifted the billowing skirt of her white organdie dress and made her way carefully down to the dock below, where her trunks and bags had been deposited earlier.

And there she stood, for half an hour, the noonday sun broiling down upon her head until she was forced to snap up her white ruffled parasol. Inside, she seethed and cursed the day Chase Lancaster was born. He was insufferable, embarrassing her in front of the captain and other passengers by yelling for her to hurry, and now leaving her standing alone on the dock like some sailor's trollop.

Oh, why had Gray insisted she travel with the lout? Why hadn't he seen what a cad Chase really was? She wasn't sure she could put up with his mockery and hatefulness long enough to find out the things Javier wanted to know. It rankled, too, that Chase was always such a gentleman around everyone but her. He was even nice to Arantxa.

Thank God he'd stayed away from her while they'd been at sea. Not that he hadn't kept a close eye on her. And she knew the reason why. He'd expected her to steal off and do something immoral with Javier like some loose hussy. His fears just went to show what kind of man he was, always expecting the worst of her and other men, probably because his own behavior left so much to be desired.

She felt the uncomfortable sensation of sweat trickling down the small of her back beneath the fine white fabric of her dress. She retrieved her dainty lace handkerchief and dabbed at the perspiration beaded at her temples. From the ship, Matamoros had looked beautiful and welcoming with its flat-topped white houses and graceful church spires rising against the blue sky. But now, as she glanced around the busy dock, the Mexican town did not seem so inviting. Several dock workers with swarthy skin and dirty clothes, sharing a bottle of tequila, returned her glance with leers.

One, the dirtiest creature Carlisle had ever laid eyes on, gestured toward her, then made a remark in an unfamiliar Spanish dialect. She couldn't understand the words, but the way his companions guffawed made it fairly obvious that his observation was insulting. Never before had she been left standing by herself in a public place frequented by ruffians! Her brothers had always insisted she take her maid along when she went to Marshall Field's store or driving in Lincoln Park. She breathed a sigh of relief when she saw Chase sauntering toward her, apparently unconcerned about her safety or her long wait.

"Where have you been?" she demanded. "I'm burning up out here in the sun! And those men over there have been calling out rude things to me!"

Chase glanced at the trio, then shrugged. "I thought you liked men to notice you."

"They're hoodlums! Or worse!"

He ignored her, grinning as he surveyed the far end of the cobbled street that ran parallel to the waterfront. She followed his gaze to the contingent of horsemen and closed carriage now clattering toward them.

"There's our ride now," he said, taking hold of her arm. "Esteban's right on time."

"Who's Esteban?" she asked, half running to keep up with his long, hurried strides. He didn't deign to answer, and Carlisle had suddenly had enough of his incivility. She jerked her arm away from him and stood her ground.

Chase frowned down at her. "Now what's the matter?"

"I will not be dragged about by you and treated like some prisoner you're towing off to jail! I refuse to go another step until you tell me who that man is." She stopped, suddenly remembering that her duenna was nowhere to be seen. She looked back at the ship. "And where is Senora Alvarez?"

Chase's deep blue eyes raked over her flushed face. "Esteban's an old friend of mine, and the foreman of my ranch. He's come to escort us there. As for the senora, she decided to sail on to Tampico, where she's to visit her son's family."

Carlisle was stunned. "But I thought you said it was necessary for me to have a duenna while I was in Mexico!"

"No, that's not what I said," he answered, a rakish grin curving his lips. "What I said was you needed a duenna while Javier Perez was around. There'll be no need now that you're traveling with me and my friends."

"Well, I happen to think differently," she returned furiously. "You're a lot more dangerous and ill-mannered than Javier. At least he's never taken advantage of me."

"Glad to hear it, Senorita Kincaid. But you have no reason to fear me. Once we get to the ranch, my mother will take you under her wing. The two of you should get along fine, since she disapproves of my manners as much as you do."

When he took her elbow, Carlisle had no choice but to be pulled along with him. She pressed her lips into a tight line, deciding that being alone with him was even worse than she'd imagined. As they crossed the cobbled wharf, the man leading the armed riders halted those behind him with a raised right arm, then swung off his horse and strode toward them, grinning widely.

"Esteban!" Chase called out, obviously overjoyed to see his friend. He released Carlisle and greeted the other man with a warm *abrazo*.

"It's been too long this time, *amigo!*" Esteban answered.

"*Sí, compadre.* I wondered if you'd tear yourself away from that beautiful wife of yours long enough to come meet me!"

"*Caramba,* your ugly face is little comfort after three nights away from my hot-blooded Conchita. She is visiting her kin near the river while I'm away. They're camped in their usual spot. Here, I have brought your riding clothes."

"*Gracias.*" Chase took the worn saddlebag Esteban handed to him, laughing and slapping his Mexican friend on the back.

"How's Mother and Tomas? Did they come with you?"

"Your mother, she has gone home to Mexico City. Your brother, Tomas, thought only of the toros, so she took him away to where he'd carry the schoolbooks instead of the cape. He is as eager to fight the bulls as we were in the old days, eh, *amigo?*''

Chase laughed again, clapping his friend's shoulder. *''Sí,* but he is already much better than we were. I have the scars to prove it!''

As the two men continued to joke and reminisce, Carlisle bristled at how incredibly rude Chase Lancaster could be. She felt like an utter fool, standing to one side like an unwanted stepchild. She flushed with heat and anger. He probably would never have presented her if his friend, Esteban, hadn't looked curiously at her.

''Oh, yes,'' Chase said, glancing at her. He had forgotten her, the idiot! ''This is the *muchacha* I telegraphed you about. Senorita Carlisle Kincaid. She'll be our guest for a time. Carlisle, allow me to present Senor Esteban Rivera.''

Esteban swept off his wide tan sombrero and bowed from the waist. He was unusually tall for a Mexican and dressed in a loose white shirt and travel-stained riding breeches. A red scarf was tied around his neck, and he wore both a pistol and a long hunting knife hanging from his belt.

''My pleasure, senorita,'' he said in heavily accented English. ''I am pleased you honor us with your lovely presence. My woman, Conchita, will be your maid. She is lonely at the rancho.''

Thank goodness, a gentleman! Carlisle thought gratefully. And there would be a woman to talk to! Her spirits revived considerably, and she gave Esteban Rivera her most winsome smile.

''Senor Rivera, I am most pleased to make your acquaintance. It's refreshing to find I will be traveling with a gentleman, at last.''

Esteban looked surprised and glanced at Chase, whose face, as usual, showed no trace of emotion. Carlisle really didn't care. She'd had her fill of Chase Lancaster. She'd cultivate the friendship of Esteban Rivera and his wife, and Chase could go to blazes!

4

Across from the docks, a small, whitewashed cantina lay quiet in the morning sun. While Esteban courteously led Carlisle to a small table there, Chase disappeared upstairs without a word of explanation, carrying the worn brown leather saddlebag that Esteban had handed him out on the street.

Carlisle wondered where he was going. It wouldn't surprise her one bit if he was escaping through a back door, leaving her stranded in a foreign land with a handful of men she'd never seen before.

"Chaso has made you very angry, no?" Esteban asked softly. Carlisle turned her attention away from the upper balcony and surveyed her companion with some surprise.

In spite of his rugged face, Esteban Rivera wore an expression of complete tranquility. So intelligent were his dark eyes and so gentle his smile that Carlisle felt easy in his presence. He seemed the sort of man who'd know the answer to any question she might ask and offer wise counsel on any problem. Both of his hands lay on the table, his fingers long and slender, almost delicate. Somehow she knew they could be very good friends, she and Esteban.

"*Sí*," she agreed. "We don't care for each other very much."

"I am surprised. Chaso likes women, especially the pretty ones. You are the most beautiful senorita I have ever seen. I must paint you while you're at the hacienda."

"You're an artist?" Carlisle smiled as his black eyes roamed over her features.

"*Sí*. It is my destiny. And you have the face of an angel, with hair like fire."

Carlisle had heard compliments before. But Esteban was not flirting with her. He was examining her face with serious objectivity, as if she were some unique sunset he wanted to capture on canvas.

"I'm flattered, Senor Rivera. But I must say I don't feel particularly worthy of your attention. I'm not yet used to your hot Mexican sun."

Esteban's regard drifted down her expensive white organdie outfit, his eyes lingering on the long, tight sleeves and high, lace-edged neckline. "Our *muchachas* do not wear so many clothes, especially the *gitanos*, who are gypsies like my wife, Conchita. Soon we will join her people and she will give you better clothes to wear." His gentle smile spread over his face, lighting his splendid eyes. "Conchita is wild and hot-tempered, but she treats me like I am king."

Carlisle nodded, wishing she were already wearing Conchita's clothes. Even in the deep shade of the patio, she felt constrained and overheated in the clinging white dress. It was one of her best, a design by Charles Worth, which Gray had given her for a graduation gift. Now she realized she should have listened to Chase when he'd warned her about its unsuitability for traveling. But she'd wanted to look her best while saying good-bye to Javier.

Besides, she hadn't expected them to leave for the hacienda immediately. She'd expected at least one night in a hotel where she could bathe and refresh herself after the sea voyage. She felt sticky and cross, but she decided not to voice her discomfort and irritation, because she liked Esteban.

An Indian girl wearing a cotton print skirt and low-necked white blouse glided up to their table, balancing a wooden tray containing a pitcher of cool orangeade, which Esteban called *naranjada,* and a plate of flat corn cakes he called tortillas. Carlisle sipped the sweet juice but lowered her cup as Chase reappeared on the stair. He'd changed into riding clothes like those Esteban and the others wore—dark brown suede breeches, fringed down the sides and flared at the bottom to fit over his boots, and a loose-fitting white shirt.

Carlisle stared at the black leather holsters strapped low on each of his hard-muscled thighs. The ivory-handled Colt revolvers rode near his fingertips, and he looked big and menacing with his hard tanned face and intense blue eyes. When he gazed at her, she felt a shiver fan out across the nape of her neck.

"You ready, Esteban? We have a long way to go tonight."

His attention returned to Carlisle, and instinctively, she knew that whatever he said would be mocking.

"That is, if you're ready, ma'am?"

Even Esteban appeared to notice the sarcastic

drawl, and he looked searchingly at Chase. Hot and angry, Carlisle spoke sharply.

"Perhaps I would have liked to freshen up and change into something more comfortable, Mr. Lancaster."

"Why, Senorita Kincaid, you chose your traveling apparel yourself, after I told you it wasn't suitable. Now I'm afraid we just don't have the time to sit around and let you sort through your trunks. We aren't traveling through downtown Chicago, you know. Here, in the wilds of Mexico, we have to make use of daylight, because the Comanches ride at night."

"Comanches!" Carlisle echoed, forgetting her ire. For some reason, the thought of encountering Indians while in Mexico hadn't occurred to her. Stone had told her the fierce red men rode in plundering bands on the western plains. But surely not here in Mexico, a civilized country!

"Yes, ma'am," Chase said with exaggerated patience. "Savage Indians. With red skin and scalping knives and everything. Guess you don't see many back in Illinois, do you?"

She was grateful when Esteban spoke up, though he earned a frown from Chase for his trouble. "Do not worry, senorita. The Comanches do not attack carriages surrounded by so many armed *vaqueros*. And the *guerrilleros* hide in their rebel holes in the mountains like cowardly swine. You'll be safe with us."

At the mention of rebels, Carlisle's interest sharpened. So did Chase's, for he drew up a chair and spoke in a lower voice.

"Has there been trouble anywhere here in the north since I've been gone?"

Carlisle pretended disinterest as she sipped her orange juice, but she listened eagerly, half surprised they spoke so freely in front of her. Javier was right. They didn't suspect her.

"Sí, amigo, and many rumors of *revolución,"* Esteban said. "Trouble is not far away, I think. Many *guerrilleros* are congregating in the sierra, and there have been attacks. They blew up a trestle near El Paso del Norte and a bank in Chihuahua."

"Damn," Chase muttered, his face growing harder. "In New Orleans, I heard rumors of a plot to return Santa Anna to power."

Every muscle in Carlisle's body went stiff, and her palms grew sweaty as she put her mug back on the table. Nerves jittering, she wet her lips. Suddenly she wasn't so sure she would be very good at spying. Perversely, her heart hammered with excitement.

"What's the matter with you?" Chase asked her suddenly.

Carlisle jumped guiltily. Dear God, am I that transparent? she thought as Chase's eyes narrowed.

"Nothing's the matter," she replied. "Except first you tell me to hurry, then you sit around chatting as if we have all day."

"Sorry, ma'am, don't know what I was thinking of," Chase said, scraping back his chair, amusement glinting in his eyes.

Ignoring him, Carlisle rose, glad he walked on ahead. She smiled at Esteban as he bowed slightly, then took his arm and allowed him to lead her outside to where the carriage awaited them in front of the cantina.

By midafternoon of the same day, Carlisle wished she were back in the quiet, shade-dappled cantina, sipping the cold *naranjada*. The carriage in which she rode was well sprung and as comfortable as such a conveyance could be under a broiling hot sun. For hours they'd traveled up the Rio Grande River, then headed southwest across a dry, desolate plain toward the distant foothills of the Sierra Madre.

She rode alone inside the coach, wilted by the heat and nearly choking on the dust kicked up by the rolling wheels. It swirled inside the open windows to coat the black leather seats like talcum powder. Already her lovely white dress was dingy from the horrid reddish dust and stuck to her like a wet bedsheet. She longed to tear off all the layers of undergarments, but she knew such immodesty was impossible, not while traveling with a group of men. She did resort to unbuttoning her bodice as far as was decent. She lifted her clinging skirt and waved it up and down, trying to cool her stocking-clad legs.

She thought of the cool ocean breezes that had teased her hair as she stood on the promenade deck with Javier and Arantxa. They'd laughed together as a school of dolphins leapt and played alongside the starboard bow. Javier and Arantxa had sailed on down the east coast of Mexico to Veracruz, and Carlisle could have been with them, if it weren't for Chase Lancaster. Rage against her hateful host rose inside her as she was jounced up and down and from side to side in the careening carriage. Why were they going so fast? They weren't escaping a fire, for heaven's sake!

Carlisle was simmering with anger by the time Chase edged his black stallion alongside her window.

"How's it going?" He peered in at her, insolently

eyeing her uncovered legs, which were propped in unladylike fashion on the opposite seat.

"How do you think it's going?" she snapped, hastily pulling down her skirt. "It's like being roasted in a slow oven in here, and there's dust all over me! Just look at my gown! It's ruined!"

Chase grinned at her display of wrath, running his gaze over her flushed face and disheveled hair. Carlisle folded her arms over her chest and clamped her jaw shut, wishing she could lock him up inside the hot, dusty prison he expected her to endure. She watched him unhook a metal canteen from his saddle horn and hand it through the window. Carlisle took it, ignoring him as she uncorked it and drank thirstily. The water was tepid, but at the moment, it tasted better than vintage champagne.

"Do you know how to ride?" Chase asked a moment later when she returned the canteen.

"No."

Chase frowned at her sullen answer and glanced at the yards of dingy white organdie filling the carriage seat.

"Oh, hell, strip off some of those bulky petticoats and I'll take you up on my horse with me. I'm scouting ahead for an arroyo where we can get some water. But make it quick. I don't have all day."

"Ride? With you? What makes you think I'd ever consider that?"

"Suit yourself, then." Chase shrugged carelessly. He pulled the reins, jerking his mount away, and Carlisle immediately regretted her impulsive rejection.

"Wait!" she called out the window as his stallion began to drop back. "I'm sorry! I do want to go with you!"

He spurred ahead and flashed her a lazy grin. "At your service, ma'am. But like I said, you'll have to shed all those underthings. The dress itself probably weighs a ton."

"All right," she agreed, not particularly adverse to ridding herself of layers of silk and cotton insulation. She waited for him to look away, but he continued to ride alongside the carriage, watching her through the window.

"I'd like some privacy," she said tartly.

"I won't peek, I promise," he answered with just enough scorn to make Carlisle flush.

She jerked down the tasseled window shade and began to wriggle out of her heavy petticoats. When only three lay heaped on the floorboards, she was amazed at how much cooler she felt.

"What the devil's taking you so long?" Chase's voice growled from the other side of the shade. "I'm eating dust out here!"

Good, she thought as she released the shade. "Do you really think it's proper for me to ride with you? I mean, when I'm not fully dressed."

Chase shook his head, his exasperated look making Carlisle feel silly.

"Since when have you worried about propriety? I saw a lot more of you the day you were hanging on the trellis with your skirt hiked up to your waist."

"Only because you were so ungentlemanly that you stood there staring up at me, even after I'd asked you to leave!"

Chase grimaced, obviously annoyed, judging by the restless way he raked his fingers through his gilt-edged hair. Even after such a short acquaintance, she was beginning to recognize signs of his anger.

"Look, Carlisle, if you want to ride with me, fine. If not, say so, and I'll be on my way."

Carlisle hesitated, but one brief glance around the small, dusty carriage convinced her. "How will I get on the horse with you?"

"Stand up and take hold of my neck," he ordered, unlatching the door.

Carlisle obeyed, gasping as his arm folded around her waist, lifting her sideways and in front of him as if she weighed nothing.

"Straddle the saddle. It'll be more comfortable."

Carlisle was scandalized at his casual suggestion. Even though she'd never learned to ride, she knew that proper ladies never sat astride a horse. The fact that Chase, a man, had suggested it made her feel wicked and wanton. She swung her leg over the horse's neck, then took hold of the saddle horn with both hands.

Her breath caught as Chase promptly pulled her back against his chest, holding his left hand against her midriff while he controlled the spirited stallion with his right. It was, beyond a doubt, the greatest degree of intimacy she'd ever experienced with a man, and as his muscular thighs hugged her, her face reddened with embarrassment.

"Must you hold me so tightly?"

"I must, if you don't want to end up in the dirt." He tightened his grip, spurring the horse forward with a touch of his heels. Carlisle hung on to the saddle horn as they surged ahead of the outriders.

They galloped in front of the coach toward a thick copse of straggly trees in the distance. Carlisle looked around the barren plain stretching out toward the mountains, its flat ocher expanse dotted by odd-

shaped cacti and low, scrubby bushes she'd never seen
before. They rode fast, kicking up a pillar of dust
behind them, and the wind engendered by the wild
ride whipped some of the pins from Carlisle's hair,
until the coils of heavy golden-red tresses began to
loosen and flow down her back and over Chase's arms.
Carlisle laughed aloud, just because it felt good!

"So you like riding, do you?"

Chase's mouth spoke against her temple. His lips
touched her skin, and to Carlisle's chagrin, goose
bumps rippled over her flesh from head to foot. What
was she thinking of, she wondered in sudden dismay,
to have agreed to go off alone with him in the middle
of nowhere? Hadn't Arantxa and Javier told her how
dangerous and unprincipled he was? Hadn't she
sensed it herself, from the very beginning?

After a while, they reached a verdant growth of
thick, bending willow trees that lined the edges of a
small stream, and Chase slowed his horse to walk
through blessedly cool shade. He reined up at the
water's edge, lowering Carlisle to the ground, and
then swung off the horse himself. Carlisle stood aside
as he led the lathered animal to drink. Uneasy, she
glanced around at the dense thicket of mesquite and
huge maguey plants which lined both sides of the
creek.

"Do you think Indians might be about?" she asked
hesitantly.

"No, not here."

He hadn't looked at her or given her much attention, so she knelt on the bank of the stream. Dipping
her handkerchief into the water, she bathed her face
and throat.

"Why don't you take off your shoes and wade? Or take a bath if you want. I'll stand guard."

Carlisle turned in surprise, expecting to see a mocking expression on his face. She was startled to see he was smiling with, for once, no hint of derision in his eyes. Standing there, he looked unbelievably handsome, one hand on his hip, the other idly holding the reins of his horse.

"You know I can't do that." She looked longingly at the cold water, pooling in dark blue depths at the center of the creek.

"Can't you swim?"

"Of course. When I was little, my brothers taught me at our lake house."

"Then go ahead. I promise I won't tell a soul."

He was teasing her now, so Carlisle smiled.

"Well, maybe I'll wade for a minute, but I'm not taking off any more of my clothes."

Chase pulled his rifle out of the fringed leather scabbard tied to his saddle, then squatted on the sand, casually holding the gun in the crook of his right arm.

Carlisle sat down, took off her small white pumps, then glanced at him. He was grinning, challengingly, and she raised one finely arched brow, then untied her black ribbon garter. Without looking at him again, she quickly unrolled her sheer white stockings and slipped them off her toes. She stood, bunched up her skirts, and waded to her knees in the clear water.

Finally, she gave in to her desire, rolling up her sleeves and hitching the bulky organdie skirt into her waistband. She bathed the dust from her face and arms, acutely aware that Chase still hunkered down close by, his eyes following her every movement. She felt compelled to look at him. He was no longer smiling; his gaze rested on her with the quelling intensity that always made Carlisle's throat tighten—his look was one of desire, she knew it instinctively, though no one had ever looked at her in quite the same way.

Her heart sped. They were all alone. Esteban and the others were far behind. Would Chase take advantage of her? What would it be like to lie with a man like him and let him touch her with his hands, his lips? She stared back, her eyes locked on his, mesmerized, afraid to move as a force, as tangible as a rope, held them. Suddenly, he stood, turning away from her to adjust the bridle.

"Let's go, Carly. I don't know why the hell I brought you out here."

He'd never before called her the pet name her brothers sometimes used. She was pleased he did. She moistened dry lips.

"Don't you?" she heard herself say.

Chase stopped tightening the girth but did not turn around. For some reason, she felt as if she wielded some kind of strange power over him, when usually she felt so vulnerable where he was concerned.

"Why don't you join me?" she suggested brazenly. "The water feels good against my skin."

Chase stood very still for a moment. Then he looked at her, and she saw some unidentifiable emotion move deep within his blue eyes.

"There's a proverb in my country that I think you should heed, Senorita Kincaid," he said, his gaze holding hers. " 'Charming lady be not too bold, lest you tempt like Aztec gold.' "

Carlisle flushed with embarrassment. "I don't know what you're talking about," she replied as lightly as she could.

"The hell you don't. I've gotten my share of invitations from willing women, but never one quite as blatant as the one you just flashed to me out of those big green eyes of yours. Like I told you before, Carly, someday you're going to tempt the wrong man and land yourself in very serious trouble. Believe it or not, I have enough honor left in me not to seduce my friend's sister. No matter how much she wants it." Carlisle felt her face grow hotter, but he went on with calculated cruelty. "So don't waste your virgin's teasing on me."

Abruptly, he pulled his horse toward her. Without another word, he hoisted her into the saddle and mounted behind her. As they rode back in silence, Carlisle held herself ramrod straight and haughty, but she felt foolish and naive and, most of all, angry, because every word he'd said was true. She had wanted him to wade into the water and pull her roughly into his arms. She had wanted him to kiss her again, as he had in the coach, because she craved the breathless, tingling arousal she'd felt when his mouth twisted over hers and made her moan. What was happening to her? What had he done to her?

After Chase deposited her back in the coach, damp and disheveled, Carlisle huddled in the seat, humiliated beyond belief. She'd tried to entice Chase, despite his rude, callous treatment, despite all the bad things Javier and Arantxa had told her about him. Well, she vowed resolutely as she settled back on the seat, preparing herself for a long, uncomfortable ride, it would never, ever happen again.

5

For the next three days, Carlisle avoided Chase as they trekked onward toward the mountains, spending the nights in dusty cantinas or accepting the hospitality of small hacienda owners along the way. On the fourth day, as twilight crept over the peaks looming majestically against the horizon, they finally reached the bank of the Santa Catarina River, where they were to meet Esteban's wife and her gypsy clan.

Carlisle looked around eagerly as Esteban helped her from the coach. Chase had kept his distance since they'd returned from the stream, and he barely glanced at her now as he dismounted, his attention on the encampment, where news of their arrival was beginning to circulate.

A flock of dark-haired, dark-eyed people quickly surrounded Esteban. He laughed, clasping both men and women fondly to his breast as he greeted each one by name. Most of them embraced Chase with the same unbridled enthusiasm, especially the women, Carlisle noticed, wrinkling her nose. She jerked her head around as a shrill feminine squeal rent the air.

"Esteban!"

A tiny woman, not five feet tall, came flying toward Esteban, her scarlet skirt flapping around her legs.

"Conchita!" Esteban cried, laughing with pleasure and opening his arms.

To Carlisle's shock, Conchita leapt onto him, wrapping her arms around his neck and her bare legs around his waist in the most scandalous fashion imaginable.

"You are so mean to leave me all alone for so long!" she cried. *"Mi madre* say you look for another woman!"

"So you have missed me much, eh?" Esteban swung her around until she shrieked. "Let me show you how much I have missed my sharp-tongued little Conchita!" Esteban said, pulling her head back and kissing her passionately on the mouth while his hands wantonly explored her hips and waist. Conchita's people began to clap and cheer, and Conchita made a great show of rubbing her body provocatively against him.

When Esteban's hands disappeared beneath his wife's skirt, Carlisle blushed and looked away, but she heard Chase laugh. It was just like him, she thought with a dour twist of her lips, but she could not help but peek again at the entwined couple, beginning to think she might learn the secrets of the marriage bed right then and there. Esteban, however, had already lowered his wife to her feet, and the gypsy girl was shaking a finger at Chase.

"Don Chaso! You are angry with me, no? You have given me no greeting at all!"

Chase grinned, and Carlisle was astonished again

as he kissed Esteban's wife on the lips as heartily as her husband had. Carlisle's gaze went quickly to Esteban, who only threw back his head and laughed, not seeming to mind his friend's familiarity with his wife. And, of course, Chase Lancaster didn't mind, she thought crossly. Conchita was just another sparrow to devour! Disgusted, she watched him release Conchita, who immediately rushed to Carlisle.

"Ah, so you are the *gringa* Don Chaso tell us about! And so tall and *bonita*, with all that flaming hair."

Conchita looped her arm through Carlisle's and pulled her toward the circle of wagons, chattering the whole time. "There's to be a fiesta *grande* tonight! For you and Don Chaso! We will drink and dance all through the night, *sí?* I will teach you the *jarabe*. I am the best dancer of all my gypsy kin."

"*Gracias,*" Carlisle said, wondering what the *jarabe* was as Conchita introduced her to several men who had run to meet them.

"This hombre, he is my cousin Emilio, and this one, he is Paco. They are wild with *el diablo,* so you will like them very much, yes?"

Conchita laughed knowingly, and Carlisle nodded, smiling as more gypsy hombres hovered around, all black-haired and slim, dressed in tight black pants and the long-sleeved loose white shirts called *camisas*. Brothers, sisters, aunts, and uncles, all were introduced in quick succession until Carlisle felt so deluged with Spanish names that she couldn't imagine being able to put faces to any of them. Except for the tall, bearded young man called Emilio, who looked at her with such raw, smoldering hunger that he was hard to forget.

Carlisle caught sight of Chase, who stood a short distance away, each arm draped around a pretty girl. The sight annoyed her, but why should she care what he did? Why, indeed? Except that she needed to be on better terms with him so she could garner information for Javier.

Finally, Conchita led her past several wagons, their side panels painted with murals of mountain valleys, bullrings, and ocean vistas. Each had a high driver's seat, but at the rear, the wagons resembled small cottages with retractable steps and curved shingled porches to shield the back stoop. Conchita's wagon was a brilliant azure blue with cherry-red molding and decorative trim. The painting on the side portrayed a dancing senorita in a flowing mantilla.

"You will sleep in my own wagon, Dona Carlita, so you will feel welcome." Smiling with pride, Conchita held back a silk curtain, striped with gold and black.

"I really hate to take your bed, Conchita. I—"

Conchita frowned, her fists planted firmly on her slender hips. "But I say you will! You are Don Chaso's honored guest, and he is Esteban's *patrón*. You must accept or we will be insulted, *comprende?*" Her lips curved slyly. "And Esteban will not mind. He likes to make love to me under the stars."

Carlisle could think of nothing to say to Conchita's intimate revelation, but she smiled as she ducked inside the wagon, beginning to admire Conchita's lack of inhibitions. She laughed to herself, wondering what Miss Martin, one of the strictest of her childhood governesses, would think of the hot-blooded little gypsy. But how free Conchita and her people were!

Carlisle couldn't wait to rid herself of the endless, silly rules of etiquette and be more like them.

"*Gracias,* Conchita. I mean no insult. You're very kind. Esteban is a lucky man."

Conchita's smile widened. "My Esteban, he is my life, *mi vida.* He's a good hombre, too. He never beats me like my cousins do their women." Her dark brown eyes flicked down over the tight-fitting bodice of Carlisle's full-skirted gown of lavender silk.

"You have a hard, hot journey in that big purple dress of yours, no? But *esta noche,* tonight, you must dress like the gypsy so you can dance with us!"

Conchita threw open a small wooden trunk and pulled out a lemon-yellow blouse with purple embroidery around the scooped neckline.

"*Sí,*" Conchita said, retrieving a matching cotton skirt with a wide ruffle decorating the hem. She thrust it into Carlisle's hands. "All my cousins and brothers will fight for you at the fandango! But I must go now and find my Esteban. My bed has been cold and lonely, you understand, no? I will send little Carlos with water for your bath. Then you must rest if you are tired, for our fiesta will last until *mañana!*"

Abruptly, Conchita was gone, the striped curtain waving desultorily in her wake. As Carlisle stood alone, looking around the dim interior, she was possessed by the most peculiar sensation of unreality. How incongruous that she, Carlisle Kincaid, one of the richest heiresses from Chicago, was somewhere in Mexico, in a painted gypsy wagon, seriously considering donning a costume that required no petticoats, panniers, or corselettes. And why? To dance and drink wine with a bunch of gypsies!

She laughed aloud, imagining what Gray would say.

He'd be absolutely furious with her, and with Chase Lancaster for allowing it. Her girlfriends from the convent, on the other hand, who'd spent nearly every waking moment craving exciting adventures, would be green with envy. Even Arantxa, who'd enjoyed more freedom than any of them. Well, Carlisle decided, holding the skimpy yellow blouse against her chest and peering into a dusky mirror hanging on the wall, she intended to take advantage of this night and enjoy herself, for she'd certainly not find herself in such bizarre circumstances again.

Chase stood with his back propped against a high wagon wheel and drank deeply from a skin bottle of *aguardiente*. In the clearing amidst the wagons, Conchita's clan was already laughing and singing while the *músicos* strummed their guitars and the women shook their tambourines. The dancers, men as well as women, whirled and stamped, feet bare, arms waving over their heads, castanets clicking, raven hair flying, until Chase's blood pounded through his temples in raw, primal excitement. He liked the passionate life the gypsies led; he liked to be among them. They made no pretenses, Conchita's people. They lived and loved as they saw fit, and the rest of the world be damned.

Already they'd shocked Carlisle's naive sensibilities; he'd seen the expression in her emerald eyes when Conchita had kissed him. He frowned and drank more of the white sugar cane rum. She hadn't emerged from the wagon yet. He'd been watching for her, and that irritated him—almost as much as she irritated him. She was a tease. She'd proved it again at the arroyo when she'd invited him into the water with her. But taking her on his horse with him had been his idea, and he should have known better.

Since the first time he'd felt her lips surrender under his mouth and heard her weak moan, he'd wanted to kiss her again. He couldn't deny he wanted her, but he sure as hell couldn't act on his desire. He was on dangerous ground with her. And he'd already decided that once they arrived at the hacienda, he'd let Esteban and Conchita entertain her, so he could keep his distance. She was just too damn desirable.

Chase would never have dismissed Senora Alvarez if he'd known his mother had taken his brother, Tomas, to their home, the Casa Amarilla, in Mexico City. Now it would be difficult to leave Carlisle at the ranch while he traveled on to the city, especially since she was so eager to get there herself. But journeying alone together all the way to the capital was unthinkable—not in his present state of mind.

A blazing bonfire had been built in the center of the clearing, and across from him, he saw one of Conchita's cousins, a young hombre named Emilio, rise to his feet, his eyes fixed on the back of Carlisle's wagon. Without looking, Chase knew that Emilio was watching Carlisle, and he turned to see what held the man entranced.

But he was in no way prepared for her appearance. Her low-cut yellow blouse bared soft white shoulders, and she'd unbound her hair, damn her, allowing a fiery, shimmery riot of curls to tumble down her back. Each time she moved, the leaping flames of the fire glinted through the coppery tresses. As she stopped on the back platform of the wagon to watch the dancers, Chase knew without a doubt that every man present would want her.

Muttering a low oath, he frowned blackly. Was she out of her mind, appearing among so many hot-blooded men looking like that? Was she so blind to her own beauty that she didn't realize how she affected the opposite sex? Or, more likely, he thought furiously, had she done it on purpose? No wonder Gray had seen fit to confine her to a convent. Chase was beginning to think that was exactly where she belonged.

From her place on the wagon stoop, Carlisle was glad to see Conchita rushing toward her. The tiny gypsy girl pulled Carlisle by the hand to a place beside Esteban. Several women were dancing by the fire, and Carlisle watched them, trying in vain not to feel self-conscious in the loose, unfamiliar, but unbelievably comfortable clothing. Night had cooled the air, and everyone seemed very pleased to see her, smiling and laughing and constantly refilling her tin cup with some kind of sweet white wine.

Gradually, she began to relax, the quick, riveting strum of the guitars invading her brain and making her pulse race. The gypsy women danced as if possessed, lifting their full skirts and allowing their naked legs to flash in the firelight, their faces flushed with exertion and excitement. She longed to join them, to forget propriety and modesty, to laugh and stamp her bare feet on the hard-packed earth.

"Don't drink too much of that. *Aguardiente*'s a lot more potent than it tastes."

Chase was standing beside her, hands on his narrow hips. He wore the white, full-sleeved shirt and black pants of the gypsies, and he was furious, his blond brows drawn down, his mouth set in a tight, thin line.

"You're asking for trouble, wearing that kind of outfit here," he said angrily. "Don't you have any sense at all?"

Carlisle's own ire leapt. She was tired of him telling her what to do.

"Why don't you just leave me alone? You're the one who brought me here! I wore this because Conchita wants to teach me the *jarabe,* or some such thing—"

"You're not going to dance the *jarabe.* Is that clear, Carlisle? You'll cause enough trouble among the men as it is. I'm not about to see someone knifed on your account!"

"Knifed? What on earth are you talking about?"

"The men here fight over the women they want. And the way you're being ogled right now, there'll be a whole pack of them after you."

"Don't be ridiculous. Everyone's being very nice to me. You're just afraid I might have a good time for a change!" He probably wanted her to sit in the wagon by herself all night! But he wasn't going to spoil her fun. She'd wear what she wanted to, and she'd dance if she liked.

"Ah, senorita, I have never seen such hair as yours, like the fire of the setting sun," said a voice near her ear, so soft and caressing it gave rise to a chill.

Turning quickly, she found Emilio smiling at her, his brilliant black gaze wandering over her face and hair. He picked up a fragrant lock that lay over her shoulders.

"It is like fine silk, *querida,*" he murmured.

As Carlisle stared into his handsome face, his teeth appeared, white beneath his thick, downward-slanting mustache. She'd never seen eyes that glittered so brightly, like twin obsidian disks.

"Gracias," she murmured uncomfortably, sipping her *aguardiente* and daring to glance sidelong at Chase, who had taken a seat on the ground beside her. A black scowl riding his brow, he said nothing, only tipped a skin bottle to his mouth.

As time went by, the wine took hold of the dancers, and the guitars gained momentum, rising to a throbbing, surging fever pitch. Carlisle drank more cautiously, heeding Chase's warning as she listened to Emilio's flowery compliments, which flowed without pause into her ear.

"You like our fandango, eh?" Emilio asked, and Carlisle vaguely felt his arm settle around her shoulders.

"Sí. The dancing is wonderful."

Out of the corner of her eye, she saw Chase pull a pretty girl close and kiss her. The woman was more than willing, because she caught her fingers in Chase's blond hair and pulled his head down, demanding more. Unfortunately, Carlisle knew exactly how the girl felt, all breathless and weak. She'd want him to keep kissing her, whether she liked him or not. Carlisle frowned. Chase was the one who'd probably get knifed, she thought contemptuously.

"And now, Dona Carlita!" Conchita cried suddenly, jumping to her feet. "I will show you our *jarabe* as I promised! And I am the best, am I not, my Esteban?"

"Sí, you are the only one," Esteban answered, his eyes glued to his wife as the music died. Then one

músico stepped forward and began to pluck slow, haunting chords from his guitar. Conchita only swayed at first, like a slender reed in the wind. But when she suddenly came out of her lethargy, stamping her feet and arrogantly tossing back her head, chills ran through Carlisle.

Fascinated, she watched Esteban step into the circle, his arms held behind his back, his eyes locked upon his wife as she came slowly toward him, snatching up her skirt to reveal her feet. Slowly, sensuously, she leaned up against him, so close her breasts touched the front of his shirt. As Esteban grabbed for her, Conchita whirled quickly out of his reach, haughtily turning her back, spurning him, her expression disdainful.

Carlisle's breath caught, but the onlookers cheered and clapped in time with the staccato rhythm as more guitarists joined in. Carlisle's heartbeat thudded with the riveting beat, her eyes widening as Conchita writhed and twisted, moving close to Esteban's loins and undulating her hips against him in the most indecent way possible, her eyes half closed, her mouth parted and wet.

Carlisle moistened her own lips with the tip of her tongue, an unknown sensation curling deep inside her core. She put her hand against her throat, unable to pull her gaze away. While she watched, Conchita whirled once more out of Esteban's grasp, but this time he followed, jerking her roughly around. He kissed her, hard, forcing her head back. Then, to the delight of the onlookers, he bent low, hoisted Conchita over his shoulder, and strode quickly out of the firelight and into the night.

"Conchita warms her husband's bed very well. It is *bueno, sí?*"

Carlisle stared at Emilio, shocked by his remark, but the wine she'd drunk muddled her thoughts and made it hard to concentrate. She watched Emilio pour more *aguardiente* into her cup; then for some reason she laughed as he pushed it toward her mouth, urging her to drink more. She'd had too much, and she was probably slightly tipsy, she realized suddenly. She'd never been allowed more than one or two glasses of champagne at balls or soirees, and she rather liked how relaxed and happy the wine made her feel.

"I like it here, Emilio," she cried, suddenly full of goodwill. He put his face very close to hers, and she leaned toward him, wondering how it would feel to be kissed by a handsome, black-eyed gypsy.

"Come, beautiful one," he cried, pulling her to her feet.

Carlisle went eagerly into the circle of dancers, the frenzied excitement of the other couples communicating itself to her. She laughed again, then lifted her yellow skirt and kicked off the huaraches Conchita had given her. She stamped her bare feet and whirled around, moving in cadence with the stirring guitars, snapping her full skirt the way Conchita had done. Emilio assumed his position, his head held high and arrogant as he gazed at her. Carlisle tilted her chin up and shook her head until her hair rippled like living fire, then turned her back when Emilio reached out to touch her. She laughed, moving away again. She loved it! She felt wonderful! She let herself go, losing herself in the rhythm, and the crowd grew quiet, the men pressing closer, watching intently, no longer drinking or talking, envying Emilio.

She dipped again, one side of her blouse falling to reveal the top of a softly mounding breast. When a murmur of appreciation went up, Carlisle smiled at Emilio, her hips undulating invitingly in the way Conchita's had. And while everyone watched, she lifted her hair with both hands, very slowly and deliberately, holding it off her neck as she sensuously enticed her partner with her body.

When Emilio advanced, she retreated, turning her back on him, and when the gypsy band yelled and clapped, she barely heard, lost in the steady beat, her face flushed.

She felt light-headed, but wonderful, too, more than she had in days and days, more than she ever had in her life! So when a hand suddenly closed over her bare arm and swung her around, it took a moment to focus her eyes on Chase, who stood tall and forbidding, eyes blazing like hot blue flames. To her shock, he jerked her toward him, his mouth attacking hers, hard, relentless, and so unexpected that her mind froze. He didn't stop but kept on, bending her backward, his fingers biting painfully into her arms.

Dizzily, she clung to him, forgetting Emilio, forgetting everyone and everything. A strong, overpowering sense of urgency danced over her nerves like fire igniting, and she pressed herself against him, wanting his kiss.

Then, suddenly, he let her go and leaned down. What on earth was he doing? She gasped weakly as he threw her bodily over one broad shoulder.

"Stop—" she managed to cry breathlessly as blood began to rush into her head. Vaguely she heard cheers and Emilio shouting something, then they were enveloped by darkness. She heard the hollow clump of

Chase's boots against wooden steps before she was dumped unceremoniously upon the cot in her wagon, making the wood frame creak and sway. A match flared, and she pushed her hair out of her eyes, blearily gazing up at Chase, who stood above her, his fists clenched.

"You sure as hell didn't waste any time trying to seduce some other man, did you?" he ground out, his voice so filled with fury that Carlisle tensed all over.

"What are you talking about? I was only dancing with Emilio. I—"

"Shut up, Carly. You've had too much wine to know what you're saying."

"I'm not drunk. Maybe just a little dizzy," she began, trying to stand, only to be grabbed by him and hauled roughly to her feet.

"Let me go!" she cried, struggling against his grip. "You're hurting me!"

His hold lessened, but his anger did not. "You'd better get used to it, because I intend to keep you a virgin whether you like it or not!"

At first, Carlisle thought she hadn't heard him right.

"How dare you say that to me?" she cried furiously, pushing violently against his chest, to no avail.

"I'll say it to you, all right, after watching you make a spectacle of yourself out there." He shook her by the shoulders. "You're just damn lucky I was around, or Emilio would have been the one to claim you!"

"Claim me? What do you mean?"

Chase's mouth twisted with scorn. "Why, you're mine now, Carlisle. This is the way a gypsy claims his lover. Emilio would've carried you off if I hadn't, and you'd be out in the dark somewhere with him right now, letting him have his way with you.''

Carlisle tried to comprehend all he'd said, but she couldn't think straight. Her head was spinning.

"Just go away, Chase! Go away and leave me alone—"

He cut her off in midsentence. "What's the matter, Carly? Now that you've enticed a man to your bed, are you afraid? That's usually the way it is with little virgins like you. You saw Esteban carry Conchita off and you got all stirred up. So you decided you wanted someone to do the same thing to you, and you didn't care if it was Emilio, or Paco, or even me!" He shook her again, making her long hair swirl around her face.

"Well, none of them did, did they?" she cried. "Only you, and you've already told me you're much too *honorable* to touch me!" She stressed the word with heavy sarcasm, her chest heaving with rage.

Tension stretched like a white-hot current between them, and Chase stared at her, fighting the unbelievable wave of desire that held him against his will. Carlisle felt it, too; he could read it in her burning eyes. She wet her lips, and his grip on her upper arms tightened. But she didn't cry out or try to pull away. Instead, she stared up at him defiantly, head thrown back, lips moist and slightly parted. No longer willing to hold back, he jerked her against him until their mouths nearly touched.

"Damn you, Carly," he muttered hoarsely. Then he gave in to his thundering need, and their lips forged together, burning, hungry, their kiss hard and devastating. When she pushed against his chest, he let go of her, and they stood apart, close but not touching, both quivering with desire, both knowing that what was about to happen had been inevitable from the first moment they met.

Chase took hold of her hair, both fists entangled in the silky softness, and for one long, breathtaking moment, he stared down into her huge green eyes, knowing he shouldn't be there, shouldn't do what he wanted so desperately to do, giving himself one last chance to release her and walk away. But Carlisle moaned, all the stiffness and resistance flowing out of her body. When her arms slid around his neck, he was lost. They fell upon each other like two long-separated lovers, starving, needing, desiring.

Carlisle felt him push her against the wall, pull her blouse off one shoulder, lift her off her feet, and move his mouth over her quivering, naked flesh. When his lips closed over the hard tip of her breast, the awful, awesome burst of pleasure shook her whole body, and she cried out.

Panting, she couldn't think, and her head lolled back, her eyes shut as he lifted her skirt to her waist, his hands jerking her hips against his loins. Out of control, they fell back upon the bed, her hair spreading over them and tangling around his arms, until he caught it back, his lips scorching into her mouth— and then she was lost in a strange, dark world of swirling passions and gasping, trembling needs.

He jerked her blouse to her waist, his mouth like a brand on her shoulders and breasts. He was kissing her bare stomach, his hand moving up her inner thigh to where no one had ever touched her before, caressing her softly there until she moaned weakly, her fingers convulsively clutching his thick blond hair, her eyes squeezed tight. She strained up against him, wanting something more, waiting for something, until her body jerked and held, and she cried out, a strange muffled whimper deep in her throat.

"God, oh God, Carly," Chase cried, lurching away from her until he was on his knees beside the bed. She put her hands up to draw him down again, and she could feel his flesh trembling beneath her fingers.

"What are you trying to do to me?" he whispered hoarsely. "What do you want from me? Do you want me to dishonor you completely? And myself?"

Carlisle lay on her back, staring at him, lips bruised by his mouth, body quivering from his touch. A sob caught in her throat. "I don't know what I want anymore. All I know is that when you touch me, I begin to tremble, and I feel something wonderful, something I don't understand."

"*Dios,*" he muttered, getting to his feet and pacing a few steps away. He stopped at the door, running his fingers through his hair. "Go to sleep, Carly. Tomorrow, if we're lucky, maybe you won't remember any of this."

Then abruptly he was gone and Carlisle closed her eyes, her head wheeling crazily. She sobbed again, because she didn't want him to go. Slowly, inexorably, she sank into a dark oblivion, as deep and blue as Chase's eyes.

6

The fact that Carlisle remembered nearly everything the next morning did not improve her state of
mind. Little conversation passed between her and a
sleepy-eyed Conchita, who sat across from her in the
rumbling carriage. Because of her overindulgence in
aguardiente, Carlisle had fallen asleep easily, nearly
the moment Chase had left her alone, but now as she
recalled what had happened between them, she
burned with shame. She hated him for the way he'd
treated her, and she hated herself even worse for not
only letting him, but moaning and clutching him to
her, like some kind of harlot. Lord, what was the
matter with her? Was she losing her senses?

Frowning, she settled her attention on the distant
peaks of the great Sierra Madre, rising majestic and
jagged outside the open carriage window. In front of
the blue mountains, low, rolling hills hugged the
winding dirt road they traveled. She couldn't stomach
the thought of facing Chase. The mere idea flooded
her with humiliation. Thank goodness he'd ridden

ahead with Esteban early that morning so she hadn't had to confront him.

She leaned forward, peering out the window, but he was nowhere in sight. Good, she thought. Maybe he'd stay away all day. How was she ever going to bear living in the same house with him?

Her brows drew together in a frown. She and Chase got along so badly, she doubted he'd ever tell her anything of importance. She wished Javier and Arantxa would come soon. She missed them, and she was eager to join the *guerrilleros* in the mountain hideout.

"You know what Emilio say, *chica*. He say gypsy blood run in your veins," Conchita volunteered suddenly, startling Carlisle out of her thoughts. "He say he want to make love to you all through the night, but Don Chaso claim you for himself."

Another hot, betraying flush ran like a flame beneath Carlisle's skin, darkening her cheeks. She wished she'd stop blushing. Apparently Chase had been right about Emilio's intentions.

Conchita's smile was sly. "But I do not blame you for choosing the blue-eyed one for your lover. He is *muy macho*, like my Esteban. But Don Chaso was angry, too, eh? He wore a hard face when he saddled his *caballo*." She giggled and tucked her feet beneath her. "He is jealous of my handsome cousin Emilio, no? You are lucky, *amiga*, for he is not usually so possessive with his women."

"I am not his woman, and we are not lovers," Carlisle said firmly, embarrassed now to think how he'd carried her off to her wagon like some kind of barbarian conqueror.

"Oh, that is too bad, but do not be sad. His *azul* eyes flame for you. He will make love to you soon.

Last night he watched your wagon like the eagle until you came out.''

"He seemed occupied enough to me," Carlisle replied peevishly. "He had a woman on each arm."

"*Sí*, all my *muchacha* cousins want him to choose them for his lover. He is the great *patrón,* and they say his hands make them shiver and tremble."

"I really don't want to hear any more of this," Carlisle interjected hastily, recollecting in exact detail what his hands could do.

Carelessly, Conchita shrugged a shoulder, but her dark, liquid eyes reflected a knowing look that made Carlisle uncomfortable. She strove to change the subject.

"How much farther is Chase's ranch?"

"Tonight, late, we will reach the Hacienda de los Toros."

"Is the hacienda big?"

"Oh, *sí*, many cowboys ride the cattle and train the bulls. Don Chaso's bulls are toros bravos. They're known all over Mexico for their fierceness," she added proudly. "Don Chaso, he make my Esteban the boss while he, the *patrón,* is away in the capital. But it is very lonely there, except when Dona Maria and Don Tomas come to visit us."

"Who is Dona Maria?"

"She is Don Chaso's mother, and Don Tomas is her son. He is *muy simpático*. You will like him, I know it."

"I didn't know Chase had a brother until a few days ago," Carlisle said, momentarily reflecting on just how little she knew about Chase Lancaster, except for what the Perezes had told her. She decided to see what information she might wheedle out of

Conchita. "My sister-in-law, Tyler, is Chase's American cousin, and she never mentioned Tomas."

"They do not have the same papa. Don Chaso's *padre* was a *norteamericano,* but Esteban say he was very bad, a bandit. Don Chaso's mama and grandpapa raised him. He was a great *hacendado,* and Esteban say he gave many bars of gold to the Holy Church so that Dona Maria could divorce the *norteamericano* and marry Don Tomas's father, Don Hermando. But now she wears the black again. Don Hermando died in the war."

Carlisle considered all Conchita had said, but her last remark gave Carlisle entry into the subject she wished to pursue.

"Your war was very bad, wasn't it, Conchita? I've heard many stories about terrible atrocities committed by the Juaristas."

Conchita's face whitened, and her lips stretched into a tight grimace. "No, do not say such lies! The Juaristas set our country free! I am a Juarista, and Esteban, too! The French pigs were the murderers. I curse them."

Taken aback by Conchita's viciousness, Carlisle hesitated. "But I've heard it said that the Juaristas killed innocent people." She searched the gypsy's angry face. "I heard they massacred a whole village once, one called San Miguel."

"Do not speak of San Miguel!" Conchita cried, looking as if she'd been slapped. "It is an unholy place!"

"But why?" Carlisle persisted.

"Because many suffered and died there. No one dares speak of such things in Don Chaso's presence, not even his *madre. Comprende?* It is forbidden!"

Nodding, Carlisle turned to look out the window again. Not long before, they had entered the strange, treeless foothills of the Sierra Madre, and the air had grown cooler as the coach gradually took them to higher elevations. But at the moment, the weather had little to do with the coldness she felt.

Vividly, she remembered the grisly tale recounted by Javier and Arantxa about San Miguel. Conchita's reaction gave credence to Chase's involvement. Why else would his family and friends fear to mention the mission in his presence? He was guilty. It was hard to believe, but she had no doubt he could be brutal and ruthless when he deemed it necessary. Yet how could he order his men to shoot women and children? Only a monster could do such a thing.

Far ahead of Carlisle's coach, Chase walked his horse alongside Esteban's. Gripping the reins tightly, he stared straight ahead, his mind still tormented by what he and Carlisle had done inside the gypsy wagon. Good God, he had wanted her so badly he'd actually trembled with need. It had taken every ounce of his strength to let go of her, and his hands had been shaking long after he'd stumbled from the wagon.

He gritted his teeth. Now he was angry at himself and her. Even this morning he'd behaved like a coward, riding ahead of the carriage so he wouldn't have to see her. His weakness for Carlisle appalled him. Why was she able to control him the way she did? Was she some sort of witch?

"You do not look so happy, *amigo.*"

Chase glanced at Esteban, then made a conscious

attempt to relax his tight muscles. Since last night, he'd been as tense as a trapped cat.

"Sorry. I've got a hell of a lot on my mind."

Esteban shifted in the saddle, leaning forward and propping his arm on the saddle horn. His dark eyes searched Chase's face with such a knowing look that Chase glanced away, fearing his friend could read his innermost thoughts.

"*La gringa* is like a thorn in your side, no? One you cannot pull out so easy?"

Chase's frown deepened. "I'm not in the mood to talk about Carlisle. She's the least of my worries."

When Esteban chuckled, Chase glared at him. "What the hell's so funny?"

Esteban remained unruffled in spite of Chase's wrath. He shrugged. "I just never expected to see you like this, *compadre*. Not El Gato Grande."

"Like what?" Chase asked tightly.

Esteban's dark eyes glinted. "Like a lovesick bull, pawing the ground and bellowing over the fence of the cow pen."

"Dammit, Esteban, that's not funny."

"Neither is the way you've been treating the *gringa*. Emilio told me how you claimed her."

Chase felt his face darken with embarrassment, which made him even more furious.

"Nothing happened between us, if that's what you want to know."

"I ask you nothing, Chaso. It's just that you are not yourself since you returned from New Orleans with Carlita. You say cruel things to her. You treat her different than your other lovers. I think it is very strange. Even now, you look as if you're ready to draw your gun and shoot me."

"I just might do that if you don't quit needling me about Carlisle!"

They rode in silence, and Esteban remained quiet for a few moments. Then he spoke again, ignoring Chase's bad mood.

"It is plain to me that you already love the *gringa*. Why do you fight yourself so hard? Why not just face it like a man?"

"That's ridiculous. Anyway, I'm already betrothed to someone else. You know that."

"*Sí*, but your mother arranged the marriage when you were just a boy. I know you have no desire to wed Dona Marta. You told me yourself you probably would not."

"*Por Dios*, Esteban, leave it alone, will you? I just met Carlisle a week or so ago, and we can't stand each other. I'm not in love with her, or anybody else, *comprendes?*"

"Then why do you get so riled up when you speak of her, *amigo?* It is no sin to love a woman. Do you not remember how jealous and miserable I was before my Conchita decided she would be my wife? I wore the same black look as you, my friend, and I watched her every movement, just as you do Carlita's. And the *gringa* feels the same about you."

"Shut up, Esteban. I don't want to talk about it anymore," Chase warned through clenched teeth.

Esteban only laughed. The sound grated on Chase's nerves, but as they lapsed into silence, Chase knew his friend was right. He *did* care about her. He just didn't know what the hell to do about it.

As Conchita had predicted, by nightfall the carriage in which she and Carlisle rode passed beneath a tall white archway which glowed ghostly and pale in the moonlight. They proceeded down a long avenue, through shifting patterns of dark and light created by the moon filtering through huge cedar trees lining both sides of the road.

Carlisle watched eagerly for the house, half out of curiosity and half because she was so weary of the endless, bouncing journey, not to mention Conchita's constant chatter about Don Chaso's manliness. Half an hour later, the coachman urged the horses through yet another massive entry arch with a tall gate of black iron spikes. Huge octagonal iron lamps hung on poles at intervals along a smoothly paved road, and Carlisle sat back, impressed as a low and rambling, two-story Spanish *estancia* came into view.

The carriage halted with a lurch in front of a pillared arcade, roofed with heavy red tiles and lit by many lanterns. Chase had already dismounted at the foot of a low stone staircase, and as his steed was led away by a small Indian boy dressed in white, he opened the coach door and held out his hand to Carlisle as if nothing untoward had passed between them the night before. Carlisle decided to act that way, too.

"Bienvenida, welcome, Dona Carlita," he said, his smile easy, his eyes shining like sapphires in the lantern light. *"Aquí tiene usted su casa,"* he said, "which is a time-honored proverb in Mexico. It means, 'This is your house.' "

Reluctantly, Carlisle put her hand in his outstretched one, felt an immediate reaction to his touch, then denied that her trembling had anything to do with Chase Lancaster. When Conchita started to step down, Chase stopped her.

"No, Conchita, it's been a long journey. Go home

with Esteban. Rosita will see to Carlisle's needs to-night.''

''*Gracias*, senor. *Mañana*, Dona Carlita, I will at-tend to you,'' Conchita called as the driver chucked the reins and the carriage rattled off down the drive.

''Do they live nearby?'' Carlisle asked Chase.

''Just down the road in the village of La Mesilla. Many of my *vaqueros* live there.''

Tired to the bone, Carlisle allowed him to lead her up the steps and through the arched gallery stretching across the front of the house.

The front doors, a ten-foot-high expanse of richly carved mahogany, stood open. Inside, massive beams supported the lofty ceiling of the entry salon. A great adobe fireplace filled one side, with a log fire crack-ling and popping in the grate. Directly in front of her, a wide stone staircase adorned with intricately de-signed black iron railings rose to the second floor. Near the steps, two young Indian maids stood wait-ing, wearing spotless white blouses and skirts.

Chase greeted each girl by name, and the servants curtsied and welcomed him home, while Carlisle let her gaze circle the room. A heavy Spanish table stood beside the door, carved of fine oak and covered with a beautiful white lace runner. A thick, crimson-and-gold Arabic carpet covered most of the floor, and it seemed to Carlisle that she had walked into the plush palace of some desert sheikh.

Instead of this magnificent, luxuriously furnished mansion, she'd expected a dusty cow farm with railed corrals and watering holes, such as those Gray had described to her after one of his trips to El Paso.

''Rosita, Dona Carlita is my houseguest. You will be her maid. See that she receives anything she needs, *por favor.''* When Chase spoke, his deep voice seemed to echo up into the recesses of the high domed ceiling.

Rosita looked about twelve years old and had the brown skin and flat, solemn features Carlisle had begun to identify as Indian. The girl bobbed a quick curtsy, taking in Carlisle's red hair and green silk gown as if she couldn't believe her eyes.

"I believe Rosita likes the way you look, Senorita Kincaid. Redheads are rare in Mexico."

Carlisle thought she heard sarcasm in Chase's voice, but she smiled at Rosita, who shyly lowered her gaze.

"You'll probably wish to bathe and retire now," Chase said, his polite mien making Carlisle suspicious.

Why was he being so nice? she wondered. Why was he pretending to be a gentleman? She supposed he couldn't act like a despicable cad in front of his own servants. His dark blue eyes found her again.

"I'm sorry about what went on between us last night, Carly. It was all my fault, so don't blame yourself. I promise you, nothing like that will ever happen again."

Totally shocked, Carlisle felt her jaw drop, but Chase had already turned back to the maids.

"Rosita," he went on, "show Dona Carlita to her room and draw her a bath, *por favor.* And you, Carmen, tell Dolores to prepare a light meal for our guest. *Buenas noches,* Senorita Kincaid."

Still amazed by his apology, Carlisle followed Rosita up the stairs, but at the top step, she paused with her hand resting on the iron railing. As she stood looking down into the spacious room below, a gray-

haired man dressed in a neat black suit hurried from
a doorway beneath the stairs.

"Bienvenida, patrón! You stay away from us too
long! Even *su madre* gave up and went home to the
Casa Amarilla!"

"Jorge, *amigo!* I have missed you!" Chase greeted
him, exchanging a warm *abrazo* with the old Indian
servant. "But I must leave again soon. El Presidente
has need of me in the capital."

"Sí, Don Chaso. El Presidente has sent many letters here for you. There was one today, most *urgente.*
I have locked it in the safe with the others."

The men walked toward a hallway, and as Jorge's
voice faded, Carlisle wondered what the important
message said. Could it concern the *guerrilleros?* She
would have to find out, she decided as she followed
Rosita to her bedchamber.

After speaking with Jorge for a few minutes, Chase
walked quickly to his library. He went to the safe
behind the bookcase, turned the tumbler until the
combination clicked, and retrieved the packet of letters from the president. He sank down in the chair
behind the desk, his muscles stiff and sore from the
long ride.

Opening the envelope that had arrived earlier, he
rapidly skimmed the message, then took the glass
chimney off the oil lamp and held the stiff white
parchment to the flame. The fire quickly ate a hungry
black line across the gold presidential seal, and when
the paper curled, he dropped the flaming remnants
into the copper dish atop his desk. He sighed, leaning
back in the chair, his mind recoiling from what Benito Juarez had penned in his neat, lawyer's script.

Dios, he thought, it was starting all over again, the fighting, the killing, Mexican against Mexican. A kind of sickness he'd not felt since the worst days of the war spread like a black blight over his soul. Why couldn't the conservatives see that the Juarez reform laws would allow their country to survive and grow strong?

Even his own grandfather, whom Chase had respected more than any other man he'd ever known, had been blind to the poverty and hopelessness of the peasants. Juan Morelos had ruled over his domain for his entire life like some steel-fisted feudal lord. Would the opponents of Juarez insist on war again, on inviting the intervention of foreigners, who only came to rape their country?

Slowly, inexorably, from the darkest dungeons of Chase's mind, a picture struggled against the restraining chains of forgetfulness. He rubbed his eyes, trying to force the grisly images away, but he saw them vividly: corpses everywhere; blood and gore spattering walls and floors; limbs sliced away by sharp machetes; flesh torn and blackened by gunshot blasts—old men, women, babies, every inhabitant of San Miguel. God, there had even been crucifixions. Bile rose in his gullet, and his mind shrank from the ghastly faces of the dead.

Agitated, he slid open the drawer and took out a flask of tequila. He drank deeply from the bottle, forcing his mind blank as he'd learned to do after the massacre. His present problems gave him plenty to worry about. Benito's news would affect Carlisle more than anyone. He'd heard the Perez family was involved in revolutionary activities, had even mentioned it to Gray Kincaid in New Orleans. But now their opposition to the Juarez government was a proven fact.

Roberto Perez, Javier and Arantxa's father, had been caught plotting an assassination that nearly took Benito's life. He'd failed, thank God, but one of Benito's advisors, a friend of Chase's, had been killed. Perez had been captured and imprisoned at Chapultepec Prison to await trial for treason, but the most important question concerned his children. Had Javier and Arantxa been involved? And if so, to what degree?

Carlisle wasn't involved, of course. Why would she be? But Chase knew that she'd obstinately defend her friends against his accusations. She would be loyal to the end, as she had been to Tyler when he and Gray had decided his cousin should marry. Perversely, that was one of the qualities Chase admired most in Carlisle. He had been glad she had befriended his cousin when Tyler needed an ally so badly.

But now, under the circumstances, Chase could not allow Carlisle within a mile of any member of the Perez family, not without endangering her. And his interference would make her furious. He could almost see those green eyes glow with fire, as they always did when she was angry with him.

Earlier, when he'd apologized, they'd filled with shock, but he'd meant what he'd said. All day long, riding and talking with Esteban, he'd had time to analyze his own behavior. He remembered what Esteban had said, that he was already in love with Carlisle and should face the truth like a man. And Chase had finally admitted that his *compadre* was right. He cared about her. Though she could make him furious, he understood her, probably better than she knew herself, because he'd been much like her when he was her age.

Chase could remember very well how he'd acted when he was seventeen and his mother had encouraged him to study with the priests. Instead, he had wanted to fight the bulls, as his half brother, Tomas, did now. During those days of his youth in an austere monk's cell, he'd thought of the bullring, and of women—what it would be like to touch and kiss them. Carly was no different. She was curious, sensuous, eager. Except that she was a woman, and those of her gender didn't have the luxury of living life the way they wanted. She had spent an entire year in a convent. No wonder she acted as rebellious as she did. Who wouldn't?

He heaved a deep sigh, fixing his eyes on the flickering flame, not sure what to do about his predicament. He wanted her, God help him, more than anything he could ever remember. When he'd seen her with Emilio, he'd lost control, something he'd never before done over a woman. He'd been angry, frustrated, and jealous.

And last night he'd found that she wanted him, too. He supposed she still thought herself in love with Javier Perez, but she wasn't. Even if she did love Perez, Gray would never allow such a marriage, not when he learned of Javier's involvement with a rebel faction.

Who would she marry? Chase wondered. And why did the thought of her marrying someone else leave him with a bad taste in his mouth? Lord, there were plenty of women around. Why did he hunger so incessantly for Carlisle? Any kind of relationship between them would be extremely complicated, if for no other reason than the betrothal contract his mother had arranged with the daughter of one of her friends, years ago, when the girl was a mere child. Chase hardly knew Dona Marta, but she was eminently suitable. He'd never courted her, and he'd never been sure he'd honor the agreement. As for Carlisle, no doubt Gray intended her to wed some rich American businessman eventually.

Chase drank again. At the moment, despite his growing feelings for her, Carlisle was his responsibility, and she would be for the duration of her visit. Benito had asked him to go to Saltillo and find out what he could about the *guerrilleros* purported to be gathering in the mountains there. The order gave him a good reason to escape her company for a time. Once away from her intoxicating presence, perhaps he could think straight and decide what he should do about her.

Esteban and Conchita would watch over her until he returned. If they showed Carlisle a good enough time here at the hacienda, perhaps she wouldn't be so hell-bent on joining Javier Perez. And if she didn't know they were purposely keeping her away from her friends, she wouldn't be so likely to throw a temper tantrum and try to go to them on her own.

If letters from Arantxa or Javier arrived, he would have to intercept them, at least until he learned the extent of their involvement in their father's plot. His course of action decided, Chase restoppered the bottle of tequila, put it in his desk, then took himself upstairs for some much needed rest.

7

The ringing of hoofs against cobblestones awakened Carlisle the next morning. She sat up, looking around the large bedchamber to which she'd been ushered the night before. Royal blue curtains were drawn over the closed windows, making the room very dim and cool.

Across from her, a large round gold mirror reflected her position in the middle of the magnificent canopied bed. She looked very small and insignificant framed by its immense, carved posts, with a big silver crucifix hanging on the wall above her head. She swept back the covers, pulling on her dressing gown and padding barefoot to the window. The hoofbeats of a prancing horse still clattered on the paving stones outside, and as she slid back the curtains and parted the shutter, she hoped she would see Chase.

A blast of heat hit her face, and she squinted in the bright morning sunlight, shielding her eyes as she stepped onto a small iron balcony. Below, Esteban sat astride his horse, Conchita in the saddle in front of him. He held her with one arm while he kissed her,

seemingly oblivious to the way his steed backstepped
and danced sideways.

"*Buenos días,*" Carlisle called down, leaning
against the rail and laughing as the couple broke apart.

Esteban immediately set Conchita on the ground, and
as she ran out of sight beneath the arcade pillars, he
doffed his wide white sombrero.

"*Buenos días, el ángel!* You must let me show you
the toros today! They are the bravest in all Mexico!"

"I'd like that! After breakfast?"

"*Sí.* I will be back for you!" Esteban swept his hat
through the air in a gallant salute, then spurred his
mount down the front avenue. Carlisle watched him
until he was out of sight, then looked down the road
in the other direction, eager to see Chase's hacienda
in the daylight. Impressed, she noticed neat flower
beds ringed with whitewashed rocks and ablaze with
scarlet geraniums. Yellow roses climbed the tall stone
wall that surrounded the mansion, and baskets of daisies and marigolds hung from every lamppost and
balcony rail. Carlisle turned as Conchita entered the
room and called out to her.

"*Hola,* Dona Carlita! I have your breakfast for
you!"

"Does Esteban always kiss you like that before he
goes off in the morning?" Carlisle asked, coming
back inside as Conchita placed a silver tray on a table
near the center of the room.

"Oh, *sí.* I would be angry if he did not," Conchita
answered, rushing past Carlisle to push the balcony
doors together. She opened the slatted panels to allow
light to filter through. "Soon it will be very hot. You
must keep the shutters closed so your room will be
cool for siesta."

"I won't need a siesta. I can't sleep during the day."

"Oh, *sí,* everyone at the hacienda rests when the sun climbs high. You will see, Dona Carlita, it is the custom here in Mexico. But you do not have to sleep if you do not want to. Esteban and I do not sleep."

Conchita's smug smile suggested exactly what Esteban and Conchita did at siesta. Apparently the marital bed was no torture chamber for little Conchita. And the sensations Carlisle had experienced so briefly on the bed with Chase were certainly nothing to complain about. Perhaps Conchita would tell her what would have happened if Chase hadn't left so abruptly, Carlisle thought as she sat down before a plate loaded with rice, beans, and hard-boiled eggs. She poured herself a cup of milk from the heavy pitcher.

"Is it nice, the thing between a man and a woman, Conchita?" she asked, trying to act casual.

Conchita was smoothing the rumpled linen bedsheets, but she stopped at once and looked at Carlisle. "You are so *inocente, niña.* No wonder Don Chaso watches you so close. He is like your duenna, no? But *sí,* it is very *bueno,* the thing between a man and his woman. My Esteban, he is a *fantástico* lover. His hands, they do such things to me, they make me moan and cry out, but you will see someday, when you marry and lie with a man."

Carlisle sipped the cool milk, aware that she was blushing. Though she very much wanted specific details, she couldn't bring herself to ask any more questions. Conchita's description was intriguing, to say the least. She envisioned Chase's hands, large, brown, strong, and remembered how savagely they'd pulled off her clothes and moved over her body. Just thinking about how his mouth had caressed her made her heartbeat go wild.

Angry, she shook such thoughts from her mind. Why didn't she think of Javier's hands on her body? She loved him, didn't she? Chase had only kissed and held her because he was angry about Emilio and wanted to punish her. He'd said so. Why did she always daydream about Chase? As she finished her meal, she vowed not to think about him again. But while Conchita helped her bathe and put on a lightweight dress of pale blue cotton, she was already wondering where Chase was and why he'd felt the need to apologize.

Conchita departed with the breakfast tray, and to Carlisle's chagrin, she realized she was looking for Chase when she stepped out of her bedchamber. He wasn't in sight, so she strolled along the upper porch, amazed at the huge Spanish house. The architecture was so different from what she was used to. Each room opened directly onto the covered gallery, both upstairs and down, and the building was constructed around a big garden area with great leafy trees and flagstone-paved walkways.

It was like having a yard inside the house, Carlisle thought as she descended a wide, curving stone staircase that led to the patio. She stopped at the bottom to admire a double-tiered fountain. Jets of water arced gracefully to tinkle in the shallow bricked pool surrounding it. As a faint breeze rustled the leaves of the mimosa tree just above her head, Carlisle decided it was very pleasant there. A jingling of spurs captured her attention and she turned, expecting to see Chase. But it was Esteban who approached her.

"*Hola,* Dona Carlita," he said, politely removing his hat.

"*Hola,*" Carlisle returned, smiling.

"Chaso asked me to show you the ranch, if you wish."

"Is Chase to join us?"

Esteban's dark eyes looked apologetic. "Chaso is already gone. Did he not mention it to you?"

"Gone? Where?" Carlisle asked quickly, more upset by the news than she wanted to be.

"He had urgent business, but he asked me to make you feel welcome."

"He's not going on to Mexico City, is he? He's supposed to take me there with him."

"No. I believe he's gone to Saltillo."

Carlisle froze for a second. Could Chase already know about the rebel encampment? That was something she'd try to discover when he returned.

"Chaso said he would return here. I do not think he plans to be away long."

"I see."

"I have saddled a horse for you," Esteban told her. "Do you ride?"

Carlisle shook her head. "Would you teach me, Esteban? I've always wanted to learn."

"*Sí,* everyone at the rancho rides, and the mare I have chosen for you is very gentle."

"Then let's have our first lesson now," Carlisle suggested eagerly. But when they reached the front drive, the horse in question seemed very big and intimidating.

Putting on the leather riding gloves and flat-crowned hat that Esteban provided, she hid her trepidation and listened carefully as he explained how to handle the reins. Actually, it sounded quite simple.

All she had to do was pull in the direction she wished to go.

"I ordered Dona Maria's sidesaddle for you," Esteban said. "Are you ready?"

"Sí," she said, but as she stepped up on the mounting block and placed her foot in the fancy silver stirrup, she thought how it felt when Chase had held her before him in the saddle. Settling her knee over the saddle horn, she took up the reins. The position seemed very precarious, and she waited nervously as Esteban swung gracefully atop his own mount. Her horse sidestepped when Esteban moved closer to her, and Carlisle tightened her grip.

"Bueno, Dona Carlita," he said. "You must show her who is in charge, or she will get big-headed and try to rule you. You must wear your hat, too, senorita, or your skin will burn. Our sun is very hot."

Obediently, Carlisle pulled the wide-brimmed hat from where it hung down her back and angled it to shade her face. Side by side, they walked their mounts down the paved avenue which led around the end of the house. Tall, big-limbed cedar trees shaded their way, and Carlisle found that riding was not as difficult as she'd imagined—but then, the horses were moving at a sedate pace. A wild gallop, such as the one she'd taken with Chase, would be a different story. Yet that was what she really wanted to do!

At the rear of the hacienda were the stables, a long, low whitewashed structure covered by the same heavy red Spanish tiles that decorated the main house. Beyond the practice rings, the road led to a pasture where the bulls were kept.

The bullring was large, surrounded by a six-foot-high adobe wall. Esteban led her to a thatched-roof pavilion where they could watch a young *vaquero* reining a beautiful white Arabian through a series of intricate steps and maneuvers.

"What a magnificent horse!" Carlisle cried, leaning up against the rail.

"Chaso handles him better than anyone else, though he rarely goes into the ring anymore."

Surprised, Carlisle glanced at Esteban. "Chase is a bullfighter?"

"*Sí*, he was very good, but he no longer enjoys it. Chaso saved my life once, right there." Esteban pointed to a spot against the high white wall.

"Really? From a bull?"

"*Sí*. We were only boys. My parents were campesinos and worked for his grandfather, who was the great *hacendado*. Chaso was ten and I was twelve, but we wanted badly to be matadors. The bull charged, and I froze with fear. Chaso distracted *el toro* with his cape, but the horns caught him in the thigh. He still bears the scar, and I never forget that I live and breathe because of his bravery."

"You and Chase are very good friends, aren't you?"

"*Sí*, we are closer than brothers. I would be honored to give my life for Chaso."

They watched the *vaquero* for a time, then remounted and rode past huge fenced pastures with great herds of cattle and horses. Carlisle was amazed by the vastness of the ranch. Not far from the main house, just over a small rise, they came upon a village, its adobe houses bleached by the sun.

"That is La Mesilla," Esteban told her, reining up and smiling in his gentle way. "Conchita and I live there with the other *vaqueros* and *indios* who work the fields. Come, Conchita will have *naranjada* cooled and ready.''

Carlisle nodded, eager for a rest from the hot sun and hard saddle. The little town was composed of rows of squat, flat-roofed dwellings clustered around a tidy central plaza. A twin-towered mission church with capped buttresses and high, narrow windows dominated the square, but many market booths lined the perimeter, where groups of Indians and mestizos sold their wares.

Esteban led her to a cozy house surrounded by a low brick wall. He lifted her from her horse and tied the mounts to a hitching ring beside the grilled gate. Conchita came running through the small, shady yard.

''So there you are!'' she cried. ''Come inside, where it is cool!''

When they reached the thatched front porch, Carlisle took off her hat and sat down in a wooden rocker. Conchita immediately rushed off to bring them refreshments.

''You honor us by visiting our casa,'' Esteban said, sitting down on a low wall.

''I'm pleased to be here. You have a lovely home.''

Carlisle did like the little white house. Though small, it was neat and cool, and filled with the scent of gardenias and roses.

''Chaso wanted us to live in the *estancia* with him, but I like it here in the village. I like to paint the people when they are at market or dressed for Mass.''

Carlisle had almost forgotten he was an artist. ''May I see your work, Esteban?''

He appeared inordinately pleased that she'd asked, and when he led her inside the house, she saw that all the walls were hung with his pictures, the paintings done in vivid colors, with a crisp sense of reality that made Carlisle exclaim with delight.

"You're very talented!" she told Esteban, walking to one particular picture that caught her eye.

Chase was portrayed in a bullring, resplendent in a short, richly embroidered blue jacket with gold braid, a red cape hung over one shoulder. His head was held at an arrogant angle, his blond hair shining in the sun. She'd seen him look that way several times during their voyage when he stood at the *Mayan*'s rail and gazed out to sea.

"You've captured him well," she murmured.

"*Gracias*. Will you sit for me?"

"Of course I will. Anytime you wish."

"Perhaps we can start tomorrow night? I always work at night."

A few minutes later when they'd returned to the covered porch, Conchita served the orange juice and a delicious vegetable stew which she called *puchero*. Later, after Conchita left to visit with a friend at the front gate, Esteban got out a pad and pencil and sketched Carlisle while she rocked contentedly in the shade.

"Conchita told me you asked her about San Miguel," he said unexpectedly, rousing Carlisle out of her lethargic mood.

"Yes, I did," she admitted, feeling guilty.

"It was very bad," he said then, his placid face troubled.

"If it bothers you, Esteban, you don't have to discuss it."

"No, I do not want you to think us murderers, Chaso and I."

Carlisle felt terrible, because she already liked Es-

teban and Conchita very much, and she certainly
didn't want to insult them.

"I don't think you're a murderer."

"I have killed more men than I can count, but only
in the war." He paused, then went on, his voice very
quiet. "Four years ago, the massacre happened, and
every day I pray to the Holy Virgin for forgiveness.
Chaso, too, suffers much for what happened at San
Miguel."

"Was he in command of the Juaristas that day?"

"*Sí*, but he did not order the massacre. He and I
had taken some of our men around the mountain to
find a back way into the mission. Still, he blames
himself, because his men did the killing."

Carlisle waited, Esteban's deep sorrow communicating itself to her.

"The war was terrible, with many atrocities committed. The French were butchers. The ones who died
at San Miguel were evil. They rode in bands that
plundered and destroyed the villages." His face took
on terrible, sad lines. "They were the men who raped
my poor Conchita."

"Oh, no, Esteban!" Carlisle cried.

"*Sí*. They came upon the gypsy wagons at the river
and shot many of the men. Then they took the pret-
tiest women for their *putas*. Conchita was bitter for a
long time afterward, but she gets better each day."

Carlisle couldn't hide her horror, and she looked
to the gate where Conchita was laughing and chatting. No wonder Conchita had reacted with such anger when she'd mentioned the French.

"Many Juaristas suffered and died at San Miguel
before Chaso lay siege to the mission. The French
used the old church as a prison, where they tortured

and killed our men. That is where they took my Conchita and many *muchachas* like her. She escaped, *gracias a Dios*, but others were not so lucky. Chaso wanted to destroy the evil place, but we had no cannon. The mission was well fortified, because the priests of San Miguel used to operate a silver mine there for the Church.''

Esteban hesitated, his eyes haunted. ''Each day that we camped in the plain in front of the gate, they killed one of our *compadres* and threw the body over the wall. The murders went on for many days, until the defenders were starved into surrender. When they finally opened the gate, it was as if our men went loco. It was horrible what they did to the French and Mexicans who rode with them. Bodies were dismembered, blood ran in the streets—''

Esteban's voice choked, and a sheen of tears misted his dark eyes. In his mind he saw the carnage again as he and Chaso led their men out of the mine shaft. The killing was almost over by then, but they had heard the screams of agony from inside the church. Swallowing hard, he fought the memory of what he'd seen when he'd thrown open the church doors, but the scene hit him again with the force of a blow. French soldiers, their hands nailed to the walls; corpses, hacked and bloody, piled in the aisles; even children—one small boy lay sprawled across a pew, his skull crushed by a gun butt. Sickness overcame him in a great, swift tide, and without another word to Carlisle, he got up and entered the house.

Carlisle watched him stumble away, her emotions in turmoil. No wonder San Miguel was never mentioned to Chase and Esteban. There was no doubt that

Esteban suffered deeply from remorse. Chase probably did as well.

Carlisle had been so sure Javier and Arantxa had been right, but after Esteban's painful revelations, she didn't know what to think. Both sides had been brutal, both had killed and maimed, just as they had in her own country's civil war. But one thing she did know—Esteban and Conchita weren't the bloodthirsty monsters Javier had described the Juaristas to be.

8

For the next two weeks, Carlisle settled into the routine of the hacienda, waiting for either Chase to return or Javier to come for her. She slept until midmorning as was the custom, then wandered until the sun drove her inside for siesta. Usually, Esteban and Conchita would join her for the late meal, or *comida,* as they called it, and in the evening she'd sit for Esteban.

One night in late April she again sat in Esteban's lantern-hung patio. She had donned the simple white cotton dress and lovely white lace mantilla which Esteban insisted she must wear to look like an angel. But inside, her thoughts were far from seraphic as she fumed over Chase's continued absence.

He'd probably planned to leave her like this all along, she thought crossly, to ruin her trip by insisting she come to his ranch instead of visiting the Perez family, and then strand her there alone. It'd serve him right if she left with Javier before he came back! The thought of never seeing Chase again was disconcerting, if only because she'd be cheated out of giving him a piece of her mind for dumping her off like some old dog!

She looked at Esteban, who sat before his easel, his slim body erect, his dark eyes intent on Carlisle's hair, then on his palate as he mixed the exact shade of red. She'd found that when Esteban worked, he shut the world out. Even now, his wife was muttering impatiently in her gypsy dialect, sleepy and wanting to go to bed. But Esteban seemed unaware, so absorbed was he in his work.

During the past few weeks, not only had she learned to ride, but Conchita had worked with her on her Spanish until Carlisle felt much more competent with the language. But she missed Arantxa and all the talks they used to share. And Javier. He'd told her he loved her! Where was he? Why hadn't he come back for her?

She visualized Javier astride a horse, his handsome face ablaze with patriotic purpose, ammunition belts slung over his chest while he led his gallant men to defend the Holy Catholic Church. Perhaps they even wore crosses on their tunics like Richard the Lion-Hearted and his Crusaders, she thought dreamily. The *guerrilleros* would be noble and compassionate, nothing like the cruel Frenchmen Esteban had described to her. After all, they were loyal Mexicans, fighting for their freedom and the survival of their faith. They would never hurt innocent people, like Maximilian's French troops had.

Carlisle looked up, roused from her daydreams when, across from her, Conchita suddenly smiled and jumped to her feet.

"Chaso's back!" she cried, running toward the front gate.

Carlisle froze, then turned slowly, appalled at how

her heart had risen into her throat. Chase came striding toward her, his arm around Conchita. He was dressed in a short charro jacket and fitted trousers with silver buttons down the sides. The dark blue coat was adorned with beautiful silvery embroidery, and he looked unbelievably handsome.

"Hola, Carlita," he said, his smile so warm and caressing that she melted. She'd vowed to lash out at him the moment she saw him, but with him here before her now, Carlisle couldn't pretend she wasn't glad to see him.

"Bienvenida, Don Chaso," she said. His expression told her that he was pleased she'd greeted him in Spanish.

"Esteban has prevailed upon you to sit for him, I see. He's a slave driver when he paints. I sat for him once."

"It is about time you returned, *amigo,"* Esteban said, for once drawn away from his canvas. "Carlita was wondering if you had left her here forever."

"I wouldn't do that," Chase replied, looking at her. Something in the way he said it sent a thrill of pleasure through her.

Chase sat down on a bench, unable to force his eyes from Carlisle's face. God, he had missed her. He had taken his time on his ride to Saltillo, trying to come to terms with his feelings. Stubbornly determined to rid his mind of Carlisle's face, he had stayed away longer than was necessary. All the while, he yearned to see her, wondered what she was doing and whom she was with, until he branded himself an idiot and rode home.

"Don Chaso, I have brought *aguardiente* for you," Conchita said.

Chase dragged his attention from Carlisle long enough to take the cup she held out to him.

"I am glad you are here," Conchita whispered to him. "You will make Esteban stop, eh? He does not listen to me when he holds his paintbrush."

Chase laughed, well able to understand Conchita's dilemma. Ever since they'd been children, Esteban had been fanatical about his art. When young he'd satisfied his creative urges with crude pencil etchings and watercolors, but now he nearly always fashioned portraits in oil. At times it was hard for Chase to think of his quiet, sensitive friend as the great fighter he'd proved himself to be during the war. Esteban was a man of courage on the battleground; in fact, he was one of the bravest men Chase had ever known.

When Chase had rallied to the Juarista cause after Maximilian had driven Benito Juarez and his government from Mexico City, Esteban had ridden at his side for the four long, bloody years it had taken to rid their country of the foreign interloper. He trusted Esteban with his life.

Chase raised a booted foot and propped it atop his other knee, watching as Esteban reached out and pulled the jeweled comb from Carlisle's hair. The long, shiny tresses fell from the knot she had twisted atop her head, tumbling around her shoulders. He felt a strong, absurd jealousy as Esteban carefully arranged the gleaming mass of coppery waves while Carlisle sat docilely, an angelic smile on her face.

Dios, she was exquisite, he thought. Why should one woman enjoy so much beauty? He watched, fascinated, as Esteban carefully rearranged the delicate mantilla around Carlisle's face. The gossamer white lace could not hide the gleaming golden-red hair.

Suddenly, he decided that when the portrait was done, he would persuade Esteban to give it to him.

Esteban had called Carlisle "the angel," and she looked like one. But if anyone knew she was not destined to play that role, it was Chase. From the beginning he had seen the real Carlisle. For some reason, she had never pretended with him, as she did with others. Underneath that cool and flawless exterior, she was as hot-blooded as Conchita.

While he studied her, she looked up and smiled, her small white teeth flashing for an instant, and Chase felt himself beaming back, rather stupidly, he feared. But apparently she wasn't angry with him for leaving her for so long. Suddenly eager to be alone with her, he stood and looked pointedly at Esteban.

"Let's call it a night, Esteban. Conchita's tired, and I have some matters to discuss with Carlisle."

Esteban grinned, obviously aware of the real motive behind Chase's suggestion. "*Sí.* I am sorry, *amigo.* I forget myself at times," he said, lowering his brush. He smiled at Carlisle. "Will you sit for me again tomorrow night, Carlita?"

Carlisle nodded, and Chase walked to where she sat, eager to touch her.

"Come, I have my horse outside the gate. You can ride back to the hacienda with me."

Carlisle barely had time to bid Esteban and Conchita good-bye before Chase was leading her out of the patio. She found, however, that she didn't care. She was glad he was home, glad he wanted to be alone with her. He untied his horse from the hitching rail, then looked down at her.

"I've missed you, Carly."

Pleasure ran over her like warm water, and she

realized she'd longed for him, too, more than she'd thought.

"Then why did you go off without even saying good-bye?" she asked softly.

"I wasn't sure what to say." He reached out and touched her hair, very gently. "Did you miss me?"

Carlisle felt weakness creeping up her legs. *"Sí,"* she whispered.

"Bueno, querida," Chase murmured, his fingertips lightly stroking her cheek.

Carlisle closed her eyes as his mouth touched hers, softly, tenderly.

"You told me you'd never kiss me again."

"That's what I thought, but then I saw you tonight looking like an angel, all in white, and I couldn't help myself."

Carlisle had to smile. "Perhaps you should send for Senora Alvarez. She will keep you in your place."

Chase laughed, warm and genuine, with no arrogance, no scorn, and when he put his hands on her waist and lifted her into the saddle, her stomach felt fluttery and unsettled. As he swung up behind her, Carlisle's heart lurched alarmingly. She had no defenses against him. When he touched her, whispered sweet things to her, she could not resist him. She felt like one of El Gato Grande's helpless sparrows.

As Chase walked the horse across the plaza to the road, Carlisle relaxed in his embrace, remembering the day on the journey from Matamoros when he had taken her with him to the creek. He was different now than he had been that day, she could sense it.

"Why were you gone so long, Chase? I was worried about you."

"I thought you'd be glad to be rid of me for a while."

"I don't hate you, you know," she answered, trying to make her answer sound playful.

He was quiet for a moment. "How do you feel about me, Carlisle?"

His question surprised her. She found it a difficult one to answer, because she just wasn't sure.

"Actually, I like you," she said finally, realizing she meant it.

"And I like you, too, Carly," he replied.

Realizing how childish their grudging admissions sounded, they both laughed. When they reached the big house, Chase lifted her to the ground. He smiled down at her.

"Before I left for the village tonight, I ordered *comida* for us. Will you join me?"

"*Sí,*" Carlisle answered, thoroughly enjoying his politeness. This was a different Chase Lancaster, not cold and heartless, but charming and solicitous. It was almost as if he were courting her favor. She liked this new man, she decided as he took her arm and led her to the patio.

A glass-topped iron table was already set with china and crystal goblets, and as Chase seated her, Rosita came forward with a steaming bowl of rice and frijoles.

"*Perdón*, Don Chaso, but my little sister has been waiting for you to return. She has a gift for Dona Carlita."

"Little Renate?" Chase said, obviously surprised.

Carlisle looked around for the six-year-old girl who had been following her everywhere for over a week now. She found the child in the shadows of the porch.

Renate came forward, curtsying to Chase, then handing Carlisle a small bouquet of white daisies tied together with a red ribbon.

"*Gracias,* Renate," Carlisle said, touched by the child's devotion. She hugged the little girl close. "I love daisies. They remind me of my garden back in Chicago."

"*De nada,* Dona Carlita," Renate murmured, beaming with pleasure as she was led away by her older sister.

"I see you're still winning hearts," Chase commented, seating himself across from her.

"She's very sweet. She comes to my room in the morning and talks to me while I dress."

"Sounds like a fascinating pastime," Chase said, blue eyes glinting.

Carlisle grew warm just thinking about Chase in her bedroom, watching her. Immediately, she thought of the night in the gypsy wagon when he'd nearly torn her clothes off in his eagerness to touch her. Swallowing hard, she strove to change the subject.

"Esteban said you had urgent business in Saltillo. I hope it wasn't an illness in your family?"

Chase hesitated before answering, and Carlisle wondered why. Had he learned something about the *guerrilleros?*

"No. I went there on government business. What have you been doing since I've been gone?"

"Esteban's been teaching me to ride."

"I wanted to do that."

Carlisle was surprised. "Why?"

"Because I thought you'd enjoy the freedom it'd give you."

"I do enjoy it."

"Perhaps I can take over Esteban's job now. Would you object?"

"Of course not."

"Were you lonely here without me?"

Carlisle fingered the stem of her wine goblet. "A little, but I do love it here in Mexico. It's so beautiful with all the flowers and sunshine."

Chase smiled, obviously pleased by her remarks. "Instead of going on to Mexico City, I would like you to stay here a while longer. Would you consider that, *querida?*"

Carlisle stared at him, mesmerized by the warm invitation in his eyes.

"Will you be here?" she asked.

"*Sí.* I want to spend time with you. I want to show you I'm not nearly as bad as you think."

Carlisle smiled, more pleased than she should be. "How can I refuse when you ask me in such a nice way?"

"Then you will?"

"Yes. I haven't heard from Arantxa and Javier anyway. I can't imagine why they haven't written to me. They should have reached Mexico City by now, don't you think?"

Chase looked down, then returned his gaze to her. "The post is difficult here in Mexico. I'm sure you'll hear from them eventually."

He smiled, and Carlisle gazed, enraptured, into his handsome face, suddenly much less eager to join her *guerrillero* friends. Perhaps with Chase treating her so politely, a few more weeks at the Hacienda de los Toros wouldn't be so bad. Indeed, why not enjoy herself?

* * *

For the next few weeks, Carlisle did enjoy herself. She spent most of her time with Chase, nearly always in the company of Conchita and Esteban, as well. When the four of them were together, she could see what close friends Chase and Esteban were. Always joking, they often threw outrageously rude remarks at each other, but neither of them ever took offense. At such times they reminded her of how her brothers, Stone and Gray, had acted before the war.

One night in mid-May she was filled with thoughts of her brothers as she sat in front of her mirror and arranged a mantilla over her hair. She wondered if Emerson Clan had received the letter Javier had composed for her while they were aboard the *Mayan*. Javier had promised to post it from Matamoros before his ship sailed on to Veracruz. She had also written to Gray and Tyler, but she hadn't had any correspondence from them yet. She supposed they were still on their wedding trip.

She shook her head. It was hard to believe more than a month had gone by since she had seen Javier and Arantxa. She couldn't believe they had abandoned her for so long. Something unforeseen must have happened to keep Javier from coming for her. But Chase was proving to be an excellent host, and she liked him more each day. Anyway, she had no choice but to wait for Javier to contact her.

Tonight there was a big fiesta being held in La Mesilla, and Chase was taking her there. Smiling, she realized how happy she felt. She fussed with the lace mantilla, arranging it in the most becoming angle. For some reason, Chase liked her to wear the white one Esteban had given her for the portrait, and she had chosen it to please him.

Snatching up a shawl, she hurried downstairs. Chase was waiting in the salon, dressed in a tan charro jacket and flared trousers. He turned as she entered the room, and his look alone wreaked havoc on her pulse.

"You're beautiful, *querida,*" he said, but made no move toward her. Since he had returned, he had been so formal and proper that she longed for him to stride across the floor, grab her, and kiss her just as passionately as he had at the gypsy camp. Oh, Lord, was she falling in love with him? she suddenly thought in dismay. And what about Javier? She loved him, too. Or did she?

She felt so confused that she was glad when a sudden commotion outside on the drive caught their attention. Through the open doors she could see several *vaqueros* astride prancing ponies, each man holding a burning candle.

"They've come to invite you to the fiesta, Carly," Chase told her. "It's the custom."

He led her beneath the arcade, and a young caballero guided his horse to Carlisle, then swept off his black-and-gold sombrero.

"Senorita, honor us by joining our fandango," he said gallantly, leaning down to offer Carlisle a crown of white gardenias.

"*Gracias*, senor," Carlisle answered. "I am honored."

Her answer pleased the caballero, for he smiled and bowed as his friends doffed their hats and rode on toward the village with a great deal of shouting and jingling of spurs.

"What a beautiful custom," Carlisle murmured, lifting the soft white blossoms to her nose and inhaling their sweet perfume. When Chase came up behind her, she was acutely aware of his closeness.

"The gardenias are for your hair, Carly. May I?"

Carlisle handed him the fragrant circlet, and he carefully placed it atop her mantilla.

"We should go now. It's growing dark, so they'll be shooting off the fireworks soon. And there will be dancing and singing. If I remember right," he said, leading her down the steps to their horses, "you're pretty good at the *jarabe*."

"You'll let me dance?" Carlisle asked as he helped her to mount. "After what happened with Emilio?"

"Nothing happened with Emilio, thanks to me."

Carlisle smiled, remembering instead, and with vivid clarity, what had transpired that night between Chase and her. She rode beside him to the village, quite comfortable on horseback now. She was excited to see a festive crowd of *vaqueros* and peasants jostling about in the square. Conchita and Esteban stood waiting for them at the front gate of their house, and the two couples strolled together through the milling throngs, enjoying the sights and listening to the sounds of guitars and marimbas played by *músicos* who wandered through the crowd.

"Come, Esteban, we must dance!" Conchita cried, dragging her husband off to join the couples twirling in the center of the square.

"What about you, Carly? Do you want to join them?"

"I think I'd rather stay with you," she said and was glad she did because he reached down and laced his fingers through hers.

Hand in hand, they walked along, often stopping and talking to others. Carlisle was impressed by the great respect the villagers showed Chase. After a time, they sat down together to watch the fireworks. Great fiery pinwheels spun with blazes of sparks and loud explosions, and Carlisle laughed at the way the children ran and shrieked with terror at each loud bang.

"Carly?"

She looked at Chase and found him watching her, his face serious.

"Yes?"

"I have to talk with you."

Chase glanced around as if reluctant to begin, and Carlisle sensed something was wrong. She waited warily.

"I'm sorry, but I have to leave the hacienda again."

Dismayed, Carlisle searched his face. "But why? Where are you going?"

"I have to go to Mexico City to see the president."

"But that's all right. You can take me with you, can't you? Arantxa and Javier are probably waiting there for me."

"No. I can't do that."

"Why? That was our plan all along—to visit here first and then go on to Mexico City."

"Things are different now."

Carlisle frowned. "How are they different? What are you talking about?"

"I don't think Javier and Arantxa are suitable companions for you. I don't want you seeing them."

"You have no right to choose my friends," she said quietly, once again afraid that he had uncovered information about Javier's *guerrillero* stronghold while he was in Saltillo.

"I'm sorry to have to tell you this, Carlisle, but

I've found out that the Perez family is embroiled in subversive activities. Gray wouldn't want you to associate with them any more than I do. It could be dangerous.''

Several days ago, he'd also received a telegram from Gray, alerting him that Carlisle had told Tyler she planned to elope with the Perez boy while in Mexico. Chase didn't really believe she meant to now; nonetheless, it was more important than ever to keep her out of the capital.

"I don't believe you," she lied, but her voice sounded so nervous that Chase's eyes narrowed. As his gaze moved over her face, she swallowed hard, feeling guilty and deceitful. Oh, Lord, did he suspect her, too? Carlisle thought wildly. Had he discovered that she was involved?

"It's true, Carly."

Despite the fact that he now knew about Arantxa and Javier, Carlisle realized that she felt more distressed over the fact that he was going away without her. "So you're just leaving me and I'm supposed to sit here by myself? How long are you going to be gone?"

"Probably for a month, maybe more. I can't be sure."

"Will you take me with you if I promise not to see Javier and Arantxa?"

Chase hesitated, then shook his head. "I can't. There are other obligations in the city I must attend to—"

"Then don't let me stop you!" Carlisle cried angrily, suddenly suspecting that his pleasant behavior for the last few weeks had been designed expressly to keep her from wanting to join Javier. He'd merely been performing his duty to Gray, nothing more. Trying not to show how hurt she felt, she shrugged a shoulder as if his departure meant nothing to her. "Go on, then, if that's what you want," she told him, standing up before he had a chance to answer. She glanced out at the crowd, looking for Conchita and Esteban. "I believe I want to dance after all."

Chase was frowning as she walked away, but she didn't care. As she threaded her way quickly through the revelers, tears burned her eyes, but she was determined Chase wouldn't see them. Suddenly no longer interested in the fiesta, she hurried across the plaza to the road that led back to the hacienda, intending to walk back to the big house, where she could be alone.

As she skirted the fringe of the crowd near the church, she was caught from behind, a hand clamping over her mouth so tight that she couldn't scream. She struggled desperately, but could not break free as she was dragged backward into the dark shadows of an alley.

"Carlita, do not fight so! It's me!"

Astonished to hear Javier's voice, Carlisle grew still. The moment she did, he released her. She whirled around and found Javier, with Arantxa right behind him. Both were dressed in the white shirt and pants the campesinos wore.

"Javier! Where did you come from? Arantxa, I can't believe it's you! Where have you been?"

Arantxa hugged her tightly, then spoke low and urgently. "Much has happened, but we've finally come for you. We must hurry or someone will see us!"

"Now?"

"Sí," Javier answered. "We've waited nearly three days before we could get you alone like this!"

Carlisle looked around, wondering if Chase might have followed her, but only the shouting and singing of the merrymakers broke the quiet of the night. "I can't just leave without telling anyone. And my clothes are at the hacienda—"

"We have clothes for you," Javier said quickly. "Come on, Carlita, this will be our only chance! Hurry, before we are seen and captured!"

As Javier took her arm and pulled her down dark back streets, a curious dread filled her. But why should she feel so bad? Chase was leaving, wasn't he? He didn't care enough to take her with him, but Javier did. He had come for her, just as he had promised.

Behind the church in the shadow of a high cemetery wall, a group of twenty or more horsemen awaited them.

"Here, Carlita, slip these pants on under your skirt," Javier whispered. "And here's a rebozo to wrap around your hair. No one must recognize you."

Carlisle did as she was told, eyeing the men on the horses, who sat watching them.

"Did you find out anything about Lancaster, Carlita?" Javier asked softly.

"Only that he knows rebels are gathering near Saltillo. He went there several weeks ago, but he wouldn't tell me why, except that it was government business. And he warned me tonight that your family was involved in subversive activities."

"So he does know. Hurry, Carlita, because now we are in even greater danger here! We cannot let him see us!"

Javier's voice was urgent, and despite Carlisle's misgivings about leaving without telling anyone, she mounted the horse he held for her. But as they rode away from La Mesilla and Chase, toward the mountain stronghold of the *guerrilleros*, she couldn't help but look back and feel regret.

9

As the sun appeared above the mountains, Chase rode along the road bordering his ranch on the north. In his hand Carlisle's white mantilla fluttered in the slight breeze. He looked down at the dainty white lace that had cast spidery shadows over her beautiful face the night before. Lifting it, he inhaled the faint fragrance of her sweet perfume. He shut his eyes, sick inside, his fist tightening around the fragile veil.

Dios, where was she? He looked out over the hilly, uneven terrain around him. All night, his men had combed every inch of the hacienda, but there had been no sign of her—except for the mantilla they'd found in an alley near the plaza.

Scanning the rolling rises to his right, he caught sight of a group of *vaqueros* searching the banks of a small arroyo. How could this have happened? How could Carlisle just disappear in the middle of a crowded fiesta? He gritted his teeth and turned his stallion's head toward the hacienda.

In the cloudy mists of memory, he saw her the way she'd looked the first time they'd met. High in the air, hanging precariously to a damn rose trellis, her blue skirts hitched up. The image was crystal clear, one he'd never forget, so evocative of Carlisle—willful, fiery-tempered, but with a smile so sweet, it tied a man's stomach in knots.

The ache in his gut had started the moment he'd found her missing, and it would continue until he knew she was safe. Praying Esteban had had better luck with his search, Chase urged his horse toward the hacienda.

If Carlisle wasn't found soon, if she wasn't lost somewhere on the estate, he would have to face the worst. She'd been upset with him last night when he had told her he was leaving. He had seen the hurt in her face. Perhaps she had convinced someone to take her to Mexico City in defiance of his orders. But if she hadn't been taken by someone else, either willingly or by force, she could be lying injured somewhere—a thought that made him recoil the minute it came into his head. She was all right. He'd find her soon. His gloved hands tightened around the reins.

Ahead of him, the red tiles of the hacienda's roof were gilded golden-red by the rising sun, the color of Carlisle's hair, he thought painfully. Again longing swept over him, and he knew, against his will, against all propriety, that she meant more to him than anything. He'd realized that over the past few weeks when they had gotten along so well together. One reason for his intended trip to the capital had been to nullify his betrothal to Dona Marta. Then, after he had returned to the Hacienda de los Toros and Carlisle, he'd planned to tell her how he felt about her, and write Gray seeking permission to conduct a formal courtship. And Carlisle would have agreed; he'd seen her feelings for him in her eyes. He loved her, desperately loved her.

Grim-faced, he galloped under the entry arch and down the cobbled road to the house. As he reached the pillared arcade and swung from the saddle, Conchita appeared at the front door. Chase looked behind her, hoping to see Carlisle, but Conchita stood alone, her expression uncharacteristically somber.

"Has Esteban returned?" he asked her as one of his servants led his stallion away.

"No, Don Chaso. I am sorry, but Esteban and his men have not returned from Monterrey. But every house in La Mesilla has been searched. No one see her, but many still sleep from the *aguardiente.*"

Chase frowned, massaging his forehead as he entered the salon. He poured himself a generous shot of tequila and tossed it down, then refilled the glass.

"Perdón, Don Chaso, *por favor."*

Nerves on edge, Chase spun around and saw Carlisle's maid in the doorway. Beside Rosita stood her younger sister, Renate.

"Sí, Rosita? Have you heard something?"

Rosita nodded, nudging the child forward, but the little girl resisted and hid her face in Rosita's long white apron.

"She is very frightened, senor, but she saw the senorita last night. She thinks Dona Carlita is *muy bonita* and often follows her. But she is afraid to tell me what happened, so I brought her to you."

Hope flared in Chase's heart, and he went to the child, going down on one knee and taking her hands in his.

"Renate, *niña,* surely you are not afraid of me? At Christmastide, did I not help you break the piñata in the plaza? *Por favor,* you must tell me about Dona Carlita. It is *muy importante.*''

Renate wouldn't look at him, her arm tightening around the doll she held crooked in her elbow. She finally answered, her voice so low that Chase could barely hear her.

"Un hombre took her." Renate raised her big black eyes, shining with tears. "He did this to her." She withdrew her hand from Chase's and pressed it hard over her own mouth.

Fear streaked through Chase, but he tried not to show it to the child.

"What hombre, *niña?* Do you know his name? Was he a *vaquero* here at the hacienda?''

Solemnly, Renate shook her head.

"Where did you see them?''

"Behind the church where they tied their horses.''

"There was more than one?''

The child bobbed her head again.

"Did you see which way they went?''

Renate nodded, then pointed her finger toward the south windows.

"The road to Monterrey?'' Chase asked, his tone growing more urgent.

"Sí, Don Chaso, they rode away very fast.''

"Gracias, Renate, you're a good little girl,'' he said. "You have helped me very much. Go with Rosita now, and she will give you breakfast.''

"Senor? Will *la gringa* come back?'' Renate asked, her eyes frightened.

"Do not worry, *niña.* I will find her and bring her home, I promise.''

Despite his encouraging words, Chase was gripped by cold-blooded horror. The kidnappers had to be the *gavilla de ladrones.* The armed bandits who infested the surrounding mountains were filthy cutthroats and renegades who killed, pillaged, and raped. And Carlisle, innocent, alluring, beautiful Carlisle, was in their hands. *Dios,* but he had to find her before they melted into the high sierra. He had to ride to Monterrey and find Esteban! If he had to, he'd track the bastards to the end of the earth!

Striding quickly into the hall, he meant to cross the patio and call for his horse, but the thunder of riders in the drive made him detour to the front door. Esteban leapt to the ground before his horse came to a complete halt, leaving his men to stop the animal's prancing.

"Chaso! A letter for you was nailed to the cathedral door!"

Chase grabbed the folded parchment, jerking loose the seal. He skimmed it quickly, then read it again.

"Por Dios, compadre! Tell me what it says!"

Chase looked at Esteban. "Carlisle's been taken by a band of *guerrilleros.* Goddamn it, they've taken her to San Miguel."

"Dios," Esteban muttered, his dark face flushing with anger.

Chase paced restlessly across the arcade, staring down at the letter again. "They say they control the entire valley. If we try an assault, they'll kill her."

Esteban crossed himself. "Sweet Mother of God, why? What do they want with Carlita?"

"They don't want her. They want me. They say they'll exchange her for me."

"No, *amigo,* you cannot trust them. They will kill you."

"Maybe not. They could want me to coerce Benito to their own purposes."

"You cannot take such a risk!"

"Carlisle is innocent in this, I won't let her suffer on my account."

"Hijos de puta madres!" Esteban cursed furiously. "They have chosen San Miguel only to torment us!"

Grisly visions of San Miguel rushed through Chase's mind. His flesh crawled at the thought of Carlisle in that nightmarish place among hard, brutal men.

"There's no way we can storm the mission without endangering her, even if I could get enough nacionales soldiers here in time to scale the walls. I have to go alone, *amigo.*"

"Not alone, *compadre.* I am ready. What must we do?"

Chase put his hand on his friend's shoulder, grateful for his loyalty. *"Gracias,* Esteban. I think I know a way we can get Carlisle out alive. I wish I could do it alone so I wouldn't have to involve you, but I can't."

"You think of the mine shaft, no? The one we found the day of the massacre?"

"Sí. Even if it's still flooded, I think we can use it. The rebels will never expect us to come in through the mountain. If we can find the shaft again and get inside San Miguel without raising an alarm, we can take Carlisle out the same way."

"Dios, it's a risky thing you consider," Esteban said, smiling grimly, "but then, we have cheated death many times before, *mi amigo.* And we will do it again."

"*Sí*, but we must make careful plans and move quickly. There is little time to lose."

After nearly a week of traveling by horseback over rough terrain, Carlisle knew that her romantic notions of being a *soldadera,* a camp follower, were wearing thin. In New Orleans, she had never considered how the rebels would journey from place to place, nor had she realized just how hazardous and frightening the mountains of Mexico were. Ever since they had skirted Monterrey and begun their arduous climb into the *tierra fria*—the cold country—she'd been hungry and nearly frozen all the time, with every muscle sore from riding astride a hard leather saddle. She clutched the saddle horn tightly as her horse stumbled on the rocky, narrow trail, then struggled to regain its precarious footing.

Far below, hidden by the night, she could hear a creek rushing at the bottom of the steep-sloped gorge. Arantxa called the canyons they'd been climbing for days *barrancas,* and Carlisle wished they could stop and rest. She was exhausted. Javier pushed them too hard. They traveled all day, every day, then far into the night, the lead man lighting their way with a flaming ocote torch. They rode single file, Javier just ahead of Carlisle, and Arantxa behind.

The other men followed, all heavily armed, *bandoleras* across their chests. Most of them were bearded and unkempt, and she'd been dismayed and frightened when she'd seen the guns and knives tied to their belts. They looked more like bandits than the Holy Crusaders she'd dreamed of. And she hated the way they looked at her, as if they wanted to attack her. They probably would have if Javier hadn't made it clear she was his woman.

That first night when she'd been so angry with Chase, Carlisle had been happy to see Arantxa and Javier. But now that they were so far away from the Hacienda de los Toros and Chase, she regretted not having left a note of explanation for him. Chase would be worried about her, and so would Esteban and Conchita.

Shivering in the cutting predawn chill, she wrapped the warm red shawl Javier had given her around her shoulders and up over her head. Now she wore the thin peasant pants and tunic of white cotton like all the others, but the rebozo did not keep her warm, and she struggled to pull the striped serape that she used as a bedroll closer around her. Her feet felt like ice and so did her hands, and she again wished Javier would let them stop. They had been riding since dawn.

Ahead of her, Javier was a dark silhouette against the red glow of the torch. She thought of their talks in New Orleans and aboard the *Mayan* when he'd spoken of the revolution and his bitter hatred for the Juaristas. But somehow, his heroics no longer fired her imagination. She'd met too many Juaristas who'd borne their own hardships during the war.

Twisting in the saddle, she saw that Arantxa looked exhausted, too. Carlisle faced forward again and stared at Javier's back as her horse plodded onward. Arantxa was not her usual ebullient self, but very quiet and withdrawn. They had barely talked to each other at all, not about anything, and when Carlisle had asked her what was troubling her, Arantxa had refused to say. But there was something wrong. Carlisle could sense it. Arantxa was the best friend she'd ever had; she couldn't hide her moods from Carlisle. Perhaps Arantxa, too, didn't find the role of female *guerrillero* so exciting.

If Carlisle were at the hacienda now, she would have been asleep in the soft, comfortable feather bed. What was Chase doing? Had he found her missing and begun a search? What would he think? Would he come after her?

He'd been so nice to her, so thoughtful. But just when she thought he might care about her, he had decided to leave her. Of course, it didn't matter now. When she'd left with Javier, she'd become Chase's enemy, though the idea no longer pleased her. She'd grown to care about him, she finally admitted to herself with a sinking heart. What was she going to do?

Javier reined back and waited for her. "Do not despair, *querida*," he said with a smile. "We are making good time."

Reaching over, he covered her hand where it lay on the saddle horn. Carlisle noted, rather forlornly, that she felt nothing. Yet Chase's slightest glance made her breathless. What had happened to her? When had she stopped loving Javier? He'd been as kind as ever, and it wasn't his fault she'd become disenchanted with the idea of being a *guerrillero*.

"Carlita, I missed you more than I could bear." He spoke very low so his men wouldn't hear. "You're going to make a fine *soldadera*, and when I march down the Paseo in Mexico City, victorious in our *revolución*, you will be by my side." In the smoky torchlight, his dark eyes shone with fanatical belief in his cause, but Carlisle could no longer share his zeal.

"I'm so tired, Javier. When can we stop? I don't think I can go much farther."

"I am sorry, *querida*. We will stop now, if you are so weary. I do not want you to be unhappy."

He lifted her hand to his lips, kissed it tenderly, and urged his mount forward once again. Immediately, he ordered the group to stop, then led the column off the trail into a copse of tall pine trees.

As Carlisle and Arantxa dismounted, the men began calling back and forth to one another, but they spoke rapidly and in a dialect Carlisle could not understand very well. Much of the time she had no idea what was being said by those around her, and she found it unsettling—as was traveling in the dark for hours on end to an unknown destination. As the days passed, she had begun to feel that she'd lost control of her life, that she wasn't free to choose her own destiny, which she thought she'd be once she joined the rebels. And where were the poor peasants she had expected to help find a better life? The *guerrilleros* were tough, hardened men. She couldn't imagine them being downtrodden or helpless.

Wearily, she unsaddled her horse, then flexed her back and shoulders, which were stiff from riding so long. Some of the men were building a fire and preparing coffee and rice, but Carlisle was too tired to eat. She pulled the thick wool blanket around her and lay down on cold, hard ground, every muscle in her body protesting when she tried to relax. She closed her eyes, so exhausted now that she couldn't even worry about scorpions or snakes crawling on her, as she had during the first few nights she had slept in the open air.

A few minutes later, when a whisper intruded on her dulled brain, she struggled out of a half doze.

"Carlita? Are you still awake? I want to talk to you while Javier's with his lieutenants."

Arantxa knelt beside her, peering anxiously down at her. Carlisle pushed herself up on one elbow as her friend arranged her bedroll and lay down beside her.

"I'm glad you're with us, *amiga*," Arantxa whispered. "It's been lonely for me since we left the ship. I need to talk to you about Papa. He's in prison in Mexico City, and I'm so scared for him!"

Arantxa's words brought Carlisle completely awake. She turned on her side, facing Arantxa. "Your father's in jail? Why? And why haven't you told me before now?"

Arantxa shot a guilty glance at Javier, where he knelt at the fire among his men. "Javier told me not to. He said he didn't want you to worry about it. Don't tell him I told you, or he'll be mad at me."

"What did your father do?"

"They arrested him in our house in Mexico City and accused him of treason. But it's not true! He's only fighting for what he believes in, like us!" A low, hoarse sob escaped her, and Carlisle put her arms around Arantxa. But inwardly, she was struck by the realization that she, too, could be accused of treason. For some reason, that danger had never occurred to her, and she felt frightened.

"I'm so scared for him, Carlita," Arantxa murmured against Carlisle's shoulder. "I can't bear to think of Papa being in prison."

"How do you know he was arrested, Arantxa? Were you in Mexico City with him?"

"No," Arantxa murmured, raising her tearstained

face. "We heard of it when the *Mayan* set anchor at Veracruz. Our friends there said we'd be arrested, too, if we went on to Mexico City. We didn't even get to see him! Oh, Carlita, Papa cannot live in such a terrible place. Javier says we will get him out, but he won't tell me how he plans to do it. I'm not sure we can!"

"What about your mother? Is she safe?"

"*Sí*, but she was forced to flee the country. They say she has gone to Cuba, where my uncles can protect her. Oh, Carlita, what will become of my family?"

Carlisle patted her back, but she had no reassuring answers for her distraught friend. "Perhaps Javier can negotiate his release in some way," she suggested, for lack of anything better to say. "Come, lie down and try to sleep. Tomorrow things will look better."

Arantxa lay close beside her for warmth, and minutes later, slept. Despite her own physical fatigue, Carlisle could not go back to sleep. Fear still gripped her, and she realized she should never have left Chase and the Hacienda de los Toros. She had been happy there, safe and well-taken-care-of. There, she hadn't had to suffer the awful long rides, stinging insects, and leering, uncouth men. Why had she left? Now she could never go back. Tears threatened, and her last thought before she slept was about Chase, her heart heavy with the fear that she would never see him again.

"Get up, Carlita, it's nearly dawn. We will reach our stronghold today."

To Carlisle, it seemed she had just closed her eyes when Javier shook her. She struggled up, shivering with cold, feeling dull from lack of sleep. She drew her blanket around her, gratefully taking the cup of coffee and plate of rice Arantxa brought to her.

Hungry, she ate her breakfast quickly, as unappetizing as the food was. Then she climbed into the saddle again, longing for a hot bath and a hairbrush, but more than anything, wanting to stop the endless riding up and down barren mountain canyons.

They set out again, single file, and in time Carlisle saw the morning star and was glad when the eastern sky grew pale. The mountain scenery lightened from ebony to gray, and they proceeded along in the misty silence, with only the creak of leather and the jingle of harnesses and spurs.

They rode all day, only stopping briefly to stretch their legs or eat a meal of cold tortillas and water. When Carlisle had begun to give up hope of ever reaching their destination, the trail wound around a treacherous bend and a vast valley stretched out before them, high, barren mountain peaks rimming the edges like a crown. They began to descend at once, slowly, down a steep path that snaked its way to the valley floor. Halfway there, Carlisle picked out a square bell tower rising on the distant slope.

"Where are we, Arantxa?" Carlisle turned and asked her friend.

"San Miguel. Javier made it our fortress, so we will remember our *compadres* who were murdered there by the Juaristas."

Dismayed, Carlisle looked again at the scattering of small buildings behind the tall fortress-like walls of San Miguel—the place where Chase's men had committed the massacre. As they rode across the level plain toward the old mission, she visualized where

Chase and Esteban would have set their tents during the siege. Suddenly, she could understand how San Miguel had withstood attack for so long. The back of the mission abutted a steep mountain, and the massive stone wall protected the front like a castle keep. Bodies had been hurled from that parapet every day, she recalled, horrified to think such a thing could have happened. High on the hill behind the church steeples, she could see the yawning opening of the silver mine's main shaft.

Carlisle tried to imagine what it had looked like four years ago when Chase and his men had camped in the valley and assaulted those forbidding walls. She cringed to think about how many people had died, on both sides. As they approached the great wooden gates, she was overcome by a powerful reluctance to enter the mission of San Miguel. When the gate swung inward and their horses made loud clopping sounds on the flagstones, she felt like a felon being led into a prison cell.

They stopped their horses in the plaza before the church, and Carlisle looked at the crumbling adobe houses lining both sides of the central square, where many of Javier's crude *guerrilleros* had gathered to greet them. The inhabitants of San Miguel spoke welcomingly to their *compadres*, but when they saw Carlisle, they grew silent. As they stared at her, dread touched her heart. She thought about the massacre that had taken place on the streets around her and remembered Esteban's pain, his description of blood running down the streets, of dismembered bodies. Somewhere in the quiet buildings around her, Conchita had been raped. She shuddered with horror, wanting to flee the evil place.

"How long must we stay here?" she asked as Javier lifted her from the saddle.

"Until we have crushed Benito Juarez and freed our *amigos* rotting in his prisons. And you will help us, Carlita." Carlisle pondered his cryptic statement as he draped an arm affectionately around her shoulders and led her inside the two-story adobe building built as an annex to the church, leaving Arantxa to follow behind them.

The place looked as if it had been a cloister for the priests at one time. Though very old, with patched plaster on the walls, the rooms had been made comfortable in anticipation of their arrival. Several Indian servants hovered around the arched hearth, where the spicy aromas of chilies and tomatoes emanated from the bubbling depths of a black iron pot. Carlisle looked around the big room, which had been freshly whitewashed. Exposed beams crisscrossed the ceiling, and a set of narrow wooden steps had been built along the wall, with no banisters. As Javier led her to the stairs, Carlisle began to think his manner overly solicitous.

"You and Arantxa must share a room, Carlita, but you shall have a personal maid. Inez, there in the green skirt, will tend to your needs."

Carlisle glanced at the stocky Indian girl, who stared dispassionately back at her.

"You'll have everything you need here," Javier continued caressingly. "Anything that's within my power to give you."

"*Gracias*, Javier. All I want right now is a bath and some rest."

"Of course, *querida*, forgive me. I will have Inez

bring you warm water. Do you wish something to eat?''

Carlisle shook her head, too tired to think about food. She preceded Javier up the steps, but before she followed him through one of the doors at the top of the stairs, she glanced at the room below, looking for Arantxa, who stood talking to the Indian women.

Inside the bedroom, Javier waited for her beside a white iron bed. A bright yellow-and-blue blanket woven in geometric Aztec designs lay across the footboard, and a carved wooden crucifix hung on the wall behind it. A glowing brazier warmed the room, and a low gold brocade divan was positioned before the single window, which had been left unshuttered. Through the narrow aperture Carlisle could see far out over the valley floor.

"Does your room please you, *querida?*" Javier asked softly, studying her reaction.

Somehow Carlisle sensed that he was thinking of embracing her, and she turned away, gazing out at the distant mountaintops.

"I really must rest, Javier, *por favor.*"

"*Sí.* I will see you later, Carlita."

Once he had departed, Carlisle walked to the window and gazed out across the valley where the sunset was throwing golden arrows of light from behind the towering peaks that separated San Miguel from the Hacienda de los Toros. Again she longed to be with Chase. What was he doing? Did he miss her as much as she did him?

10

A thick stand of pine trees rose on a ridge at the north side of the San Miguel valley. Chase edged his horse carefully off the trail and through the low-hanging fragrant branches, his destination the overgrown trail which led down the steep barranca. He had been afraid he might have forgotten the way, but he hadn't. Everything looked as it had four years ago when he and Esteban had searched the mountainside for a back entrance into San Miguel. As far as he knew, no one besides the two of them had any idea the abandoned mine shaft still existed.

When his horse reached the trail, its hoofs crunched and slid on the loose gravel of the incline, and Chase reined up. A moment later, Esteban appeared, leading a pack horse with ammunition and supplies, in case they were forced to hide out for a long period of time.

Urging his horse down the steep slope, Chase felt anxiety begin to eat at his heart. It had taken Esteban and him nearly two weeks to ride to San Miguel and scout out this overgrown path. They had been lucky to avoid the rebel patrols, but the *guerrilleros* had had Carlisle all that time. God, what if they'd hurt her? The thought made his stomach cramp. During the war, he'd seen other young girls who'd been the victims of lustful, cruel men. Raped, defiled, and beaten, taken on as *soldaderas* against their will, like Conchita. She'd been broken and spiritless when Esteban had met her, and it had taken many months and great kindness and sensitivity to bring her back to life.

He couldn't bear to think of Carlisle, helpless against some stinking animal. She was innocent, a virgin, for God's sake. And she belonged to him. His heart had felt cold and dead ever since he'd found her gone. Gray had put her in Chase's care and trusted him to protect her. How could he ever explain to Gray how such a kidnapping had been allowed to happen? That's why he hadn't contacted her brother yet; he'd wait until he had her back.

He was going to marry her. He'd already made up his mind. He wanted her, and she wanted him, whether she knew it yet or not. Gray would agree, especially when he found out all the strife between Carlisle and Chase had been Chase's fault. He'd played with Carlisle's emotions from the beginning, and he couldn't even say why. But he meant to make it up to her, when and if he got her out of San Miguel. The rescue would not be easy. As meticulously as he and Esteban had made their plans, a million things could go wrong.

For the next half hour, Chase concentrated on getting down the treacherous barranca to the entrance of the shaft, often having to lean far back in the saddle as his horse tried to negotiate the crumbling shale and near vertical drop.

Behind him, Esteban cursed in Spanish and gripped his saddle horn when his mount stumbled. Both men sighed in relief when they reached the place where the mountain leveled off and formed a narrow ridge. The mine entrance was not far now, and Chase rode along the edge of the cliff, glancing down at the swift-flowing stream at the bottom of the barranca.

The opening to the shaft was barely discernible against the dark, barren mountainside. The wood supports were nearly hidden by encroaching vines, and the ground was choked with thick weeds. But that was good. If a rebel patrol rode by, they weren't likely to spot the shaft.

Pulling up, Chase dismounted and flipped his reins over a branch. Not waiting for Esteban, he walked to the entrance and held back the hanging foliage. Inside, the cavern stretched out like a dark, bottomless mouth. He lit a match and ducked below the sagging timber supports. Hundreds of years ago, Spanish soldiers had whipped the backs of Indian slaves to cut the shaft through rock in quest of silver. But the mine had yielded up all its glittering wealth long ago.

"Any sign anyone's been here?"

Esteban spoke from behind him. Chase took the kerosene lamp he held and lit the wick. The ante-chamber was actually a natural cave with a man-made shaft leading up through the mountain toward the main mine. The ceiling was high enough for Chase to stand up easily, despite his height, and he walked toward the dark pool near which a hot spring bubbled. He knelt and tasted the water.

"It's still drinkable," he told Esteban.

"*Bueno, amigo.* I'll bring the horses."

Chase held the lamp out over the pool. The spring

had flooded the shaft since the war, but the water didn't appear deep. They could wade it, or swim, if they had to. He looked around, noting that several *catres,* the wooden framed beds used by the campesinos, were still there, from when the cave had been used as a wartime hideout.

Impatient, he yelled for Esteban to hurry. The longer the *guerrilleros* had Carlisle, the more she'd suffer. The bastards wouldn't kill her as long as she was useful to them. But after two weeks with such beasts, she might wish she were dead.

Chase's jaw clenched hard, and he forcibly relaxed his muscles, helping Esteban unsaddle their horses and picket them in the corner of the cave where they could reach the water.

Once their supplies were hidden and the entrance camouflaged with branches, he unbuckled his holsters and draped his gun belt over his shoulder. He waded into the warm water, holding his rifle and the lantern up before him. The water was waist-deep in the main cavern, but when they entered the shaft, Chase had to bend over slightly as the tunnel descended and the water level rose to his chest. Esteban, being of shorter stature, waded nearly neck-deep.

They proceeded in silence for what seemed an eternity, the only sounds the sloshing of water or the occasional rustle of a bat rousted from its hanging repose. In time, however, the shaft began a gradual ascent, and the warm water receded to their waists, then to their knees. Once he attained dry footing again, Chase stopped and waited for Esteban to reach him.

"If I remember correctly," he said softly, "the shaft turns off to the right and eventually meets the main tunnel. After that, we might run into someone, if they're using the mine." He rebuckled his gun belt and tied down both holsters. "With any luck, they'll be down on the plaza, and that'll mean we can get in and out without a lot of trouble. We need to find out where the guards are and where they're holding Carlisle."

Esteban nodded, and Chase crept forward cautiously, his rifle in readiness. When the passageway forked, Chase paused to extinguish the lantern. He set it aside, allowing his eyes to adjust to the pitch blackness. In minutes he could make out a small square of light far ahead. There was no one in sight, and they crawled along until they came to a stack of wooden crates just inside the opening that led out to San Miguel.

"Dynamite and rifles. French-made, the bastards," Chase muttered harshly.

"*Caramba,* there's enough here to supply a small army," Esteban answered softly. "With this much arms and ammunition, they can launch attacks all over the north."

Keeping low, Chase skirted the boxes until he could see the tiled roof of the church. The mission was laid out in a U-shape, with the open part of the U forming a plaza. Armed men sauntered around the well or stood in groups under thatched pavilions. Most of the rebels were dressed in the white cotton tunic and loose pants of the campesinos, but all were armed and most had *bandoleras* slung across their chests. Chase scanned the front wall where two guards walked back and forth, watching the valley road for intruders.

The old mission church was decrepit, the adobe walls crumbling in patches on the bell towers on ei-

ther side of the arched front door. Chase looked away
from the church, forcing down memories he didn't
want to think about. Most of the atrocities had been
committed inside the walls, on hallowed ground.

Across the courtyard, a group of camp followers
squatted around cooking fires, and he looked in vain
for a glint of coppery hair. His gaze moved to a long,
low structure which he assumed housed the soldiers.
Ten or twelve men sat on the covered porch, gambling
and drinking. Everyone seemed completely at ease,
unprepared for attack or siege. And why shouldn't
they feel secure? The French butchers had held San
Miguel for weeks before Chase's men could break
through the gates. The mutilations flashed across his
mind, and just as quickly, he banished them.

"She's probably in the casa by the church," he
whispered, focusing his spyglass on the front porch.
"I can see guards there—one by the steps and another
under the tree."

Chase surveyed the house for a while, wishing he
could see Carlisle. He felt so damn helpless, knowing
she was somewhere close by, possibly being brutal-
ized. But there was nothing he could do until the sun
went down.

"We had better separate and search for her," he
said, very low. "It'll be safer that way, and quicker.
It'll be dark soon. We'll move then."

They settled across from each other where they
could see anyone who might approach. Chase glanced
at his friend, glad Esteban was there with him. They
had been through many battles and skirmishes when
they'd ridden together during the war, but never before had they been so outnumbered as they were at
the moment. He knew, and he knew Esteban knew,

their chances of getting in and out of San Miguel undetected were next to nil.

"It's going to be dangerous this time, Esteban. We'll need the luck of the saints to get Carly out."

Across from him, Esteban smiled and rested his rifle across his bent knees. "Ah, but we have looked death in the face before, no? It will be the same this time." He chuckled. "Anyway, you have to get me out alive. Conchita will kill you if you don't."

Chase's smile was grim. "*Sí.* And you should be home in bed with her now, instead of here."

"I wish I was. But still, you are my brother, *compadre,* and Carlita's your woman. Would you not help me rescue my Conchita from these stinking men? I do not forget that you faced the bull for me. That jagged scar on your thigh, it gave me my life."

Chase grinned. "Oh, hell, Esteban, you've already made that up to me a dozen times. After this, we'll call it even. Then I won't have to hear all this undying gratitude you're always spouting."

Esteban laughed softly, but Chase checked his revolvers, then turned his attention back on the square below. Despite their jokes, the next few hours would be wrought with danger. It would be a miracle if something didn't go wrong.

When the sun finally dropped below the mountains, darkness descended quickly. Chase was encouraged to see a bonfire being lit in the middle of the square. Guitar music filtered up to them, and Chase's hopes leapt. A fiesta would mean drinking and carousing, and two extra bandits mingling in the crowd might go unnoticed. He forced himself to wait a while longer, giving the pulque and *aguardiente* time to flow. Then he crouched low. "I guess this is it," he murmured to Esteban, suddenly feeling quite calm.

Esteban made the sign of the cross on his chest, then clasped Chase's hand. *"Vaya con Dios,* my brother."

"You, too," Chase whispered. Then they struck out in opposite directions, Chase's destination the casa by the gate, Esteban's the soldiers' barracks.

Alone, Chase pulled his sombrero's brim low and drew his pistol. He draped his serape over his shoulders to hide his guns, then kept to the shadows, hunched over to disguise his unusual height.

By the time he reached the waist-high stone wall that encircled the plaza, the dancing had begun with a great deal of handclapping and shouting. Chase squatted in a shadowy spot beneath a tree, remembering how jealous he'd been when Carlisle had danced with Emilio.

Scanning the crowd for her again, he tensed every muscle in his body when he saw Carlisle come out on the porch. A man was pulling her by the arm, and she was resisting. Rage roared alive, hot, lethal, and his finger tightened on the trigger of his revolver. He couldn't see them well now; they'd passed behind a group of men. Chase inched down the wall in their direction, wanting to kill the bastard who was forcing Carlisle to go with him.

Realizing that he'd have to move out into the open if he was to keep them in sight, he did so, keeping his head down and his hat low. The man still held Carlisle's arm, and Chase's face took on harder lines as she jerked free and started to turn away, as if she meant to run. Chase stood up, ready to follow her, but as the fire lit Carlisle's face, he froze.

She was laughing. Carlisle wasn't struggling to free herself, to run away. She was getting ready to dance. Disbelief hit him like a fist as she raised her arms over her head and began to sway as she had with Emilio, the fire turning her hair into a golden-red blaze. Rage came swiftly, pure and deadly, as Javier Perez stepped up to dance with her.

Damn her to hell! Chase thought, blind anger overtaking him. She was with Perez! She was one of them! She had been from the beginning!

God, he'd come here for her. Thrown all caution to the wind, risking his life and Esteban's for the goddamn bitch.

Overcome by fury and the shock of her betrayal, he backed into the shadows again, damning her viciously as he turned, ready to find Esteban and get the hell out of there.

All he saw was the gun butt swinging toward his face. Then there was a sickening thud, a white flash of agony, and he was swallowed up in a gaping black pit.

Carlisle was glad when one of Javier's lieutenants ran up and whispered some urgent message. She hadn't wanted to join the fandango in the first place, and wouldn't have if Javier hadn't dragged her out into the plaza. She'd finally laughed and agreed to join the dancing, but her heart wasn't in it. Her heart wasn't in anything, anymore.

Whatever Manuel's problem was, Javier must have deemed it important, because his expression had grown serious, and he'd quickly excused himself and hurried away. She wondered what was so pressing, but she didn't care much. She was bored, bored with all the strangers around her, bored with their beliefs, which were not her own.

Sighing, she sat down on a low stone wall beneath a tall pine tree. At the moment, no one paid much attention to her. All the *guerrilleros* and *soldaderas* were drinking and dancing, as they did every night. From the beginning, Carlisle had felt out of place among them, unlike the way she'd felt at Chase's ranch, with his friends. She'd felt at home there.

A great sadness welled up inside her and made her spirits plummet even lower. She bit her lip, feeling deep, cutting regret. Why had she left? Why had she ever wanted to join this bunch of ragtag bandits? She didn't like the men—they were uncivilized and crude, always fighting among themselves and making obscene, insulting remarks to her. She found it hard to believe they cared one whit about the poor people of Mexico.

Across the cobbled square, on the other side of the covered well, Arantxa appeared in the throng, dancing wildly with the young hombre she'd taken up with, a slim young hidalgo from the city of Querétaro. She and Arantxa had grown apart in the fortnight at San Miguel. Arantxa didn't even seem concerned about her father anymore, and Carlisle didn't understand why she wouldn't be. Javier seemed to have convinced his sister that he had a way of freeing their father, but neither of them would tell Carlisle, which made her feel even less a part of their revolution.

Carlisle preferred to spend her time alone in her room, looking out over the wide valley instead of training in the plaza with the other *soldaderas*. For a while, she'd practiced shooting a gun and learned to grind and shape tortillas on the stones called metates.

But Javier hadn't allowed her to ride out of the mission on any of the frequent patrols that kept the valley secure.

Secretly, she was glad. She wished Chase would come for her, but she knew he wouldn't. He didn't even know where she was. Neither did Gray or Stone. Her brothers would be frantic with worry if Chase had contacted them about her disappearance. Why hadn't she at least left Chase a note?

Agitated by her thoughts, she stood and slowly strolled the length of the adobe wall, looking for Javier. Perhaps he'd allow her to send a message to the Hacienda de los Toros, just to let everyone know she was safe. He was nowhere in sight, and she glanced up at the old church, which he'd made his headquarters. A dim light flickered in the high arched windows, and, suddenly depressed, Carlisle left the fiesta and made her way through the trees lining the side of the casa. She'd go to bed, she thought, where she wouldn't have to think.

Suddenly, she sensed a presence behind her, but before she could turn, hard fingers dug into her shoulder. She started to scream, but her cry of distress died in her throat as a pistol was cocked near her ear, its barrel pressing on her right temple.

"I will kill you, Dona Carlita, if you make one little sound."

Carlisle recognized Esteban's soft, melodious voice at once. When he released her, she tried to turn, joy filling her. She winced and groaned as he grabbed her hair and jerked her head back. The gun pressed painfully against her cheek.

"I would like to kill you right now, *gringa* bitch,"

he ground out, his voice low and icy. "But first you're going to help me get Chaso out of here."

"What? Chase's here? Where?"

Her question enraged him. "Do not take me for a fool! I will not hesitate to pull the trigger after what you've done!"

Carlisle could feel the hairs on the back of her neck rise in response to the razor-edge harshness of his voice.

"*Por favor,* Esteban. I don't understand! How did you get here? Where's Chase?"

"Your friends have him in the church, if they haven't already killed him."

"Killed him?" Carlisle cried, shaking her head in confusion. "What are you talking about?"

Esteban's fingers tightened around her arm, hurting her. "He came here for you, *puta.*"

"How did he know I was here?"

Esteban made an impatient sound in his throat, clamping his hand over her mouth as a pair of *guerrilleros* stopped nearby, drinking from a bottle and shoving each other in a heated scuffle. He held Carlisle tightly against him until the altercation was over and the men slunk away in opposite directions.

When he removed his hand, Carlisle grabbed the front of his shirt. "I don't know what you're talking about, Esteban, you must believe me! I came here with Arantxa and Javier, my friends from New Orleans! We planned it long before I ever came to the hacienda. I swear it! I didn't even think Chase knew where I was! How did he find me?"

"Because he got a ransom note, as you well know."

"What? You must believe me, Esteban! I knew nothing of that, nothing!"

Esteban hesitated, but his grasp on her arm did not loosen. "Then you can prove it by helping me free him. But," he said, pressing his gun into the softness of her cheek, "if you try to warn anyone, I will kill you, *comprende?*"

"*Sí,* Esteban. I'll do anything you say! Is Chase really in danger?"

Esteban didn't answer, but pulled her along as he skirted the plaza, hunched low and keeping her down beside him as they crept in the shadows of the trees. When they reached the walled enclosure surrounding the church, Esteban stopped and peered through the darkness where a guard stood on duty, revealed by the lantern hung above the stone doorway. Suddenly a man's scream pierced the night. The yell had come from inside the church.

"Oh, my God, Esteban, was that Chase? What are they doing to him?" Carlisle cried, grabbing his arm.

Esteban ignored her. "We've got to get in there! Will the guard let you in?"

"I don't know! I can try!"

"I warn you, do not betray me. I will be at your side with this." The gun barrel jabbed her ribs.

"I won't, Esteban! I'd never do anything to hurt Chase!"

"*Vamos.*"

Sombrero brim down, Esteban pushed Carlisle ahead of him across the dirt yard. The man leaning indolently against the wall straightened from his slouch as they drew near.

"*Buenas noches,*" Carlisle said, realizing her voice shook. She tried desperately to control the quivering.

"Buenas noches, senorita."

"Is Don Javier inside? I must see him. It's urgent."

"Sí, senorita, he is there, but you cannot go in."

"But why not? He won't mind."

The guard was big, with beefy, muscular arms, and when she tried to go around him, he stepped in front of her, completely blocking the doorway.

Carlisle gasped as she felt Esteban move, heard a muffled thunk, then saw the big man crumple at her feet. As Esteban dragged him out of the circle of light, Carlisle opened the door a crack and peered into the church.

No one was in the narrow vestibule, but as they crept quietly inside, voices filtered in to them from the chancel. Several doorways led to side aisles, and Esteban pulled her to the one on their left.

"Stay here," he whispered. "I'm going to try to surprise them."

Carlisle obeyed him, watching him move off on his hands and knees toward the front of the church. She peeked around a pillar, trying to see Chase.

The sanctuary was dark except for one large iron candlestand bright with dozens of burning candles. Javier stood with his back to her, but two other men were holding Chase's arms outstretched against the wooden crossbeam behind the altar. Although his head hung down, he wasn't unconscious, because Carlisle could hear him groaning.

"Now you know how my brother felt, you bastard," Javier ground out, his voice echoing slightly in the empty nave.

Carlisle strained to see what they were doing as Javier grabbed a handful of Chase's hair and slammed his head brutally against the wall.

"I knew you'd come here for Carlita, Lancaster. I saw the way you looked at her. But she never once cared for you. She came with me willingly. We're lovers, you know. I'm a lucky man, am I not? She is beautiful, her skin as soft as a rose petal. She moans and cries out each night when I take her."

Carlisle shut her eyes, sickened by Javier's lies. She wished Esteban would make his move.

"Hijo de tu puta madre," Chase gritted out between clenched teeth.

"Manuel, do the other one," Javier ordered. "And don't be so gentle this time."

Carlisle looked again as Manuel stepped forward. Chase struggled, and Carlisle watched, transfixed with horror, as the *guerrillero* rested a six-inch spike against the palm of Chase's right hand. Then, quickly, he raised the hammer in his fist and hit it hard, sending the nail slicing through Chase's flesh and deep into the board behind it.

Chase screamed in agony, and, sick to the depths of her soul, Carlisle jumped up, oblivious to anything but preventing Chase from being hurt anymore.

"No! Stop it, Javier!"

Cursing, Esteban came to his feet a good distance down the aisle and pointed his gun at the three men as they whirled around to face Carlisle.

"Back away from him, you sons of bitches," Esteban growled, moving forward, his eyes trained on their guns. "Keep your hands up and get down on the floor! Pronto!"

Carlisle hardly heard him as he quickly raised the butt of his rifle and slammed it against the nearest man's head with a dull thud. The rebel fell forward face first, and Javier and his other lieutenant dropped down to the floor. Esteban took their pistols and stuck them into his belt as Carlisle ran to Chase where he hung against the wall, a nail driven through each palm, blood dripping down his wrists, staining his shirtsleeves red. She put her hands on his face, lifting his head gently. He'd been beaten. His handsome face was nearly unrecognizable, already swelling and badly bruised.

"Oh, Chase, Chase, what have they done to you?"

Tears ran down her face, and she wiped them away as Chase lifted pain-glazed eyes and tried to focus on her. He seemed to realize who she was then. He struggled weakly against the spikes.

"Help me," he groaned out.

Behind her, Esteban barked out orders while he held his gun on Javier and the others, his voice shaking with anger and anguish. "Get him down, dammit! Get him the hell down from there!"

Carlisle's stomach twisted at the sight of Chase's hand. The nail had been hammered deep into the beam, leaving barely enough for her to grasp.

"Oh, God, God," she moaned as she curled her fingers around the nail and pulled as hard as she could. The spike was slippery from Chase's blood, making it hard to hold. Another sob escaped her as she realized that the nail was embedded too deep to move.

"I can't pull it out, Esteban! Help me! I can't get it out!"

"Pull my hand off it," Chase grunted, groaning with effort as he tried to force his palm up off the spike.

Moaning with horror, Carlisle held on to his wrist with both hands and pulled. Chase cried out in stark agony as his hand came free, blood gushing from the open wound. He ground his teeth as he jerked his other hand off the nail. Chase staggered and almost fell, but when he grabbed the gun Esteban handed him and turned to face his torturers, she'd never seen such black lethal hatred. With no compunction, he pulled the trigger, the bullet slamming into Manuel's chest. Javier lunged away, diving behind a pillar before Chase could shoot him.

Cursing, Chase started after him, firing again as Javier ran down the side aisle toward the back of the church. Chase stopped and took cover as several *guerrilleros* burst through the front doors.

"Kill the bastard!" Javier yelled, and the men dropped down behind the back pew and began to shoot.

Carlisle cowered to one side as Esteban crawled on his elbows to the center aisle. He returned their fire, shot for shot, hitting one of the *guerrilleros*, who screamed and fell backward. A moment later, Chase was at her side, hunched low. He grabbed her arm and pulled her out through the side door. Esteban backed out behind them, pinning the *guerrilleros* down with his fire before he turned and ran after them.

As Chase dragged Carlisle along, despite all the danger and confusion, the only thing she could think about was his hands. He was groaning, and she knew he must be in terrible pain, but he was single-mindedly making his way up the steep path behind the church, keeping low, his breath labored. She climbed after him, sliding in the gravel, but each time she stumbled, Esteban pushed her on.

Alerted by the shots, a man came running toward them. Chase lifted his rifle and fired. The *guerrillero* fell, and Carlisle stifled her scream as he tumbled head over heels down the steep trail, his body precipitating a small rock slide. She lost her footing, regained it, then scrambled up the rest of the way on her hands and knees, terrified when she heard the shouts of pursuers only yards behind them.

At the top of the path, Chase had already attained the shaft. He pulled her into the entrance as Esteban came running, panting heavily with exertion. Ten yards inside, Chase pulled her down, then moved forward to meet Esteban, who'd picked up a lit lantern outside and was running with it, making shadows careen crazily around the walls of the mine.

"Is it bad, *amigo?*" Esteban asked, looking down at Chase's hands.

Chase nodded, holding out his maimed palms. The jagged puncture wounds bled profusely. "I'm losing a lot of blood. Give me your neckerchief."

Esteban pulled the scarf from his neck, quickly wrapping it around Chase's right palm, and Carlisle hastily ripped the hem of her skirt for a bandage.

"Come on, we've got to go on," Chase grunted as Carlisle bound up his other hand.

A shot rang out from the entrance, ricocheting off the stone walls, and they ducked and retreated farther into the darkness, leaving the lamp between their pursuers and themselves.

Carlisle watched Chase clumsily attempting to hold his rifle. He lay on his stomach and inched up level to Esteban's position, so that one of them was on either side of the tunnel. Carlisle huddled a few feet behind him, wishing she had a gun, wanting to kill Javier herself for what he had done to Chase.

More gunfire erupted outside, the echo reverberating hollowly down the shaft, but Chase and Esteban waited until a *guerrillero* crept into the light of the lantern before they opened fire. The man fell, face forward, and there were scrambling sounds of retreat in the dark behind him.

"Go on, Chaso, take Carlita out," Esteban whispered. "I can hold them off. Then I'll follow."

"Forget it," Chase said. "Why should you get all the pleasure of killing the bastards?"

To Carlisle's shock, Esteban gave a low laugh. "If you had not got yourself captured, Chaso, we wouldn't be in this mess, *amigo.*"

"You owed me one, didn't you?" Chase muttered thickly, cradling one hand against his chest. "You've been telling me that for years. So now it's time to pay up."

Carlisle shut her eyes, amazed that they could be having such a stupid conversation. My God, she thought, Chase was hurt, badly.

For about ten minutes, there was complete silence. Then Javier's voice echoed out from the other end.

"Carlita, *por favor,* come out here with me. I love you. He deserved what I did to him. I did it for my brother. Come to me so you won't get hurt."

She didn't answer, feeling sick as he tried again to persuade her. A short silence ensued, then something came rolling toward them.

A stick of dynamite landed two yards in front of Chase, the fuse burned down to a fraction of an inch from detonation. For one awful, heart-stopping instant, all three of them froze; then Esteban scrabbled on all fours, lunging past Chase.

"No, Esteban!" Chase yelled, rising to his knees.

A blinding white light froze Esteban in the act of

throwing the dynamite back at the *guerrilleros,* followed by a deafening blast that sent both Chase and Carlisle flying backward as the roof of the shaft came crashing down upon them, plunging the mine into darkness. Dirt and timbers broke loose and fell with a great roar. Then there was only silence, broken occasionally by the sound of rocks raining down atop the rubble and debris.

11

Chase tried desperately to open his eyes, to remember what had happened, where he was. His first awareness was of a burning sensation. His eyes felt as if hot coals were lodged tightly in each socket. Groaning, he put his hands to ears which seemed stuffed with gauze. He coughed, tasted dirt and blood, spat it out, then rubbed his aching eyes as he forced them open. All he saw was deep, impenetrable black.

Weakly, he shoved himself upright, his palms throbbing with jagged blades of pulsating pain. From the spikes, he thought dully. Then he remembered the explosion, saw Esteban holding the stick of dynamite just before it went off. Oh God, Esteban's dead, he thought, his heart welling with grief.

Fear hit him, then panic, sudden and overwhelming. Where was Carlisle? She'd been with them. She'd helped them, hadn't she? Groggily, he rose to his knees.

"Carly? Can you hear me?"

His shout reverberated eerily. The blackness was complete, the only sound the sifting of sand and rocks from the ceiling of the tunnel. He could feel the dirt raining down on his head. He groped in a circle around him, grunting again as he dug his legs out from under debris. He felt weak, disoriented, making it hard for him to think coherently.

He had to find Carlisle, he thought, and Esteban. . . . No, Esteban was dead, he remembered in horror, buried in the cave-in. He felt sick inside, physically ill. But Carlisle wasn't dead, she couldn't be. He had to find her!

"Carly!" he yelled, choking on the dust still hanging in the air. He crawled on his hands and knees, grinding his teeth as pain erupted in his injured palms. With every movement, crumbling dirt and pebbles dropped on his back.

Timbers creaked threateningly, and he realized the shaft might give way again and bury them alive. Urgency took over, and he no longer thought of his pain as he stretched out his arms and felt through the rubble in a wide arc in front of him. Oh, God, his eyes. What was wrong with his eyes?

After a moment of searching, his fingers touched skin, a bare leg, and frantically, he felt his way up to Carlisle's shirt. She was half buried, and he dug desperately to free her, grabbing the front of her blouse and jerking her head up.

"Carly! Can you hear me?" He touched her, calling her name again, shaking her, but she lay as still as death. Rigid with fear, he laid his ear against her chest. Her heartbeat was very faint, but discernible. He cradled her face, saying her name until she sputtered for air and moaned.

"Come on, Carly, we've got to get out of here,

now!'' Chase hoisted her as best he could, trying to ignore the fire flaming behind his eyeballs.

"What happened?" she muttered groggily, and he half carried, half dragged her as he felt his way farther down into the tunnel.

"The shaft collapsed, and it could go again. Can you walk?"

She coughed, then moaned again as she struggled to move. "I don't know. My leg hurts. It's bleeding, I think."

"Come on, try to stand up."

One arm around her waist, he pulled her to her feet. Carlisle groaned, but she was regaining her senses now. She clutched his arm with her fingers. "What about Esteban?" Her voice grew shrill as she began to remember. "Where is he, Chase?"

"He's dead," he said, but he choked on the words, anguish hitting him like a blow to the head. He started off down the tunnel, blindly, feeling his way along the walls.

"Is there a way out?" she asked from somewhere behind him.

"Just come on, dammit," he said harshly, remembering that Esteban was dead because of Carlisle. He heard her sob, but he was unaffected. Esteban was gone.

Moving slowly down the gradually sloping floor of the shaft, he barely noticed when Carlisle grabbed the back of his shirt in order to keep up with him. He thought only of getting out into fresh air where he could breathe and see; it already felt as if his lungs were packed with dust and grit.

He knew his eyes were badly hurt—burned by the blast. The pain made the hurt in his hands seem insignificant. Finally, after what seemed like an eon, his boots sloshed in the water, and he knew they'd reached the right tunnel. He knelt, splashing water on his face, trying to cool his eyes.

"Is the shaft flooded?" Carlisle asked, her voice low and frightened.

Chase put out his hand through the darkness and touched her. "It's not much farther, down through the water, then we'll get out."

He felt her cringe, but she didn't complain or ask any more questions. Moving into the water, he heard her gasp as she followed, still clinging to his shirt.

"It's so warm," she said, her voice setting off subterranean echoes along the water-filled passage.

Chase didn't answer, but proceeded through the blackness, feeling his way along. The wall was rough and damp with slime, but he knew he was getting closer to the cave. Carlisle held on tightly, wading behind him as the water gradually grew deeper.

"It's over my head!" she cried a few minutes later.

"Just hold on to me, and I'll tow you. It's not much farther."

After that, she said nothing and only soft splashing sounds interrupted the tomblike quiet. A short time later, Chase waded out inside the cavern, the cool, fresh air making him shiver after so long in the spring. Carlisle followed, her teeth chattering loud enough for him to hear, and he felt his way to the wall where they'd left the lanterns. He found them after a few moments, but by now his hands were numb and nearly useless.

"You're going to have to light the lantern. I can't do it," Chase said, then sat still as Carlisle felt her way toward him in the dark. He heard her fumbling with the tin of matches, heard the scratch of a match.

Carlisle sobbed in relief when the match fired. The tiny flame painted the cavern with darting lights, and her eyes found Chase where he stood at the edge of the water. The sight shocked her. His battered face was grotesquely swollen now. He'd lost his makeshift bandages in the water, and blood oozed from his hands. While she watched, he put his fingers to his eyes, leaving traces of crimson on his dirt-smeared face.

"Oh, dear God, Chase, you're losing so much blood!" she cried, sick to the core. "We've got to get your hands bandaged."

"Just get the goddamn lantern lit so we can see!" he demanded furiously, and Carlisle stared at him in dismay as he came toward her, feeling his way with outstretched arms. "What's taking so long? Light the damn thing!"

"Oh, my God, Chase," she said, horrified as the truth dawned. "It's burning now. Can't you see it?"

She watched him stop where he was and stare in her direction. His eyes were so bloodshot, the whites were no longer visible. His eyes were blood-red.

"Bring the light to me."

Carlisle obeyed, and when she came close, he reached out and touched her.

"Do you have it?"

His voice was quiet, but tense.

"Yes, it's right here in my hand." She held it up close to his eyes, but he only stared straight ahead.

"Hold it closer," he ordered.

"I can't, Chase. It's right in front of you!" she

cried, her heart breaking as he reached out, blindly knocking into her.

"Oh, God," he muttered, turning and stumbling a few feet away from her. "The explosion did it. I looked right into the blast," he said very low, as if explaining it to himself. "I'll be able to see in a few hours. Dammit, we'll have to stay here until I can."

Carlisle remained silent, but for the first time, she looked around the cave. Three horses were tied in the far corner, and a large pile of supplies was stacked on a rough bed frame against one wall. She went there, then stopped in her tracks as Chase whirled around.

"Where the hell do you think you're going?"

He was staring at a spot several yards in front of her, and for a moment she was overwhelmed with sorrow, knowing it was her fault he was blind and helpless.

"To get bandages for your hands," she answered, but her voice broke with emotion. She hurried to the saddlebags and sorted quickly through the food, whiskey, and clothes, pausing when she saw some of her own things, a skirt and blouse, even undergarments. He'd come for her, she thought, and he'd been hurt so much. And gentle, sensitive Esteban was dead because of her. Biting her lip to keep from crying, she went back to Chase.

"We have to clean the wounds," she said hesitantly. "And your shirt is wet and covered with blood. Let me help you."

He stood silently while she struggled to strip off his shirt; then he waded back into the spring, bathing his face and arms. Thankfully, the water was crystal clear. Carlisle stood at the edge as he returned and sat a few feet away. Without speaking, she began to wrap the strips of cotton around his palms, her stomach turning at the sight of the punctured flesh.

"I'm sorry, Chase," she said, tears running down her face. "I'm so sorry about Esteban."

He didn't look in her direction. "Why did you decide to help us? I don't understand why you didn't let them kill us in the church."

"Do you really have to ask me that?" she cried. "Because I care about you! I couldn't bear to see them hurt you!"

Chase looked away, and Carlisle felt panic rise inside her breast, making it hard for her to breathe. "I didn't know about the ransom note, Chase. You have to believe me! I only went with them that night because they were my friends, and I knew you were leaving the hacienda. Arantxa and I planned to join the rebels last year at the convent, before I even met you. I didn't know they wanted to hurt you, please believe me!"

"Esteban's dead because of you," Chase said in a leaden tone, then got up and felt his way slowly to the old makeshift bed. While she watched, he found several bottles of whiskey in the pack. He sat down, his back propped against the wall. Clumsily, using both hands, he lifted the whiskey and took a deep draught.

Carlisle sat still, but in her mind's eye she saw Esteban running toward the dynamite, heard the explosion again. She knew that Chase had every right to hate her. She closed her eyes and felt deathly sick, but she thrust her nausea away and walked back to the supplies. She got out several blankets and clean clothes, trying not to think about anything.

She took them back to the water, glancing at Chase. He still lay on the *catre,* drinking whiskey steadily. The bottle was already half empty. She knelt, realizing every muscle in her body ached. Removing her filthy, torn clothes, she waded into the spring, checking her arms and legs for cuts and bruises. She found plenty, but she knew she was lucky not to have fractured a bone or suffered a concussion. Why should she be the one to emerge unscathed? she thought as she washed the grime from her hair and body, the hot water feeling good. After drying off, she donned clean clothes and wrapped herself in one of the blankets. Huddling against the wall, she watched Chase drink himself into oblivion.

For two long hours, there was total silence in the cavern, neither Chase nor Carlisle uttering a word. Carlisle watched with a heavy heart as again and again he brought the bottle to his lips for long draughts of the mind-numbing liquor. She knew his eyes were hurting him, because he rubbed them often. Several times he went to the pool to bathe them with his unbandaged fingertips.

Every time she shut her own eyes, she saw the sharp spikes pinning Chase's hands to the wall, and each time the haunting vision made her want to retch. How could Javier do such a savage thing? How could she have misjudged him so completely? They'd used her, sent a ransom note to lure Chase to San Miguel.

Chase had come to rescue her. He did care about her, or he had. Now he hated her. Now Esteban was dead, and Chase was blind. Again she felt terrified. Oh, Lord, his loss of sight had to be temporary. But what if Javier and his men came for them before it returned? And what if his eyes *didn't* heal? She couldn't bear the thought of Chase being blind for the rest of his life! Tears fell again, and she laid her head on bent knees, suffering in silence. He'd never forgive her, never. Even if she hadn't known Javier's real intentions, she had gone with him willingly, and Chase would never understand that. He'd only remember that she'd lured Esteban to his death, and Chase to agonizing torture. He wouldn't care if she'd acted unwittingly or not.

Never before in her life had Carlisle felt such dreadful remorse. Her heart ached as if it were being squeezed by a gigantic vise.

A glassy clink broke the silence, and Carlisle looked up as the empty whiskey bottle rolled across the earthen floor. Chase sprawled on the *catre,* sunk in a drunken stupor. When he groaned she went to him.

He was restless now in his pain, turning frequently. She sat down beside him, tucking a blanket around him, lifting his hand into her lap. The bandages were already blood-soaked. She knew the wounds should be sutured. They were deep, and jagged on both the palms and the backs of the hands because of the way he'd jerked them off the nails.

When he lay still for a few moments, she decided to rebandage them. She tore more strips from the shirt she'd used before, then found enough whiskey in the bottle to cleanse the wounds. He didn't move when she poured the liquor on his left hand, then tightly rewrapped it. But when she dribbled the liquid over his other palm, he flinched with pain and tried to draw his hand away. Rousing groggily, he tried to sit up as she swiftly bound the wound.

"Carly?"

He felt for her, and Carlisle's heart tightened at the sight of his beautiful dark blue eyes now reddened and blind.

"Yes, Chase, my darling, I'm here," she whispered, tears coming again.

"What's the matter?" he asked, the whiskey slurring his words.

"I'm sorry, Chase, I'm so sorry."

He frowned as if trying to understand, then laid his head back. Carlisle felt so alone, so guilty and forlorn, that she huddled down close beside him and wept, for him and Esteban—and for herself, because she loved him so desperately and knew that now he'd never hold her again.

Chase jerked awake, aware immediately of only pure, riveting pain. At first, he didn't understand why he couldn't see. His head, hands, and eyes all throbbed with fiery agony. He couldn't think where he was or who he was, and he didn't care. He only wanted the pain to stop.

He groaned, then tender hands touched his face, comforting hands that did not hurt him. He heard the voice, sweet and disembodied, and a picture erupted inside his head of shining golden-red hair and eyes like emeralds. The hands came again to soothe him, and he gave up his thoughts and sank again into the deep, midnight-blue ocean of sleep where he found peace.

When next he struggled up from those blurry depths, the voice returned, quiet and welcome.

"Drink this, my darling. It will help the pain."

His head was lifted very gently, and a cup pressed to his lips. The whiskey went down strong and potent, and he swallowed more. Eventually the liquor dulled his thoughts, his aching palms, and soft hands returned to touch his eyes with a cool cloth, bathing his forehead and cheeks, wetting parched, dry lips, soothing and comforting. Then he smelled fragrant hair as it brushed his mouth, felt soft lips upon his cheek, and tried desperately to see.

"Carly," he muttered, the name alighting in his brain like a butterfly on a rose, bringing with it a sense of contentment and, curiously, an awful dread which remained coiled in his subconscious like a cobra ready to strike.

The drink was offered again, and he took it gratefully, sinking gradually into his cocoon of dreams.

When he awoke the next time, he was completely lucid. The pain was still there, but now a dull, persistent throb. His memory of San Miguel came flooding back, his torture, Esteban's death, Carlisle's betrayal. He sat up quickly and paid the price. His head pounded as if he'd been hit by a board.

"Chase! Lie back, please!"

It was Carlisle, he realized, her hands upon his chest, pressing him back down. His skin crawled as if a serpent writhed across his flesh.

"Get away from me," he snapped, unable to see her, unable to see anything.

Her hands immediately withdrew. He sat tense, a wave of rage rising inside him, higher and higher in a swirling, mind-encompassing flood, washing away reason and deluging him with bitterness. The pain intensified almost at once, especially in his hands, until it felt as if he held them buried in piles of flaming embers.

Carlisle's voice came again from the darkness, soft and trembling and full of sorrow.

"Please, Chase, let me help you. You need me now. There's no one else here. Let me make it up to you."

"I don't need anybody. Is it night or day?" he demanded, hating the perpetual blackness, trying to see even a glimmer of light, anything.

"It's morning."

After she'd answered him, Carlisle said nothing else, but he felt sure she stood very near, well within his reach. He could sense her presence, detect the scent of her hair. He felt a sudden, almost overwhelming need to reach out and touch her, to draw her near and run his fingers over her beautiful, traitorous face, so he would know he wasn't living alone in some awful, terrifying nightmare. It was like an ache, his desire to hold her, as vivid as the one throbbing in the palms of his hands. He sat still, fighting it, listening for a sound that would reveal her whereabouts.

"Are you hungry?" she asked after several minutes, and he quickly jerked his head toward her voice. He hadn't thought about food, but now he realized his stomach felt shriveled and shrunken.

It was then, for the first time, that Chase felt his helplessness, his dependence on the woman who'd led him to ruin. He gritted his teeth, vividly remembering the last time he'd seen Esteban, the last time he'd seen anything. A flash of bright light, then absolute darkness. His sight would come back, he told himself firmly. In time he would see again. He had to believe that.

"How long have we been here?" he asked, turning

his head in the direction where he thought Carlisle was standing. When she answered from a different spot, he muttered a low oath, angry that she could move around silently, watching him. The feeling of dependence on her mounted, and he hated it. He hated it worse than anything he'd ever experienced.

"Three days," Carlisle said at last.

Injured as he was, the wheels in his head began to spin. Would the rebels come searching for them, or would they assume them dead? He thought of trying to make the trip back to the hacienda, and realized immediately that it would be madness in his present condition. Carlisle had no idea how to get there. He could only hope that if Perez sent out patrols, they'd have one hell of a time finding the other end of the shaft. Later, when his eyesight returned, he'd try to reach friends in the area. Later, he'd ride back to San Miguel and avenge Esteban's death.

"Chase," Carlisle said softly, "you have to eat something to keep up your strength. You've lost a lot of blood."

He didn't answer, but he knew she was right. He felt unwell and shaky—and trapped. It was an awful thing to be isolated in darkness.

"I found rice and beans in your saddlebags." She hesitated again. "I cooked them for us. They're still warm on the fire. I'll feed them to you if you like. I know you can't use your hands. They're too swollen."

Since when did Carlisle know how to cook? Chase wondered. Probably part of her training as a *soldadera* during her weeks at San Miguel. A surge of vicious anger rent him.

"Just hand it to me," he snapped.

He heard her move away, and, for the first time, the crackling of a fire. A moment later, she placed a small cup in his hands. He held it in the crook of his elbow, trying to grasp the spoon with his fingertips. He listened to see what Carlisle was doing, but she was making no sound. She watched him from somewhere, Chase knew it, and it made him uncomfortable.

Carlisle *was* watching him from her seat beside the small fire she'd built with such difficulty, tears running down her face. She had longed for and dreaded the moment when he would awaken and remember that he hated her.

She wiped the wetness from her cheeks, sick to see the way his bandaged hands fumbled with the spoon. She ached to help him. He needed her now so desperately, but his pride and anger ruled him. He'd called her name over and over when his mind was subjugated by whiskey—her name and Esteban's—and she'd begun to hope that he did care about her enough to forgive her, someday when his grief over Esteban had diminished and his wounds had healed.

Helplessly, she watched him bring the spoon to his mouth, and she remembered the first moments in the mine shaft after the explosion. She'd opened her eyes to pitch blackness, and she could remember how frightened she'd been. She wondered if Chase was scared. It was hard for her to imagine him being afraid of anything.

Dear God, she thought, he might never see again. The realization was like a knife in her heart. When a muffled sob escaped her, Chase looked in her direction, then set the bowl on the floor and lay down, as if he'd suddenly lost his appetite.

"Chase? will you let me change the bandage on your hand? The wound needs cleaning."

Carlisle's voice was soft and hesitant. She was so sweet now, so sorry and eager to wait on him, to make up for everything. But Esteban was gone, blown to bits and buried in rubble. Pure grief gripped him, and he clamped his teeth.

"Chase? Can I, please?"

"Go ahead, dammit! You know I can't do it myself!"

She said nothing, and he stiffened when she suddenly touched his leg. She was kneeling between his knees, he realized with a start, so close he could detect the faint scent of her skin. She took his right hand and carefully began to unwrap the bandage. Every muscle in his body went tense. He wanted to reach out and touch her hair. He wanted to *see* her, dammit—*damn her!*

"They're so swollen, Chase. If only I had a needle I think I could stitch them."

Chase didn't answer. He wet his lips, realizing he still wanted her, even after all she'd done. When she touched him, gently, soothingly as she was now, he wanted to pull her close and make love to her. He groaned as Carlisle poured whiskey on his palm, the sting sharp enough to bring tears.

"Good God, Carlisle, hurry up!"

"I'm sorry," she murmured, rewrapping his palm, then starting work on his other hand. A few minutes later, she was finished, but she remained where she was, leaning up against his legs. Chase knew she was looking at him, and he wanted to push her away but didn't trust himself to touch her. He went rigid when

Carlisle laid her palm gently alongside his jaw. He shut his eyes.

"Chase, I'm so sorry," she whispered, her voice trembling with regret and sorrow. "I know how you felt about Esteban—"

His friend's name was enough to kill Chase's desire for her. He pushed her back with his arm and stood, stumbling a few steps away.

"Stay away from me, damn you," he gritted out hoarsely. "I don't want to hear your voice. I don't want you to touch me."

Blindly groping for the bed in his haste to get away from her, he stumbled over a boulder and went down hard on his hands and knees. Agony shot up both arms, and he cradled his hands to his chest.

"Oh, Chase, please, let me show you!" Carlisle cried, close beside him.

"I don't want you to touch me," he repeated viciously. "*Comprendes,* Carlisle? It makes me sick."

Several days later, Carlisle sat outside the entrance to the cave, looking down at the stream rushing through the bottom of the canyon. Since their argument, she and Chase had lived together in virtual silence. It was torture for her to be in the company of the man she loved, wanting desperately to talk to him, to touch him and make him forgive her. But his hands were beginning to heal, and he had learned the interior of the cave and was able to get around better without her help.

The sunlight felt good after so long in the cool, dim reaches of the cave, and she scanned the far slopes for signs of riders. There was no one, and she wondered how long they'd have to remain there and whether the *guerrilleros* were looking for them. A slight scraping of rocks alerted her to Chase's approach, and she scrambled up as he appeared in the beamed entrance. He stood there for a moment, his head cocked as if he were listening.

"I'm right here, Chase," she said softly, feeling certain he'd come in search of her. "Is anything wrong?"

"No, I just wanted some air."

He walked a few steps outside, very slowly, moving into the shade of a pine tree. He was shirtless, and she could tell he'd just bathed in the spring, because his hair was still wet. Her gaze went to his broad back as he turned to face out over the valley. She swallowed, wishing she could run to him, embrace him from behind and lay her cheek against the smooth brown muscles of his back. Tears threatened again, but she bit them back. Tears did no good.

He was bearded now, the facial growth several shades darker than his blond hair, and he still wore the terrible, hard expression on his face, one she feared would never leave him. After a while, he turned and disappeared into the cave again, and loneliness crushed down on her. Never in her life had she felt so alone and afraid.

In that moment, it seemed that she'd always been adrift with no one to love her. She thought of her brothers, Gray and Stone, and wondered where they were and what they were doing. They'd tried so hard to take care of her, ever since she was a little girl, and she'd tried just as hard to evade their supervision. Now she longed for them. She'd even welcome one of Gray's stern lectures.

Suddenly, she desperately wanted to go home to

her house on Lincoln Avenue in Chicago, where she'd be safe again. Maybe there she could forget that Chase hated her. Yet even as she made the wish, she knew she wouldn't leave Chase—never, not as long as he let her stay with him. He needed her now, no matter what he said. But would he still need her when they managed to return to the Hacienda de los Toros? What would he do with her then?

12

Chase lay on the blanket-padded *catre*, his eyes closed. Although his muscles were relaxed, every fiber of his body was quivering. With the heightened sense of awareness that blindness had given him, he listened to what Carlisle was doing. Now, in his world of darkness, every sound, every smell, every touch had to be examined and savored.

His eyes were better. The pain had lessened, and he'd begun to hope his sight would eventually come back. He opened his eyes and strained to see Carlisle where she was preparing to bathe in the spring. She followed the same routine every night when she thought he was asleep. His jaw clamped tight.

In his mind he saw her again, the way she'd looked the night she'd danced, her hair swinging down her back, all coppery bright and silky, her exquisitely beautiful face glowing with color.

He stiffened. She was undressing now. He could hear the flutter of her clothes. His imagination took over, and he visualized her pushing her skirt down over her hips and off her bare legs, pulling loose the drawstring on her blouse and letting it fall to her waist.

Wetting dry lips, he thought of how sweet her skin had tasted beneath his mouth, how silky the flesh he'd caressed so intimately had felt. He fought himself, grinding his teeth until he thought they'd crack, as soft little splashes told him she'd stepped into the water.

He heard her sigh, the same soft murmur he'd forced from her with his kisses. Oh, God, he hated her for what she could do to him. She was treacherous, a traitor, and now his body trembled with the desire she set afire inside him.

Had it been the same way with Javier? Javier had taken great pleasure in telling him she'd been his lover. He wondered if it were true. The thought made him sick to his stomach. He turned his head away from the spring, ignoring the need eating at his gut.

The rippling of the water each time she moved made his chest heave. He imagined her raising one arm, the water trickling in rivulets down her soft shoulders and naked breasts. Furious, he realized his hands were trembling with the need to touch her. It wasn't Carlisle he wanted, he told himself firmly. He just needed a woman. He needed someone in his arms, someone warm and willing. But not Carlisle— anyone but her.

Unable to stand it another moment, he shot to his feet, his body straining toward her.

"What's the matter? Did you hear something?" Carlisle's voice was low, afraid.

Chase took a step closer, and he knew she was naked. With glistening droplets of water covering her skin. He fought a battle that he could never win; then, muttering a curse of defeat, he moved toward her, past the fire, into the water where she bathed.

"Chase? What is it?"

Carlisle's whispered entreaty led him to her, and he groped in the water, oblivious to the fact that he was soaking his clothes and bandages. When he felt slick, wet flesh, he grabbed her up by the arms, lifting her until her nakedness was pressed tightly against him.

"Damn you," he groaned hoarsely, before his mouth sought blindly for her lips, his fingers clutched in her wet hair.

He found her mouth, parted, willing, as hungry as his own. Her arms came up to encircle his neck as she clamped herself against his body.

"Chase, I'm sorry. I love you so much—" She gasped, her lips moving against his whiskered cheek.

"Shut up," he muttered, and his mouth made sure she did. He was totally out of control. He knew it, but he couldn't help it. He slid his hands over her back and hips, welcoming the feel of her, inflamed by the way she met his embrace eagerly, her own passion equaling his thundering desire.

It was she who pulled him down so that they lay half in the water, half on the smooth sandy floor. Chase rolled atop her, his hands holding her head, his mouth attacking her lips.

Dios, he wanted her, he was desperate for her, and that was all he could think about, with Carlisle in his arms, Carlisle pressing kisses on his shoulder and along his jaw. He didn't care what she'd done or said. He didn't care about the betrayal. She wanted him. She moaned and pressed herself up, her fingers clutching his arms, hungrily pulling his lips down against hers. Their tongues met, and, heart thundering, his sense of touch excruciatingly acute, he let his desire control him. Beneath him, she writhed and cried out with pleasure.

"I love you, I'll always love you," she kept whispering, but he didn't believe her. And then he couldn't think at all.

Carlisle clasped him to her, moaning as his mouth left her lips, his head lowering to her breasts. He took them hungrily, and the exquisite rush of joy made Carlisle gasp, her fists tight in his hair as he continued to say her name, muffled against her skin, bringing her body alive with his hands and mouth.

From then on, Chase's own arousal dictated his actions. He stripped off his clothes and carried her to the bed, pinning her there, his elbows supporting his weight, his fingertips entwined in her hair. She welcomed him, ignorant as to exactly what he sought from her so urgently. His breathing came fast and hard against her ear, and when she felt him position himself over her, she was afraid, but she didn't struggle. She cried out as he entered her, but Carlisle held back any other sound as the sharp pain faded. She clutched him to her, because this was what she wanted, this man moving inside her and making her his own.

She shut her eyes, instinctively matching his movements, finding them strange and different. But she liked the way he held on to her so tightly and moaned against her hair as if she were giving him the greatest pleasure he'd ever known. When he tensed his body and groaned her name, she knew he was experiencing something wonderful, something she'd given him.

When he finally lay still, his arms still wrapped

around her, she wept and held him to her, never wanting to let him go.

Chase lay wide awake, Carlisle's warm softness pressed intimately against his side. She slept peacefully, her breathing deep and even, and he shifted her in his arms until his nose and mouth were buried in her hair. He squeezed his eyes shut, trying to stem his feelings. He wanted her again, as he always wanted her. His whole body was aware of the way her small hand felt lying innocently atop his chest.

Why shouldn't he use her for his pleasure? he thought bitterly. He'd lain with other women for that reason. Carlisle deserved no more. His mouth tightened as he thought of Esteban. He missed him. Sometimes he couldn't believe his friend was really gone. And he swore to God, if it was the last thing he ever did, he'd get Javier Perez. He'd not rest until he saw the man dead. His fingers flexed convulsively, making his palms hurt.

He sat up, wondering if it was morning yet. Carlisle stirred behind him, but he went stiff, all thoughts of her vanishing. His heart stopped, and he sat very still, his eyes intent on a very faint patch of gray.

"Dios," he breathed.

"What?" Carlisle asked, her voice thick with sleep.

Chase stood up, then walked slowly toward the light. His heart pounded faster as he realized it was sunlight pouring through the entrance. He could see! His sight was returning! An overwhelming sense of relief hit him, and he leaned weakly against the wall.

"Chase? What's wrong?"

He turned around. Carlisle still sat upon the bed,

a vague, blurry gray form, but when she swung her legs over the side and pulled a blanket around her nakedness, he could see her every movement, as if he were looking through a smoky glass.

"I can see the light," he said, emotion roughening his voice. "My sight's coming back."

He heard her gasp; then she ran to him, putting her arms around his waist and laying her cheek against his chest.

"Oh, thank God!"

Chase felt her tears wetting his skin, but he couldn't see her clearly. Everything was very wavery and out of focus, and he shut his eyes, afraid he'd lose what sight he'd regained.

As Carlisle reached up and touched his face, very tenderly, he found himself weakening toward her. He wanted to grab her up and swing her around, to laugh and share his joy, his relief. But then he remembered the way she'd danced with Perez, the way she'd laughed up at him. Then he saw Esteban blown to bits in the mine shaft. He took hold of her shoulders and put her away from him, all desire blotted out.

"What happened between us last night meant nothing to me," he said coldly.

Carlisle shivered as he walked outside into the morning sun, then pulled the blanket closer. She felt so desolate now that Chase's arms were no longer around her. She'd given herself so willingly, wanting him to understand how much he meant to her. She couldn't, wouldn't, believe the tenderness they'd shared meant nothing to him.

Trembling, she moved to the edge of the cave and saw him where he stood gazing out over the valley.

"He'll leave me now," she murmured brokenly to herself. "As soon as he can see."

The rest of the day she worried herself sick about what would become of them. They'd be leaving the cave soon to make the trip back to the hacienda. When they got there he'd probably send her home to Gray, as if they'd meant nothing to each other. She couldn't conceive of going to Chicago and living under her brother's roof, not after all she'd seen and done. How could they expect her to sit down and stitch on embroidery with her friends in her Dorcas Society? How could she attend balls and dance with men who meant nothing to her? Chicago wasn't her home anymore. Mexico was her home. Chase was her home.

She looked across the fire at Chase, who lay on the bed. She wanted to be in his arms, she thought dismally, here in his country, at the Hacienda de los Toros. She wanted to cook and sew for him. She wanted to make him happy. She stifled a hopeless sob.

Chase turned his head and looked at her. She couldn't tell if he could see her, but his eyes glowed very blue in the firelight. She got up and walked across the earthen floor until she stood directly in front of him.

"Can you see me, Chase?"

"Not very well."

She untied the drawstring of her blouse and let it fall to her waist. He flinched perceptibly, but she didn't stop. She unbuttoned her skirt.

"Make love to me again, Chase."

He shut his eyes, and a muscle twitched spasmodically in the lean contours of his cheek.

"Stop it, Carlisle. I told you, last night was a mistake."

"I love you. I can't help it."

For the first time, he showed anger, lunging to his feet and grabbing her by the shoulders.

"Don't you understand, dammit? Every time I see you I think of Esteban! I think of these!" He held up his hands, palms toward her.

Carlisle's eyes filled with tears. "I don't care. Just don't send me away."

"Stop crying, Carly. Just stop it!"

Chase shook her, and when she sobbed, her head falling back, he emitted a groan of frustration. Then he was kissing her, taking her down to the bed with him. She kissed him passionately, her fingers buried in his thick blond hair, his hands closed on her waist, lifting her up until his mouth could find her breasts.

She cried out weakly, writhing with pleasure. His mouth was hot and seeking every inch of her flesh, and she eagerly met each touch and caress as if it were the last. Their lips came together with a terrible kind of anxious desperation, and then he rolled over, his hands holding her head, his hard brown body straddling her.

He held her there, his eyes on her face as if he was trying to see her, his breathing hard and uneven. Then he was kissing her with draining relentlessness, as if he meant to punish her, though he was only pleasing her more.

He caught her hands and held them imprisoned beside her head, but he did not hurt her, and she was overcome by desire and need, until nothing else mattered, because then it happened, the glorious explosion of pure raw pleasure, the release she'd sought, the ecstasy she'd known they'd share from the first moment they met. This was meant to be. The two of them were meant to be one, no matter what else happened. They were a part of each other now. She could never leave him.

Over the next few days, Chase's eyesight improved steadily. Although he couldn't tolerate bright sunlight without pain, the blurriness was less pronounced. He kept inside during the day, watching near the cave entrance for any sign of rebel activity or of the government troops which should have been dispatched to Saltillo when he'd notified Benito Juarez about the revolutionary stronghold at San Miguel. At night, he sat by himself outside the cavern.

He was there now, in position as usual as dusk descended like a gauzy gray blanket over the chasm below. Carlisle was inside, asleep on the *catre*. He'd made love to her, fiercely, desperately every night since he'd waded into the spring and possessed her for the first time. But during the days, he hated himself for his own weakness, and he'd sit alone, away from her, and listen to her muffled weeping. She was as unhappy as he was.

Dios, what was he going to do about her? Gray would probably kill him. In good faith, Gray had put his sister in Chase's care—and look what had happened to her. Most of it was her own fault for getting involved with the Perezes, but her welfare had been Chase's responsibility. He'd failed to protect her, and now they were lovers and enemies, both at the same time.

Grimacing, he stood and walked to the boulder that overlooked the arroyo. Far below, on the trail winding to the mine, he saw movement, then froze as three heavily armed horsemen rode into sight. *Guerrilleros,* he thought, on a direct route to his position. He scanned the bottom of the canyon for other riders, saw a group searching along the sandy banks of the stream. Cursing, he ran for the cave. He dragged tree branches against the entrance, trying to disguise the opening. Hurriedly, he buckled on his gun belt, then slung several ammunition belts over his shoulders as he yelled to Carlisle.

"Get up, Carly! *Arriba,* quick!"

Carlisle sat up, wearing only his shirt. Her eyes widened with fear as a man's shout came from outside. It was too late to get to the horses, so Chase pulled her into the water. They waded quickly into a dark, deep passage where the tunnel wall turned back into the mountain.

"Not a word, Carly, do you hear?" he whispered, very low, and she nodded, holding tightly to his arm as voices sounded at the mouth of the cavern. Chase flattened himself against the wall, gun barrel pointed up and resting against his shoulder.

"El capitán was right. They have been here," a deep voice muttered in Spanish. "You, Pablo, go down and bring the others. We will search the cave for them."

Chase waited tensely, cursing inwardly for letting himself be trapped inside the mine shaft. He listened as the two men searched through their supplies and then led the horses outside, the hoofs clomping hollowly on the dirt.

In a minute the men returned, speaking softly to each other. Chase heard an ocote torch hiss and flare, then the sloshing of water as they waded into the spring. They were coming toward them, intending to search the shaft.

Thrusting Carlisle behind him, Chase moved back as far as he could, but a few seconds later, a gleam of light appeared in the darkness and one of the men rounded the corner, his rifle pointed directly at them.

Chase squeezed his trigger. The rebel looked faintly surprised as a bullet ripped through his chest. Then he reeled backward and fell in the water, extinguishing the torch in his hand. When the cave was plunged into blackness, Chase moved, wading out into the main pool, his heightened sense of hearing helping him locate the other man by the loud splashing he was making as he tried to escape. He fired his pistol twice, and a scream pierced the dark, followed by a commotion in the water and a gurgling sound.

Chase stood still for a moment, every sense alert, praying the third man had not heard the gunfire. A frightened whimper spooked him, and he swung around, ready to shoot, then relaxed as he realized it was Carlisle.

"Carly? We've got to get out of here before they bring the others!"

Standing still, he heard her making her way through the water toward him, and he took her arm, his gaze fastened on the entrance. His vision was blurred again. "Can you see anybody outside?" he whispered.

Carlisle shook her head. "No, but the horses are tied up just outside."

"All right, *vamos!*"

Squinting in the deepening dusk, he took the lead. Thankfully, he could see the horses. He lifted Carlisle into her saddle, then swung up onto his own mount, hoping Carlisle could handle a horse on the treacherous mountain trails.

The *guerrilleros* would come up from the arroyo below, so he'd have to skirt the slope and climb to the higher ridges toward Saltillo.

The track was narrow and more hazardous than the one below the cave, but he knew it well from past patrols during the siege of San Miguel. The *guerrilleros* would find it hard to discover their tracks in the rocks and loose gravel, especially at night. But they'd have to travel hard.

For several hours, he guided them in a gradual ascent, always looking behind for lanterns or any sign of pursuit. By the time they reached the wide trail that followed the crest of the ridge, Carlisle slumped wearily in her saddle, shivering in her wet shirt. But he knew they couldn't stop, not until he had put more distance between them and their pursuers.

The moon rose and painted the path with a faint silvery mist, making travel easier, and Chase pressed on hard, riding as fast as he safely could. Finally he guided his horse into a thicket of cedars where they couldn't be seen from the road.

"What are we doing?" Carlisle asked as Chase dismounted and untied the blanket from the saddle pack. He wrapped it around her shoulders.

"We'll rest for a while and get an early start in the morning."

She stood uncertainly in the darkness as he positioned himself against a tree trunk facing the road, his rifle across his knees. But when she sat down close against him, she was trembling with cold.

"You'll warm up in a minute," he said.

"My clothes are still wet," she answered weakly.

Chase put his arm around her and pulled her close. "We can't risk a fire, but lean against me and it'll be warmer."

She did so, and despite the mosquitoes and chilly night air, it wasn't long before she slept, her cheek against his chest.

By dawn, they were riding again, and Chase found the trail he'd been searching for, one which would give him a vantage point of the winding dirt paths on which Javier Perez and his men would have to follow them. There was no sign of riders, however, and he veered back down again through a forested trail where the soft groundcover of pine needles hid their tracks.

Carlisle said nothing in the long hours they spent riding, and very little during the brief rest they had the next night. By the third day, she began to cough and shiver, and Chase realized she'd caught a chill. She hadn't complained, not one word, but her eyes were feverish, and when he took her on his horse with him, she lay listlessly against him, her skin hot, flushed, and dry to the touch. He pushed on harder, and late that night he finally reached the house of his old *compadre*, Gilberto Gomez.

As he approached the long front veranda of the mountain hacienda, a dog began to bark. All the windows were dark, but as Chase slid off his horse, Carlisle cradled in his arms, Papa Gilberto appeared in the doorway with a lantern. When Carlisle moaned and writhed in her delirium, Chase quickened his step.

"Chaso? Is that really you?" the old man exclaimed as Chase climbed the steps.

"*Sí, compadre,* I have come to you for help. My *amiga* here is very ill."

"Come quick, then, into my room. My *niñas* are all sleeping."

Chase followed him, lowering Carlisle to the bed, and Papa Gilberto set the lantern on the table beside her. He bent over her, lifting her eyelids and feeling the pulse in her throat.

"I think it might be malaria," Chase told him. "We've been on the run for several nights."

"*Sí.*" Papa Gilberto shook his gray head. "It looks like it. I must give her my *remedio* to help her rest better."

The old man hurried out of the room, and Chase sat down on the edge of the bed. He touched Carlisle's face and found it burning hot. She tossed her head from side to side, and Chase rose and looked around until he found a pitcher, bowl, and stack of clean towels on a bureau across the room. Frowning, he poured water and soaked one of the cloths, then wiped the sweat from Carlisle's brow. He wished Papa Gilberto would return. She was very sick.

"Here, support her back and we will see if we can get some of this down her," Papa Gilberto said, coming up behind him.

Chase obeyed, watching his friend give her the medicine a drop at a time. Afterward, he lowered her to the bed again and bathed her face.

"She will sleep more peacefully now," Papa Gilberto told him, but his eyes searched Chase's face. "What has happened to you, *amigo?* Your eyes, they are very bad and filled with blood. And your hands, how did you injure them?"

"There's been an uprising in the mountains north of here. At San Miguel."

Papa Gilberto crossed himself. "The place of evil?

Come," he said, picking up the light again. "She will be all right. Let me look at your eyes and hands."

Chase followed him out onto the porch and sat down on the steps while Papa Gilberto retrieved his medicines. The old man had been the healer of the area for many years. Most of the people relied on him for any illness or injury they might suffer. He had fought with Chase and Esteban during the war. At the thought of Esteban, Chase felt sorrow rise in his heart. He tried to block the memory out. He didn't want to think about Esteban's death now.

Papa Gilberto shuffled out of the house again and held the lantern up while he examined Chase's eyes.

"*Dios, mi hijo,* surely you cannot see so good?"

"*Sí,* now I can, but not at first. I looked into a dynamite blast."

"*Caramba,* the rebels are that strong?"

"*Sí.* I have to get to Saltillo as soon as possible. I sent word to Benito to send troops there. We need to get back to San Miguel before the *guerrilleros* decide to abandon it and find another place to hide."

"Lean your head back, Chaso," Papa Gilberto ordered.

Chase obliged, and the clear drops his friend applied to his tired, strained eyes felt cool and soothing.

"There is little else I can do for your eyes. But take these drops with you. Use them often, and I think it will help clear them."

"*Gracias,*" Chase said as his friend began unwrapping the filthy bandages around his hands.

"*Por Dios,*" Papa Gilberto muttered when the puncture wounds was revealed. "What devil did this to you?"

"Javier Perez, damn his soul to hell."

"I will have to sew up your palm, *amigo,* and the other hand, too. Then they will heal." The old man carefully laid Chase's hand down. "I will get you pulque to drink, first. It will lessen the pain."

When Papa Gilberto returned with the jug of agave wine, Chase drank deeply, the crude liquor burning down his throat into his empty stomach. He swallowed more, watching Papa Gilberto thread the needle, then set his teeth and looked away as the old man inserted it into the open wound and began to sew.

The process took a long time, and Chase groaned with relief as Papa Gilberto finally splashed the pulque onto his palms.

"Who is the *gringa?*" Papa Gilberto asked him as he applied clean bandages.

"A friend," Chase answered. "I have to get to Saltillo to meet the Nacionales, and I can't wait for her to get better."

"*Sí,* she is much too sick to travel. My *niñas* are good nurses. They will take care of her. But you must rest for the night. Saltillo is a long ride. Tomorrow Juana will fix you food and drink to take with you."

"*Gracias,* my friend. I owe you a great debt."

"You owe me nothing, Chaso."

Chase nodded gratefully, then went back into the room where Carlisle lay, spread a blanket out on the floor beside the bed, and was asleep as soon as he closed his eyes.

When Carlisle awoke, she saw the face of a pretty, little raven-haired girl. She felt sore all over, and when she tried to sit up, the girl became excited and ran from the room. Frowning, Carlisle looked around. She lay on a *catre* padded with soft blankets and pillows. The room was composed of whitewashed adobe walls with one square window, built high up near the thatched roof. The plain wooden shutters were open, and a large horsefly flew in, its buzzing loud and angry.

Too weak to support herself any longer, Carlisle lay back just as half a dozen young girls descended on her bedside from the next room, all chattering at once and leaning over to look at her. She stared up at them, wondering where she was. And where was Chase? She asked the girls about him in Spanish, appalled at her own gruff, gravelly voice.

"Don Chaso has gone to Saltillo. He left you here with us. We're to take care of you for him," one said, and the others tittered their agreement. They quieted as a wizened little man entered the room, and opened a path to the bed for him, as if he were royalty.

Carlisle began to feel dizzy and was racked by a fit of coughing. The man sat down beside her. His gnarled hands felt cool on her burning forehead.

"Cómo está, niña?" he asked her.

"I'm very weak," she answered, still so disoriented she had trouble concentrating. "Is Chase all right?"

"Sí. He has gone for help. I am Senor Gomez, but everyone calls me Papa Gilberto, and you are safe here in my casa. You have been very sick with the fever."

"When will Chase come back for me?" Carlisle croaked out, afraid he'd never return and she'd be left to die among strangers. She began to weep tiredly. Her tears brought concerned cries from her flock of young nurses.

"Don Chaso will come for you, you must not

worry," one of the older ones reassured her. "He was very afraid for you when he brought you here! He was very tired and his eyes and hands were so bad that Papa had to treat them with his healing salve."

"*Silencio*, Adela!" the old man barked sternly.

"You must not worry, senorita. We will take care of you." He supported Carlisle's back and held a cup to her lips.

The water was cool and tasted wonderful to her sore throat, but caused her great pain when she tried to swallow. Very thirsty, she drank again anyway.

"How long have I been here?" she asked when the old man lowered her back against the bed.

"Nearly four days and nights now," he answered, smiling as two of his daughters immediately set about fluffing and rearranging Carlisle's pillows. "You must be patient with *mis hijas*," he told Carlisle with an indulgent smile. "They do not see many travelers here so high in the sierra. They think you are *muy bonita*, and they think of Don Chaso as their favorite uncle."

Six dark heads nodded agreement, causing many different braids to shake and wave, but Carlisle found herself unable to think coherently any longer. She closed her eyes and fell into troubled dreams, in which Chase hung against the wall, sharp spikes protruding from his palms, and Esteban stood poised with a flaming stick of dynamite in his hand, where Chase looked at her from blood-red, blind eyes, until she cried out, moaning and calling his name in despair, over and over.

13

Tomas Ricardo Jimenez y Morelos pushed his brocaded black sombrero off his head, letting it hang by its strap against his back. The slight breeze dried the sweat on his forehead and ruffled through his dark brown hair. Scowling darkly, he sat upon his bay mare and peered up the trail ahead, which wound its way through pine trees in a long, gradual ascent. He was furious with Chaso for burdening him with this difficult climb. And for what? To fetch some invalid *muchacha* Chaso had left with Papa Gilberto.

Escorting his half brother's women around was not the reason Tomas had made the arduous trek to Saltillo with Capitán Luiz and his Nacionales. He'd come there to fight the *guerrilleros,* though his *madre* had thought his only intention was to find Chaso and persuade him to come home to Mexico City.

His mother, Dona Maria, worried too much about her older son, whom she'd borne to the *norteamericano* named Lancaster. She considered Chaso to be wild and unpredictable, with too much of his gambler father in him. But in Tomas's eyes, Chaso was *muy macho,* the kind of man Tomas wanted to be.

Not only had Chaso been hailed as a great hero when the Juaristas had driven out the French, but now he was an important government official, as well. And the most sophisticated and beautiful senoritas in the capital vied with one another for his attentions.

Sí. Tomas wanted to be just like Chaso. After all, Tomas was no longer a boy—he was sixteen, nearly a man now. The time had come to put away his schoolbooks and leave the *universidad.* He wanted to fight in the bullring and against the enemies of his president, Benito Juarez. He was tired of the way his *madre* coddled and protected him.

At times, even Chaso forgot Tomas had become a man. He was deeply piqued that Chaso had sent him with the squad of soldiers to fetch the *gringa,* instead of letting him ride with Chaso to San Miguel to crush Javier Perez and the *guerrilleros.*

Glancing back at the eight men riding behind him in their sweat-soaked tan uniforms and white sombreros, he wished he sported the proud insignia of a Nacional so he could avenge his own father's death at the siege of Querétaro. But again his mother had intervened to thwart his wishes, and Chaso had concurred with his mother's desire for Tomas to become a licenciado, as Tomas's father had been. But Tomas was not interested in studying the law! Why couldn't she understand that he was bored to tears by the heavy statute books filled with small print and endless legal terms?

Tomas jammed his hat back on his head, then leaned forward and urged his horse up a steep rise in the trail He'd become an expert horseman while living at the Hacienda de los Toros. He'd loved his life at Chaso's rancho, where there were no books or *profesores* to endure. After he delivered Chaso's woman to his mother in Mexico City, perhaps he'd go there again.

The journey to Mexico City with the *gringa* promised to be long and difficult, especially since she was ill. Chaso had procured a traveling coach in Saltillo in which she was to ride to the capital, but the narrow trails where Tomas now guided his horse wouldn't support a mule cart, much less a coach. As it was, if she couldn't ride, they'd have to carry her down the mountain on a stretcher. Chaso had said the *gringa* would be very weak.

More upsetting to Tomas, Chaso himself had not looked so good. In fact, Tomas had been shocked the first time he'd seen his half brother. Chaso had ridden up to their camp on the outskirts of Saltillo, his eyes so bloodshot they looked entirely red. But, thank God, he was no longer blind.

A surge of pure rage shot through Tomas when he thought of Chaso being nailed to the wall like some animal hide. Damn the rebel swine! More than anything, he wanted to help Chaso avenge himself on Perez!

Frowning, Tomas prodded his mare onward. Up ahead, he recognized the point where the trail leveled off and led through shady trees to Papa Gilberto's hacienda. The ride had been long and hot, and he was ready to rest on the hammocks strung from the porch rafters and look out over the cool, pine-forested hills. And he was eager to see all of Papa Gilberto's *niñas*. He'd always gotten along well with them. Of course, they were mere children, the oldest barely twelve, but their father had taught them to ride and rope as well as any *vaquero*. The Gomez family never missed the branding fiesta that Chaso hosted annually at the Hacienda de los Toros. The celebration was known far and wide in the state of Nuevo León and was looked forward to by many *hacendados* in northern Mexico.

As he led the small column of riders out of the broiling sun and into a deep river of shade, the white adobe house came into sight. His thoughts returned to the *gringa*. Chaso had said little about her, had almost been evasive. He'd only told Tomas to take her to Mexico City, then arrange passage to New Orleans as soon as she was able to withstand an ocean voyage.

But Tomas had noticed the way Chaso's face had hardened when he spoke her name, as if he didn't like her very much. If that were the case, why did he go to so much trouble to arrange for her safe passage? The whole situation was rather mysterious, but soon Tomas would know more, for he intended to find out the answers from the *gringa* herself.

When he entered the grassy yard, there was a flurry of activity beneath the long, thatch-roofed porch as several of the Gomez girls ran down the steps and eagerly called out greetings to him. He grinned, foolishly pleased by their fond reception. He did like the pretty, raven-haired *muchachas* with their happy, giggly ways.

"Tomas! We did not think Don Chaso would send you for Carlita!" cried the oldest one, named Juana. "Can you stay here for long?"

"No, *niña*," he said, dismounting and rumpling her shiny black hair. "Only long enough to rest and

have something to eat. Chaso wants the *gringa* taken
to the city, pronto.''

"Come, we will tell Papa that you're here," she
said as the soldiers dismounted behind Tomas with a
great deal of creaking leather.

Juana's sisters greeted Tomas with equal enthusiasm, then went on to the young Nacionales, who were
more than happy to be served cool milk and frijoles
by such pretty girls.

Instead of taking Tomas around the side of the
house to the kitchen, Juana led him up the front steps
of the veranda, then around to the side of the casa
which faced the mountain valley. Papa Gilberto sat
there in his big wooden rocker, and Tomas pushed
his hat back as the old man rose. After the customary
abrazo, Papa Gilberto held Tomas an arm's length
away, shaking his grizzled head as if he could not
believe his eyes.

"You have grown, *mi hijo,*" he said, his voice full
of affection. "You will someday stand as tall as Don
Chaso."

"Chaso sent me here for his friend," Tomas said,
but inside, he was very proud of Papa Gilberto's compliment. Any comparison to his half brother pleased
him immensely. "Is the *gringa* better, Papa Gilberto?
Chaso said she was very sick."

Papa Gilberto's brown skin was as tough as leather,
and his face became grave, twin furrows cutting into
his weathered brow.

"She has had a bad bout with the malaria fever.
You must take her to a doctor in the city. I have given
her my *remedios,* but she does not get back her
strength. She is very sad and lonely, even here, with

all the *niñas* to cheer her. Come, I will take you to her."

On the porch spreading across the back of the house, a red-and-green serape had been hung from the rafters as a privacy screen. When Papa Gilberto held back the curtain, Tomas saw the girl where she lay in a net hammock. At first, he was struck by how small and frail she seemed, lying motionlessly in the wide swing.

"Carlita?"

Papa Gilberto addressed her softly, and the girl turned her head and looked at them. As if thunderstruck, Tomas stared at her face. Never in his sixteen years had he seen anyone who looked like Chaso's *gringa*. He found himself embarrassingly tongue-tied as her huge green eyes settled on him. She was so incredibly lovely, she didn't seem real, with all that shiny red hair framing her pale face.

"Carlita, Don Chaso has sent Tomas for you."

Interest sparked in the girl's eyes, Tomas could see it clearly, but he still stared mutely at her. A moment later, he remembered his manners and bent at the waist in a courteous bow, trying to hide how profoundly her beauty affected him.

"*Buenos días*, Dona Carlita. I am Tomas Ricardo Jimenez y Morelos. Don Chaso is my brother. Well, actually, he's my half brother, and I have come to see you safely to my mother's casa in Mexico City."

Carlita smiled slightly, and her even white teeth made her even prettier, despite the pallor of sickness and the violet shadows beneath her eyes.

"You are Tomas, the matador?" she surprised him by asking. "Esteban told me once that you were very good with the bulls." Her expression suddenly looked pained. "Esteban is dead now, did you know? I feel so sorry for poor Conchita."

Tomas nodded, a wave of sadness rolling over him, but when she suddenly looked away, wiping her tears, he was filled with compassion for her suffering. He surprised himself by wanting to put his arm around her thin shoulders and comfort her.

"Do not worry, Dona Carlita. Chaso has gone to punish the *guerrilleros* for killing our friend."

Her delicately arched brows drew together with worry, and her extraordinary eyes searched his face. "Is Chase all right?"

"*Sí*. He has taken troops to San Miguel. I wanted to go with him, but he said he needed someone he could trust to escort you."

To his disappointment, she didn't seem overly impressed with his reliability.

"Can he still see all right?"

"*Sí,* but I think his eyes hurt him very much, even though he does not complain."

The *gringa* looked to the distant hills. "And his hands? Are they better?"

Tomas stiffened with anger. "*Sí*. The *guerrilleros* will pay for what they did to all of you. Chaso will not rest until they are dead."

Their gazes touched again, briefly, and her expression was so strange and desolate that Tomas was filled with unsettling questions. Who was she? What part had she played in Chaso's life? Was she his latest lover? As much as he wanted to know the answers to these questions, he could not bring himself to ask.

"Did he say what was to become of me?" Her voice was so filled with hopeless despair that Tomas's heart was touched. She watched him closely, as if what he said was very important, and he became desperate to reassure her.

"Do not be afraid, *por favor,* senorita. You will be safe from the *guerrilleros.* There are many soldiers who will accompany us to Mexico City."

His answer didn't seem to be the one she was hoping for. Perhaps she was eager to go home to the Estados Unidos, he realized suddenly, and was quick to put her mind at rest. "And then you're to go home at once. I'm to book passage for you at Veracruz to the port of New Orleans."

Her face fell, and he knew at once that he had said the wrong thing. Moisture gathered in her eyes, and one tear rolled down her cheek as she wearily laid her head back against the hammock. Papa Gilberto took his arm and led him down the porch.

"Dona Carlita weeps often. It is not your fault. It is the sickness that makes her melancholy. We will let her rest now while we join the *niñas.* Will you stay the night with us? We would be honored."

"No, we must go as soon as possible. There is a carriage waiting for Dona Carlita in Saltillo."

"*Bien,* but she will have to be carried there. She is much too weak to ride. And I will send Juana to nurse her, for the journey will be long and tiring for the poor *gringa.* "

A little over two hours later, Tomas bade the old man and his pretty *hijas* adios, and reined his mare to one side of the litter Papa Gilberto had fashioned by securing a blanket between two sturdy tree limbs.

Juana walked beside her patient, and without appearing to, Tomas observed Dona Carlita from beneath the brim of his sombrero. She no longer wept, or spoke at all, but her sadness showed plainly on her face.

As they made their slow descent, Tomas's fascination with the *gringa* grew. He'd met a good many *norteamericanos* since Chaso had been the foreign advisor to El Presidente, but none of the ladies looked like Dona Carlita. No woman he'd ever seen compared with her. He wondered how old she was. He wanted to ask, but the potion Juana had fed Carlita made her sleep during the entire trek to Saltillo.

They spent the night in a small hotel in the town, and in the morning Carlita was so racked by chills and nausea they could not continue until the following afternoon. Tomas paced the hotel arcade endlessly, though Juana assured him Carlita had survived many other attacks of the malaria. When they were finally able to lift her into the feather bed stretcher across the interior of the coach, her face looked so ashen and drawn that Tomas was afraid. What if she did not survive the journey?

"Juana? She is truly all right? She will not die, will she?"

Impatiently, Juana shook her head. "You do not listen so good, Tomas. I know what to do. Papa taught me. She will be better when she wakes up, so do not look so scared, like a lovesick *novio.*"

"I am not scared, Juana," Tomas said sharply, but Juana only laughed at him as she climbed into the coach.

At midday, they stopped at a small hacienda for food and rest, and Carlita felt well enough to step down and stretch her limbs. Tomas made certain he was there to support her.

"I am so relieved you are feeling better, senorita,"

he said gallantly as he ladled a cup of cool water for her from their host's spring-fed well.

"The fever comes and goes, Don Tomas," she answered. "Juana said it will stay with me for a long time."

Tomas watched her drink, pleased she used his name so familiarly. "You have been through much since you came to my country. You will be happy to go home, no?"

"No, I won't be happy to leave." Sighing, Carlita looked down into the tin cup she held. "Chase hasn't told you much about me, has he, Tomas?"

"No, senorita. He said nothing, except that you were very sick."

Tomas felt himself leaning forward, anxious for her to speak again. To his disappointment, she stood.

"I'm so tired. Would you help me to the coach so I can lie down?"

"Sí, senorita."

He helped Juana settle her comfortably in her makeshift bed, then decided he had to know more about her. He'd ask her more questions the next time they stopped, especially about her relationship with Chaso.

In the days and nights that followed, however, the *gringa's* condition worsened, and more often than not, she writhed in her fevers and terror, calling often for Chaso, and with such desperation that Tomas realized with sharp dismay that she must care deeply for his brother.

Despite Juana's excellent nursing skills, Tomas was relieved when they topped the last bend of the sierras and were able to see the great plain of Mexico spread out below them. The lakes shone in the afternoon sunlight beneath the twin volcanic mountains that reared up behind them. He hurried his small troop onward, eager to reach the Casa Amarilla and enlist his mother's aid in caring for Dona Carlita. She would know exactly what to do.

The Casa Amarilla was in Tacubaya, a suburb of Mexico City reached by the long, wide avenue called the Paseo. When they finally clattered to a stop at the foot of a hill where the large yellow mansion had stood for many years, he pounded on the outside gate until the *portero* swung open the doors and allowed the caravan into the inner courtyard. He yelled for his mother, but it was Adolfo, her old Indian retainer, who came running, his wide-browed face alarmed.

"Dónde está mi madre, Adolfo? Where is she? Dona Carlita needs a doctor!"

"Calm yourself, Tomas," came his mother's cultured voice from where she stood in the open door of the salon. Dona Maria Jimenez y Morelos was a small woman, barely over five feet, with gray-peppered black hair parted in the middle and swept back in elegant wings to a heavy bun at her nape. Her face was relatively unlined by age, though she was nearing fifty. Her eyes were black and perceptive, and at the moment, she was frowning at the uproar her son had created inside her quiet domain.

Tomas was relieved she was at home and not out on some social call. "Mama! I have brought Chaso's *amiga* here, and she is very sick!"

"Then why, *mi hijo,* is she still out in the carriage? Have her brought inside the casa at once."

Her cool directive made him feel young and foolishly incompetent, but he was more than willing for her to take charge. He was very worried about Carlita's condition.

"Mama, Juana has come with us, too. Papa Gilberto asked for your hospitality for her."

"Well, of course, his *niñas* are always welcome in my house. But why has Papa Gilberto been caring for this girl? Who is she?"

Juana was already on the sidewalk, and she curtsied respectfully the moment she saw the older lady.

"Dona Maria," she said. "It is very good to see you again."

"*Gracias,* Juana, and welcome to the city," Dona Maria replied with a gracious nod. But she gasped when she caught a glimpse of the girl inside the coach.

"Tomas!" she exclaimed in dismay. "What are you thinking of? The child should not have been traveling in such a condition! Run and fetch the doctor quickly! And, Juana, *muchacha,* go tell Adolfo to ready a bedchamber for the poor child."

Relieved now that his mother had taken over, Tomas swung atop his bay and rode at a gallop for the nearby dwelling of their family physician.

Dona Maria supervised from the foot of the elaborately carved pine bed as two of her young Indian maids fussed with the crisply starched bedcovers. They tucked and plumped vigorously, though the girl lying in the sea of white linen remained oblivious.

The *gringa* was striking, she thought, even as sick as she was. But who was she? And why had her son put her into her care? Chaso was so unpredictable!

"Dona Maria? I came as soon as I could."

Dona Maria turned as her old friend, Dr. Francisco Alvarado, hurried into the room. He had been her family doctor for many years, even before he had delivered Tomas into the world. He was tall and lanky, his long, wavy hair liberally streaked with white, and he had an aristocratic grace about him, though he often worked in the outlying villages of the city, tending the campesinos free of charge.

"*Gracias,* Doctor. This poor girl arrived here very ill. I hope you can help her."

Dr. Alvarado frowned, peering intently at his patient as he set down his weathered medical bag. "It looks like the *paludismo* fever, but I'll have to examine her."

"Oh, no, malaria? Poor *niña.* I will wait outside."

By the time Dona Maria motioned the servants out of the room and shut the door behind them, Dr. Alvarado had already removed his black frock coat and was leaning over the girl. She found Tomas outside, his handsome young face twisted with concern.

"How is she, Mama?"

"The doctor will tell us that soon enough." She looked him up and down, then arched a brow in disapproval. "For shame, Tomas. You look as if you have not bathed for days. Cecilia, prepare a bath for my son at once, but first, Tomas, come with me. I have much to ask you about Chaso."

Tomas seemed reluctant and gave one last look at the sickroom door before he followed her down the carpeted hallway to her private sitting room. Dona Maria seated herself on a low blue damask couch beside the pink marble fireplace. As her younger son sat down in the tall-backed chair opposite her, she studied his face.

Tomas appeared very tired and worried. He should not have accompanied the soldiers to Saltillo. She had made the wrong decision. But when Tomas had accused her of treating him like a baby, she had known he was right. She was often overprotective of him. Tomas had always been such a sweet child, so easy to love and care for. Completely unlike Chaso, who had been wild and headstrong since the moment he'd begun to walk.

For a brief instant, she allowed memories to swirl around her, memories she rarely let surface, of Chaso's father, Burl Lancaster. They'd both been so young! And so foolish to defy her father and run away together. Burl had been so handsome then, with every woman telling him so, just as the ladies told Chaso now. But she'd been naive and blind to Burl's faults— the drinking and insatiable wanderlust, the obsessive gambling.

For eight years she'd put up with his unstable, dangerous way of life, because she loved him. She'd made her home with him in America, on the decks of steamboats and in seedy dockside inns, until she could stand no more and had returned with Chaso to her father's great hacienda.

Her annulment had cost her father dearly, but his gold had persuaded the Church to allow her to marry again. Thank God, the man her father had chosen for her had been kind and good. Poor Hermando had never stirred her passion the way Burl Lancaster had, but he had been quiet and wise, and he had treated Chaso as his own son, helped to raise him in a stable environment of wealth and privilege.

''Tell me about Chaso,'' she said brusquely. ''Where is he? Is he well?''

Tomas's brown eyes evaded her gaze, and Dona

Maria felt her muscles grow stiff. *"Dios mío*, Tomas, tell me what has happened to your brother!"

"Chaso is all right now, Mama," Tomas reassured her quickly, but his mother waited warily, every nerve on edge. "He was captured by the *guerrilleros.*" He studied the flowers on the carpet.

Ghastly tales of the atrocities suffered during the war filled Dona Maria's head. She was stricken with terror for her older son. "What did they do to him, *mi hijo?*"

Tomas obviously did not want to answer, and he stood, moving agitatedly around the room, his face flushed with anger. "They tortured him," he said, his voice choked. "They drove nails through his hands, like the blessed Cristo."

Sick horror rushed like a torrent through Dona Maria, bringing her to her feet. She took a few jerky steps toward the windows. Chaso, her beautiful son. How could such things still happen? Why did the suffering continue? The war was long over! She fought to calm herself.

"Are you sure Chaso is all right now? Do not be afraid to tell me the truth. I must know."

"Sí, Mama. Esteban rescued him from them, and the girl upstairs, Carlita, she helped Chaso when he couldn't see."

Dona Maria blanched. "Couldn't see? Tomas, what do you mean?"

"His eyes were injured in an explosion when they escaped. But now he is all right."

"His sight is back? You're sure?"

"Sí, Mama. His eyesight is still weak, but he is no longer blind."

"Oh, *gracias a Dios,* but where is Esteban? Is he watching over Chaso?"

Tomas shook his head sadly. "I am sorry, Mama, but Esteban is dead. The rebels killed him."

"Oh, not dear Esteban! I don't understand any of this! Why was Esteban not at the ranch with Conchita?"

"Chaso would not tell me everything, but some of the Nacionales say the *guerrilleros* took Carlita from him, so Chaso and Esteban had to rescue her. She has suffered very much, Mama."

"I believe others have suffered even more," Dona Maria said coldly, noting with consternation the flush of angry color that rose in Tomas's cheeks.

"Dona Carlita is very sick and very sad, Mama. Surely you cannot blame her for what happened to Chaso and Esteban?"

"And do you have a reason why I should not?"

"Chaso does not blame her, or he would not have sent her here to you."

"And did he say what I am to do with the *gringa?*"

Tomas looked disconcerted. "He said to send her home to America. But that is out of the question now, while she is so ill."

For some inexplicable reason, Dona Maria was relieved to hear Chaso's orders concerning the girl. But the look on Tomas's face told her he didn't feel the same way. Instinctively, she knew he already liked the *gringa* too much. But before she could question him further about the girl, the doctor arrived to apprise her of Carlita's condition.

"Don Francisco, sit down, *por favor,* and I will have refreshments brought to you."

"*Gracias,* Dona Maria," Dr. Alvarado answered.

While she rang for the maid, Tomas asked him about his patient.

"She is very weak, Tomas, and we must take good care of her. The malaria has run its course, I believe, because of Papa Gilberto and the *niña's* care. But I fear the child will complicate matters and make her recovery take longer."

"Child? What child?" Dona Maria asked at once, perplexed by his remark.

"Why, the *gringa* carries a baby, Dona Maria, for quite some time now, I believe."

"But Carlita is not married!" Tomas interjected quickly. "You must be mistaken, Don Francisco!"

Embarrassed by her son's naiveté and rudeness, Dona Maria dismissed him. "You must be tired from your journey, Tomas. Cecilia will have your bath ready by now. I will join you when we dine later this evening."

Tomas looked annoyed, and more upset over the pregnancy than he should. Why? He hadn't even known the *gringa* before he escorted her from Saltillo! As he left the room, a maid entered with a tray of coffee and sweet cakes. Dona Maria waited for her to leave, then questioned the doctor further.

"Were you able to speak to her about the baby?" she asked.

Shaking his head, Dr. Alvarado watched her pour the steaming brew for him. "She did not know she was expecting a child, but the campesina—Juana's her name, I believe—she suspected it. She has helped care for the *gringa* for weeks now. The chills and fever have passed for the time being, but they will come again every day or so until we can affect her recovery with quinine."

"And will her sickness hurt the *bebé?*"

"I cannot say. It is very early in her confinement, so perhaps she will regain her strength. We will have to take extra care with her."

"*Sí,* and we will, Doctor," Dona Maria answered, gazing at him thoughtfully. "Is she well enough for me to speak to her?"

When he nodded, she rose and left him to finish his *café con leche* at his leisure. She walked directly to the *gringa's* bedroom, then crossed the floor to where Juana sat in a chair beside the bed.

"Juana, *niña,* you must be hungry and tired, too. Run to the kitchen and my cook, Cirila, will see to you."

"But what about Dona Carlita—"

"Do not concern yourself. I will sit with her until you return."

Although a trifle hesitant to leave, Juana obeyed, and after she was gone, Dona Maria sat down on the edge of the bed.

"Dona Carlita? Can you hear me?"

The *gringa's* eyelashes fluttered, revealing pure green eyes bright with fever.

Leaning forward, Dona Maria pushed the girl's damp hair off her burning forehead. She smiled reassuringly. "You are safe now, *niña.* I am Chaso's mother, and we will take care of you here at the Casa Amarilla."

"*Gracias,* senora," the girl mumbled, but her face was flushed and tears wetted her cheeks.

Dona Maria wiped them away, her heart troubled. "You must not weep. Everything will be all right. But there are things we must know in order to help you. Would you like us to notify someone for you?

Your husband, perhaps? He will be very concerned about you and your child?''

Carlita moved her head from side to side, but despite her obvious weakness, she reached out and clutched Dona Maria's hand.

''Chase doesn't know about the baby!'' Her voice rasped faintly, and a sob caught in her throat. ''He'll be so angry! He won't want the baby because he hates me! He sent me away because of Esteban!''

Dona Maria put her hand on the distraught girl's shoulder, murmuring comforting words. But inside, she was appalled at Carlita's revelation. Chaso, the father of the *gringa's* baby? Could it be true? But the girl was hardly in the mental condition to tell lies about the paternity. Already she had begun tossing restlessly again.

''Oh, my Chaso,'' Dona Maria murmured under her breath. ''What have you done to this poor *niña?*''

Suddenly angry with her son for sending the girl to her without a word of warning or explanation, she set her teeth. Her older son was used to having women on his own terms, she knew that. She'd heard the tales of his liaisons with different ladies. But in the past, most of them had been older and much more sophisticated than the mere child lying before her. How could he think of using a young girl so vilely, then ordering her exile the way he had? It was abominable behavior, unlike Chaso, even if he didn't know she carried his child!

There was probably much more to this girl's story than Dona Maria knew, but that would not be the case for long. If Chaso was the father, the *gringa* carried Dona Maria's own first grandchild. Her face settled into determined lines, and she leaned forward to stroke the girl's hot cheek.

"Do not fear, *niña*. I will take care of you and your baby. I can promise you that."

14

For the first time in weeks, Carlisle was up from her sickbed. Fully dressed, she stood at the tiny balcony off her bedchamber. A low iron grill crossed the bottom half of the window, and she held on to the rail, lifting her face to the warm golden sun of early September. But she felt very tired and empty, and sorrow hung over her heart like a shroud. She carried Chase's child, one he wouldn't want. Even though he'd been kind those last days when she was ill, he'd made it clear he wanted her out of Mexico, and out of his life. She knew she should write Gray and explain all that had happened between Chase and her, but she couldn't bring herself to do it. She was ashamed of the things she'd done and the pain she'd caused Chase.

A wave of nausea rose in her throat. The morning sickness was familiar to her by now, and she put her handkerchief over her mouth and waited for it to subside. Sometimes she couldn't believe a baby grew inside her. But Juana had suspected Carlisle was with child early in their journey from Saltillo, a trip of which Carlisle remembered very little. And Dr. Alvarado had verified her condition.

Moment by moment, like quicksilver, her feelings about the baby changed. Sometimes she was terrified to the core to contemplate her situation, alone in a foreign country, unmarried, and pregnant by a man who hated her. Despite the circumstances, neither Tomas nor his mother had treated her with anything but respect. In fact, they'd been very considerate and concerned during her convalescence. Especially Tomas.

Every morning he visited her before he left for his studies at the *universidad,* never failing to bring her a bouquet of fresh flowers, usually gladioli and lilies he'd picked from the well-tended beds in the spacious patio. She liked him very much, but he was completely different from Chase. Although he was just two years her junior, she felt much older after all she'd experienced during her months in Mexico.

Nausea gripped her again, and she hurried inside to the pitcher and bowl to bathe her face with cool water.

"The sickness will leave you soon, Dona Carlita. Then you will begin to feel like eating again. You are much too thin, you know."

Dona Maria had come into her room, quietly, without knocking, and Carlisle immediately felt self-conscious and embarrassed. Though Chase's mother had been solicitous, she had also been exactingly formal, and she'd visited Carlisle much more infrequently than Tomas.

"I cannot seem to keep anything down," Carlisle said in Castilian Spanish, and the older woman smiled.

"We will speak English, *por favor*. Everyone in my house is quite comfortable with your language."

"*Gracias.*" Carlisle could think of nothing else to say, and she turned away when she felt nauseous again. Droplets of sweat formed on her forehead, and she stifled a sick moan.

"Come, sit down, Dona Carlita. You must breathe deeply and think of other things, and it will be easier. I remember well the early days of my own confinement."

Carlisle did as Dona Maria suggested and revived somewhat. She sat down across from the breakfast tea cart that had been brought up to her room earlier. She'd been unable to touch the food.

"You really must eat something," Dona Maria urged. "You must think of my grandchild."

Carlisle felt herself tense. She met the other woman's gaze. "How do you know Chase is the father?"

Dona Maria poured a liberal amount of *canela* into a china cup, then handed the fragrant cinnamon tea to Carlisle. "You told me yourself, the first night Tomas brought you here. Do you not remember?"

Carlisle shook her head. "I remember little about the first few days."

"You were deathly ill. We were all quite worried. Tomas, in particular. He has become very fond of you. Are you aware of that?"

"*Sí*, Dona Maria. Tomas has been wonderfully kind to me. I am grateful to all of you."

"And my other son? Was Chaso kind to you?"

Carlisle could feel her face heat as a warm flush colored her cheeks. She kept her eyes downcast, unable to meet Dona Maria's gaze.

"*Sí*, senora, he was kind to me."

Nervous with the subject, she sipped from her cup, but the spicy tea only made her stomach heave. Quickly, she placed it in the dainty white saucer.

Dona Maria's keen dark eyes were still leveled on her, and Carlisle feared her next question. How could she talk to Chase's mother about what had gone on between Chase and her? Their relationship was so mixed up and confused, she didn't understand it herself.

"I have sent to the Hacienda de los Toros for your personal belongings. Of course, the seamstresses here will have to alter your clothes for your confinement. Today I sent Juana to purchase suitable dresses for you to wear until your own wardrobe arrives."

Carlisle searched Dona Maria's face, unable to hide her surprise. "You don't mean you intend for me to stay here, in your house?"

The expression on Dona Maria's thin, aristocratic features did not change. "Why, of course you will stay here. Where else would my son's child be born?"

Carlisle hesitated, somewhat intimidated by the stern, erect woman across from her. "But Chase told you to send me home. He'll be angry if I'm here when he returns."

"Obviously, he did not know you were carrying his child when he gave those directives. More than anything else, I've tried to instill a sense of honor in both of my sons. He will do his duty to you, Dona Carlita. I can assure you of that."

"I'm afraid there's much you don't know about the two of us," Carlisle told her warily.

"Then perhaps you should tell me."

"Chase might prefer to tell you himself."

"But Chaso is not here, and probably will not be

for some time yet. There is no need for you to be afraid to speak. I am well aware that my son can be quite impossible at times. He inherited that unfortunate trait from his *gringo* father.''

Dona Maria had not smiled during her remarks, but somehow Carlisle knew Chase's mother would not be judgmental. For so long, Carlisle had held all her torment inside herself. Now she felt the need to speak her fears aloud to someone who'd understand and advise her. Still a little frightened to bare her innermost thoughts, she took a deep breath and forced herself to meet the perceptive dark eyes watching her so intently.

"I hardly know where to begin, Dona Maria," she ventured hesitantly.

Chase's mother waited silently, and finally the words came pouring out of Carlisle.

"It's so strange between us, Dona Maria! From the first moment we met, I felt as if I were out of control of myself. I didn't even like him much then, and I tried to hide the fact that he affected me. But when he looked at me, he made me feel ways I'd never felt before! I told myself he was arrogant, that I hated him, but I didn't! I never hated him!" To her humiliation, she burst into tears.

Dona Maria took a crisp white handkerchief from her sleeve. "I understand, *niña,* more than you know. Chaso is very much like his father."

Her words were gentle, and Carlisle dabbed at her eyes, feeling better already.

"How did you meet my son? And why are you here with him in Mexico? As you can tell, Chaso does not see fit to keep his family informed of his business."

Carlisle twisted the handkerchief in her fingers,

thinking that in the past few months she'd shed more tears than in her entire life.

"We met at my brother's house in New Orleans. Gray had brought Chase's cousin, Tyler MacKenzie, there, and Chase was to bring her here to Mexico."

"My niece, Tyler, is here?"

"She didn't come because my brother decided to marry her, and Chase gave his consent. It's a long story, I'm afraid." Her lips curved into a sad smile. "It seems everything in my life has become very complicated."

"I remember Tyler well. She was Burl's sister's child, a beautiful little thing with the oddest red-brown eyes." She shook her head, as if enjoying some long-ago memory. "I can remember visiting her father's plantation, Rose Point, I believe it was called." She smiled faintly. "Tyler used to follow Chaso around like a little lost puppy."

Carlisle listened quietly, finding it hard to believe that the elegant, gracious lady opposite her had been married to Tyler's unscrupulous Uncle Burl. Chase had never once spoken of his father other than to condemn the way he'd raised Tyler.

Suddenly Dona Maria seemed to shed her reminiscent mood and return to the present. "But enough about Tyler. Did Chaso invite you to visit him?"

Again Carlisle fought off her unwillingness to explain. In retrospect, all her actions seemed so silly and immature. "I was supposed to visit Arantxa Perez. We were best friends at the Sacred Heart Convent, but Gray wouldn't let me come to Mexico unless Chase was my chaperone."

"*Dios mío*, I guess he hadn't heard about Chaso's reputation with women."

Carlisle shook her head. Then her words began to flow faster, and her heart suddenly felt unfettered. She wanted to tell it all and have someone absolve her from the guilt shackling her soul.

"Arantxa's brother, Javier, told me awful things about Chase and what he'd done in the war. He told me the Juaristas were murderers. I thought I loved Javier then, and I believed everything he said. But, Dona Maria, I was so wrong! About everything! I know that now. But it's too late, because I left the Hacienda de los Toros and went willingly with Arantxa and her brother. That's when Chase and Esteban came after me. And now Esteban's dead because of me. And Chase—they hurt him so bad. Oh, God, they drove nails into his hands! And it was my fault, all of it!"

She buried her face in her hands, muffling her words. "I never wanted them to get hurt. You have to believe me. I saw Esteban die. I saw Chase hanging up against the wall, and it haunts me day and night. I see it over and over, and I know that Chase despises me. Even afterward, when he made love to me, I know he blamed me."

Sobs overwhelmed her, and when Dona Maria rose and laid a comforting hand on her back, Carlisle put her arms around the other woman's waist and wept into her black silk skirt.

"You must not cry, Carlita. You have been through many terrible things. But you are not alone anymore."

After a time, Carlisle calmed, her sniffling diminishing until she was able to lean back against her chair, feeling weak and drained. When Dona Maria silently offered her a fresh cup of *canela* tea, Carlisle drank it and felt better.

"I'm just so confused, Dona Maria. My life seems over, when just six months ago I thought only of escaping from the nuns and being free to do whatever I wanted. That's why I wanted to come here to Mexico. But I've hurt people, and I've hurt myself. I can't bear to tell my brother Gray about all the wrong things I've done. And most of all, I can't bear to think of never seeing Chase again." Her voice faltered, and she couldn't speak.

"Forgive me for asking, Carlita, but are you sure, without a shadow of a doubt, that Chaso is the father of your child?" Dona Maria asked gently.

Carlisle nodded, her throat clogged. "I've never been with any other man. I swear it."

"Then you shall see Chaso again, my *niña*. I will make sure of it."

"Why are you being so kind? You have no reason to believe me."

"No one could disbelieve words uttered with such pain and bitter regret." Dona Maria patted her hand. "And I understand the way you feel. Long ago, I, too, was young and eager to live my life as I wished. I, too, became enamored of a man who took my breath away. Chaso is like his father. He has broken many hearts before yours, *niña*. It is hard on the women who love such men. And you do love my son, don't you, Carlita?"

Carlisle shut her eyes and nodded, her lips trembling. "Oh, yes, I love him. I love him so much it hurts inside."

* * *

Chase put his hands over his ears as the gunner lit the fuse and took cover. The cannon recoiled as the powder ignited, sending the cannonball toward San Miguel with a booming explosion. Watching with satisfaction, he saw the missile hit its target, knocking down another portion of the outside wall.

A week after he'd ridden out of Saltillo with Captain Luiz and his Nacionales, they'd trapped the *guerrilleros* in their lair and laid siege as they'd done four long years ago. But this time they'd had access to heavy artillery. Hauling the cannon up the mountain trails had been difficult, but he'd known it was the best way to capture Perez without undue casualties among his men.

They had been bombarding the walls for weeks now, and the *guerrillero* stronghold was ready to fall. He sent a rider to demand surrender after each assault, but if he had to, he'd continue firing until he'd destroyed the whole place.

After several more direct hits, he signaled to stop the barrage, then waited for the reverberating echoes of the big gun to die. He sent a rider forward to call for surrender, with no quarter given.

Triumph overcame him, and he smiled grimly as the front gate of the mission slowly opened and a white flag began to wave. Perez was his, the bastard.

"Captain Luiz," he said to the officer standing with him, "secure the buildings and line up the prisoners in the plaza. There will be no killing, *comprende?* Make sure the men know it. Under no circumstances will there be another massacre, or any atrocities committed. The *guerrilleros* are to be taken to Mexico City for trial."

The soldier saluted smartly, then swung himself

into the saddle. Chase mounted more slowly, his gut tight with emotion as he followed the first wave of his men through the battered gate. He had dreamed of this moment, hungered for his revenge. Now he savored the elation he felt. Esteban's death would be avenged. He had sworn it, and he meant to see it to the end.

Inside the mission, the effect of the cannon fire was evident in the crumbling walls and fallen roofs. The church had nearly been destroyed, one whole wall knocked out. Chase had ordered the guns directed on the bell towers. No one would ever be tortured inside its walls again. No rebels would ever use San Miguel as a sanctuary. He meant to bombard it to rubble before he marched his troops from the valley.

The *guerrilleros* had been herded into the square. Near the spot where Carlisle had danced with Javier, he thought, bitterness biting into his heart. Many of them were wounded and being helped along by their women, the *soldaderas* who'd fought at their sides. He searched for Javier Perez's face among the prisoners, then went rigid when he found him—standing straight and defiant while his sister, Arantxa, cowered on the ground beside him.

Chase's teeth came together hard, and he dismounted near Captain Luiz. "There, the man with the girl at his feet. He's their leader. Chain him and bring him here. The girl, too."

Coldly, unfeelingly, Chase watched his orders being carried out. When the Perez twins were thrust to their knees before him, Captain Luiz took Javier's hair and jerked his head back, forcing him to look up at Chase.

Javier's face contorted with hatred, and Chase

wanted to grab him by the throat. He wanted to squeeze his fingers around his neck until the last breath left his body. He wanted to kill him more than anything he'd ever wanted in his life. He'd killed many times in the war, but never with the brutal, violent onrush of hatred he now felt. Appalled by his own savagery, he stood unmoving, finding it hard not to succumb to the desire to strangle Perez with his bare hands.

"And where is my little *gringa* whore, Lancaster?" Javier asked, his teeth clenched. "Will she join us in prison? Or have you already taken her for your lover? How does it feel to be betrayed by the woman you love? She and I laughed about it when we were in bed together."

His words were cut short as Chase grabbed him by the front of his shirt and jerked him up, his face red with rage. He drew his gun and put the barrel against Javier's head, ready to pull the trigger.

Javier laughed. "Go ahead, make me a martyr. You Juaristas are known for your brutality. The people expect it of you."

Javier's taunt struck home. Chase was suddenly dead calm again. He released his hold on Javier, and the man fell back to his knees.

"No, Perez. You'll be tried according to the laws of Mexico, as will all your men. And when you're found guilty, you'll be shot for treason. Just like your father was."

Beside Javier, Arantxa gave a grief-stricken cry. Chase looked coldly at her as one of his men shackled her wrists together.

"Prepare them for traveling," he ordered, then turned and walked away.

* * *

Nearly a week after Chase had watched San Miguel razed to the ground, he reached the Hacienda de los Toros. He didn't stop at the big house but rode on to La Mesilla and the task he had dreaded for so long. Just the thought of telling Conchita about Esteban's death made him sick to his stomach. He should have told her before now, but he had been at San Miguel the whole time. And he had not wanted her to find out from a letter. He had to be the one to tell her. He owed Esteban that much. *Dios,* why did it have to happen? Why did Esteban have to be the one to die? Even capturing Perez had not given Chase peace of mind.

When the public square of the village came into view, he slowed his horse to a walk, his eyes on the rose-draped wall of Esteban's house. How many times had he made the trip, eager to see Esteban after a long separation? How often had they dined and laughed together at the old wooden table on the porch? Oh, God, he'd never see Esteban again. He'd never be able to ask for his advice or help.

By the time he had tethered his horse and entered the front gate, Conchita had seen him and come running in her usual ebullient way.

"Don Chaso!" she cried. "At last you have come home! But where is my Esteban?" She glanced up and down the street.

Chase swallowed hard. He tried to smile, but couldn't. "Let's go into the house, Conchita," he said.

"*Sí*, you are tired, no? I have tortillas and *aguardiente,*" she told him as they crossed the porch and entered the front room. "But first, *por favor,* tell me about Esteban. Where is he? I have missed him so much.''

Chase had trouble finding the words. Then he found it difficult to say them.

''I'm sorry, Conchita,'' he began, and Conchita's lovely dark eyes grew still, a terrible look of stark fear taking over her face. Chase forced himself to go on. ''There was an explosion in the mine at San Miguel.'' Chase's voice cracked as he remembered the last time he'd ever seen his friend. ''Esteban was killed in the—''

''No! No, I do not believe you!''

Conchita began to scream and pull at her hair. Chase grabbed her, holding her until she quit struggling and went limp in his arms.

''No, no, not my Esteban,'' she kept saying, sobbing hysterically against his chest.

Chase held her tightly, his throat clogged with so much emotion that he couldn't speak, not even to comfort her. He shut his eyes, wishing there were something he could do. When he opened his eyes again, his gaze riveted on the portrait hanging on the wall opposite him.

Carlisle stared back at him, dressed in white and looking as much like an angel as any mortal possibly could. Esteban had even painted a pale aura around her head as if she wore a halo. Damn her, he thought, rage shooting through him like a caustic acid. Carlisle had killed Esteban as surely as if she had put a gun to his head. Chase would never forgive her for it. Never.

In the days following Carlisle's heart-to-heart talk with Dona Maria, she was treated as an honored guest in the Casa Amarilla. Once up and around, she realized Dona Maria's house was a favorite gathering place for the socially elite of Mexico City. A steady flow of well-dressed matrons, with marriageable daughters and nieces in tow, entered the arched gate to converse or take *comida* with the elegant Dona Maria, hoping her two handsome sons would be present. If not, they were equally desirous of inspecting her beautiful and mysterious *gringa* houseguest.

On these occasions, Dona Maria introduced Carlisle as her son Chaso's good friend from the Estados Unidos. No whisper of scandal concerning her friendship with the Perezes or her misadventures in San Miguel was ever heard.

Just as often, Tomas would accompany Carlisle on long afternoon drives when she felt tired of company and weary of spirit. During these jaunts, they'd drive down the wide Paseo into Mexico City, where cobbled streets wound past wide-eaved adobe houses, private and quiet inside their tall walls.

Carlisle found the old city a fascinating place with its graciously ornate colonial buildings, their hand-carved stone facades like ancient filigree. She was awed by the great Basilica of Our Lady of Guadalupe and the huge amphitheater called the Plaza de Toros, where crowds of Mexicans watched the fierce bullfighters.

All around her, society danced and flirted, rode in the Paseo or walked in the Alameda, and Carlisle took it all in with interest. But her heart was never truly engaged unless Chase was mentioned. Often, there was news that he still fought to quell the northern uprising, and she would shake with fear. What if he were captured again, and tortured? They'd never let him live, and that thought left her terror-stricken.

She was contemplating such horrors one afternoon as Tomas sat beside her in his mother's finest carriage. They had ridden far out of the capital to the outlying villages of the valley, where the air was thin and clear, the sunlight blinding, and the shadows deep and chilling. Lakes dotted the plain, and when they reached the village of Amecameca, huge, snow-covered volcanoes loomed up, protecting the rim of the valley like gigantic sentries.

"That one is Popocatepetl, the Smoking Mountain," Tomas told her. "And the other is Ixtacihuatl, the White Woman. Aztec legends say he is a jealous lover watching over his frozen mate."

"They are beautiful," Carlisle agreed dutifully, but she was really thinking that the shadows against the icy peaks were the same dark blue as Chase's eyes. Almost at once, her mind conjured up the awful red they'd been just after the explosion, and she bit her lip, wondering if they still gave him pain.

"You looked very sad just now, Dona Carlita," Tomas commented.

"I'm sorry, Tomas," she said, facing him. "I was thinking of Chase."

"You think of him often, *sí?*"

"*Sí.*"

They rode in silence for a while; then he spoke, obviously extremely embarrassed by the subject matter.

"Mama intends to make Chaso marry you. Is that what you want?"

Momentarily, a ripple of shock coursed through Carlisle, because Tomas had never before made mention of her baby. Neither had Dona Maria discussed Chase with Carlisle since the day Carlisle had poured out to her their whole sordid story.

"Chase will never marry me," she answered quietly. "No one could make him, not even your mother."

"Mama has her ways. She has already quietly begun plans to nullify his betrothal with Dona Marta. She would never have done that unless she was sure he would marry you."

Carlisle froze. "Who is Dona Marta?"

"She is a friend of the family, and she was to marry Chaso someday."

"Is he in love with her?" Carlisle felt sick as she asked the question.

"Oh, no, he hardly knows her. She is younger than I, so do not worry about her."

Carlisle felt better and she smiled, grateful for his continued support. At the moment, he seemed older than he had the day they'd met at Papa Gilberto's. Today he looked very tanned and handsome in his fancy gray charro suit and big black sombrero.

During her weeks in the capital city, she'd grown used to seeing the men in tight trousers and short, heavily embroidered jackets. Her own clothes had arrived, but she'd lost so much weight during her illness that there had been no immediate need to let out the waistlines. She put her hand on her stomach, awed to think a life was forming inside her.

"I hope Chaso refuses to marry you," Tomas said tightly.

Shocked, Carlisle's eyes filled with dismay. "Oh, Tomas, do you blame me, too?"

"Oh, no, never! If he refuses, then I am duty-bound to wed you in his stead." He removed his sombrero, his brown eyes shy. "I would be very honored to have you for my *novia,* Dona Carlita."

His face was so earnest that Carlisle's heart was touched. "Tomas, you are so sweet and good to me."

The boy grinned, apparently pleased by her answer, and Carlisle reached over to touch his youthful cheek. "But I'll be all right, I promise. You and your mother have made me feel strong again. Whether Chase marries me or not, I'll still be happy to have his baby."

"But if you are not married, your reputation will be ruined. No one will associate with you. It is the way here in Mexico."

"That is the way it is everywhere, Tomas."

Carlisle looked north, toward the dark, jagged peaks in the distance. Somewhere behind those high rugged barriers, Chase fought the *guerrilleros.* Did he ever think about her?

Chase *was* thinking of Carlisle. As he walked his horse down the narrow, cobbled hill toward his mother's mansion, his bewhiskered face grew tight with long-contained anger. Exhausted, physically and spiritually, he thrust the vision of Carlisle from his mind.

She was gone, thank God, and now that she was, perhaps the hell she'd thrust them all into would end. But the ache of betrayal stirred deep in his heart. Why couldn't he just forget her? Damn her green eyes which haunted him day and night!

Furious, but too tired to give in to his rage, he rode on, stone-faced and haggard, to the arched carriage door of the Casa Amarilla. He jerked the bellpull outside the porte cochere, impatient that he had to wait.

"Don Chaso!" cried the boy who finally threw open the gate.

"*Hola,* Paco," Chase answered the mestizo groom, walking his horse into the inner courtyard. He dismounted slowly, his muscles aching from several days in the saddle. He'd traveled the mountain roads from Querétaro alone and fast, in order to make better time.

His men would follow at a slower pace, now that their job was done. They'd taken San Miguel bravely, destroyed it and what it stood for. But there had been no massacre or atrocities this time. Their prisoners were being marched to Mexico City for trial.

Paco swung the gate closed, barred it, then ran to take Chase's reins. He grinned, revealing a large space where his two front teeth were missing.

"*Buenos días,* Don Chaso! We did not know you were coming today!"

"*Gracias. Dónde está mi madre?*"

"Dona Maria is in her room, senor. She will be so happy to see you."

Chase nodded, then walked across the paving flags to the low stone wall that separated the stables from the lush, shade-dappled patio. After the heat of the midday sun, the shade from a eucalyptus tree immediately cooled him, and he walked past the central fountain, which was encircled by big, blade-leafed maguey plants. The tinkling jets of water brought him to a stop. The spot was so peaceful.

For one swift instant, he felt overcome by emotion, by sheer thankfulness to be home again in a haven protected against all the evil he'd seen. Inside his mother's inner sanctum, with its quiet elegant walks and sweet-smelling gardenias and azalea hedges, no one suffered awful pain and ghastly mutilations. He felt the need to lie down in the deep, cool shade and weep out his grief for Esteban—and for Carlisle's treachery. He'd loved them both, and both were gone from him, forever.

Appalled at his own weakness, he set his jaw at a determined angle and walked on. *Dios,* what was the matter with him? He'd seen atrocities during the war, and bitter betrayal.

"I'm just too goddamned tired to think straight," he muttered hoarsely. He needed sleep. In a real bed, free of the never-ending nightmares of Esteban being blown apart, of nails being hammered slowly through his palms. An icy chill rippled up his back, and he flexed his newly healed hands as he climbed the patio steps to the open door of his mother's bedchamber.

She sat at her white desk with its curved cabriole legs, and again he was overcome by sentimental yearning for the long-past childhood days when he'd run to her with his scrapes and bruises, and she'd taken him onto her lap, soothing him with her soft hands and gentle voice. He wanted to be comforted, he realized suddenly, despite the fact that he was a grown man.

"Mama?"

His mother looked up, then quickly dropped the pen she'd held in her hand. She rose to her feet, her fingers gripping the edge of the desk.

"Chaso! *Gracias a Dios!*" she cried, then hurried to him.

Chase put his arms around her shoulders, so frail but so strong, and breathed in the faint lemony scent that had been her essence as long as he could remember. They said nothing as she sobbed against his chest.

He held her, surprised, because he'd never seen her cry before, except when Tomas's father had died.

"Shh, Mama," he said. But she found his hands and held them palm-up so she could examine the jagged, raw weals where his flesh had torn.

"Oh, I cannot bear this, *mi hijo,*" she whispered brokenly.

Chase led her to the bed, and they sat side by side. Dona Maria swiftly regained her composure, as Chase knew she would.

"I have been so worried about you," she said, her voice taking on a scolding tone. "Why did you not send word that you were safe?"

But even as she spoke, her hands touched his cheek gently, pushing back his hair, which had grown shaggy in the past few months.

"The fighting has been hard, and high in the sierra. I had no time to send out letters."

"And you are here to stay? The rebellion is over?" she asked fearfully.

"The *revolución* is crushed. We've broken their strength and captured their leaders."

"My prayers to the Holy Virgin have been answered. And you are safe!"

"*Sí,* Mama."

She searched his face. "Are you really all right, Chaso? You look so weary. You must lie back and rest. I will get food and wine for you."

Chase did as she said, then went rigid at his mother's next words.

"Chaso, you have not asked about Dona Carlita. She was very ill when she came—"

"I don't want to hear about her!" he interrupted harshly, shocking his mother into silence. He shut his eyes again as she moved away with a soft rustle of silk. And then the sleep he'd cheated for so long pulled him into its embrace.

It was nearly dark by the time Carlisle and Tomas returned to the Casa Amarilla. Dona Maria was waiting for them at the grilled gate.

"Buenas noches," Carlisle called to her, totally unprepared for the first words out of Dona Maria's mouth.

"Chaso has come home."

Carlisle's smile faded, her heart stopped, and a peculiar mixture of fear and joy seized her.

"Where is he?" she whispered breathlessly.

"He's exhausted. We barely had time to talk before he fell asleep."

"Does he know I'm still here?" Carlisle asked, her breath held captive in her throat.

"He was too tired to discuss it."

Carlisle saw the way Dona Maria averted her gaze, and her hopes fell.

Tomas's relief was evident in his voice. "Is he all right, Mama?"

"Sí." Dona Maria hesitated. "His body has healed, but there is a look in his eyes that frightens me."

Carlisle knew that expression. In the cave, she'd seen it often—cold, empty, disillusioned.

"I want to see him," she said. *"Por favor,* Dona Maria," she added, suddenly desperate to look at him, to touch him, before he found out she was there and sent her away.

Dona Maria took Carlisle's hand, her eyes very serious. "He is still fighting inside himself, *niña*. It might be better if you give him time to find peace."

"I won't waken him, I promise. I only want to see him and make sure he's all right."

Dona Maria sighed, shaking her head. "He's resting in my room."

"I will go with you," Tomas offered at once, but as Carlisle hurried away, his mother put a hand on his arm.

"No, *mi hijo,* this is something they must solve between themselves. You are not needed there."

Carlisle was grateful that Dona Maria had prevented Tomas from following her. She lifted her skirts and ran up the stairs, then stopped before the door, filled with dreadful anticipation. She turned the door handle.

The drapes and shutters were closed, but even in the semi-light she could see him sprawled across the wide bed, still dressed in travel-stained riding attire. She walked across to him, careful not to make a sound. He lay on his back, one arm flung out palm-up, the other curved above his head. He slept heavily, without moving.

He looked so handsome, so peaceful. A rush of tears threatened. Oh, God, why couldn't things have been different for them? Why had everything gotten so mixed up? Why couldn't they have met at a ball or across a tea table? Then they could have gotten to know each other, been friends, courted like other couples. Now she couldn't imagine why she'd disliked him at first, or why she'd put her trust in Javier and Arantxa. She'd been so stupid.

Chase stirred and murmured something unintelligible. Carlisle sat down on the bed, reaching out and touching her fingers to the thick dark growth on his chin. His beard was much darker than his hair, she thought irrelevantly, then slid her fingertips up to where his hair curled behind his ears. He needed a barber.

Her gaze moved to his open hand, and her heart lurched. She lifted it, cradling it gently. She stared down at the awful red scar and felt deep, bitter sorrow.

"Carly?" Chase mumbled groggily, raising himself up on his elbow, his eyes bleary with sleep. His other hand found the back of her head, his fingers tangling in the loose chignon. Carlisle went eagerly, gladly, as he pulled her down against his chest.

"Oh, Chase, I've missed you so much," she whispered, breathless as his mouth found her lips. Then her words were taken. He was aroused, his hands seeking entry into her clothes, and Carlisle knew he was still dreaming. But it felt so good to be held in his arms, to hear him murmuring her name against her hair. His lips sought hers again, almost desperately.

"I love you, Chase. I love you so much," she murmured as she slid her arms around his neck.

She felt his shoulders tense, then gasped as his eyes flew open. His fingers closed cruelly over her arms and thrust her away from him. He was up off the bed before she could catch her breath, combing trembling fingers through his hair as he leaned shakily against the bedside table.

"Dammit, what the hell are you doing here?"

Chase hadn't looked at her yet, as if he couldn't bear to, and his sudden coldness slashed Carlisle's heart like a saber. She tried to gather up her pride and use it as a shield, but she found she had very little left. Her voice shook when she tried to answer.

"I was too sick to leave at first, then—"

"I don't give a damn! I told Tomas to put you on a ship out of here!"

Carlisle could see fury flashing in the blue of his eyes now, and even though his terrible anger was intimidating, she knew in her heart he didn't really hate her, which had been her greatest fear. He still wanted and needed her. He'd shown that when he'd been half asleep and unaware, before all the guilt and blame had descended on his conscious mind. She took a deep breath.

"I know you don't want me here, and—"

"You're damn right I don't. And Tomas better have a hell of a good excuse for you still being around."

"Tomas did not make the decision. I did." Dona Maria stood in the doorway, drawn up to her full height. "And I'll not let you blame your brother or your *novia.*"

Chase looked as if he'd been struck by a thunderbolt.

"My *novia?*" he repeated, then laughed so coldly that Carlisle shivered. His amusement was short-lived. "She is not my fiancée, or anything else. She is nothing to me."

Carlisle lowered her eyes, fighting tears of humiliation, but Dona Maria's voice was calm.

"There you are wrong, *mi hijo.* Dona Carlita is the mother of your unborn child."

The silence was long, and so heavy that the room seemed smothered by it. Carlisle could not bring herself to meet Chase's eyes.

"And what makes you think the child she carries is mine?" Chase asked at last, his voice brittle.

"Chaso! How dare you speak so to Dona Carlita?"

"You do not think my question legitimate under the circumstances, Mother?"

"I think your question is insulting. Do you deny the possibility that you could be the father?"

"I can't deny that, and she damn well knows it. But I won't be trapped into a marriage, like some schoolboy."

At that, Carlisle found the tattered shreds of her pride.

"Nor will I," she said. "I will leave this house tonight."

"You will do no such thing," Dona Maria replied at once. "And this bickering will solve nothing. We will speak of it again when my son is rested and refreshed, and can behave like a gentleman. Come with me, Dona Carlita. Tomas awaits us for *comida*. Chaso will join us later."

Chase muttered a furious curse, and Carlisle bit her lip, distressed, as Dona Maria led her from the room.

15

Chase paced back and forth across the floor of his bedchamber, his gut knotted with nerves. Since he'd found Carlisle in his house, claiming to be with child, he'd felt sick inside, tormented in heart and mind.

Worse, he'd found he still wanted her desperately. Touching her again, holding her in his arms, had made him forget for a moment all she'd done. Damn her for coming to him when he'd been so weak, his guard down. Even now, as he tried to focus only on her crimes, his mind rebelled and all he could think about was the texture of her hair, the way the thick golden-red strands slipped through his fingers as fragrant as flowers, as soft as silk. *Dios,* she could drive a man insane!

Steeling himself, he conjured up Conchita's grief the day he'd told her about her husband's death. His anger returned in quick, staccato surges, like a pulse driven by a pounding heart. He left his room and descended to the patio. As he reached the dining table on the arcaded porch, he was thankful that rage gripped him, because Carlisle sat beside his mother, so beautiful under the candlelight that his breath was snatched from him. She wore a serene, seraphic look, entrancing but deceiving.

He cursed her inwardly, and avoided looking at her. Instead, he bent and kissed his mother's cheek.

"Buenas noches, Chaso,'' his mother greeted him. "Now that you've bathed and rested, I trust you are more yourself.''

"Sí,'' Chase replied, ignoring her subtle rebuke. As he sat down, he glanced at his half brother. *"Hola,* Tomas.''

"Aren't you going to speak to Dona Carlita?'' was Tomas's curt demand.

Surprised, Chase observed his brother for a moment. He shrugged. "Why should I?''

His remark angered Carlisle—he could see her eyes flare—but she only lowered her lashes. Tomas was not so circumspect about his opinion.

"How dare you treat her in such a way?'' he cried furiously, coming to his feet.

Tomas's extreme reaction was unexpected, but Chase was careful not to show his concern. He looked at Carlisle instead, who seemed as startled as he by Tomas's behavior.

"Sit down, Tomas, and quit acting like a ruffian,'' his mother said. "I am beginning to wonder what kind of sons I have raised. Have both of you forgotten your manners?''

His face still flushed a mottled red. Tomas sat down again.

Water tinkled musically from the fountain as the maids moved around the table, serving enchiladas and rice. The silence between the diners continued, and Chase drank his wine, noting with some satisfaction that Carlisle seemed robbed of appetite. He watched her surreptitiously, then realized that Tomas did the same. *Dios*, he realized, Tomas is infatuated with her, too. She had wasted no time enticing the boy into her silky web.

"Why the hell didn't you do as I told you?" he said tightly to Tomas, a black frown on his face. "You were to send her home immediately. If you'd done that, none of this would be happening."

Tomas glared accusingly at him. "She is to have your child! What kind of man are you to use her, then thrust her aside?"

"Stop it," Carlisle cried, her face drained of color. Her mouth trembled as they all looked at her. "I won't listen to this any longer. And I won't stay here, Chase. You have no need to worry. I intend to leave in the morning. I made the decision earlier, and there's nothing any of you can do to stop me." Her gaze sought Dona Maria. "You have been very kind, senora, and I'll always remember that. But I don't belong here."

No one spoke as she walked away, her head held high. Even her decision to leave annoyed Chase. He was further irritated by Tomas's next pronouncement.

"If you are not man enough to do the honorable thing toward Dona Carlita, Chaso, then I will. I intend to ask Dona Carlita to become my wife."

"Tomas!" his mother cried, shocked.

Chase only laughed. "Don't be ridiculous. You're only a boy."

"I'm not a boy. I'm sixteen, and I won't let you dishonor poor Dona Carlita. She is so sweet—"

Chase slammed his fist down on the table. The resulting thud rattled the dishes and upset his mother's wineglass. His blue eyes burned with fury.

"Poor Carlita betrayed me! She got Esteban killed! I was crucified because of that sweet girl!"

Tomas looked as if he'd been struck across the face, and tears shone in Dona Maria's eyes as Chase stood, trying to control his anger. It took him several minutes.

"If she is pregnant," he said at length, his voice strained, "and if the baby is mine, then I will consider the options."

"The baby is yours," his mother said quietly. "She has not lain with any other man. She told me herself, and I believe her."

"Javier Perez says differently," he returned coldly. "He enlightened me with a great deal of relish while he tortured me."

"And he has certainly proved himself the most trustworthy of men, hasn't he, my son?"

His mother's sarcasm made Chase flush.

"I don't care whose baby it is! I love Carlita!" Tomas said heatedly. "If you don't want her, I do. I'll marry her tonight and claim the baby as mine."

Astonished, both his mother and brother turned to stare at him.

"Don't be absurd," Chase muttered.

"What's so absurd about it?" Tomas demanded. "At least I know my duty as a man. Apparently you've forgotten what honor is!"

"Shut up, Tomas," Chase said harshly. "There's no way in hell you'll ever marry Carlisle, *comprendes?*"

His voice was so dangerous now that Tomas clamped his lips together, his expression mutinous.

"I'm not so sure Tomas's suggestion is a bad one, under the circumstances," Dona Maria said, flabbergasting Chase. "Dona Carlita is close to his age. It is a convenient solution, Chaso, since you obviously intend to shirk your responsibility to her."

Furious, Chase turned on his mother. "I won't be manipulated into marrying a woman I despise." His voice was low and lethal.

"And I will not abandon my first grandchild to the life of a bastard," Dona Maria said, very calmly, but displaying the same stubbornness as her son.

Chase glared at her, a muscle twitching in his tanned cheek.

"I will do as I see fit with Carlisle," he said tightly, "and I'll tolerate no interference from either of you, is that clear?"

Without another word, Chase turned and stalked away in search of Carlisle.

Still trembling with anger, her hurt and longing momentarily forgotten, Carlisle slung several of her gowns into the trunk she'd dragged from the adjoining dressing room. Chase didn't care about her or the baby. He didn't care about anything. She'd go home to Chicago, where she belonged, and have her baby there!

That thought sobered her and made her weak-kneed. She sank down in front of her mirrored dressing table and stared into her own frightened green eyes. What would Gray and Stone say when they learned she was pregnant out of wedlock? They'd be appalled and disappointed and hurt. Both of them had protected her virtue so diligently.

They'd be furious, too, although she knew they

would forgive her eventually and hush up the scandal.
And Carlisle knew Tyler would stand by her. Tyler
was very loyal to those she cared about. Chase would
be the one they'd condemn. They'd blame him for
everything.

Suddenly the idea of going home didn't seem so
awful. Up until now, she'd put off writing Gray out
of shame. Now she realized they'd all have to know.
But what if they insisted Chase marry her against his
will? The idea was so repugnant, she shuddered.

"Never. They can't make me do that," she vowed
in a whisper, horrified to think what an enforced marriage to Chase would be like.

"Make you do what?"

Carlisle's gaze flew up to where Chase was reflected in the looking glass. At once, and without
mercy, the old pull of his magnetism began—the
strange, inexplicable hold he had on her. She stiffened, preparing herself when she recognized the carefully controlled expression on his face. It signified a
dangerous, unpredictable mood. She moistened her lips
with the tip of her tongue, nervous, aware that they were
alone in her bedchamber. She drew her dressing gown
together at the throat as his dark blue eyes raked over
her figure.

"What do you want? I'm not dressed," she said,
trying to sound cold, but she was embarrassed when her
voice quivered noticeably.

Chase barked a laugh totally devoid of humor. "Why
this sudden shyness, Carly? If you'll remember, I'm no
stranger to your body."

Carlisle dropped her gaze, again plagued by an awful urge to cry. But she wouldn't, not with him watch-

ing. She'd keep her self-respect, even if he took everything else from her.

"Go away, Chase, please. I don't want to fight. I'm leaving in the morning. Isn't that soon enough for you?"

"Perhaps it would be if you hadn't seen fit to seduce my little brother first."

His remark shocked Carlisle. She finally met his accusing stare. "What do you mean? Tomas has been kind, and he's treated me like a lady. He's my friend, and I care about him."

"And you have beguiled him, as you did so many other men." His voice dropped to a husky whisper. Carlisle grew wary. He lifted one long, curling lock from where it lay on her back. Her heart raced and she shut her eyes. Why did she have to turn into a quivering mass of jelly when he touched her? Why did she have to love him so much?

"In fact," he went on slowly, caressing a strand of her hair between his thumb and forefinger, "he wants to marry you. Is that what you had in mind?"

Carlisle couldn't mask her astonishment. "Of course not. He's just a boy."

"He doesn't seem to think so."

Carlisle could sense there was something more, and she felt a strange terror well up inside her.

"What do you want, Chase? I'm tired, and I don't feel well."

She stood, intending to move away from him so she could control her reaction to having him so close. Still, after all his cruel words of rejection, she wanted him to hold her and kiss her. She barely got a step away when he grabbed her by the shoulders and spun her around.

"I'm tired of playing games with you, Carly. I want to know if the baby you're carrying is mine."

Carlisle blanched, then tried ineffectually to push him away. It was like trying to shove a brick wall. "How dare you ask me such a thing? I've never known a man before you. Javier never touched me like that, not once, and I never wanted him to. I was a virgin that first time in the cave, and you know it."

She twisted again, but his fingers tightened around her upper arms.

"And all these months I've been gone? How many lovers have you taken here in Mexico City?"

Appalled by his crude accusation, she stared unflinchingly at him, letting her contempt show in her eyes. His face remained impassive, but he suddenly released her. The tears that Carlisle had fought for so long came in a flood now, and she turned away.

"I'm leaving, aren't I? I don't want anything from you! Please, just go away and leave me alone!"

"If that is my baby, do you really think I'll stand by and let you find some other lover to raise my son?"

Furiously, Carlisle turned on him. "What do you expect me to do? You've made it clear that you can't stand the sight of me!"

"Unfortunately, I suppose I'll have to tolerate your presence here, at least until the baby is born."

A great seething rage roiled up within Carlisle. "But I don't think I can tolerate yours. I don't have to be humiliated by you. I'm going home, Chase, and you can't stop me."

"Oh, can't I, Carlisle?" he answered with a smile of disdain, his eyes as hard as arctic ice. "You will stay here and become my wife, because I'll not have my son born a bastard. But don't expect me to ever share your bed again. And don't think I'll ever love you or forget your treachery."

"And I have no say in the matter?"

His smile was frigid. "Not one word, *querida*. Not a single word."

Their gazes held for one long moment; then he took himself out of the room with long, angry strides, leaving her leaning weakly against her dressing table.

The door slammed hard enough to jar the hinges, and Carlisle shook with anger. But deep in her heart, a different emotion fought to fly free. He'd been angry, his words purposely laced with cruel barbs, but he no longer questioned that the baby was his. He was willing to marry her and give the child his name. More than anything in the world, that was what Carlisle wanted. Her baby would know his father.

Chase was still filled with rage and bitterness, but she could not blame him. She had to make him see how much she loved him, how sorry she was that she'd caused him such suffering. He wanted the baby growing inside her, and someday, God willing, he'd want her again, too.

As twilight drifted down like a silver-gray mantle over the tiled red rooftops of the city, Carlisle sat alone on the elaborate velvet bench at the foot of her immense four-poster bed. Her heavy satin gown, the color of old ivory, lay against her knees in graceful, glistening folds, with hundreds of seed pearls gleaming among the exquisite swirling lace.

As she contemplated her imminent wedding to the man she loved, she realized she was afraid. Abruptly, she stood, her quick movement causing her voluminous skirt to rustle around her ankles. A nosegay of white roses lay on the small mirrored stand where twin candles burned. She took it in her hand.

Earlier in the day, Tomas had brought the bouquet to her. She fingered the soft silk ribbons dangling from the silver holder, remembering how sweet he'd been. Since Chase had told her how Tomas felt, she'd been careful not to encourage him in any way, determined to alleviate any kind of strife between Chase and his brother. It hadn't been easy for her, and her teeth caught at her lip as she recalled his hurt looks when she'd pointedly avoided his company during the past two weeks since Chase's return.

Thank goodness, all the preparations were at an end. Although Carlisle hadn't been expected to worry herself with the wedding details, and since Chase had absented himself from the Casa Amarilla as much as possible, Dona Maria had happily taken matters into her own capable hands.

She'd discussed with Carlisle the importance of keeping her condition secret, pointing out that the discovery would ruin Carlisle's reputation in the city. She'd therefore arranged for Carlisle to spend the last months of her confinement in the city of Puebla with Chase's aunt Isabella, who lived at the great hacienda of the Morelos family. That way, she'd explained, no one would know the exact date of the baby's birth.

Another problem Chase's mother took in hand was the breach of Chase's betrothal with the Moreno family, old and honored *gachupines* with pure Spanish bloodlines. When questioned, she'd quietly assured Carlisle that the contract had been voided.

In the quiet room, Carlisle's sigh was forlorn. More and more, she'd been plagued by the fear that she was doing the wrong thing. If Chase felt trapped into marriage because of the baby, what kind of life could she possibly hope to share with him? Would she always be the object of his scorn? Perhaps she should flee now, before it was too late, back to her brothers. Gray and Stone would take care of her.

But how could she do that? She had not even had the courage yet to send word that she was expecting a child. Gray would be furious, and he'd probably come to Mexico, which would make everything between Chase and her that much worse. No, she would wait until she was married, perhaps even after the baby was born. Then she'd tell them everything. They knew she rarely wrote letters—even when she had been in the convent. Her brothers had always scolded her about that, though if truth be told, they were hardly what you'd call devoted correspondents themselves.

Carlisle looked toward the door as someone tapped for admittance. Dona Maria appeared, adorned in a lustrous, high-necked gray silk gown. Draped carefully over one arm was a long ivory mantilla of beautiful Spanish lace.

"The carriage awaits us at the door," she said, hurrying across the room toward Carlisle. "Are you ready, my *hija bonita?*"

Carlisle was touched that she called her daughter. No one had ever done so before. She hardly remembered her own mother, who had died when Carlisle was very small. Despite Dona Maria's kindness, Carlisle's smile was apprehensive.

"I'm afraid I'm doing the wrong thing, Dona Maria."

"Ah, *niña,* you must stop all this worrying and put

a smile on your face. This is your wedding day, and you are marrying the man you love, no?''

"But he doesn't love me! He told me he could never love me!''

"But that is because he is *un hombre, querida*. It is the fierce pride of our Mexican men that makes them so hard and unyielding. Inside here," she said, putting her fingertips to her breast, "my son knows what he really feels. One day he will tell you.'' Her dark eyes sparkled. "And then he will come to me and thank me for showing him his duty. I know Chaso, *niña*. You must believe me.''

Carlisle did feel better. She hugged the older woman lightly. "How lucky I am to have you on my side. At first, I thought you'd hate me.''

Dona Maria cupped her palm against the elegant curve of Carlisle's cheek. "You are very hard to hate, Carlita, and I think my stubborn son will find that out very soon." She drew back suddenly, carefully displaying the fragile veil in front of her. "But look, I have brought this lovely mantilla for you to wear in the ceremony. It has been in my family for six generations. I would be pleased if you'd wear it when you become my only daughter.''

Touched, Carlisle laid her fingers on the old lace, so soft and precious. "I would be very honored," she said softly. *"Gracias,* Dona Maria.''

"You honor me, and my son. But you must not weep. Chaso will be humiliated if you appear with swollen eyes. Now turn around and let me help arrange your mantilla.''

Carlisle obeyed, watching as Dona Maria slid a white, emerald-encrusted Spanish comb into Carlisle's elaborately coiled chignon.

"And this is my wedding present to you. It, too, is a family treasure. It is said that long ago, in Spain, one of our ancestors, a beautiful lady with blond hair and dark blue eyes just like Chaso's, wore it when she wed a brave conquistador who sailed with the great Cortez. Someday you and Chaso will present it to your own daughter." She patted Carlisle's hand. "There, now you are even more beautiful. Chaso will be very proud."

Carlisle stared at the winking emeralds as Chase's mother arranged the ivory lace lovingly over the comb and shadowed her face with its intricate designs.

"I pray he will be proud," Carlisle murmured, not at all sure he would be.

"Chaso is a man, is he not? He will be struck as if by a thunderbolt when he sees you at the altar. But we must hurry or he will be angry with us for making him wait!"

Chase was angry, all right, though his bronzed, handsome face showed no trace of such emotion. He stood tall and straight just inside the front rail of the ancient Basilica of Our Lady of Guadalupe. Beside him, Tomas stood as his *padrino,* frowning as if he were not his brother's best man but a felon awaiting execution. In his hands, he twisted the heavy emerald ring Chase would soon slide on Carlisle's finger.

Chase looked out over the great, cavernous nave where hundreds of very curious, elaborately costumed guests had already found their seats. Inside the mantilla-covered heads of the ladies, he had a feeling the most deliciously wicked conjectures were taking shape about why he'd embarked on such a sudden alliance with a *gringa.*

Of course, none would dare speak the questions aloud for fear of bringing down the wrath of Dona Maria Jimenez y Morelos. Instead, they'd whisper in their walled patios behind fans, and spend the next nine months scrutinizing Carlisle's waistline. And they would not be disappointed in their scandalmongering.

Damn, where was she? Didn't she know she'd only add fuel to the bonfires of gossip by showing up late for the wedding? His mother surely knew the consequences of her tardiness. He resisted the urge to pluck the gold pocket watch from his black velvet charro jacket and check the time.

Jaw clenched, he gazed at the astonishingly lavish adornment of the altar, glittering with gold carvings and statues of angels. Slowly, inexorably, a different altar superimposed itself over the scene, less decorative, crumbling and shabby, but with a similar cross and crucified Christ. Again he felt the wall behind his back, saw Javier's brown eyes fill with triumph and hatred. In his mind he watched them hold the mallet, felt the jab of the spike against his palm just before the hammer sent it slicing through his flesh.

His fists balled, hard as rocks, enclosing the scars he'd wear for the rest of his life. But at least he was alive, which was more than he could say for Esteban. A familiar pain cut through his heart. He thought of him every day. Esteban was to have been his *padrino*. They'd laughed about it the night Esteban had made Chase admit he loved Carlisle. He felt a curl of nausea in his stomach, but he thrust his thoughts away as a faint murmur swept like a storm wind through the church.

At the back of the rose-strewn center aisle, between

long lines of flaming candelabras, Carlisle stood in the soft glow, all white lace and satin, golden-red hair gleaming like the setting sun. Esteban's angel, he thought bitterly as she began her slow, decorous walk to the altar. She moved gracefully, looking almost as if she floated toward him, her eyes on him and nowhere else, her exquisite face solemn and lovely. As quick as a flash flood, and despite all she'd done, a wave of pure, overwhelming pride hit him.

When Carlisle reached him, she stopped, and Chase read the uncertainty in her wide green eyes. She showed her emotions more than she used to. Now he could easily see her hopes, her fears, her hurt, when before, he'd only been able to guess.

Reaching out, he offered her his hand. Then to his shock, she bent and pressed her lips to his scarred palm. Whispers rippled through the guests, and Chase swallowed hard, his heart pounding as he drew her with him to the altar. They knelt together before the priest, and inside, Chase felt torn by conflicts he couldn't come to grips with. He still loved her, God help him. He loved her too much. But he also knew that Esteban's death would always stand between them.

The Mass began. While the padre recited the ancient Latin words, Chase thought about the child forming inside Carlisle's slender body. Would the baby be a boy? Or a daughter who would possess Carlisle's extraordinary beauty? But could anyone, even her own flesh and blood, rival Carlisle's coppery hair and emerald eyes?

The priest's voice droned on and on, and when Chase felt Carlisle sway weakly beside him, he braced her back with his arm. She leaned against him, turning her head slightly toward him. Through the sheer, delicate lace he could see the perfection of her features, and he knew that if he lived to be old and white-haired, he'd never forget the way she looked at that moment.

16

For one brief moment during the ceremony, Carlisle had seen love shining in Chase's eyes. Though the warm look had disappeared quickly, she still held the memory close to her heart as she stood with Chase and his family on the marble dais in the magnificent ballroom of Chapultepec Castle.

Tomas had once brought her there on one of their afternoon drives, and she'd been fascinated by the immense palace built like a crown on the high hill where Montezuma once held his court and bathed in crystal pools fed by high mountain aqueducts. More recently, Austrian Archduke Maximilian and his wife, Carlota, had called themselves emperor and empress, and had opened the castle terraces and gardens for glittering balls honoring their French allies and the Mexicans, like the Perez family, who supported their reign. Now the hundreds of guests filling the candlelit ballroom were the Juaristas whom Maximilian had failed to subdue.

"Do try to pay attention, Carly. We're supposed to act blissful."

When she looked up at Chase, surprised and hurt by his unprovoked sarcasm, he shifted his gaze away from her. She craved another soft look, warm and unguarded. She loved the way he smiled, when his deep dimples framed his mouth. He'd grinned so often when they first met, usually at her expense. Now she'd welcome his teasing and the sight of his eyes glinting with amusement.

She wished they didn't have to stand in line and meet people who looked at her as if she were some exotic butterfly on display. Sadness descended, and her heart weighted her down like a millstone. She stiffened as Chase suddenly put his arm around her waist and drew her close to him. He smiled at her as she'd been dreaming he would, but his eyes weren't warm, so the gentle look didn't matter.

"Querida, allow me to present Senor Ernesto Moreno and his daughter Dona Marta."

Carlisle's gaze darted to the young girl beside the tall, silver-haired man who was dressed impeccably in black. Chase's former betrothed was very pretty, with huge brown eyes and sun-streaked brown hair. She was quite young, only twelve or thirteen, Carlisle guessed, and she noticed at once the way Dona Marta studiously avoided Chase's eyes.

"How do you do, Dona Marta," Carlisle said when Chase presented her, feeling as self-conscious as the other girl looked. She wondered if Dona Marta hated her for marrying Chase in her place, then felt a flood of embarrassed color rise when she realized they might know she was already pregnant.

Dona Marta curtsied gracefully, then moved on to where Tomas stood with his mother.

"I wish you a very happy and prosperous life, Don

Chaso,'' Senor Moreno said, exchanging with Chase the customary *abrazo*. Then he bowed gallantly to Carlisle. When he passed on to converse with Dona Maria, Carlisle breathed easier, thankful the Morenos were the last guests in the reception line.

"It's customary for us to begin the dancing," Chase told her. His words were short and abrupt now, as if he were angry. When he took her fingers and pressed them to his lips, she knew it was for the benefit of all the people watching them. Carlisle felt she couldn't bear another minute of this tense sham. She wanted to run away, but Chase held her arm firmly.

As the *músicos* began to play, Chase took her in his arms and began to waltz, slowly, gracefully, elegantly. She'd never danced with him before, and for some reason, it made everything worse. A wedding wasn't supposed to be an awful ordeal strained by cold politeness that made her heart break. Tears formed in her eyes, and she could not stop one from escaping down her cheek.

"Stop crying, Carly," Chase ordered softly, nodding at those watching and applauding.

"I can't help it!" Carlisle wiped at her tear, but a stifled sob escaped her.

Chase swung her to a halt near the open terrace doors, smiling as he signaled the other couples to join the dancing. He led Carlisle outside, where the night was cool and dark, and she dabbed at her tears with the fine linen handkerchief Chase handed her, aware she'd embarrassed him in front of his family and friends.

"Are you all right?" he asked, standing a little apart from her, his voice gentler now.

"I'm sorry. I'm just so tired," she managed to say, sniffing. "I haven't been sleeping well."

"No, *I'm* sorry. I was inconsiderate. Here, sit down." He drew her to a bench and helped her pull her bulky skirt out of the way. "Would you like a drink or something to eat? You've lost a lot of weight, and Mother says you aren't eating enough to keep a bird alive."

His concern made her want to cry harder, but she refused to dissolve into tears. "No, thank you. I felt strange meeting Dona Marta. You were supposed to marry her. Why would she put herself through the humiliating experience of attending our wedding?"

"Don't worry about Dona Marta. She was relieved to be released from the marriage contract. According to Don Ernesto, she's terrified of me. She'd heard the silly accounts of El Gato Grande, I suppose."

"Wasn't her father angry that the betrothal was broken?"

"It seems little Marta's had a crush on Tomas since they played together as children, so Don Ernesto was eager enough to substitute my brother for me."

"Does Tomas want to marry her?"

"He will accept the arrangement in time."

Neither spoke for a few minutes. At last Carlisle could not bear their estrangement any longer. She wanted him to understand, to forgive her.

"Chase, please, let's talk about Esteban—"

The minute she said the name, Chase stood, interrupting her. "We've been out here too long. If you're feeling better, we should go in. El Presidente has honored us by bringing his family to the wedding. We'll speak with him for a moment, then I'll make our excuses early so you can get some rest."

Carlisle had no choice but to go along, and the instant they entered the ballroom, they were surrounded by well-wishers, who clapped Chase vigorously on the back and kissed Carlisle's hand.

Slowly, Chase made their way around the edge of the dance floor to where the dark, somber-faced President of Mexico sat on a red velvet sofa with his wife. Carlisle was overcome by nervousness, and she hung back as Chase was greeted affectionately.

Benito Juarez stood at once, his calm deep eyes fixed upon Carlisle's face as he extended his hand.

"It is my sincere pleasure to meet you, Senora Lancaster."

Her new name startled her, but she returned his smile. He was not striking in appearance, not when she remembered all the reforms for the people of Mexico that Dona Maria and Tomas had subscribed to him. But somehow she sensed his greatness, and knew that his wide forehead and inscrutable Indian features would long be remembered by the Mexican people.

"I am not a dancer of ability, Dona Carlita. You have only to ask my dear wife, Dona Margarita." He glanced affectionately at the gray-haired woman sitting beside him, who nodded graciously at Carlisle. "But I would be pleased if such a beautiful bride as yourself would grant me one turn about the room."

"I would be honored, El Presidente."

The president led her out onto the floor, and she found she was nearly as tall as he. Though stocky and obviously uncomfortable with dancing, he managed the footwork of the waltz quite well. He was silent, but in an agreeable way, and suddenly Carlisle felt the need to earn his goodwill.

"I hope you can find it in your heart to forgive my part in the terrible things that happened at San Miguel. I was foolish to believe the lies I was told about you."

Benito Juarez smiled gravely. "You are now the wife of my most trusted foreign advisor and very good friend. My family and I welcome you to our country."

His words were sincere, and she realized how the man had attained the adoration of his people. She could understand Chase's loyalty and deep respect for his president.

"*Gracias,*" she said as the music came to an end.

Chase had waltzed with Senora Juarez, and after a few more minutes of exchanging pleasantries, he was able to lead Carlisle out of the crowded ballroom. Much laughter and ribald banter concerning their early departure followed them, and suddenly Carlisle began to hope. Finally they'd be alone together again. She'd longed so often to talk to him. She wanted to explain everything, how she felt, how terribly sorry she was for all the pain she'd caused him. Now that they were married, perhaps he'd listen to her.

Chase handed her into the coach, then paused to give instructions to the driver before he followed, settling into the seat opposite her. She frowned slightly, wishing he'd taken a place beside her. She wanted so desperately for him to hold her.

Chase said nothing, only stared at her so intently that her nerves began to jump. What was he thinking? Was he glad they were man and wife? Or did he really hate her?

"Chase, could we talk now, please?"

"What about?"

She shifted uncomfortably. Now that they were alone, his voice had a hard edge again.

"About us, of course."

"What about us?"

"Oh, please, Chase, let's not fight. We're married now. Why can't we try to make it work?" She reached out to touch his knee. "I love you, Chase. You must know that."

She was in no way prepared for his reaction. He pushed her hand away from him. "Don't say that to me, *comprendes?* I don't want to hear it."

"But why? Why won't you let me tell you how I feel?"

"Because I'm angry," he said, uttering each word with slow succinctness. "I'm so angry my guts are tied in knots, every day, every night." He leaned forward and took her by the shoulders. "And you know why, Carly? Because Esteban's dead." He opened his palms and thrust them out in front of her eyes. "And because Perez did this to me."

"I didn't want that to happen, Chase! Why won't you believe me? What do I have to do to make you see how sorry I am?"

"I wanted to kill you when I saw you dancing with Perez. But then you took care of that, too, didn't you? You had to help save my life so I couldn't even put my hands around your neck and enjoy that revenge. And now as the last slap in my face, you carry my child, and I'm damned to see you everyday, to relive it all, over and over again."

Carlisle sat frozen.

Raising his hand, he beat on the ceiling with his fist to signal the coachman to stop. When the carriage halted with a lurch, he thrust open the door and leapt to the ground.

"Wait, Chase, where are you going? It's our wedding night!"

"A wedding night is not required to give my child a name. Sleep well, Carly."

The door slammed, and Carlisle strove desperately to fight off her hurt. She knew he blamed her. At least he'd finally accused her to her face. Perhaps this outburst would help drain away the anger festering inside him.

Despite her attempts to be reasonable and try to understand Chase's cruel behavior, she felt deep, razor-sharp humiliation when she stepped down in the courtyard of the Casa Amarilla and faced the servants alone, abandoned on her wedding night.

Valiantly, she smiled and endeavored to act as if her heart were not bleeding. Everyone was quiet and asked no questions, but she saw the sympathy in their dark eyes, so she avoided speaking to them, lifting her gown and hurrying upstairs.

Like that of a wounded doe wanting to die in her den, her first impulse was to seek the sanctuary of her own bedchamber. Chase's suite had been prepared as the bridal bower, and some innate streak of defiance made her pause before its open portal.

Fresh flowers had been collected into huge, showy bouquets—so many that the sweet scent of roses and gardenias permeated the room. Tears burned, but she quickly recovered herself as Juana appeared from the adjoining bathing chamber. The girl seemed surprised to see her.

"Dona Carlita? I did not hear you come in. Are

you ready to bathe? Or will you and Don Chaso wish time alone?''

"A bath, *por favor. Gracias,* Juana.''

Juana turned to her chore, and Carlisle stopped her with a second request.

"And would you prepare the sleeping potion you gave me when I was ill? I want only to sleep and forget everything that's happened.''

"Sí, Dona Carlita,'' Juana answered, but her eyes were troubled as she hurried off to draw the bathwater.

Carlisle set about making her mind as blank as humanly possible. She carefully removed the delicate mantilla and lay it over a chair. She wouldn't think about Chase, she decided, because when she did, she was either miserable or angry. She felt numb and empty, but those feelings were preferable. Damn Chase, anyway.

With difficulty, she unbuttoned her dress, feeling a twinge of regret as she set it aside. Last year when she was in the convent, how could she ever have imagined what a horrible wedding day she'd have, already pregnant by a man who hated her?

Sighing, she thrust Chase from her mind again and entered the elaborate bath. Since her first days in Mexico City she'd marveled at the palatial marble fireplaces and sunken tubs of the Casa Amarilla. She slipped out of her chemise and stockings, moved across the blue-and-white mosaic tiles, then stepped down into the deep, round pool in which wispy steam rose from the warm, rose-scented water. Her tight muscles began to relax, and she leaned her head back and closed her eyes.

"I have the potion, Dona Carlita,'' Juana said from

where she knelt beside her. "It will relax you, and
then later, you will sleep long and deep, and have
wonderful dreams. Drink. Then I will turn back your
bed and bring your nightgown."

"*Sí*, Juana, *gracias*," Carlisle said, taking the cup.
She drank the brew quickly, wanting Juana's concoc-
tion to plunge her into immediate oblivion.

Instead, her whole body grew warm, beginning at
her toes and moving slowly upward like a low-grade
fever. But with it came the most wonderful sense of
contentment. Soon she felt suspended in a netherland
of dreams, warm, cloudy, and beautiful. She did not
know how long she drowsed there before voices in
the next room compelled her to open her weighted
eyelids.

Chase stood in the doorway, Juana behind him, and
Carlisle knew she had to be dreaming.

"Leave us, Juana," her husband ordered, without
looking at the Indian girl. Carlisle's delicate brows
drew into a mild frown. Damn Chase, he even tormented her while she slept!

"Go away, Chase, and leave my dreams alone,"
she muttered, her voice thick with sleep. "You're not
even real."

"The hell I'm not," he answered, his deeply tim-
bered voice echoing through her drug-muddled brain.

The fact that he answered her brought Carlisle
closer to awareness. She struggled to sit up, sloshing
waves against the walls of the marble tub. She endeavored to blink away her fuzzy vision as he approached her, not completely sure if he was real or
imagined.

"Why are you here?" she asked, confused.

"I changed my mind and decided to enjoy my wedding night, after all."

To Carlisle, it seemed he spoke from the far end of a tunnel. So it is a dream, she thought. Chase would never come back. Through a misty haze she saw him unbutton his shirt and the lightly furred, sunbrowned muscles of his chest emerge. Then he unbuckled his belt. She watched with dreamy fascination as the rest of his clothes disappeared and he stood naked before her.

"Why do you have to look so good, like some big Viking god?" she asked peevishly, groggily surprised when he gave a low laugh and stepped right down into the water with her! He wore the old, slow smile, with deep dimples grooved into his tanned face. She loved that smile so much, she thought. Then a low moan was torn from her lips as he pulled her body tight against him. Bare flesh, slickened by warm water and scented oil, met and slid together, his muscles as hard as rock against her naked breasts. Then his fingers threaded their way up beneath her heavy coil of hair, pulling her head back until her throat arched.

Breathless and dazed, Carlisle parted her lips, and Chase's mouth came down on hers, so hungry, so tender, and all a wonderful dream.

"Make love to me, Chase," she whispered thickly when his mouth let up in its erotic search of her tongue and lips. "I love you, I love you—"

Everything was indistinct now, all wavery and blurred as if they embraced beneath a tranquil sea. From somewhere far away, his muffled words reverberated in her somnolent mind.

"*Dios,* Carly—"

What a wonderful dream, Carlisle decided. She really loved this dream, and she loved Juana for giving her the potion that made it possible.

"I love you," she murmured to her handsome bridegroom, sliding her hands over the bronze skin of his shoulders as he leaned her back, his forearm supporting her head. "I always have, you know, from the first moment I saw your beautiful blue eyes."

Her conjured lover groaned, his lips seeking hers again, very gently, as if he feared he'd bruise her. How real his palm felt sliding over her bare hip! If only Chase had really come, were really on his knees, sliding his arm beneath her waist and lifting her from the water so he could taste her breasts.

"Oh, please, let you be real!" she cried, writhing and clutching her fists in his soft blond hair. Her head dropped back, more of her pins and combs coming loose, more silken hair tumbling over his arms. "I can't bear it if you're not real!"

"What in God's name did Juana give you?" she heard him say. Then he laughed softly when she pulled his head down and kissed him passionately.

After that, vaguely, she felt him carry her to the softness of the bed, felt him kiss her all over until his body covered her own, his elbows braced on either side of her head. Her hands found his shoulders and slid down his back, her fingers outspread and clutching the molded, rippling muscles. Convulsively, her fingernails curled into his skin, and she arched up to meet his movements, sheer ecstasy controlling her as they moved together, their bodies joined, his anguished cry muffled against her cheek.

"Oh, God, Carly, I loved you! I loved you so much! Why did you have to betray me?"

Carlisle felt her heart clutch, for she had no answer, and Chase did not wait for one as his mouth covered hers. She wrapped her arms around his neck, wanting him to be real, to be making love to her and giving her the pleasure that was so intense that the wild beating of her heart shook her limbs and made her lips tremble.

"Please be real," she cried one last time before the sweet release rocked her body, spiraling deep into her quivering core, racking through her like a series of small shocks, until she lay limp and shivering, weak and satiated. When he groaned, his own cry of wonder loud in her ear, she was pleased. Then she gave in to the cloying, sticky strands of sleep tangling her thoughts and slept, her hands still clutched tightly in her husband's gilt-burnished hair.

Chase jerked in his sleep, awakening with a start. It was early morning, and sun creeping through the shutter slats painted a mosaic of bright white bars on the dark blue bedcovers. Carlisle was cuddled close to his side, his arm resting atop her naked shoulders. Her small body felt warm and soft, and strands of her long coppery hair lay like satin banners across his chest. Gently he brought a fistful of the silken-textured tresses up against his face. The sweet, flowery fragrance invaded his senses, and when his arms tightened around Carlisle, she stirred sleepily, emitting a soft moan.

God help him, if he'd ever had a weakness in his life, it was Carlisle. Even when he hated her, he wanted her. The night before, he had fully intended to let the beautiful *cortesanas* of Los Angeles erase Carlisle from his memory. He'd wanted to hurt her by leaving her alone on their wedding night. He'd measured his words with cruel deliberation and had triumphed when he'd seen pain in her eyes.

But after she had gone, he'd visualized her humiliation when she was forced to face the servants alone, and felt a strong wave of guilt. He had no compunction about hurting her privately—she deserved it for her treachery against him—but her public embarrassment was different. She was his wife now, and even the most loyal servants gossiped with their counterparts in other houses. His slight to his wife would have been found out, and he had not wanted that. So a block away from the elegant bordello, he'd turned back toward home and Carlisle.

Now, with her in his arms, he wasn't sorry he'd come. He was tired of fighting his own need for her. He wanted to be free to love her again, the way he had before Esteban had died. He wouldn't think of San Miguel or Javier Perez, and he'd let himself love her the way he used to. That's what they both wanted.

Carlisle stretched, then snuggled contentedly into his arms, her lips against his chest, her gentle breath soft upon his skin. The drug still held her in its spell. Juana had made it strong. He stroked Carlisle's bare back, drawing the cover over her, then slid his palm over the deep indentation of her waist. Her stomach was still flat and firm, but his child grew inside her. If not for the baby, she would have been gone, back to America and her brothers.

Despite all the protestations of opposition to her presence that he'd hurled at his mother and Tomas, the thought of never seeing her again pierced him like a thorn. He wanted her there with him. He'd married her to keep her with him.

Shifting onto his side, he turned her face so he

could look at her, marveling at the length of her curling eyelashes. *Carlita has a face as sweet as an angel.* Esteban's reverent voice echoed out of the mists of Chase's mind.

"Oh, hell, why did Esteban have to die?" Chase said aloud, squeezing his eyes shut. Along with his grief, all the anger he'd wanted to forget came flooding back into him. No matter how much he wanted to forget it, Esteban's death was Carlisle's fault. She was as much to blame as Javier, who'd tossed the stick of dynamite into their midst.

Fury engulfed him, and he sat up abruptly, releasing his hold on his wife. She rolled back and slept peacefully, her golden-red hair spread out on the pillow like a cloud of fire. Reluctantly, almost against his will, he uncurled his fingers and stared down into his palms where the ugly red scars still bore witness to his crucifixion. He felt the agony, heard his own screams, and the remembered torment brought him out of the bed and away from Carlisle.

By the time he'd shaved and dressed, he'd managed to subjugate his anger, tamp it down and hold it inside himself as he'd done so often in the past few months. When he was ready to leave his chamber, he paused at the foot of the bed. Carlisle lay on her back, the bedclothes caught around her waist, baring her long slender legs.

Chase's fingers caught the carved wood of the bedpost, squeezing hard enough to make his fingers go white; he fought the urge to jerk her up and kiss her brutally until she put her arms around his neck and surrendered with the weak mewling sounds he'd forced from her throughout the night. With incredible effort, he turned away and left the dusky bedchamber, closing the door softly behind him.

Outside, away from Carlisle's mesmerizing presence, he felt in control again, but the casa was quiet and deserted. Out on the patio, near the big fountain, he found his mother breakfasting with Tomas.

"Chaso! Have we disturbed you?"

"No," Chase answered in a noncommittal tone which discouraged any further questions. He poured himself *café con leche,* then glanced briefly at Tomas, whose brown eyes rested on him with haggard hostility. The poor boy was in love with Carlisle, and Chase knew how helpless that could make a man feel. But Tomas would have to get over her, and fast. He was betrothed to another girl now, and he had better get used to it.

"Tomas, I need to talk to you. It's *muy importante.*"

"Is it about Carlita?" Tomas asked eagerly.

Chase's face darkened with annoyance. "Now that Carlisle is my wife, your preoccupation with her will have to stop," he said bluntly.

Tomas flushed, a deep, angry red. "She is still my *amiga,* Chaso, and she always will be. And she needs friends now, the way you treat her. It wouldn't surprise me if the marriage wasn't even consummated."

"Tomas!" Dona Maria cried, shocked. "You speak out of turn!"

Chase's blue eyes looked deadly. "The marriage was consummated. A number of times. But with the bride already with child, it hardly matters, does it, Tomas?"

Tomas frowned, and with effort, Chase kept his burgeoning anger in check. Tomas's infatuation with

Carlisle would cause trouble for all of them. Suddenly he was glad he'd decided to marry Tomas to Dona Marta. Still, Chase was reluctant to tell Tomas about his new *novia*, dreading the boy's reaction.

"A decision has been made concerning your future, Tomas," he began.

Tomas interrupted. "What gives you the right to make my decisions, Chaso?"

"Because I'm the head of this family, and you're my brother. I thought you considered me as such."

"That was before I saw the way you behaved to Carlita. She doesn't deserve to have to marry you and be treated like dirt."

"She was perfectly willing to marry me," Chase answered as calmly as possible, within inches from losing all patience. "Perhaps you'd do well to analyze why she did so, Tomas, since you're obviously so besotted with her you can't think straight. Despite what you think or what you want to believe, Carlisle loves me and wants to be my wife."

"But you don't love her, do you? If she were mine, I'd treat her like a queen."

"Well, she isn't yours, goddamn it!" Chase roared. "And she never will be! You had better accept that, because I won't tolerate you lusting after her in my own house!"

"The Casa Amarilla is Mama's house, not yours!"

Dona Maria leaned forward as if to speak, but Chase began first.

"*Bueno,* then, Tomas," he said between clenched teeth. "I'll take Carlisle to the Hacienda de los Toros and leave her there so you won't be around."

His threat silenced Tomas, and Chase's frown grew more pronounced. They were already arguing, in a way they'd never done before, and he hadn't even broached the subject of Dona Marta.

"As you are aware, there was a betrothal agreement between Dona Marta and myself," he said, forcing his voice down.

"*Sí*, and you treated poor little Dona Marta as shabbily as you have Carlita. Marta's my friend, and now she probably hates you, too."

With difficulty, Chase reined in his growing desire to throttle his little brother.

"I'm very pleased to hear that you consider Dona Marta your *amiga*, because her *padre* and I have agreed that you should take my place in the betrothal agreement." Tomas's face drained of color, then grew mottled with scarlet blotches as Chase continued. "The whole purpose of the arrangement was to ally our families by a marriage. You'll do as Dona Marta's bridegroom as well as I would have, probably even better."

"I won't wed her!" Tomas cried furiously. "Carlita's the only woman I'll ever marry!"

"*Sí*, Tomas, you'll marry Dona Marta, or you'll be cut off from the family."

Tomas's jaw went rigid. "Now I understand. .You want to rid yourself of me so you won't have to share Mama's inheritance—"

Chase shot to his feet. "Enough, Tomas!" he ground out harshly. "This wasn't even my doing! I went to Senor Moreno ready to offer a cash settlement for my breach of the betrothal contract. This was the girl's idea. According to Don Ernesto, she's already in love with you."

"What? That's absurd. She's just a *niña*, with freckles all over her face."

Chase raised a brow. "She's near your age."

"But I'm a man. She's just a girl. I could never marry her. She's skinny."

Dona Maria shook her head, as if fed up with her sons' argument. "Dona Marta was at the ball last night, *mi hijo,* and she did everything possible to draw your attention away from Chaso and Carlita. If you'd even glanced at her, you would have seen she's blossoming into a lovely young woman."

"I don't want to see her!" Tomas shouted defiantly. "And I won't marry her! Carlita's the only woman I'll ever love. Someday she'll leave you, Chaso, and I'll be there for her!"

Chase felt his jaw clench, then his fists. "Dammit, Tomas, you go too far! If you want to live here in the Casa Amarilla, you'll keep your distance from my wife!"

Tomas stalked angrily from the table without another word. Furious, Chase shook his head as his mother hurried after him. He cursed under his breath, blaming Carlisle for Tomas's adolescent behavior. Until Tomas had met Carlisle, he'd been a fine, obedient boy. Now she'd possessed him as she'd possessed every other man who'd ever laid eyes on her!

17

As Juana moved around the bed, setting flame to the tall white tapers on the bedside table, Carlisle awoke, alarmed but not certain why. She sat up, clutching the coverlet against her nakedness, her red hair tousled in ringlets down her back. She frowned slightly at the darkness pressing like black velvet against the balcony door.

"Oh, Juana," she murmured, disappointed. "The potion didn't last long enough." Reclining languorously against the pillows, she smiled. "But the dreams were wonderful, just as you promised." A sensual tremor rippled over her as she remembered all the exquisite things Chase's hands and mouth had done to her during their imaginary lovemaking.

"Bueno, Dona Carlita, but I was very frightened when Don Chaso came," Juana said in her quiet way. "He seemed angry that I had mixed the potion for you. Will he send me home to Papa because I gave it to you?"

Carlisle stared uncomprehendingly at her maid. "Chase came here?"

In turn, the Indian girl looked confused. "*Sí*, Dona Carlita, do you not remember? He came last night when you were in the bath."

"Last night?"

"*Sí*. You have slept the whole day through."

Carlisle stared at Juana. "Chase wasn't a dream?"

"Oh, no, he came soon after you did. He told us about the meeting with El Presidente that detained him at Chapultepec Castle."

A pleased smile spread over Carlisle's face and warmed her inside. Despite all the unkind things he'd said and done, Chase had come to her. Now she was sorry she'd taken Juana's drug, because her recollection of the wedding night was too fuzzy to suit her. Perhaps, though, he was ready to forgive her at last. Perhaps he already had. Why else would he have come to her after telling her he wouldn't?

Anxious to find out, she quickly performed her toilette, then allowed Juana to help her dress in a lightweight apricot silk gown. By the time she descended to the patio, she was apprehensive about facing Chase. If only she could remember everything he'd said. When she found Dona Maria sitting alone by the fountain, relief and disappointment mingled inside her.

"Carlita! So you are up at last! I've been waiting supper for you." Dona Maria signaled to a serving maid, who immediately hurried away to notify the cook. "But the long rest will do you good," she continued with a smile. "I realize the wedding was exhausting for you."

Carlisle took her customary place and glanced warily at the open doors of the book-lined library, where Chase sometimes worked.

"Aren't Chase and Tomas going to join us?" she asked hopefully.

Dona Maria looked chagrined. "No. This morning my bullheaded, stubborn sons stormed out of the house in a temper." She sighed. "I knelt in the chapel for many hours today, praying to the Holy Virgin that they will stop their quarreling."

"What's wrong between them?"

Dona Maria suddenly became inordinately interested in her dinner plate. "Chaso told Tomas that he must marry little Marta. She is really a lovely *niña*. Tomas will soon see reason."

Carlisle fingered the heavy white linen napkin on her lap. "I'm sorry, Dona Maria. Tomas has been angry with Chase ever since I came here."

Dona Maria shook her head, picking up the heavy crystal pitcher of orange juice and filling Carlisle's goblet.

"You must stop blaming yourself for the actions of others. The will of God is always done. You were meant to wed Chaso, and Marta is the right *muchacha* for Tomas." She smiled, but Carlisle could detect a shadow of sadness in her dark eyes. "Both my sons are very headstrong. But you mustn't concern yourself. We must be glad that you are safely married and will soon present my son with his heir. Chaso loves you. I see it in his blue eyes each time he looks at you."

Dona Maria paused as she poured *naranjada* into her own glass. "You must be very patient with him, *niña*, for Chaso still grieves for Esteban. They had a special friendship that few people are fortunate enough to experience, closer even than brothers. Ever since they were small boys, they were inseparable.

But, in time, he will accept Esteban's death, and the two of you will be happy. You must believe that.''

Carlisle wanted desperately to have faith in her mother-in-law's encouraging prediction, but when she saw Tomas striding across the flagstones toward the table, her sense of foreboding increased. She knew at once that he was still angry.

''Buenas noches, Carlita, Mama,'' he greeted them, but his manner was stiff, his smile unnatural.

''Sit down, Tomas,'' Dona Maria said. ''We are ready to be served.''

''What about Chaso?'' was his sullen answer as he slumped down in his chair. ''Are we to be honored with his almighty presence?''

''Sí, he will come soon. He was called to meet with El Presidente on a matter of importance.''

''Does Chaso still intend to ruin my life?''

''Chaso is the head of this family, Tomas. You have always known we would arrange your marriage,'' Dona Maria reminded him. ''I don't know why you suddenly choose to be so disagreeable about it.''

''You know why,'' Tomas muttered, glancing at Carlisle. ''And Marta is such a child.'' His mouth settled in a stubborn line. ''She's gawky, all arms and legs, and she's a pest. All she ever did was follow me around and beg me to teach her to fight the bulls! I don't want to marry her. Anyway, I'm not ready for marriage yet.''

Dona Maria remained unimpressed by his arguments. ''Chaso did not say you had to wed her now. In fact, her father intends to send her to the convent school in Madrid to ready her for marriage and motherhood. When she returns, I daresay you'll see a big difference in her behavior.''

Inside herself, Carlisle cringed, pitying Dona Marta. Why did men always assume that locking a girl away in a convent would teach her to be a lady? Often, living in such austere circumstances only made girls all the more eager to rebel and taste life. Look what had happened to her.

"The wedding isn't imminent?" Tomas was asking, looking very much relieved.

"Of course it's not," Chase answered from behind them. "Dona Marta is to spend at least two years in Spain, and she won't be leaving Mexico City for Madrid for several months."

Carlisle's heart raced at the sound of her husband's deep voice, and she turned to watch him approach on the path from the stables.

His dark blue eyes found her briefly, but Carlisle's hopes for reconciliation disintegrated as he glanced coldly away. She stiffened her spine. He had come to her last night, she reminded herself. He did love her, she knew that.

A moment later, as a maid served them from a platter of steaming arroz con pollo, Carlisle found out what had caused his bitter look. He turned in his chair to address her, his handsome face devoid of emotion.

"Your friends, Arantxa and Javier Perez, have arrived in the city for trial."

Carlisle felt the color drain from her face, because she was sure the news must have brought all Chase's rage roiling up to the surface again.

Dona Maria voiced the question that lay poised on Carlisle's lips. "What will happen to them, Chaso?"

A muscle flexed in Chase's cheek. "They committed treason. They'll be tried, found guilty, and shot by firing squad."

Carlisle gasped, unable to hide her dismay as she thought of Arantxa's laughing face.

"Oh, Chase, not Arantxa, too?"

Chase's expression revealed not an ounce of compassion. "*Sí*, Arantxa, too." Without having touched the food on his plate, he stood, bowed toward his mother, and ignored Carlisle. "I have business elsewhere tonight, Mother. Adios."

As he strode away, Dona Maria appeared angry at his abrupt departure, but Tomas seemed pleased. Carlisle made certain no emotion showed on her own face. He was angry, but he'd been angry last night, and he'd eventually come to her. She understood his fury, and she didn't blame him. But it was so hard to watch him walk away, not knowing where he was going or when he'd be back.

"Are you feeling unwell, *querida?*"

Carlisle went weak with pleasure at Chase's whispered concern. She shook her head, but she was grateful for his supporting hand around her waist. They stood together in the long line of diplomats queued up to meet the United States ambassador. Since their marriage several weeks before, her husband had escorted her to many such social functions, his important post in the Juarez government requiring their presence.

As Chase presented her to an American diplomat and his wife, she realized, with some surprise, that she had become accustomed to hearing conversations carried on entirely in Spanish. Now as she exchanged pleasantries in English, her native tongue seemed almost alien.

Músicos, dressed in black charro suits with bright

red sashes, strummed guitars and played violins and trumpets as they strolled among the guests, many of whom spilled outside in small groups to enjoy the walled terraces of the ambassador's great *estancia* in the suburb of San Cosme.

As Chase led her into the large salon, for the first time in months Carlisle found herself wanting to kick off her satin pumps, lift her garnet-colored silk skirts, and dance the *jarabe*. That night they'd camped on the river with Conchita's gypsy band seemed so long ago. Sorrow touched her when she thought how in love Esteban and Conchita had been and how lonely Conchita must be now in their cozy little casa in La Mesilla.

She looked up at Chase. He was so devastatingly handsome. If only he could forget, they could be happy. Though he no longer showed his anger so readily, he intentionally held himself away from her. The core of his emotions was protected by impenetrable walls he'd constructed between them, as if he could not bring himself to trust her with his feelings.

A young English officer, resplendent in his red-and-gold uniform, passed nearby, eyeing Carlisle with an appreciative smile, and she recalled having been introduced to him at a reception the previous week. Chase's arm tightened around her waist in a proprietary way that thrilled Carlisle. She leaned closer to him, enjoying the intimacy while she could.

He loved her—she had to keep telling herself that. He just couldn't yet bring himself to forget about what had happened to Esteban. And he wanted her. Even though he absented himself from home on the nights they had no social obligations, he'd often come to her very late, after she slept. She'd awaken while being pulled roughly into his arms, his lips demanding her surrender. Then he made love to her with such gentle, overwhelming passion that she had no need to hear the words of love he refused to utter.

Carlisle put her hand against her belly. Although she was now over three months pregnant, she still had not begun to show much, except for a slight thickening at her waist. She wondered if he'd find her unattractive when she grew large and awkward. Would he seek his pleasure elsewhere? Just thinking about Chase with another woman made her feel disconsolate.

"Benito has arrived. I should join him for a moment or two," Chase said at her side, his gaze on the crowd across the room that had gathered around the presidential party. "There's no need for you to stand in line again. Why don't you sit down and rest until I come back?"

"*Sí, gracias,*" she agreed, taking a seat on a small red velvet settee in front of a tall mullioned window overlooking the garden.

"Will you be all right here alone?" Chase asked, and their eyes met and locked. Carlisle wondered if he could tell how much she wanted him. But when she saw desire flare in the depths of his eyes, she knew he had seen the love she no longer even tried to hide.

As he moved away, she watched the other guests idly, glad to sit quietly for a time. She tired easily of late, but at least the horrible queasiness that had plagued her so in the beginning had passed.

Eventually, she would face the long ordeal of confinement inside the high yellow walls of the Casa Amarilla. Somehow, the thought was not completely repugnant. To sit on the cushioned benches in the lovely dark shade of the patio or loll in the wide net hammocks hung on the cool recesses of the arcaded porch would be wonderfully peaceful. While the soft rustling of graceful palm fronds and tinkling of fountains soothed her mind, she would think about her baby.

Although she knew she shouldn't be afraid, she did dread giving birth. How often had she heard horrible stories of breech birth and childbed fever? And worst of all, stillbirth? She shivered, not wanting to think about the possibility of something going wrong. She wanted her baby so much. She wanted to give Chase a child.

"*Perdón,* but you are Dona Carlita, Don Chaso's wife, *sí?*"

"*Sí,*" Carlisle answered, recognizing at once the pretty young girl standing in front of her.

"I am Dona Marta Moreno," the girl continued. "May I speak with you?"

Carlisle strove to hide her shock, for she had never expected to be approached by Chase's former fiancée.

"*Sí,* Dona Marta. Sit here beside me, if you wish."

Dona Marta did so, fussing with her white chiffon skirts as if mightily annoyed by their cumbersome dimensions. Her dark brown hair was twisted into twin spiral braids over her ears, and large pearl earrings suspended by thin gold chains danced around her jaw. She looked at the people near them, as if she expected them to eavesdrop on her conversation with Carlisle.

"Tomas won't speak to me now that we are betrothed," Dona Marta began without preamble. "Does he hate me?"

Carlisle heard the vulnerability beneath the boldly uttered question. "I don't believe he dislikes you at all, Dona Marta. He just doesn't think he's ready for marriage yet."

"Oh, I know how he feels! But if Papa makes me marry someone, I want it to be Tomas. Tomas never, ever treated me like all the other *muchachos.*" Angry, she shook her head, making the earbobs swing wildly. She looked speculatively at Carlisle. "I am very glad Don Chaso fell in love with you. I never really wanted to marry him, you know, though all my *amigas* thought I was very lucky to be his *novia.*"

Carlisle smiled, impressed with her honesty. "I was afraid you'd be angry with me."

"No, of course not. I can see why Don Chaso chose you. You are as beautiful as he is, no? I am not pretty enough to be the wife of such a man."

"But that's not true," Carlisle protested quickly. "You are very pretty."

Dona Marta's answering smile was shy, but pleased. *"Gracias,* but I know I am plain. That is why I have decided to make myself beautiful so Tomas will want to make me his bride. Soon I go to convent in Madrid, where I will learn to act like a great lady. For Tomas," she added, then looked at Carlisle, obviously seeking approval.

"I think Tomas is lucky to have you as his *novia,*" Carlisle replied in all sincerity.

This time Dona Marta veritably beamed. Her gaze circled the room almost furtively, then she retrieved a folded parchment from the white satin reticule dangling at her wrist.

"My cousin asked me to deliver her *carta* into your hands, but no one must see. She is very unhappy."

"Your cousin?"

"*Sí*, but you must not tell anyone that I carried her note to you. Papa would punish me. Now I must go, before Papa or Mama see me here with you. Adios."

With that, Dona Marta melted away into the crowd. Carlisle looked after her for a moment, then unfolded the tiny scrap of paper. Her gaze went to the bottom first, seeking the identity of the writer.

Arantxa!

Her heart skipped a beat, and she looked around guiltily. Chase was nowhere in sight, and almost fearfully, she began to read.

Dear Carlita,

I am writing by candle in my horrid cell at the Chapultepec Prison. I am so lonely and afraid, here in this dreadful place. But I have bribed my jailor with the diamond ring that Papa gave to me, so he will take this letter to my cousin Marta. I pray she will be able to deliver it into your hands without being seen. I beg you to visit me here, Carlita. I know the idea must be distasteful to you after all you have been through because of me. But I must clear my conscience before I die. I love you as my own sister, though I know you must hate me. I implore you to come to me. It is my last wish before I die. Please have pity on me, please.

Arantxa

Blurred with tears, Carlisle's eyes remained on the letter for a long time before she hastily refolded and hid it in her velvet purse. Poor Arantxa, Carlisle should at least go see her. But how could she? Chase would never allow it.

The next day, Carlisle returned to Chapultepec Castle and walked beneath the thousand-year-old ahuehuete trees on the same ground the last Montezuma had walked. The prison was located in an isolated corner of the immense, sprawling palace, far from the glittering gold-and-white ballroom where she had danced with Benito Juarez. Tall, pockmarked limestone walls rose like a towering fortress, forbidding and frightening. A shudder skidded over Carlisle's flesh as she envisioned ghosts of tortured, wailing prisoners on the other side of the cold stones, clawing to be free. She drew her black rebozo closer around her face as she peered around the courtyard. After Chase had left for the Palacio Nacional, she'd sneaked out of the Casa Amarilla alone, on the pretext of visiting the flower market.

A flutter of fear erupted in her stomach as she approached the massive wooden gate hung with great iron hinges. An eerie premonition struck her like a strong wind in the face, and she felt an extreme reluctance to enter the ancient place of suffering and despair.

Drawing in a deep, steadying breath, she pulled the rope affixed to a bell, then waited until a burly man with great downward-thrusting mustachios opened a small door cut into the larger one.

"What do you want?" His voice was gruff, his words muttered in a dialect Carlisle had trouble understanding.

"I have come to see a prisoner."

"No visitors. *Mañana*—"

"I am the wife of Don Chaso Lancaster, the foreign advisor to El Presidente. Must I report your rudeness to him?"

Carlisle's eyes did not waver, and her imperious tone made the turnkey's small black eyes dart around uncertainly. She waited, terrified he might attempt to contact Chase for verification of her identity. The idea appalled her, but her fear was short-lived, for in seconds he opened the door with a great clanking of metal. Stepping through the portal, she was relieved when the man removed his visored military cap and held it in one bearlike hand.

"Senora Lancaster," he said with a deep bow from the waist, "which prisoner do you wish to visit?"

"Arantxa Perez, *por favor.*"

At that the guard's hesitancy returned. "My orders say she is to see no one before the trial, Senora Lancaster."

"My husband sent me here to see her," Carlisle lied boldy. "Do you question his authority, senor?"

"No, senora," he answered, then looked apologetically at the basket she carried.

Carlisle pulled back the scarf covering the contents.

"I have brought bread and cheese and clean clothes. You may examine them, if you wish."

The guard poked through the foodstuffs and garments, then replaced the scarf.

"Come with me, senora."

Carlisle followed him across an unevenly paved courtyard, aware that many other soldiers watched their progress from the walls and covered porches that ran along one side of the prison cells.

Across the plaza, they entered an arched doorway.

As they left the hot sunlight, the dank, cold gloom hit her, and it felt as if she had stepped into a tomb. Carlisle pulled her rebozo closer, steeling her resolve as a terrible stench of sweat, urine, and unwashed bodies assailed her senses. She forced herself to follow the big man down the dark passage.

The walls were a foot thick with heavily barred doors lining the stone corridors. She could hear groaning behind one, then stifled a cry of fright as a shrill scream shattered the silence. Ripples of fear coursed through Carlisle.

A few paces farther, the guard stopped. "She is here, senora."

Carlisle swallowed hard, her gaze locked on the small grate set in the thick wooden door. What if she went inside and he never let her out again? she thought wildly. No one was aware she'd come to the prison. Who'd know if they kept her here? Panic rose, but she quickly collected her wits, realizing the guard had no reason to do such a thing.

When he shoved up the heavy square bar, then pushed the door inward, Carlisle stepped to the threshold and bent to peer into the dusky interior. High on the opposite wall, a foot-long, rectangular aperture sent an elongated patch of light down upon the straw-littered floor. Arantxa sat huddled on a small *catre*, her arms wrapped around her knees. Carlisle was appalled at her appearance. Her dark hair was dirty and matted, and she had lost so much weight that Carlisle hardly recognized her. When she saw Carlisle, the girl leapt up and fell sobbing in her arms.

"Carlita, you came. *Gracias, gracias—*"

"Shh, Arantxa, please don't cry."

"I cannot help it! This place is so horrible. It's so cold and dark, with terrible smells and rats scratching at night until I think I'll go mad. You know how much I hate even mice! Remember how I screamed when I saw one at the convent?"

"*Sí*, I remember," Carlisle answered soothingly, drawing Arantxa down on the bed.

"They put shackles on my feet and hands, Carlita! Look at my wrists!"

Carlisle took Arantxa's cold hands. Her beautiful nails were all broken and ragged, her slender wrists black-and-blue, as if she wore bracelets of bruises.

"How could they be so cruel?" Carlisle cried, sick to think of Arantxa being treated so harshly.

"They treated us all the same, *muchachos* and *muchachas.*"

"Oh, Arantxa, why did you have to lie to me? Why did you tell me all those terrible things about Chase? I thought you were my friend, but you were using me."

Arantxa began to cry, her face hidden in her palms. "I didn't know, Carlita. Javier told me those things were true. I believed him, just as you did."

"Is Javier here in the prison, too?"

"*Sí*, but they will not let me see him. And Papa is dead! They shot him! Senor Lancaster told us at San Miguel!" She lifted her face, stricken and miserable. "And they're going to shoot us, too, Carlita!" Her voice grew shrill and hysterical. "They're going to shoot us!"

Appalled, Carlisle put her arms around Arantxa and tried to comfort her. "No, maybe they won't! Maybe if I tell them you're innocent. Maybe if I talk to

Chase, I can make him understand that you don't deserve to die!''

''*Gracias*, but *por favor,* you must hurry and tell them! I am so scared, Carlita! I don't want to die!''

''Hush now, and listen to me. I'll help you, I promise!''

For the first time, hope flowered in Arantxa's pale, tearstained face. ''And Javier? He did an awful thing to Chaso, I know, but he regrets it now. I know he does. You must talk to Chaso about him, too! Promise me you will!''

Carlisle squeezed her friend's hands. ''I can't, Arantxa. I can't ask that of Chase. He's too bitter about all that happened. He hasn't forgiven me yet.''

Arantxa put her head in Carlisle's lap and began to sob.

Carlisle fought her own tears. ''Look, Arantxa, I've brought you some food and clean clothes. Is there anything else you need? Please, try not to cry.''

''Just come and see me, Carlita. Come often. Say you will.''

''Senora?'' the jailor said from the cell door. ''You must go now.''

Carlisle stood, feeling sick to her stomach. Arantxa clutched her arms as if she'd never let her go.

''I'll do everything I can to help you. I swear I will,'' Carlisle promised. She bit her lip as Arantxa fell facedown on the *catre,* her moaning and weeping heartbreaking.

Carlisle hesitated, but when the guard grunted and gestured impatiently, she forced herself to leave the cell. She was shaking all over from disgust at the surroundings and dismay for her friend's plight.

Nausea came, wrenching through her stomach, and

she staggered on after the tall jailor, wanting only to get out of the dreadful place so she could breathe. They were almost at the outside door when her vision faltered and she crumpled to her knees. The last thing she heard was the guard's voice calling for help.

When Carlisle opened her eyes, she was lying in her own bed at the Casa Amarilla. Chase sat in a chair drawn up next to her, and Dona Maria and Tomas stood behind him. At first, Carlisle was confused.

"What happened?" she asked, trying to raise herself.

"You fainted," Dona Maria answered gently. "At the prison."

"The guards summoned Chaso and he brought you home," Tomas added.

Carlisle lay back, looking guiltily at Chase. He didn't seem angry, but his face was somber.

"I'd like to speak to my wife alone now, if you don't mind," he said quietly.

Dona Maria moved away at once, and Tomas followed her, although with a good deal more reluctance. When the door closed after them, Chase sat down on the edge of the bed and took Carlisle's hand.

"Are you all right, Carly?"

To Carlisle's dismay, she burst into a torrent of tears. First Chase looked faintly shocked, then he pulled her into an embrace. Carlisle laid her cheek against his shoulder and wept while he stroked her hair. When she finally quieted, he spoke softly against the top of her head.

"Why did you go to the prison, Carly?"

Another sob caught in her throat, but she could not bear to lie to him.

"Because Arantxa sent me a note begging me to come to her. I had to go, Chase! We were best friends. She was almost like a sister to me."

"It's all right. I'm not angry because you went. But you should have let me take you there."

His understanding opened the floodgates of her emotion even more. "Oh, Chase, you should see her. She doesn't deserve to die. She believed all Javier's lies about you, just as I did. Please have mercy on her. I beg you! I'll do anything you say if you'll just let her live!"

"Hush now, Carly, you're making yourself sick."

Carlisle quieted, but a vision of Arantxa in the dank cell haunted her.

"Please, Chase," she whispered. "She's so frightened."

Chase remained silent, and a moment passed before he spoke. "I'll do what I can, but under no circumstances will I intervene on Javier's behalf."

"Thank you, Chase."

"And I don't want you going back there. *Comprendes?*"

"But I told her I would. She's so desperate, I had to."

"I'll see if I can have her transferred to a more humane cell. I don't believe she played any active part in the *revolución.*"

"She didn't! Neither of us did! Please believe me, Chase, and forgive me! I'm so tired of living like this, never knowing if you really care about me!"

Carlisle was immediately sorry for her outburst,

because Chase released her and stood. He looked down at her.

"Dr. Alvarado is probably here by now. Try to rest, and I'll send him up to examine you."

As he left, Carlisle buried her face in the deep, silken pillows, weeping for herself, for Arantxa, and for all that had gone wrong between Chase and her.

18

On the first day of November, the morning of the Perez trial, Carlisle sat with Dona Maria beneath the big eucalyptus tree in the patio. Chase had forbidden her to attend the court proceedings, and Carlisle did not dare disobey him. He had promised to intervene for Arantxa, but he could not guarantee that her friend would be treated leniently.

Unable to sit still, Carlisle rose and fussed with the roses and chrysanthemums she'd arranged to perfection only moments before. She kept thinking how thin and frightened Arantxa had looked in the foul-smelling cell. Javier had tortured Chase, he'd killed Esteban, and Carlisle couldn't dredge up an ounce of pity for him. But Arantxa was different. Despite all the trouble she had caused, Carlisle couldn't bring herself to hate the girl with whom she'd lived, laughed, and shared so many confidences. For all she knew, even now Arantxa might be standing against a bullet-scarred wall across the courtyard from a firing squad.

"Please don't let that happen," she whispered beneath her breath.

"What did you say, Carlita?" Dona Maria asked, looked up from her knitting.

"Nothing. I'm just worried about Arantxa."

"I believe Chaso is pained that you still try to protect the Perez family. They committed terrible crimes against us." A shadow of pain passed over her face, and Carlisle knew Dona Maria was thinking of her son's hands.

"I know, but Arantxa took no active part. We both thought that joining the rebels would be a wild, wonderful adventure. We'd been at the convent for months, and when Javier arrived in New Orleans and invited us to ride with his *guerrilleros,* the idea sounded romantic and exciting. We didn't even know Chase then. And when Chase came to America to pick up Tyler, Javier took advantage of my family's association with him. Arantxa and I didn't know Javier's plans. We didn't know about war, and the blood and pain and terrible suffering it brings."

"That's the way of the world. Women will always be the victims of men," Dona Maria remarked, laying aside her half-finished yellow baby's shawl. "I, too, feel pity for the Perez girl. Her father and brother used her vilely, as they used you, Carlita."

"I'll never forgive myself for being so naive and trusting."

"You must not torment yourself with what is past, *niña.* Once, long ago, I thought I could never forgive Chaso's father." Her face assumed the bemused expression that usually appeared when she mentioned Burl Lancaster. "But now it seems I only remember the good things about him."

"Tyler told me lots of stories about him. She loved her uncle Burl very much."

"Burl was nothing but a rogue," Dona Maria replied sharply. "Thoroughly unscrupulous." She shook her head. "But I loved that man with all my heart." Her gaze sought Carlisle's. "I see the same adoration in your eyes, Carlita, when you look at Chaso."

"Sometimes I think I'll die from the pain of loving him so much."

Dona Maria gave her rare, wise smile. "You'll not die, *niña*. Though at times after I left Burl, I thought I would. Tomas's father was a wonderful man. Hermando was good to me, and he loved me. He gave me my splendid Tomas, but I never loved him the way I loved Chaso's father."

"How could you ever have left him?" Carlisle whispered.

Chase's mother drew in a deep, regretful breath. "I left him because I had Chaso to consider. He was eight years old, and he idolized his father. Burl would have corrupted him. I couldn't let that happen."

"I wouldn't want my child subjected to that kind of life, either. But oh, Dona Maria, it must have been difficult for you."

"*Sí*, it was the hardest decision I ever had to make."

Dona Maria looked fondly at her daughter-in-law. At that moment Carlisle saw Chase at the patio wall. As he looked straight at her, Carlisle jumped to her feet.

"Arantxa Perez is to be sent into perpetual exile. She will join her mother in Cuba, never to return to Mexican soil." His voice and manner were brusque.

"Javier and the other rebels will be shot for treason at dawn tomorrow."

"*Gracias,* Chase," Carlisle said softly. "I know it must have been difficult for you to intercede on Arantxa's behalf."

"I only recommended leniency for her. The judges made the determination."

But Carlisle knew the weight his opinion carried in the Juarez government. Chase had saved Arantxa's life, so perhaps his bitterness over San Miguel was waning. Perhaps when their baby was born and he saw his infant son or daughter, all his remaining resentment would disappear forever. She would hold that hope in her heart, for she had nothing else to cling to.

It was still dark the next morning when Chase walked down the corridor of Chapultepec Prison to Arantxa Perez's cell. She had been transferred to a more comfortable part of the jail, as he had promised Carlisle. From the beginning, he'd doubted if Arantxa had actually participated in her father and brother's subversive activities. That's why he'd agreed to ask for special treatment for her.

Stopping outside the door, he gestured the guard on duty to bring the key. It rasped in the lock, and the moment he stepped into the room, Arantxa came to her feet, a frightened expression on her face.

"There's a carriage outside that will take you to Veracruz," he said. "It's time to leave."

"What about Javier?" she whispered.

Chase hesitated, aware that she already knew the verdict had called for her brother's execution.

"I thought you'd rather leave now, before dawn."

Tears glistened in Arantxa's eyes. "I said good-bye to him last night, but I thought, I mean, I was hoping that you'd change your mind and show him mercy."

"I'm sorry, Arantxa. The sentence has already been passed. There's nothing I can do about it. Come on, your journey's a long one."

Arantxa wiped at her tears, but she picked up her meager belongings. They didn't speak as they walked together to the courtyard.

"I had some of your personal belongings brought from your parents' house." Chase gestured at several trunks roped together at the back of the coach.

Arantxa bit her lip, tears welling again. "Will you tell Carlita good-bye for me, and that I am sorry for the suffering I caused her?"

Chase nodded, taking her elbow and assisting her into the carriage. Arantxa peered out the window at him, her tearstained face full of misery.

"*Gracias*, Senor Lancaster, for showing mercy on me."

"You were not guilty of treason."

"I have to say one thing to you before I go," Arantxa said. "For Carlita and you. I heard what Javier told you about Carlita and him, and it's not true. They were never lovers. I shared Carlita's room every night she was at San Miguel, and she was rarely even alone with my brother. I don't think she liked him much after he brought her to San Miguel."

Chase looked at her and nodded, then signaled to the driver. The vehicle clattered across the cobblestones, surrounded by four armed riders. Chase turned away, a wave of compassion for Arantxa rising inside him. How unfair life could be, he thought. Arantxa was a victim of her own family. And he knew that what she'd told him was true. Carlisle had been a virgin in the cave when they'd made love the first time. He had known it all along, but that didn't change the fact that she had gone willingly with Javier and set the whole tragedy in motion. He couldn't forgive her that.

As dawn gilded the distant rooftops of the city, he climbed the stone steps to the narrow parapet from which he was to witness the execution. President Juarez stood there already, with several of his advisors.

Chase took his place beside them at the high balustrade as Javier was brought forward by a priest, feet shackled, hands bound. While the padre blessed him, he stood against the wall, tall and straight as twelve soldiers filed in and stood at attention across from him.

When the black-robed priest backed away, the captain of the guard saluted the president, then called for his men to prepare to fire.

Javier looked up to Chase, and his voice rang out, echoing hollowly against the stone walls.

"Viva Santa Anna! Viva the Holy Catholic Church!"

The command to shoot was given. The report of a dozen rifles cracked in the quiet morning. Javier Perez crumpled to the ground.

Chase had watched silently and was shocked to find that he did not exult at Perez's death as he had expected to. Although he'd done his duty and avenged Esteban, the sight of an eighteen-year-old boy lying lifeless in the dirt did not fill him with joy.

Instead, he felt sick to his stomach, and curiously empty. He only wanted war and rebellion to stop. He wanted to live his life and serve his country in peace. He wanted to forget Perez and everything that had happened. More than anything, he wanted to be happy with Carlisle, to eagerly await their baby with her as other husbands and wives did. But could he? Oh, God, could he?

During the month of November, Carlisle settled into a pleasant daily routine. Time seemed to help Chase, that and perhaps the fact that the men who'd tortured him had been punished. Generally she tried not to think of San Miguel or her days there with the Perezes. Instead, she began to prepare for the baby's birth, genuinely enjoying sewing the tiny clothes and bonnets.

One day in early December, as she busied herself folding fluffy baby blankets and soft infant sacques, she stopped to admire the room they'd chosen for the nursery. She walked to the new white wicker cradle, where Dona Maria had hung the long christening gown that the baby would wear when baptized. Carlisle ran her fingertips over the old, fragile lace, smiling to think that her big, six foot three husband had once been small enough to fit into the tiny garment.

From the table beside the bed, she picked up an ivory music box. The tinkling melody reminded her of the ball she'd attended in New Orleans on Gray and Tyler's wedding day. An eternity ago, it seemed. How silly and immature she'd been, pretending she didn't find Chase attractive. She felt as if she'd been a mere child then, though it had not yet been a year ago. Now she was a woman expecting her firstborn child.

"Carly? What are you doing?"

As always, her heart leapt at the sound of Chase's voice. Her smile was eager and full of welcome.

"*Hola,* Chaso. *Buenos diás.*"

Chase's grin carved the familiar, beloved grooves in his lean cheeks. "You have learned our language well, *querida.*"

Carlisle was pleased by the warmth in his eyes and the endearment he'd used. But was she really his beloved?

"I have a surprise for you," he said, and Carlisle was flooded with silent delight that his mood was so light. He was hiding something behind his back.

"What? Tell me."

Grinning, he brought out a bundle of envelopes. "Letters from Tyler and Gray."

"Chase, really? Quick, give them to me!"

"They've been at the hacienda all this time," he explained as he handed them to her. "No one thought to send them until now."

"I've been so worried about everyone at home," Carlisle began, hugging the precious letters close to her breast. But Chase only laughed and pulled her close. Instantly and without reservation, Carlisle forgot all about the long-awaited correspondence, enjoying Chase's thorough exploration of her lips. She didn't think coherently again until the warmth of his mouth caressed her temple, muffling his words.

"You looked so beautiful when I came in a moment ago. Like an angel—"

She felt him tense slightly, and she knew he had thought of Esteban's painting. Before he could remember and pull away from her, she took his hand and eagerly led him to the chair in front of the window.

"Let's read them together, Chase! Look, this one's from Chicago!"

Chase stood behind her as she sat down, excitedly tearing open the first letter.

"It's dated November." She flipped over to the last page. "And it's from Tyler." She began to read. " 'I am writing with the most splendid news. I am expecting a baby in the spring.' " Carlisle raised her face to Chase, her eyes shining. "Can you believe it, Chase? Tyler's to have a baby, too. Isn't that wonderful?"

"*Sí*. It's good she sounds so happy about it. What else does she say?"

Carlisle immediately returned to Tyler's childlike handwriting. " 'Gray and I are very pleased about the impending birth, and, Carly, I am so incredibly happy. Gray is the most wonderful man alive.' "

"She seems to have adjusted well enough to her marriage, just like I told you she would," Chase interjected. "I guess Gray and I didn't make such a bad decision after all."

Carlisle nodded, in complete agreement with his assessment, then resumed reading. " 'I'm afraid, dear Carly, that I also have a few pieces of unpleasant news for you. We had a fire here in Chicago on October 8 that destroyed thousands of buildings—though, thankfully, ours was spared. But before I tell you the next thing, I urge you not to blame yourself. Both Gray and I understand that you had the very best motives. Of course, you had no way of knowing your letter would cause such problems for us.' "

"What letter?" Chase asked, frowning. "What the devil did you do, Carly?"

Carlisle frowned, quickly skimming over the next

few paragraphs without reading the words aloud. Her heart sank lower with every word Tyler had penned.

"What's happened?" Chase demanded, leaning forward to look over her shoulder.

Stricken, Carlisle could not hide her guilty conscience. "Oh, Chase, I didn't dream anything like this could happen!"

"Dios, Carly, tell me what you're talking about!"

Carlisle handed him the letter, unable to look at him while he read it.

"Tyler thinks you wrote a letter to a man named Emerson Clan, summoning him to Chicago. Did you?"

"Yes," Carlisle admitted miserably. "I did it to help Stone, but I never thought anyone would get hurt."

Chase sat down and put his arm around her. "All right, tell me exactly what happened."

Filled with remorse, Carlisle bit her lip. "Stone is my other brother, the one you haven't met. During the war, he was captured and sent to a prison camp in Andersonville, Georgia, because a man named Emerson Clan betrayed him. Ever since the end of the war, Stone's been obsessed with finding him."

Her voice broke slightly. "I only meant to help him, so when Tyler told me how your father tricked a man into coming to him in one of his swindles, I tried to do the same thing. I wrote a letter to Clan's cousin in Alabama. I told him that Clan's uncle had died in Chicago and left Emerson Clan money, but that he had to go there to collect it. You see, I thought if he went to Chicago, Stone would be able to capture him. And it worked, except that after Stone had him arrested, he escaped from jail during the big fire. He kidnapped Tyler, Chase! And Gray was shot when he and Stone tried to rescue her. Oh, Chase, what if Gray had been killed?''

"Tyler says Gray's fine now. When did you send the letter, Carly?''

"Javier drafted it for me on the *Mayan*,'' Carlisle admitted reluctantly.

Chase tensed at the name, but he didn't appear to be angry. "Well, it's over now, and everyone's all right.''

"But don't you see? It's all my fault.''

"It sounds to me as if Gray and Tyler have already forgiven you.''

"And what about you, Chase?'' she asked quietly. "Will you ever forget I was the one who caused Esteban's death? Will you ever love me the way you used to?''

Chase froze, as he always did when she brought up the subject. At length, he answered.

"I don't think I can ever forget it, Carly.''

Deep inside Carlisle, something gave way. She felt as if she couldn't bear to face a lifetime like this— never knowing from one minute to the next whether Chase would treat her lovingly or withdraw into cold, bitter silence and condemnation.

"I want to go home,'' she said thickly, "to Chicago, where people love me and won't keep punishing me like you do.''

Chase's face went white with anger. "No. I forbid it.''

"I won't stay here. I can't bear to be held and kissed one minute and hated the next! I can't stand it, I tell you!''

"After the baby is born, you can go wherever you

damn well please. But my child stays here in Mexico with me, *comprendes?*"

Carlisle watched him stalk from the room. With trembling hands, she realized he could do anything he wanted with her and the baby. Perhaps that was the only reason he had married her—to keep her at the Casa Amarilla until the baby was born, then get rid of her. He'd said as much, she thought in horror, and he'd said the same thing when he'd first come to Mexico City and learned she carried his child. "I suppose I'll have to tolerate your presence here, at least until the baby is born," had been his exact words the night he'd agreed to marry her. She hadn't wanted to believe him then, but now she did. Carlisle's face drained of color, because nothing had ever frightened her as much as his icily uttered threat to take her baby from her.

Lovingly, Dona Maria took her elder son's engraved silver baby cup out of its black velvet case and placed it carefully on the crocheted doily she'd laid across the nursery bureau. Smiling, absorbed with many fond memories of both her sons, she laid the exquisitely designed miniature silver comb and brush alongside the cup.

Soon, she'd once again brush silken curls atop a tiny head and rock her grandchild in the heavy mahogany rocker which Morelos mothers had used to lull their babies for generations.

The heirloom rocking chair had been brought down from the attic the day before. Now Dona Maria seated herself in it, listening to the familiar creak as she rocked to and fro. She had spent many hours in such fashion with Tomas in her arms, humming lullabies and comforting him when he cried. In a few months Carlita would have the same pleasure, a joy a mother would cherish long after her children were grown.

She picked up her knitting needles, and soon they were clicking rhythmically together as the white yarn began to take the shape of a tiny bootie. Of late, her thoughts had been full of Chaso and his beautiful *gringa* wife. If only they could be happy together! They were so fortunate to love each other so passionately.

Carlisle, bless her, admitted her feelings openly, but Chaso remained infuriatingly silent and unyielding. She knew him so well that she found it easy to see how much he loved his wife. Was his grief still so painful that he could not forgive poor Carlita? Or was his attitude merely stubborn pride? The baby's birth would make all the difference in their troubled marriage. She truly believed that. The child would heal the terrible breach between them.

For long hours, she'd prayed on her knees before the altar in her room, said countless rosaries and Hail Marys for a total reconciliation between Chaso and Carlita. The Holy Virgin would hear her entreaties and touch Chaso's heart with forgiveness. Suddenly impassioned by that hope, she raised the rosary tucked into her belt and pressed it to her lips.

"Dona Maria?"

Opening her eyes, she found the object of her prayer standing before her. Carlita's lovely green eyes were red from weeping, her face sober and determined.

"Forgive me for interrupting your prayers, but I must talk with you. *Por favor,* it's very important."

"Of course. Carlita, you look so very tired. Are you feeling ill again?"

"No."

Carlita sat down on a chair a few feet away. When she remained silent, Dona Maria endeavored to help her.

"Is Chaso angry with you again, Carlita?"

Carlita nodded slightly, and Dona Maria frowned. "Oh, men can be so foolish!"

When her daughter-in-law did not answer, Dona Maria tried to cheer her. "Your *niño* will make your marriage strong."

Slowly, Carlita turned her face toward the window until her finely chiseled profile was outlined against the white wall.

"I must have your help, Dona Maria. I'm very sorry to have to ask you, but I have no choice."

Alarm clamored like a bell inside Dona Maria's breast. "You are like my own daughter. I'll help you in whatever way I can."

Carlita looked at her, and again Dona Maria sensed her resolve.

"Will you help me even if it entails going against your own son's wishes?"

Startled, Dona Maria shook her head. "I could not interfere in such a way, Carlita, you must know that. But if you tell me what has gone amiss between the two of you, I will gladly speak to Chaso on your behalf."

Carlita's smile became cold, cynical in a way Dona Maria had not seen before.

"Everything is amiss. Everything will always be amiss because Chase cannot forgive me." She suddenly leaned her head back against the chair, as if too tired to hold it up. "And I cannot stand the strain of it any longer. I have tried very hard, but I cannot continue living this way.''

"But the *niño* will bring you back into Chaso's heart!''

"I'm not sure I want that anymore. Today Chase told me that after my baby is born, I can go anywhere I want, but the child would stay here with him.''

"He must have been angry, Carlita. My son could not be so cruel.''

For the first time Carlita became agitated. Her hands clenched tightly over the carved arms of the chair. "Yes, he can. He can be very cruel. Esteban's death changed him. It changed all of us.''

Her voice faltered slightly, but she did not weep. Instead, her face grew even more unwavering. She lifted her chin.

"I am going home to America, where Chase can never take my child away from me. If he truly loves me, if he ever forgives me, then he can come there and tell me so.''

At first, Dona Maria was so horrified by Carlita's pronouncement that she could not utter a word.

"You cannot believe my son would take the baby from you,'' she whispered at last.

"I will not take that chance. My baby's all I have left. Surely you understand that.''

"Of course I understand,'' Dona Maria answered gently. "But you mustn't ask me to help you steal a child away from his father. It's against the laws of God.''

Carlita smiled sadly. "You did it yourself, Dona Maria.''

Stunned, Dona Maria stared at her, and Carlita's

voice softened. "You took Chase away from Burl Lancaster."

"But Chaso is nothing like his father was. Burl was a thief, a swindler who would have made his son the same . . ."

Her words petered out as she thought of those terrible, haunting days when she had struggled with the same decision Carlita was contemplating. She had loved Burl to distraction, but she had not wanted to remain with him and watch their love decay. Her heart twisted.

"But don't you see what you're asking? You want me to give up my own grandchild. I've waited so long—" She stopped, her throat clogged.

Carlita got up and knelt in front of her, holding both her hands. "I would never do that. You know how much I've grown to love you. I never knew my own mother, and no one could have been kinder to me than you have been. But if I wait here until the baby is born, I'll never be able to go home again. Chase has already forbidden it."

She continued, her voice more urgent. "What if Burl had not allowed you to take his son home with you—even for a visit? Could you have gone away and left Chase behind?"

Ashen-faced, Dona Maria stared at Carlita. "No," she whispered. "Never."

"Then please help me, I beg you. Arrange for me to travel to Veracruz and take passage to New Orleans. I swear to the Holy Virgin that I'll never keep my child away from Chase. Surely you know that I'd give my life to make him love me the way he used to, but I can't." Carlisle bit her lip, tears coming to her eyes. Overcome by sorrow, she lay her head in Dona Maria's lap and sobbed.

Dona Maria stroked Carlita's soft hair, her heart aching.

"Don't cry, Carlita," she whispered. "Together, we will find a way for you to go home."

Dona Maria kept her promise, and just over a week later, Carlisle stood on a windy seaside quay with Dona Maria and Tomas. Chase thought they were visiting his aunt's house in the city of Puebla, but instead they had traveled on to Veracruz, where the Yankee steamer, *Sentinel*, lay at anchor in the harbor. The ship was now being loaded with cargo for its homeward trip to the United States. Tomas had already bought her ticket to New Orleans, and now all that was left were their good-byes. She looked at her mother-in-law, emotion roughening her voice.

"*Gracias*, Dona Maria. I'll never forget what you're doing for me."

Dona Maria shook her head, embracing Carlisle tightly. "Oh, my *hija*, I will miss you dreadfully. I'm so afraid I'm doing the wrong thing to let you leave Chaso like this. He loves you so much. I know he does."

"I must go. I have no other choice." She looked up past the flat-topped buildings of the city to the mountains beyond. "It is very hard for me to leave Mexico." Her voice lowered. "I've grown to love your country as much as I love your son."

Dona Maria withdrew her handkerchief and wiped her tears.

"You'll write and tell me when the baby's born, won't you?" she asked, patting Carlisle's back. "And you must remember to be careful while you're aboard the ship. Please don't go out on the decks in rough weather or you might fall. Juana,'' she said, turning to the young girl who stood a few steps away, ''you must take good care of Carlita, promise me?''

''*Sí*, senora.''

Dona Maria hugged Carlisle again as the bell on the passenger launch rang. She extended a small box she had been holding in her arm.

''Here, *niña*, these are for the baby. It's some clothes I made for him, and a few shawls and blankets. Chicago is very cold, no?''

''*Sí*. *Gracias*. I'll treasure them. Oh, Mama, I'll miss you!'' Carlisle cried as they embraced again.

A sob escaped Dona Maria as she turned and hurried back to the coach, and Carlisle's own tears began to fall.

Tomas had been standing a little way apart from them, and he came close now, handing Carlisle his handkerchief. She wiped her eyes with it.

''Tomas, I'll miss you, too, very much. I'll never forget you and all you've done for me.''

''I'm afraid I will never see you again,'' Tomas said, his eyes so forlorn that Carlisle swallowed hard. She feared the same thing, but she tried to smile.

''You could always come to America to visit me. You and your mother both.''

''I think Chaso is loco.''

Carlisle hugged him tightly. ''I'm going to write to you, Tomas. You'll answer my letters, won't you?''

''*Sí*,'' he answered, his own eyes growing misty. ''Adios, Carlita.''

Carlisle walked down to the boat with Juana and was assisted inside by one of the uniformed sailors.

She sat down, tears burning her eyes. As she lifted her hand and waved to Dona Maria and Tomas, who stood beside their carriage, she felt as if she were leaving her whole life behind her. And she was, because she was leaving Chase.

Two days before Christmas, Chase rode his horse down the road to Puebla. His journey had been long and tiring, but now that he could see the slender spires of the cathedral, he knew his destination was at hand. His grandfather's great hacienda outside Puebla was a beautiful, peaceful place, and he meant to spend Christmas Day there with Carlisle. It had been nearly two weeks since his mother had taken Carly and Tomas to visit his *tía* Isabella. When they'd left, he'd told Carlisle not to be gone longer than a week, and to his annoyance, he hadn't heard a word from her since that day.

At first, he'd been glad to have Carlisle out of the house. Then he'd found himself pacing the floor of their bedchamber each night, missing her and wanting her with him. He'd had little peace since she left, and it galled him to admit he needed her.

More difficult still was living with the knowledge that he'd treated her badly and said spiteful things to her, things that he really didn't mean. Sometimes he wanted to hurt her, but when he saw the pain darken her eyes to jade, he felt worse than she did. He'd felt that way when they had argued about her visiting her family in Chicago, and Carlisle's face had reflected her wounded feelings.

He knew why he'd forbidden the trip. He was afraid she'd never come back. But he'd already decided how to make it up to her. They'd spend Christmas together at Tía Isabella's, and he'd give her the diamond necklace and matching bracelet he'd purchased.

The city of Puebla was very old, set on hills with narrow, winding cobblestone streets. He hardly noticed the pedestrians in the market stalls as he spurred his mount along, irritated with himself for the eagerness he felt. Damn Carlisle and her hold on his heart!

Within ten minutes, the *estancia* where his aunt lived came into sight. The front walls were high and bleached white from the sun, and when he pounded on the door, the *portero* immediately admitted him.

"Buenos días, Don Chaso!" he cried. "How are you?"

"Bien, Tomacinto. Where is my mother?"

"Dona Maria is in the patio, senor."

"Gracias," Chase said, handing over his reins. He took off his sombrero and slapped it against his thigh to rid it of dust, then strode across the courtyard to the walled garden. A few moments later, he discovered his mother and aunt sipping *cánela* tea in the shade. His mother looked shocked to see him.

"Chaso! What are you doing here? We had no idea you were coming!"

Chase smiled, bent to kiss his mother, then his short, plump aunt. *"Buenos días,* Mama. Tía Isabella, you are looking *muy bonita."*

"Gracias, Chaso," his *tía* answered, looking so distinctly uncomfortable that Chase's eyes lingered on her for an extra moment. He helped himself to a glass of orange juice from the pitcher on the table, then sat down on a bench near the women.

"Where's Carly, Mother? Resting?"

Tía Isabella seemed aghast at his question, and his mother quickly picked up a plate of *buñuelos.*

"Would you care for something to eat, Chaso?"

"*Sí,*" he answered, looking at the paper-thin pancakes dripping with honey. He realized his stomach was empty, since he'd left the Casa Amarilla before breakfast. His aunt seemed overly thrilled that he was hungry.

"Then I will bring you tortillas and eggs as well," she cried, jumping up and rushing away.

Chase watched her leave, then turned inquiring eyes to his mother.

"What's wrong with Tía Isabella?"

"She's just pleased to have you visit her. You haven't been here in over a year, you know." His mother smiled, but her eyes watched him, a distinct wariness lurking in their black depths.

"Is something wrong with Carlisle?" he demanded, suddenly alarmed by their strange behavior. He sat up straighter. "She's not ill, is she? Is it the baby?"

"Oh, no," his mother reassured him quickly. "She's fine, but I imagine she's a bit uncomfortable now that she's beginning to show."

Chase nodded and got to his feet. "What chamber does Carly have? I'd like to see her."

His mother poured more tea into her cup. "I must say your concern surprises me. You've gone to great lengths in the past few months to make her miserable. Why do you wish to see her now?"

Chase frowned at his mother's uncharacteristic rebuke. Because I missed her so much I couldn't shut my eyes at night, he wanted to say. He didn't.

"Because she's my wife," he replied, his tone frigid enough to make his mother lower her gaze. He glanced up at the second-floor veranda, where the bedchambers were located. "Now, where's Carly?"

His mother hesitated, then spoke, low and sorrowfully. "Carlita's gone, *mi hijo.*"

Chase's frown deepened. "You shouldn't let her go off visiting alone in her condition. When will she be back? Is she with Tomas?" he added as an afterthought, annoyed to think of the two of them alone together somewhere. Tomas was already too infatuated with his wife.

"I'm sorry, Chaso, but Carlita won't be back. She's gone home."

"To Mexico City? When?"

"Not to the Casa Amarilla. Home to America."

Chase's heart stopped. "What?"

His mother moistened her lips. "Tomas and I took her to Veracruz last week. She and Juana set sail on a steamer to New Orleans."

At first, Chase could only stare at her; then his face grew purple with rage. "Why the hell didn't you stop her?"

His mother raised her chin. "I didn't want to stop her. She asked for my help because she had nowhere else to turn."

"Goddamn it, Mother, she's my wife! She has no right to leave without my permission! How could you do this to me?"

Dona Maria stared at him calmly. "I did it because you deserved for her to leave you. You've treated her abominably ever since you married her."

"She's my wife!" Chase shouted, outraged at her interference. "She'll do as I say!"

"Apparently not, Chaso. If you've lost her, you've only yourself to blame. For the first time in your life, your actions shame me. You remind me of your father.''

Shocked to silence by her words, Chase turned around and paced a few distracted steps away. A bird chirped on the branch above the table, but that sound was the only noise in the quiet patio as Chase wrestled with his emotions. Carly gone? Fled from him?

"You shouldn't have helped her go, Mother," he said thickly. "She'll never come back."

"You disappoint me, my son," Dona Maria answered. "You speak of her as if she were dead, when, in truth, she is only a sea voyage away."

"Perhaps, but I'll be damned if I'll go chasing after her." He looked coldly at her. "I hope you're happy, Mother, because now you'll probably never lay eyes on your first grandchild."

Dona Maria looked down as Chase stalked away and yelled furiously for his horse.

19

Tyler MacKenzie Kincaid rubbed her fingers in a circular motion, trying to dislodge the lacy frost covering the windowpanes. Outside in the frigid January night, Lincoln Avenue was deserted, the corner lamplight revealing huge snowflakes falling as softly as goose down.

"Gray, what could be taking them so long?" she cried, turning to look at her husband. "I told you we should have taken the sleigh to the railway station!"

Gray smiled at her from where he stood with one elbow propped on the mantelpiece, his calm demeanor in direct contrast to his wife's excitement. "And I told you, my love, that I won't allow you outside on icy sidewalks in your condition. Be patient. Carly and Chase will arrive as soon as they can."

"But we haven't seen them in months! I'm having a baby, I grant you that, but I won't melt if I get a little wet!" she retorted, placing her hands on her hips. "I'm not made of sugar, you know!"

Amusement flickered in her husband's blue eyes.

"Well, now, sweetheart, I suppose that's a matter of opinion."

Tyler had to laugh as Gray came toward her, and she met his embrace eagerly, always happy when his arms were around her.

"I want you to quit worrying, Tyler," he murmured, his chin resting atop her soft auburn hair. "They'll be here soon. I'm as eager to see Carly as you are, but I have no doubt that Chase is taking very good care of her. He's managed to put up with her headstrong ways for all these months down in Mexico, hasn't he? If he can handle that job, I trust he can get her safely home from LaSalle Street Station, just four blocks from here."

"But it's been so long! And so much has happened since we left New Orleans last spring! I'm going to give them both a piece of my mind for not writing to us. We haven't had a letter from Carlisle since she arrived at Chase's hacienda!"

"Carly doesn't like to write letters. She's always too busy, or at least that's what she says."

Tyler disentangled herself from Gray's arms and took her place on the window seat again. She just couldn't wait! She and Gray had both been surprised when Carly's telegraph message had arrived Tuesday with the news that she was in New Orleans and ready to take the train home.

Although Carlisle hadn't mentioned Chase in her wire, Tyler knew he must be with her. He'd never have allowed her to travel alone. They must have decided to come when they got her letter informing them of her pregnancy!

Impatiently, she scratched at the ice crusting the

glass, her eyes sharpening when she caught sight of a sleigh turning into the side driveway.

"Gray! They're here!" she cried, whirling and rushing past her husband.

Gray reached out and stopped her, his grip gentle but firm.

"Remember what Charles said about running? He is your doctor, you know."

"Yes, yes, I'm sorry, but come on, hurry. I can't believe you're not as excited as I am! She's your sister! And I know how much you've missed her!"

Gray laughed and allowed her to pull him into the hallway that led to the side portico, where they could hear the jingle of bells as the sleigh came up the driveway. Tyler threw open the door just as the driver assisted Carlisle from the covered cutter.

"Carly!"

Tyler ran down the steps, disregarding her husband's concerned frown. A heavily cloaked Carlisle met her at the bottom of the stairs, taking her hands and squeezing them as they both laughed with delight.

"Thank God you're here, Carly, so Tyler will quit worrying about you and give me some peace," Gray said, putting his arm fondly around his sister's shoulders and kissing her cheek.

"But where's Chase?" Tyler cried, looking past Carlisle to see if her cousin was still in the sleigh. The only person she saw was a young girl with dark skin who shivered and rubbed her hands together.

"Chase didn't come with me," Carlisle told them. "This is my maid, Juana. Juana, this is my brother, Gray, and my sister-in-law, Tyler."

Gray nodded to the young servant, frowning

slightly. "You'll both freeze out here in this weather. Come on, let's go inside where it's warm."

Tyler slipped her arm through Carlisle's and walked with her into the brightly lit hall while Gray helped Juana up the steps.

"Oh, Carly, it's so wonderful to see you again! Here, let me take your cloak, then we'll go into the parlor! We've got a nice hot fire burning."

Carlisle unbuttoned her cape, and Gray helped her out of it. Tyler gasped when she saw that Carlisle was big with child.

"Oh, no," she cried without thinking, turning horrified eyes to her husband's face. Gray's jaw hung slack, and when Carlisle saw his expression, she spoke quietly.

"Chase and I got married while I was in Mexico," she told them, and when Tyler and Gray continued to stare at her in astonishment, she turned to her maid. "Juana, would you go upstairs and unpack our things, *por favor?* The kitchen is through those doors behind the staircase. Someone will be there to show you the way."

As the Indian girl hurried away, Carlisle faced her family again, almost as if they were a panel of judges.

Tyler suddenly realized how embarrassed Carlisle must be. "Why, Carly, you and Chase! That's the most wonderful news in the world!" Sincerely pleased by the unexpected development, she took Carlisle's cold hand. "Why didn't you write and tell us? Why, it must have been months and months ago! You're farther along than I am!"

Her innocent observation was followed by an extremely awkward silence, during which Carlisle's face turned bright pink. Tyler glanced up at her husband as he muttered something unintelligible under his breath.

"Where the hell is Chase?" he demanded furiously. "What's he thinking of, letting his wife travel alone when she's about to give birth?"

"I've left him," Carlisle admitted.

"You've what?"

"Because he never really wanted to marry me. He had to."

Tyler watched the telltale tic in her husband's cheek, the one which consistently foretold his rage.

"Damn him! I trusted him to take care of you, and look what he did!" Gray muttered in outrage.

When tears welled in Carlisle's eyes, Tyler glared at her husband. "Gray! Can't you see how tired and upset Carly is? She needs to rest before you start shouting at her and questioning her as if she's some sort of criminal! I'm sure there are reasonable explanations for everything!"

Gray was still furious and showing it, so Tyler put her arm around Carlisle's waist and led her to the steps.

"Come on, Carly, we'll get you settled in your old room. Then later, we'll join Gray for supper." She glanced over her shoulder at her husband. "Gray, darling, will you have Hildie bring up a pot of tea for us?"

Her husband's frown didn't lessen, but he turned and strode off toward the kitchen. At least she'd saved Carlisle from his wrath, she thought, relieved, as she helped her sister-in-law up the steps. Poor Carlisle looked unhappy enough.

* * *

A short time later, when the two women sat sipping chamomile tea in the window seat of Carlisle's childhood bedchamber, Carlisle recounted all that had happened to her during her stay in Mexico. Tyler sat silently, listening. The snow built into a deep drift on the windowsill behind them as Carlisle talked on and on, sometimes interrupting her story with her own weeping. When she'd finished, Tyler shook her head sadly.

"Carly, I just can't believe all those terrible things happened between you and Chase. Gray and I never once worried. We thought you were having a wonderful time and just didn't have the time to write to us."

"I love Mexico," Carlisle said. "It nearly broke my heart to leave."

Tyler's cinnamon-brown eyes brimmed with sympathy, and she leaned forward to embrace Carlisle.

"I'm so sorry, Carly. Is there anything I can do? Do you want me to write to Chase for you? If you left without telling him, he must be terribly worried."

"I had to. He couldn't forget I went with the Perezes. I think he wanted to. I think he tried, especially after we were married, but he just couldn't. And I couldn't stand seeing the cold look come into his eyes. Most of all, I was afraid he'd send me away after the baby was born."

"Oh, no, Carly. He'd never do that. He might have gotten angry and said he would, but I'm sure he didn't mean it."

Carlisle sighed. "I was afraid, and I wanted to come home to have my baby."

Tyler smiled. "I'm so glad you did." She rested her palm on her own swollen belly. "Our babies will

be cousins, and they'll be good friends, like we are."
She pressed Carlisle's hand. "I've not told Gray, but
I'm a little scared. I've heard frightening stories about
childbirth. But I've been talking to Dr. Bond, and he's
explained everything that will happen to me when the
baby is born. And he's promised to let me accompany
him to a birthing so I can see it firsthand. If I know
what to expect, I don't think I'll dread it so much.
One of his patients is due in the next couple of weeks.
Would you like to go with us? He says I can help him
deliver the child if I want."

"I don't know. Perhaps. Won't Gray mind?"

"He doesn't know yet. But he'll let me if I really
want to, especially if he thinks it'll make me feel
better about having my own child. He worries about
me too much anyway, so please don't tell him I'm
uneasy about the birth."

"I won't. I know how you feel because I've had
the same thoughts. I was deathly sick every morning
at first. Were you?"

"Oh, yes! I was violently ill when I first woke up,
but then the nausea just went away. I feel wonderful
now." Her whole face lit up. "And I felt the baby
move for the first time just a week or so ago. You
should have seen Gray's face when I put his hand on
my stomach and let him feel it."

Carlisle felt the most awful sensation of loss. Chase
had not felt his baby move, nor would he.

"I'm sorry, Carly, that was so insensitive. I wasn't
thinking."

"No, I'm glad you and Gray are happy together.
You weren't when I saw you last."

"We went through a lot, but we loved each other

so much that we worked our problems out. You and Chase will do the same thing."

Carlisle nodded, but she was not at all sure Tyler's prophecy would come true.

"Last summer when we were living at Rose Point Plantation in Mississippi, I met a woman named Bess Rainey," Tyler told her. "She was carrying a child, and one day she let me feel her baby kick. I can still remember the wonder I felt that day. And now I feel it every time my own baby moves. It's such a miracle to carry a separate little life inside you."

Somehow Tyler's words gave Carlisle comfort, more than anything anyone else had said. "I'm glad now that I came home, Tyler. I felt alone in Mexico, even though Chase's family treated me well. But this is home, and I feel safe here."

"You *are* safe here! We'll take good care of you until Chase comes. And I know he will. Until then, we'll be together and plan for our babies. It'll be wonderful to have another mother to talk to." Tyler paused, smiling. "Remember how afraid of the wedding night we were, Carly? We were both so innocent and unworldly then. But we were scared for nothing, weren't we?"

Carlisle tried to remember how she'd felt in New Orleans. But now when she thought about it, all her actions just seemed frivolous.

"I was so foolish then, and it seems like a million years ago," she told Tyler. "I don't know how Gray used to put up with me. All I thought about was myself."

"Don't look so sad, Carly. You were just gay and happy. You helped me when I was having a hard time with Gray." Tyler lowered her eyes. "Actually, I was the silly one. Even now, after all these months of marriage, I'm horribly ashamed that I wore black to my own wedding. I can remember Chase telling me that someday I'd look back on that day as one of the happiest of my life. And he was right. Now it hurts when I think how much I must have humiliated Gray by acting that way. I wish I could go back and make our ceremony beautiful and happy, the way weddings are supposed to be.''

"Gray understood. He loved you so much he didn't care.'' Carlisle fiddled with the emerald wedding ring that she hadn't removed since Chase had put it on her finger at their own strained wedding. "Gray's angry and disappointed in me. I could always see it in his eyes, even when I was a little girl. But Stone will be on my side; he always is. Is he here or working out in Denver?''

Tyler averted her gaze, and coldness ran through Carlisle's body. "Oh, dear God, Tyler, has something happened to Stone?''

"We don't know for sure where he is or what he's doing. We're all very worried about him.''

"I don't understand. When was the last time you saw him?''

Tyler's reluctance to pursue the subject became more pronounced. "Gray intended to tell you all this himself. He didn't want to put it in a letter.'' She hesitated, then went on. "Stone's missing, Carly. Did you get my letter about Emerson Clan and the Chicago fire?''

Carlisle nodded, her face stricken, as Tyler continued. "Unfortunately, Clan escaped when the city was burning and everything was so confused. There was nothing any of us could do to dissuade Stone from going after him.''

Tyler paused, looking distressed. "Early in November, he left on a train heading toward Denver. Gray got word a few weeks later that it was attacked and burned by Indians somewhere out on the prairie.'' Carlisle gasped, and Tyler quickly reassured her. "Stone wasn't listed among the dead, so we think he managed to escape. But no one knows where he is.''

"Could he have made his way to Denver? He knows the area well because he's worked out there on some of our railroad construction crews.''

"But why wouldn't he send word to us? Gray's already sent out search parties and private detectives. He wanted to go himself, but he was afraid to leave me here alone, in case Clan came back.''

"I was such a fool to send that letter to Clan," Carlisle said morosely. "You told me not to, but I just didn't listen.''

"Everything turned out all right. I'm fine now. You can see that for yourself. And we'll find Stone. I know we will.''

"Did Clan try to hurt you, too?''

"When he thought I'd lured him here so Stone could capture him, he tried to kidnap me. Stone and Gray rescued me during the fire. That's how Clan got away.'' She shivered, as if the memory upset her. "Oh, Carly, Clan is so evil. I've never seen such a cruel man.''

Tears burned like pinpricks behind Carlisle's eyes. "I'm to blame. I've done so many stupid things. I've hurt so many people. Chase, and poor Esteban—how can I ever forget all the trouble I've caused?''

For the first time in many days, Carlisle felt her

strength ebbing away. She leaned her head against the cold windowpanes.

Tyler patted her shoulder. "You must think of the future and your child. For a long time I fought with my conscience like you're doing, over the things I'd done to Gray and other people, but I've learned to live with myself. Gray has helped me see that it doesn't do any good to dwell on your past mistakes. Chase's love will help you. You'll see."

Carlisle listened to Tyler's gentle words and let them soothe her troubled heart. Everything would be all right. It had to be. Stone had to be safe. He'd come back to Chicago soon, and he'd laugh at their fears. She was at home with her family now, where she belonged. They would take care of her until Chase arrived. And he would. She had to believe that.

The next morning when her older brother knocked on her door, Carlisle was still in her dressing gown. She quickly bade Juana to admit him. He would still be angry, but she realized with some surprise that she really didn't care. She was a grown woman now, married and with child—not just his little sister.

"Good morning, Carly," Gray said after Juana had gone downstairs to join the other servants for breakfast.

"Good morning."

"May I sit down? I'd like to talk with you."

"Of course."

She led him to the chairs before the hearth. After they were seated, Gray smiled.

"I'm really glad you're home."

"I am, too," Carlisle answered, but in her heart, she wished she were back in Mexico at the Casa

Amarilla, with the warm sun and gardenias, and Chase.

"Tyler told me what happened down in Mexico," he began. "Carly I'm sorry. I thought Chase would take care of you, I swear. It never occurred to me that he'd take advantage of you. I ought to kill him for what he's done!"

"Please don't blame Chase. It's not his fault."

"But he dishonored you—" Gray sputtered furiously.

"Chase is the most honorable man I've ever met," Carlisle defended staunchly.

Her remark caused Gray to rise and begin pacing in front of her. In contrast, Carlisle remained calm. Poor Gray, she thought. Now she was causing him more grief and pain. Would it never end?

"How can you stick up for him after what he's done to you, Carly?"

"Because I love him. None of the things that happened were his fault. I'm the one who got him involved with the Perezes."

"The baby wasn't your fault!"

"Well, I had something to do with it, wouldn't you say?"

"Good God, Carly, what happened to you down there to make you change so much? I hardly know you anymore."

Carlisle almost smiled. "I grew up, I suppose. And I guess I didn't do a very good job of it. But I'd appreciate it if you'd let me stay here until the baby is born, and then I'll decide—"

"Let you stay here?" Gray repeated, looking dumbfounded. "What in God's name do you mean by such a ridiculous question? Of course you'll stay here! This is your home! We're your family!''

"Thank you, Gray." She'd almost said *Gracias,* she realized. Spanish now seemed more natural to her than English.

"I'm going to send a letter to Chase demanding that he live up to his responsibilities—"

"No, you're not!" For the first time, Carlisle became emotional. "Please. Don't contact him. I left him, don't you see? He doesn't love me. Any feelings he had died when Esteban was killed because of me."

Gray sat down beside her. He shook his head. "I wish there were something I could do, Carly. I should never have let you go to Mexico."

"You had nothing to do with what happened between Chase and me. I'm trying to be responsible for myself now. Please let me."

"All right, if you'll agree to one thing."

"What?"

"I want you to stay with Tyler and me. We want you here." He leaned back, grinning. "Tyler is absolutely ecstatic to have you in the house. She doesn't have any close friends here in Chicago yet, except for the Bonds. She's lonely, and worried about Stone."

"Stone's all right," Carlisle said firmly. "I'd sense it if anything bad happened to him. I know I would."

"Actually, I've had the same feeling all along. Stone's always been able to take care of himself."

"I guess it's in our blood," Carlisle said. "Kincaids know how to survive."

Gray gave her a hug. "That's right. Don't forget it," he said as Tyler opened the door, fully dressed, her face beaming with happiness.

"Breakfast it ready! Come on, Carly, I have so much to tell you! And I'm starved, aren't you?"

Gray and Carlisle smiled at each other. Then the three of them walked downstairs together to marvel at the deep snowdrifts that had piled up nearly to the eaves during the long winter night.

A fortnight after Carlisle arrived in Chicago, she held her skirt in one hand and carefully followed Tyler down the shiny marble staircase of the palatial new store owned by Gray's good friend, Marshall Field. She paused to look at a beautifully crocheted pale yellow baby's shawl, which reminded her of the one Dona Maria had knitted for her. She sighed, her spirits plummeting despite Tyler's cheerful attempts to brighten her day with shopping and her own bubbly company.

Nothing made Carlisle happy, but somehow she felt more at peace living in the familiar rooms of her childhood home. She felt safe in the house on Lincoln Avenue, her family's affection soothing her wounded soul. But even in the company of Gray and Tyler, and other well-meaning friends, she was lonelier than she'd ever been in her life.

Gray and Tyler had been kind—especially Tyler, for she understood Carlisle's pain. But when Carlisle saw the married couple smile lovingly at each other or share stolen kisses when they thought she wasn't watching, her heart twisted as if her lifeblood were being wrung from it. She yearned for Chase so violently that she felt physically weak. Why did everything have to go so wrong? her heart cried out at night when the house was quiet and she lay in bed alone. Why did she have to make so many stupid mistakes?

And why did Chase have to be so unforgiving? Why didn't he come after her?

"What a beautiful shawl," Tyler said, coming up beside her. "Let's buy one for each of us. And look, Carly, here are matching bonnets and booties! We'll need plenty of these. Chicago always has a windy spring, doesn't it?"

Spring seemed very far away, Carlisle thought, nodding, as Tyler chattered on. "Look how tiny these little mittens are! There are just so many things we need for our layettes, even though my friend, Harriet, and I have been sewing for months now. Thank goodness we have the driver along to help us carry our purchases. And now that you're home, we'll need another crib, too."

Pausing, she dimpled winsomely. "Gray has given us no spending limit, so we better get everything we need before he receives his first bill. Just wait until you see the children's wear section. There are tables and tables of the most beautiful clothing, and toys from England and Italy and all over the world."

Carlisle made an appropriate remark and followed dutifully in Tyler's wake, not wanting to dampen her sister-in-law's happiness. But once she saw the children's display room, she began to share Tyler's enthusiasm. Rows of small tables and chairs decorated with rabbits and ducks, miniature buggies and donkey carts, and every type of plaything imaginable made the room seem almost magical. Carlisle exclaimed over different items with as much delight as Tyler did.

"How precious," she murmured, kneeling beside a tiny but intricately designed rocking horse. "This reminds me of the one I had when I was a little girl. I can still remember how Stone used to hold me on the saddle and push me back and forth. I'd hang on to the mane and squeal until he laughed."

Her throat closed at the thought of her missing brother, and Tyler laid a comforting hand on her shoulder. "We'll hear from him soon, Carly. And from Chase, too. My cousin will be here in time for your baby's birth, I'll lay odds on it. But right now, we must have two of these darling little horses so our babies can go riding together in the nursery."

Carlisle merely smiled, but she was very pleased when they purchased the small painted ponies, one blue, the other red. They browsed for a while longer, then Tyler signed for their bountiful purchases. When they stopped in the front entrance to the store, Carlisle and Tyler stood aside, holding their prized rocking horses as Johnny, Gray's driver, carried their boxes and bundles to the waiting sleigh.

"It's snowing again," Carlisle said, shivering. "After so long in Mexico, I'd forgotten how cold Chicago can be."

"I'll never get used to the awful wind off Lake Michigan," Tyler replied. "I wish I were more like Gray. He's invigorated by the cold. Sometimes he even throws open our bedroom windows in the dead of winter!"

Carlisle, too, remembered Gray's penchant for opening windows in winter, and she laughed as they picked their way carefully across the snowy sidewalk, leaving two sets of small footprints behind them.

Moments later, they were nestled under the blankets and soft lap furs, as Gray's red-and-white cutter flew over the hard-packed snow of Randolph Street. They had almost reached Lincoln Avenue when Carlisle heard excited shouts above the cheerful jingling of the harness bells.

Tyler sat on her right, busily retying the bow around the neck of one of the rocking horses, and Carlisle looked past her. Only yards away from them a runaway carriage was careening into the intersection and straight for them. Horrified, Carlisle screamed as one of the horses pulling the coach skidded on the icy street and went down with a harsh braying, the coachman knocked from his perch just before their sleigh was struck broadside. The cutter jerked sideways on impact and went into a reckless spin. Clinging desperately to the seat, Carlisle could not hold on and felt herself being thrown into the air. The last thing she heard was Tyler's terrified scream, before she landed in something cold and icy, and knew no more.

20

The spiraling snow had turned into sleet by the time Chase Lancaster stepped from the hired hack that had brought him from the railway depot. He tilted the brim of his beaver hat to protect his face from the icy pellets as he stood at the curb and looked at the house in which his wife had taken refuge.

Even after the long, anxious days aboard the steamer and the stuffy, cigar-reeking train car to Chicago, he was angry. But no longer was his rage directed at Carlisle. His initial fury over her abandonment had fled long ago. Now he was only angry at himself for being so incredibly stupid.

He loved her. He'd loved her from the beginning. He'd never acted rationally where she was concerned. Now he dragged his feet like a recalcitrant child when confronted with facing her again, not sure she'd want to return to Mexico City with him. But she'd have to, he thought, steeling his resolve. He would demand that, as his wife, she must return.

Then he shook his head. No, he didn't want to force her. He'd *ask* her to come. He'd tell her he loved and needed her. If that didn't work, then he'd order her to come with him.

Decided, he opened the gate and walked up the snowy walk, his gaze on the second-story windows. Nearly every room was aglow in the night, and he wondered which one was Carlisle's. Anxious to see her, he quickened his stride, shrugging off his heavy wool cape as he reached the wide stone porch. He removed his hat, then saw the black wreath on the door. He stared at it in dismay, unthinkable explanations rocketing through his head. Carly hadn't been feeling well before she'd left Mexico City. What if the voyage made her worse?

"Oh, God," he muttered, hastily banging the gold knocker against the door. When no one answered, he tried the knob and found it unlocked.

Fear made his heart hammer as he stepped through the small vestibule into the large, elegant foyer. The big mansion was quiet, and no one was in sight. Not until he heard low, muffled weeping did he see the young maid in a black dress and white apron, huddled on a bench under the stairway.

"What's happened here? Why is the wreath on the door?" he demanded, going to her, tension making his voice harsh.

The girl was so upset she could hardly speak, but she jumped to her feet, her face swollen and blotchy. "Oh, sir, it's just so awful! The poor little babe came so early that he hardly even had a chance to live! And now our poor lady is near death herself, stricken with the childbed fever!" She cried pitiably through her words and had barely finished her explanation when Chase took the steps three at a time, suffocating with dread and disbelief. It couldn't be, not Carlisle, not their baby! Oh, God, don't let her die!

At the top of the steps, he looked frantically down the long silent hall with its line of closed doors.

"Carly!" he yelled. "Carly, where are you?"

Panic-stricken, he opened the first door he ran to, but the room was empty. Shouting his wife's name again, he came to a standstill when a door opened a short distance down the corridor. Carlisle stepped out, weeping into her cupped palms, but her sobbing stopped when she looked up and saw him.

Relief, pure and cleansing, swept through him. Carly was safe; his child was safe. Joy such as he'd never known before overwhelmed him, making him choke back his own sob.

"Chase! Chase!" she cried, running toward him. He met her, picking her up and holding her tight. He shut his eyes, thanking God as Carlisle clutched him, her cheek against his chest.

"You came," she wept brokenly against his shirtfront. "Oh, Chase, I've missed you so much."

Chase's hands trembled as he stroked her soft hair. *"Gracias a Dios,* you're all right. The girl downstairs said the baby died, and oh, *Dios,* Carly, I thought it was ours. I thought I was going to lose both of you." His voice was gruff with emotion.

"No, it's Tyler's baby." Carlisle began to cry again. "It happened nearly a week ago. A coach hit our sleigh."

"You were in an accident? Are you all right?" he asked quickly, holding her at arm's length to examine her tear-streaked face.

"Yes. I had a few bruises, but I landed in the snow. I was lucky, but Tyler, poor Tyler . . . When the

sleigh overturned, she was thrown into the street.
Chase, I don't think I can bear this! Please hold me!''

Chase's arms tightened around her. ''Shh, my love,
I'll hold you. Are you sure you're all right?''

She nodded, and Chase hesitated. ''Where's Tyler's
room?''

''Down there, at the end of the hall. Gray's with
her, and the doctor and his wife, Harriet. She's Tyler's
best friend.'' Carlisle pulled back to look at him, tears
running down her cheeks. ''The baby lived for three
days, but the poor little thing was just too tiny to
survive. Dr. Bond worked and worked to save him,
but he just couldn't, Chase. We lost him this morning, right before dawn.''

Carlisle suddenly grabbed his coat, her eyes full of
anguish. ''Tyler was holding the baby when he died,
and now she won't give him up. She won't let anyone
touch him, not even Gray. I tried to talk to her, to
make her accept it, but she's so sick with the fever
that she won't listen.''

Chase shut his eyes, feeling helpless and sick to the
depths of his soul. ''Poor Tyler. Take me to her.
Maybe I can help.''

Carlisle wiped her tears, and Chase supported her
with his arm as she struggled to pull herself together.

''I'm just so worried about Tyler,'' she cried. ''She
was so happy about the baby. She and Gray both
were.''

Inside the master bedchamber, the gas lamps were
turned very low. Gray sat on the edge of the bed,
leaning over Tyler, while the doctor and his wife hovered anxiously on the other side of the bed. Chase
led Carly to the foot of the four-poster. Tyler looked
very small and pale in the huge bed, her long auburn

hair tangled on the pillow. Chase swallowed convulsively as he saw the tiny, still bundle wrapped in a blue shawl and clutched tightly against her breast.

"Tyler, sweetheart, please let me hold the baby for a while. You need to rest now. You're very sick." Gray's voice sounded flat and dead; his face was haggard and drawn, with several days' growth of black beard.

Chase felt the most terrible knot of sorrow tighten inside his chest. It could easily have been Carlisle lying there holding her dead child, he thought, and he knew the pain that Gray was experiencing. Beside him, Carlisle wept, and he held her gently against him as the doctor tiptoed to them, his face grave.

"I'm Carly's husband," Chase told him in a hushed tone.

"Then you're Tyler's cousin? Good, I'm glad you're here. She'll need all of us, poor lamb. Gray finally persuaded her to take the laudanum, so she'll sleep soon. Then we should be able to remove the child from her." The doctor's lined face suddenly fell and he took off his wire-rimmed glasses and wiped his eyes.

Deep inside, Chase's own cry of grief fought to be heard as Tyler began to mumble to Gray again, her voice slurred by the sleeping drug.

"He has such pretty black hair, just like yours, Gray," she said. "I told Carly he'd look like you. Didn't I, Carly?" She frowned, turning her head groggily. "Carly? Are you here?"

Carlisle moved quickly to the bedside and picked up Tyler's hand.

"Yes, darling, I'm right here. He's beautiful, just like you said he'd be."

Tyler smiled a little, her eyes burning with fever. "Yes, he's the most beautiful little boy in the world," she said proudly. Then her eyes closed, and her breathing became less labored.

Carlisle bent over Tyler's hand, sobbing quietly. Harriet wept behind her, consoled by her husband. Chase watched Gray, who sat like a man of stone, staring down at his wife and son. After some time had passed, Dr. Bond moved behind Gray and laid a hand on his back.

"She's asleep now, Gray." He paused. "We're going to have to take the baby now. I'm sorry."

Gray didn't answer, didn't move. Carlisle raised her face, but no one else stirred. A moment later, Gray reached forward and put his hands on the baby. Tyler's arms tightened instinctively, and a deep, tortured sound was torn from Gray's throat.

"I don't think I can do it," he said, his voice so hoarse that it was nearly inaudible.

"Here, Gray, let me help you," Chase said quietly, but Gray didn't seem to hear. Again he attempted to take the baby, and this time Tyler's arms fell away. Very gently, Gray lifted the child into the crook of his right arm. He held it there for a long moment, gazing down upon its face, then turned quickly and handed the swaddled bundle to Dr. Bond. Without another word, he left the room with long, hurried strides.

As Harriet retucked the covers around Tyler, Carlisle cried against Chase's chest, and he was suddenly very concerned about her own condition.

"You need to rest, Carly. How long have you been up?"

"I don't know. Ever since the baby began to fail."

"She's exhausted. Put her to bed. I'll stay here with Tyler," Harriet Bond told him.

At the door, Dr. Bond handed him a dark green bottle containing laudanum. "Let your husband give you a dose of this, Carly, you hear me? We don't want you getting sick, too. Get some sleep and let Harriet and me worry about Gray and Tyler. God knows, you've done your part."

Carlisle walked obediently at Chase's side, her tears finally spent. She made no complaint as he helped her out of her gown and into bed.

"Take this. It'll help you sleep," he told her, measuring out a spoonful of the medicine. "You must think of our baby, too."

She accepted the laudanum, then reclined wearily against the pillows.

"Lie down beside me, Chase. I need you to be close."

Chase was more than ready to oblige, and he joined her in the bed, drawing her up against him. He kissed the top of her head. "I'm here now, *querida*, and I'll take care of you. Just relax and try to sleep."

"I'm afraid to close my eyes," she murmured. "I'm afraid you're a dream and you'll be gone when I wake up."

"I'm no dream," he whispered. "I'll be here, I promise you."

She slept almost at once, her body pressed against his side, and after a while, he felt his child move inside her. His grip on her tightened, and he knew he'd never leave her again, not as long as he breathed.

A soft tap on the door awakened Chase, and he sat up, groggy with drowsiness. The rapping sounded insistently, and as Chase stood up, Carlisle struggled into a sitting position.

"What's wrong? Is it Tyler?" she cried urgently, and Chase's hand found her in the darkness while he fumbled for the lamp. It flared, illuminating Carlisle's frightened face.

"No, *querida,* but someone's at the door."

"Carlisle? Mr. Lancaster? Please, you must wake up!" called a voice from outside.

"That's Harriet," Carlisle said, hugging her shoulders in the chill air as Chase quickly crossed the room and admitted the older woman.

Harriet carried an oil lamp, and the light cast flickering shadows on her tired, worried face. She was dressed in a long white flannel nightgown.

"Please forgive me for intruding, Mr. Lancaster, but I didn't know what else to do. Charles must stay with Tyler."

"Tyler's not worse, is she?" Carlisle cried from the bed.

Harriet shook her head. "No, Carly, dear, she's still sound asleep, the poor child. But Charles says she's much better. It's Gray I'm worried about. Hildie woke me a moment ago, scared to death. She says he's been drinking all night in his office, and now he's locked himself in the nursery. He won't let me in, and I don't know what to do."

"Stay here, Carly," Chase told her. "I'll see about Gray."

"But I should go! He needs me!" Carlisle protested.

"Not if he's been drinking too much. Please, Carly, I can handle this better than you can."

Leaning over her, he kissed her lips, then covered

her again before hurrying outside to where Harriet waited by the banister. Several of the gas jets were burning, and faraway, muffled crashes and the breaking of glass could be heard at the rear of the house.

Harriet led Chase toward the nursery, and he tried the brass doorknob. As Harriet had said, it was locked.

"Gray?" he called, banging on the door. "It's Chase. Let me in!"

There was no answer, and Chase turned to Harriet. "There should be a skeleton key for this door. Do you know where it's kept?"

"No, but Hildie does." She turned to the young, freckle-faced maid huddled on a nearby chair. "Run and fetch it, Hildie. Hurry!"

The sounds of destruction coming from inside the nursery continued until the maid ran up the steps again a few minutes later, the key in her hand.

"Go on now, both of you. I'll try to get him undressed and into bed."

Chase waited for them to move off down the hall. Then he turned the key and pushed open the door.

One gas jet glowed in its wall sconce near the window, though most of the large room was cloaked in deep shadows. Gray was staggering around, very drunk, clutching the neck of a whiskey bottle in one hand. He nearly tripped on the small crib lying on its side in the middle of the floor. Then as Chase watched, he flung out one arm, clearing the top of the dresser with one hard sweep, sending the neatly stacked blankets, baby cups, and toys flying in every direction. Gray cursed, lunging for the lightweight changing table, raising it over his head and sending it splintering against the wall.

Chase stood very still while Gray continued his grief-stricken rage. He knew how it felt, the hopelessness, frustration, and pain. He'd felt that way when Esteban had died saving his life, and he'd felt it when Carlisle had walked out on him.

There was nothing he could do to stop his friend's suffering, and no words would comfort him—not now, just hours after he had lost his firstborn son. Chase shut the door behind him and leaned against it, watching Gray until the distraught man stopped to catch his breath and tip the whiskey bottle to his mouth.

"Gray, you've got to stop this," he said calmly. "You're going to wake up Tyler. You don't want to do that, do you?"

His voice seemed to permeate Gray's stupor, and he lost his balance when he tried to take a step toward Chase, staggering to one side and peering blearily toward the door.

"Get the hell out of here, damn you!" he roared hoarsely. "Just leave me alone!"

He took a deep draught, and Chase moved closer. Gray was a big man, well over six feet. Ordinarily, Chase could hold his own against him, but at the moment, Gray was drunk and violent. Warily, Chase stopped a few feet away from him.

"I know this is hard, Gray, but you've got to get hold of yourself. Tyler needs you to be strong for her."

All the anger and animosity drained from Gray's face, replaced by raw, biting anguish.

"Tyler. Oh, God, Tyler wanted this baby so badly! I shouldn't have let her go out in the sleigh, but she begged me! Goddamn it, why did I have to let her go? She'll never get over this, never!''

Chase winced, aching for the bereaved man. "Yes, she will. You both will. It'll just take time—''

Gray's head jerked up, and Chase ducked as Gray suddenly hurled the bottle at him. It hit the door with a crash, spattering whiskey and shards of glass everywhere.

"What the hell do you know? You didn't lose your son, damn you to hell!''

He kicked out furiously at a small blue rocking horse, sending it skidding across the carpet to smash against the wall, then lost his balance and nearly went down. Chase grabbed his arm, and Gray let out a bellow of rage and swung a fist blindly at Chase's head.

Adroitly, Chase ducked the blow and managed to get behind Gray. He slid his arms under Gray's armpits and locked his fingers across Gray's chest. Gray heaved and bucked against Chase's grip, but his drunkenness hampered his movements, and Chase was strong enough to immobilize him. Gray cursed harshly, then collapsed to his knees in front of the window. Chase went down with him, still holding him from behind.

"Calm down, Gray, and I'll let you go. Dammit, listen to me! Tyler needs you! It's almost dawn! The sedative's going to wear off, and you've got to be there for her!''

Gray's muscles went slack, and he laid his face down on the window seat. "Oh, God, Chase, what if she dies, too? What will I do without her?''

A tortured, drunken half sob, half groan followed, and Chase let go of Gray and put a hand on his arm.

"Tyler's not going to die, Gray. Harriet says she's better," Chase told him gently, looking around until he saw the nanny's bed against the opposite wall.

"Come on, Gray, you're exhausted. Get a few hours' sleep before Tyler wakes up."

Gray seemed to come to himself then. He sat up, but was too drunk to stand. Chase got a grip on him and heaved him to his feet. Somehow he maneuvered him to the bed, and Gray collapsed on it.

"God, Chase, we wanted him so much. Why did this have to happen?" were the last words Gray muttered before he was granted the peace of unconsciousness.

Chase stood up, looking down at his grief-ravaged brother-in-law, knowing that what the exhausted man needed most was sleep. He'd gotten rid of his rage; he'd be calm in the morning.

Now Chase was the one who felt sick—an awful, lonely diminishment of spirit that threatened to shrivel his soul. He hurried back to Carlisle, and when he entered the bedchamber, she immediately sat up on the edge of the bed, looking worried.

Chase walked straight to her and dropped to his knees before her, clasping his arms around her waist and laying his cheek on her extended belly.

"Oh, God, Carly, I'm so sorry about all I put you through. I love you. I don't want anything ever to happen to you or the baby. I don't ever want to be without you again."

Her arms came around his head, and he closed his eyes as she threaded her fingers through his hair.

"I'm sorry, too, for so many things," she whispered, her lips against the top of his head.

Chase felt a desperate need to talk to her and make

her understand. "When Esteban was killed, I blamed you, because if I didn't, I would have to admit it was my own fault that he was dead. I took him there. I asked him to help me get you out. He'd still be alive if I hadn't taken him to San Miguel."

"Javier and the *guerrilleros* killed him, not you, and not me. They did it, and now they've been punished."

"I know, but I almost lost you. You don't know how I felt when Mother told me you were gone. I was angry and hurt, and afraid you wouldn't come home again. Will you, Carly? Will you come back to Mexico with me?"

"Yes, of course I will. I love you. All I want is to be with you."

Under Chase's ear, the baby kicked, a hard, hollow thump, as if he concurred with all they'd said. Chase smiled, again thanking God his child was healthy and strong, then climbed into bed and gratefully pulled his wife into his arms.

One week after he had died in his mother's arms, Gray and Tyler Kincaid's firstborn son was buried. The day was windy and cold with low, heavy snow clouds seeming to press down on the rooftops and the hearts of the mourners. Carlisle stood between Chase and Harriet Bond at the gravesite, her black mourning cape flapping while the priest presided solemnly over the tiny, foot-long casket.

Dry-eyed—for she had no more tears—she watched her brother scoop up a handful of dirt, his handsome face as bleak as the sky above them. He squeezed the half-frozen soil tightly in his fist for a moment, then dropped it into the small, oblong grave.

"Dust to dust, ashes to ashes," he repeated quietly. Then he turned and walked back to the waiting funeral coach.

Chase took Carlisle's elbow. She leaned gratefully against his arm as they followed Gray. Chase had been very protective of her, and she welcomed his new solicitousness. She needed her husband's love and support, because she ached inside for Tyler and Gray's loss. She wanted Chase to take care of her for just a little while, until she felt strong again.

The ride home from the cemetery passed in silence. All the words had been said already. No more could be done. Only time would heal the pain in their hearts.

At the house, Carlisle was glad the driveway was empty. The friends and acquaintances who'd come all through the day to offer their condolences had dispersed after the funeral. Tyler was still too weak to be up, and Gray had received the mourners by himself, standing for hours beside his son's coffin. He was exhausted.

In the foyer, Gray excused himself to join Tyler, and Chase led Carlisle into the private parlor at the rear of the house. The maids had prepared a cold repast for the family, but Carlisle could not face the prospect of food. She sat down wearily on the sofa by the fireplace, feeling chilled, both in body and in spirit.

"Do you think Gray's going to be all right? He's hardly said a word to anyone since the baby died."

Chase nodded as he picked up her black shawl and draped it around her shoulders.

"This has to be the coldest damn place I've ever

been in," he grumbled, leaning down to shovel coal onto the grate.

Carlisle smiled. The climate was a shock after the warm weather of his country, she thought. The rugged mountains, sunny patios, and balmy breezes of Mexico seemed very far away. At times she felt as if she lived in a dream. She'd longed for him, and now he was with her, gentle and attentive in a way he'd never been before. She watched him stoke the fire, his profile chiseled and beautiful, and beloved.

While she watched, he straightened and replaced the poker in its rack. He picked up a small, gold-framed photograph from those displayed on the mantel. He laughed and brought it with him when he sat down beside her. It was Gray and Tyler's wedding portrait, taken in New Orleans just after their marriage. Smiling, Carlisle looked down at her own likeness, thinking she looked absolutely livid. Tyler was dressed all in black, and Gray had an equally dark frown on his face.

"You're the only one grinning," she said to Chase.

"That's because I caught the bouquet."

"You mean you stole it from me. I was furious with you for snatching it out of my grasp the way you did."

"That's why I grabbed it—to see your green eyes snap. But as it turned out, it didn't matter which one of us caught it. Who would have thought then that we'd end up marrying each other?"

Carlisle smiled sadly. "It's hard to believe I disliked you so much and accepted Javier's stories about you and the San Miguel massacre. I was so idealistic then and eager to help the peasants of Mexico that I didn't even consider asking you what happened at the mission.''

Chase sighed. For a few moments he stared silently into the flames. ''San Miguel was a tragedy, one I don't think I'll ever get over. I'll always blame myself. *Dios,* sometimes I can't believe my own men were capable of such carnage.'' His expression changed, pain appearing clearly as if he were seeing the atrocities again.

Carlisle put her hand over his, wanting to comfort him. ''It really wasn't your fault. If you could, you would have prevented the massacre. Nothing like that happened the second time you captured San Miguel. And God knows you had good reason to take vengeance then.''

''I had a cross erected at the mine entrance as a gravestone for Esteban, did I tell you that? I hate to think of him up there alone. He should be buried at the Hacienda de los Toros. He loved the ranch so much.''

Carlisle nodded with sympathy, realizing how deeply her husband still mourned for his friend. But hadn't she felt the same awful fear and grief when she thought Tyler was going to die?

''Loving someone can be so painful sometimes,'' she murmured.

Chase put his arm around her. ''I never knew how much I would miss him.'' He reached out and touched her cheek. ''And it was even worse when you left me. I felt completely dead inside.''

''I didn't think you'd come after me,'' she said softly. ''I thought you'd be glad I was gone.''

Chase smiled and kissed her temple.

''I was mad as hell at first, believe me—at you and

Mother both. Then, after a couple of weeks of Mother and Tomas giving me disgusted looks, I realized how stupid I'd been. After that, nothing in the world could have kept me away from you."

He pulled her head against his shoulder. "Don't ever walk out on me like that again, Carly, even if I deserve it."

"I was afraid you'd send me away after the baby was born," she whispered.

Chase stroked the back of her hand. "I know. I drove you away. You hurt me, and I wanted to hurt you back. So I did and said stupid, spiteful things. But all that's over now. I'll never hurt you again, Carly, not if I can help it."

In the days that followed, Chase proved true to his words. He was good to her, thoughtful of her needs, and he held her in his arms at night, close and tender. During the daytime, they'd walk together and talk, more than they ever had before. Often they'd play chess in front of the fire, but she had yet to beat him at the game. Frequently, he put his hand atop her stomach to feel the baby move, and though she was deliriously happy, a cold, hard place in her heart wouldn't melt, for she grieved for Gray and Tyler, and for her little nephew who'd never see his mother's happy smile.

One day several weeks after the funeral, the same melancholy thoughts possessed her. Both Gray and Chase had gone on an errand, and she sat in the family parlor in a roomy ladder-back rocker. On the lawn outside the window, a deep carpet of snow glittered like millions of diamonds. A scarlet cardinal flew low to perch on the shoulder of a stone shepherdess in the

garden, and the scene reminded Carlisle of the day
Tyler had shown her a beautiful red bird she'd embroidered on a sweater for her baby.

For the last month while Tyler had recovered, Carlisle and everyone else in the house had tiptoed
through the rooms. Gray was with his wife often, but
when he wasn't, he became a silent, brooding stranger
whom Carlisle hardly knew. He guarded Tyler's sickroom like a dragon, allowing Carlisle and Chase to
visit for just a few minutes each day. The only good
news was the brief note they'd received from Stone,
informing them he was all right and on his way to
San Francisco—with a nun, of all people! But at least
he was safe, and they didn't have to worry about him
anymore.

Carlisle looked up as Harriet Bond came in from
the kitchen. She had grown to like the older woman.
Harriet was always kind and agreeable, and she was
absolutely devoted to Tyler. Actually, Harriet reminded Carlisle of Chase's mother, although Dona
Maria had a much more regal, authoritative manner.

"Good afternoon, Carlisle. Isn't it a bit chilly in
here for you?"

"No, it's really rather pleasant. The sun shining
through the windows makes it feel warm. How's Tyler
today?"

"She's feeling much better. We had a nice long
visit. In fact, she'd like you to come up and see her.
Hildie and I helped her into a chair. Gray will probably have our heads when he finds her out of bed, but
Charles insisted it would do her good. She's eager to
talk to you."

Carlisle hesitated. "Do you think she'll feel bad,

seeing me? I'm so big now. I wouldn't want to make her sad again.''

Harriet smiled. ''Tyler's a good bit stronger than you think. She won't begrudge you your child, dear. She'll mourn her own for a very long time, but she'll be happy for you.''

They walked together to the front stairs. Harriet went to join her husband in the parlor, while Carlisle proceeded upstairs alone. She continued down the hall, pausing at the open door of the nursery. All the glass and debris had been swept away and the furniture righted and repaired. Chase told her what had happened, and she shivered every time she thought about it. Never in her life, through all the years he'd raised her, had Carlisle ever seen Gray drunk.

She knocked on Tyler's door, then entered, finding the invalid in a tall-backed wing chair in front of the French doors that led to the upstairs porch. A bright yellow-and-blue patchwork quilt lay across her lap. Tyler smiled.

''Carly! I was hoping you'd come. Sometimes when Gray's working, I get so lonesome.''

Carlisle walked across the room, acutely conscious of her condition, especially when Tyler's gaze fell to her swollen stomach. She pulled a straight chair up close to Tyler and sat down, feeling shy and guilty for not having lost her baby, too. She looked up as Tyler took her hand.

''How are you feeling, Carly? You haven't been sick, have you?''

''No, I'm fine. It's you we're all concerned about. You must rest and take care of yourself.''

''Actually, I've felt much better the past couple of

days. I'm still too weak to walk by myself, but it feels good to sit here where I can see the street."

Carlisle glanced out the panes into the bare branches of trees, then down to Lincoln Avenue far below, appalled at how uncomfortable she felt. She couldn't even think of anything to say for fear of upsetting Tyler. She sat in tense dread, terrified Tyler was going to mention the baby.

"He was beautiful, wasn't he, Carlisle?" Tyler asked, her eyes on the trees outside. "He would have grown up to look just like Gray, don't you think?"

Carlisle's throat tightened, and she felt tears well in her eyes much too quickly to stop them. When her own baby moved restlessly inside her, she felt even worse.

"Tyler, please, don't," she began, dabbing at her eyes with the corner of her handkerchief. "You mustn't dwell on it, you know. The more you talk about it, the longer—"

"But I must! Don't you see? No one will talk to me about him. Not Gray, not Charles. And Harriet still grieves for her own children, so I can't talk to her about it. Everyone acts as if my baby never even existed. And he did. He was here. I held him, if only for a few days!"

Tyler sobbed, but her tears stopped almost at once. She leaned down and pressed her cheek against Carlisle's hand. "Please, Carly, I want to talk about him."

Carlisle's heart wrenched, but she stroked Tyler's hair. "Yes, he was beautiful," she whispered, forcing back her own emotion. "I got to hold him for a long time just after he was born, when Charles was tending to you. He was a good little baby."

"He didn't cry much, did he?" Tyler lifted her face, her eyes glowing with gratitude. "I was very sick, but I can remember that." She paused, then went on. "I'm just so grateful that God let me hold him and love him before he died."

"You'll have other children, Tyler," Carlisle said when Tyler began to cry again.

"But none of them will be like him. He was special because he was conceived when I first realized how much I loved Gray. He'll always be special in my heart."

"I know what you mean, Tyler. I really do. I feel that way about my baby, too. And now I know how fragile life is and how quickly things can happen. I don't know why my baby's still alive when yours isn't, and sometimes I feel so guilty about it."

Tyler looked down, biting her lip. "It shames me to say it, Carly, but at first I had such thoughts, too. Thank God, they passed quickly. My baby's gone, and though I know I'll probably envy you yours, I know I'll love him, too, because he belongs to you and Chase. But you must be very careful. You mustn't do anything dangerous."

Tyler pulled back and looked into Carlisle's tearful face as she went on. "Crying like this always makes me feel better. But when I look at Gray, my heart aches. I can see the pain in his eyes, though he won't talk about our son with me. He won't even discuss having other children. He's afraid to, I think."

"He's afraid of losing you, Tyler. I know he is. I saw him that night when you were so sick, and I'll never, ever forget the terrible look on his face."

"Then you've got to help me convince him that I'm

fine now. You must stay here and have your baby. Promise me you will.''

Carlisle nodded, unable to bring herself to refuse. ''Are you sure my confinement won't be painful for you?'' she asked hesitantly.

''Nothing you do can make the pain I feel go away. It'll always be with me. But maybe, if you have your child here, Gray will be able to see how happy a time it can be.''

''Then we'll stay, if you're sure.''

''Thank you, Carly, for understanding. Can we talk about him some more, just for a little while? Were his eyes blue?''

''Very dark blue.''

They spoke together for a very long time, smiling, weeping, and comforting each other as no one else could.

21

Carlisle hurried to the bed and snuggled under the downy bedclothes. The sheets were toasty and comfortable from the long-handled pewter bed warmer which Juana had used only moments earlier, and Carlisle wriggled down farther, watching as Chase built up the fire, then moved about the room extinguishing the lamps. Smiling at her, he undressed, then pulled the bed-curtains together to block out the chill emanating from the frosty windows.

"Oh, you're cold," Carlisle said as he joined her in the bed.

"Then you can warm me up."

Chase pulled her into his arms until they lay very close together, noses nearly touching. He began to kiss her, and Carlisle sighed contentedly, slipping her arms around his neck. They continued for a long time, enjoying the closeness, the intimacy, until the baby began to stir. Chase put his hand on Carlisle's hard belly.

"He's not sleepy," he whispered.

"He never is," Carlisle answered, laughing softly. "And you know what?"

"What?" Chase asked, his lips moving along her neck.

Shivering, Carlisle met his mouth again, their lips mingling in a tender kiss before she could continue. "We have to name the baby. We can't keep calling him 'he,' you know."

" 'He' Lancaster sounds all right to me," Chase murmured, making her laugh.

She slipped her fingers through his soft blond hair, her eyes serious. "I thought we'd name him Esteban. Would you like that?"

"Esteban would be pleased and honored." Chase smiled. "But what if he's a girl?"

"I'd like to name her after our mothers. Maria Christina. Do you like that?"

"*Sí.*"

"Oh, Chase, I can't wait to know whether we'll have a son or a daughter. What do you think will happen?"

"I think you need to be more careful. Juana told me you went out to the gate today."

"I only went to meet the letter carrier, and the walk was cleared of snow."

Chase tightened his arms around her. "I'm just so afraid you'll fall or have another accident," he muttered into her hair.

"Don't worry so much, Chase, really. I'm being extra careful," Carlisle reassured him. "And I don't think I'll have much trouble having the baby. Gray says that childbirth came very easy for our mother. He said she had me so fast they didn't even have time to call the doctor. My father delivered me. I hope I'll have that easy a time, too."

"Yes. I just hope you and the baby will be all right."

They kissed again, and Carlisle closed her eyes, feeling so warm and secure in her husband's strong arms that she drifted off into slumber, despite the way her child moved and kicked tirelessly inside her.

A few nights later, Chase sat in the dining room. He drank from his crystal water goblet and listened to Gray explain the details of their newly negotiated contract to Tyler and Carlisle. When Tyler had first come to Chicago, a little over a year before, she had intended to rook Gray out of enough money to buy back her father's plantation. Her plan had been as ingenious as it was dishonest, a scheme she had learned from Chase's own unscrupulous father. Luckily, Gray had seen through her deception, but now, with an ironic twist of fate, her plot had become a lucrative reality for both Gray's railroad enterprises and the government of Mexico.

"So, my love, your idea to lay railroad tracks between Monterrey and the Texas border wasn't such a bad one," Gray said, smiling at his wife.

"It seems so much longer than a year ago that Harriet and I tried to swindle you," Tyler said, blushing slightly. "Instead, I fell in love with you. Whoever would have thought things would end up this way?"

Gray raised her fingertips to his lips. "I'm a lucky man."

"If there's a railroad to the Hacienda de los Toros, you can come visit us without having to take a steamer," Carlisle interjected eagerly. "And Gray's private car would make it a comfortable trip for you. You do intend to come see us, don't you?''

"Yes, but I hope you're still planning to stay here for a while after the baby's born," Tyler said seriously, looking first at Carlisle, then at Chase. "We'd be so pleased if you would."

"We'll stay as long as Carlisle wants to," Chase answered, "though eventually I'll have to return. I've been making some important contacts for President Juarez here, but I'm still neglecting my duties in Mexico City."

"It won't be long now," Carlisle murmured, smiling at him.

Chase looked down to where her slender hand rested on the mound of her abdomen. She was nearing her time, and he wasn't sure if she could grow any larger. In fact, he wasn't at all sure he'd ever seen any other woman quite so big with child. Nor had he seen one who looked so incredibly beautiful during her pregnancy.

Once Tyler had started to feel better and join the family downstairs, Carlisle had settled down and begun to behave like her old self. His dread of the birth had lessened to some degree, but the mere thought of Carlisle going through the excruciating pain shook him to the marrow. And her time was close. On and off for the past few days, she'd had cramps and false alarms. Although Charles Bond was standing by for their call, Chase felt more anxious with every passing day.

He reached for Carlisle's hand beneath the table. She smiled into his eyes and squeezed his fingers. His heart melted, and he struggled with his need for her. He wanted to make love to her desperately, but he didn't dare. *Dios,* each night since he'd come to Chicago he'd slept with her in his arms, tortured by the feel of her satiny skin and silky hair. But he wouldn't dare do anything to hurt her or the baby. After what had happened to Tyler, he wasn't about to take any chances.

"Now if only we would get another letter from Stone—" Carlisle began, then stopped in midsentence.

Chase sat up, alarmed when her grip on his hand tightened considerably.

"What is it? Cramps again?"

"No, it feels different this time."

When Carlisle suddenly doubled over at the waist, groaning, Chase began to panic. He shot to his feet, quickly helping her out of the chair, while Gray and Tyler both rose in concern.

"Good God, it's time!" he cried. "Carly, can you walk? Should I carry you?"

Carlisle clung wordlessly to his arm as the pain continued to rip through her, and Tyler took charge, coming around the table and supporting Carlisle's elbow.

"Gray, hurry and fetch Charles! And bring Harriet, too! Chase, come on, we'll get her upstairs and into bed. Carly, dear, do you think you can walk?"

"I don't know. Oh—"

Without waiting a moment longer, Chase scooped his wife into his arms. As Gray ran for the stables, Chase hurriedly carried Carlisle up the stairs. She writhed against him as another pain gripped her, and he rushed down the hall to their bedchamber, surprising Juana, on her knees, lighting the fire. He ignored the shocked maid, striding to the bed, which had already been turned back for the night.

"It's going to be all right, Carly. The doctor's coming," he told her, lowering her gently to the bed. "I'm right here, and so is Tyler."

Carlisle clutched his hand. "Chase, I'm scared. It hurts so much."

Her words were swept away by pain, and she held her belly, her face contorted with agony.

"Oh, dear God," Chase muttered, holding both her hands and looking around frantically for help.

Behind him, Tyler calmly ordered Juana downstairs for hot water and towels, then moved to a place across the bed from Chase. Carlisle reached out to grasp Tyler's hand, and her pain seemed to ease. Almost at once, however, she cried out, squeezing tightly.

"Chase! It's coming now, it's coming now, I tell you! I can feel it!"

Ashen-faced, Chase looked across at Tyler and found his cousin's face mirroring his own distress.

"*Dios,* Tyler!" he cried frantically. "What are we going to do?"

Tyler looked at him, then began to roll up her sleeves. "We're going to get her ready for Charles, I guess, and if we have to, we're going to deliver your baby ourselves."

"Chase, Chase!"

Carlisle's cries made Chase forget about Tyler. He leaned down and held his wife as another contraction racked her. He smoothed her hair away from her forehead and tried to overcome his own fear.

"We're right here, Carly. Everything's going to be all right, sweetheart. Just try to relax." Aside to Tyler, he hissed impatiently, "Send someone else after the goddamn doctor, for Christ's sake!"

"There's no time," Tyler told him as she loosened the buttons on Carly's gown and began to untie the ribbons of her petticoats. "I don't know why it's coming so fast, but apparently she's having it right now! Quick, pull off the top sheet. I'll get her undressed so I can examine her."

"Oh, God, Tyler, do you know what you're doing?" Chase cried, jerking back the top sheet.

"Yes, of course. You know I've helped Charles with several birthings. Usually the pains last for hours, but it looks like Carlisle is going to have her babies as fast as her mother did. Just hold on to her and talk to her so she doesn't panic." As she finally managed to pull away Carlisle's garments, she gasped in dismay. "Oh, Lord have mercy. Hildie!" She turned to her maid. "Fetch me my sewing scissors. Run, run!"

Chase looked down at the foot of the bed where Tyler worked, her face flushed and worried.

"Oh, God, please," he muttered, then shouted at the maid hovering at Tyler's elbow. "Juana! Where's the blasted doctor? Go see if he's coming!"

"No, Juana, don't!" Tyler countermanded firmly. "Stay here in case I need you. The baby's coming right now. He's not waiting for anybody. Talk to Carly, Chase. Tell her it's going to be all right."

Chase felt the unfamiliar pangs of complete helplessness, but all he could think about was the horrible pain racking Carlisle's slight body.

"Carly, hold on to me, sweetheart. We're going to do this together. Tyler's helping us, and Gray and the doctor will be here any minute."

Carlisle tossed her head from side to side, her face

lined with perspiration. "It hurts so bad, Chase. I don't think I can stand it—"

"Yes, you can! I'm going to help you!" He breathed easier as the hurt subsided and Carlisle collapsed weakly against the pillows. He quickly bathed her face and throat with the wet towel Juana thrust into his hands.

"I can see the baby's head," Tyler cried excitedly. "But she's going to have to help, Chase! When the next pain comes, tell her to try to push. Charles told me that once the head emerges, it's easier for the mother. I remember him saying that."

"Oh, my God, this is it. I'll never touch Carly again, I swear it! I'll never put her through anything like this again," Chase muttered hoarsely as Carlisle jerked spasmodically in his embrace, her face twisted with effort. He put his arms around her shoulders.

"You've got to help, *querida*," he whispered. "You've got to try to push so Tyler can get hold of the baby. Carly, can you hear me?"

"Yes, yes, I'm trying!" She moaned again, teeth gritted, every muscle straining as she bore down.

"That's right. That's good," Chase murmured, wiping more sweat off her face. But as soon as her agony faded, it began afresh.

"God in heaven, Tyler, how long does she have to suffer like this!"

"Just a little more, and I can help her. Push, Carly, dear, you have to. Try again."

Carlisle strained until her face turned dark, crimson red.

At the foot of the bed, Tyler cried out in wonder, "Oh, Chase, it's a boy!"

As Tyler quickly wrapped the baby in a soft blanket, Chase looked down at Carlisle, so relieved he could barely find words. A weak, gurgling cry filled the room, and he smiled, gently wiping Carlisle's tears.

"It's over, *querida*. We have a son."

"Is he all right?" Carlisle whispered, wetting parched lips.

"Yes, he's fine," Tyler answered as she laid a tightly swaddled bundle in Carlisle's arms. Carlisle opened the blanket, smiling weakly when she saw the little face.

"He's got red hair like me, Chase. Look at him, he's beautiful."

Chase looked at the beet-red, wrinkled face of the wriggling infant, thinking his son looked like a tiny old man. But the wonder of what he'd witnessed began to sink in. He reached down to touch the tiny fingers, and the small hand squeezed hard upon his fingertip.

"Chase? Tyler! Something's wrong!" Carlisle gasped, and when she succumbed to another spasm, every ounce of color drained from Chase's face. Handing the child to Juana, he took Carlisle's hands again as Tyler ran to the end of the bed.

"My God, there's another one!" she cried in disbelief. "It's coming now, Chase! Help her!"

"Another what? Another baby?" Chase shouted stupidly.

"Yes, of course! Tell her to push!"

"Oh, God, God, I hate this. If we get through this. I'll never let her have any other children, I swear it!" Chase mumbled, then leaned over Carlisle, his voice softening. "Carly, *mi amada*, I'm sorry, just hang on. There's another baby coming. We've got to do it again." He groaned himself. "Push, love, you can do it. It'll be over soon."

Five minutes later, the high-pitched cry of another infant joined the shrill wailing of the one in Juana's arms. Carlisle collapsed again into Chase's embrace, totally exhausted, and Tyler laughed and held up the child. "It's another boy, Carly! You have two sons, beautiful twins!" While she worked to clean the baby, Chase held Carlisle tenderly.

"It's over, sweetheart. You can rest now." He stroked her hair gently, looking over his shoulder as Juana, Hildie, and Tyler exclaimed over his screaming sons.

"Hush now, sweetings," Tyler was crooning soothingly to one of the babies. "I know, you're a hungry little boy. You just want to meet your mama, don't you?"

At that point, Charles Bond rushed through the bedroom door, Gray on his heels.

"Don't worry, everyone! I'm here!" he cried, then looked astounded as he heard the crying infants.

Carlisle smiled weakly, and Chase and Tyler both laughed at the doctor's tardy reassurance. While the two newborn boys continued to yell loudly across the room, Chase let the others take care of the babies as he sat on the edge of the bed. He lifted Carlisle's hand to his lips.

"You made it look almost easy," he lied, smiling as he pushed back damp, curling tendrils of golden-red hair.

"I think I was made to have babies, lots of them," Carlisle whispered. But she was tired, so tired she could barely move.

"You should sleep now. You've certainly earned it, giving me two sons in one day."

Carlisle smiled, then reached out her arms as the doctor came forward with one of her children.

"He's healthy and hungry as a hunter," Dr. Bond decreed, handing the squalling child into her arms.

Carlisle took the child and opened her gown. The baby nuzzled frantically at her breast, then found her nipple with greedy, suckling noises. As she nursed her son, her husband hovered over her with a proud smile, and the most wonderful contentment descended over her. Thank you, God, she said inside her heart. Thank you for giving me these tiny little boys.

At once, her gaze went across the room to Tyler. Gray stood beside his wife, watching as Tyler wrapped Carlisle's other son in a soft white receiving blanket. The baby was still bawling at the top of his lungs, but as Tyler picked him up and snuggled him close, he quieted. Gray put his arm around Tyler as if to comfort her, but Tyler looked only at the baby, a gentle smile on her face. After a moment, she walked across the room. Beside the bed, she hesitated as if reluctant to give the baby up, but as it gurgled a protest, she sighed and looked down at Carlisle.

"They are so beautiful," she murmured, placing the child in Carlisle's other arm.

Carlisle held her two sons, pleased and happy, but her heart bled with compassion when she saw a sheen of tears in Tyler's eyes.

"Would you help me, Tyler?" she whispered. "I'm so very tired, and I'm not sure I have the strength to hold them both right now."

Tyler wiped at her eyes, then leaned low and kissed

Carlisle's cheek. Her murmur was close to Carlisle's ear.

"I should have known you'd have two, just so I'd have one to hold."

As Tyler took the child at Carlisle's breast, Carlisle looked into her brother's azure eyes. He thanked her and told her he loved her, without uttering a word. Then, when Tyler moved away with the crying baby, he leaned down and squeezed Carlisle's hand.

"Thank God, you're safe," he muttered thickly. "I was afraid for you."

As her second child began to suckle at her breast, Carlisle watched him join his wife on the sofa in the sitting area of the bedroom, draping his arm around Tyler while she cuddled the tiny babe.

"I love you," Chase said, reaching to touch his son's soft cheek. "I love you and our little ones."

"And I love you," she whispered, her heart full of joy. Their life had just begun, as had their sons'. And as she closed her eyes and welcomed her husband's gentle kiss, she knew it was going to be a wonderful life, one filled with love and warmth and wonder.

Epilogue

June 1872
Chicago, Illinois

The LaSalle Street Station was bustling with every conceivable kind of coach, dray, and freight wagon. The farewell party stood next to one of the hissing, southbound trains, and Carlisle hugged Tyler one last time.

"I wish you and Gray would change your minds and come to Mexico with us right now," she said, gazing imploringly into Tyler's eyes. "You've helped me so much these past three months, I don't know what I'll do without you."

Tyler laughed. "We'll follow within the month, I promise. But I'm worried about you and the babies. You're a born mother, just as you always said. And look at Chase—he absolutely dotes on those boys."

Carlisle followed her gaze to where Chase held their children. Both her sons slept soundly in the crooks of his arms as he and Gray said their good-byes.

"He's particularly partial to them, I must agree. That's one reason we're going home. He can't wait to show them off to his mother and Tomas." Her eyes searched Tyler's. "I hope you won't be lonely without them."

Tyler's lips curved. "I guess it's time I told you." She lowered her voice to a whisper. "I think I might be pregnant again. I haven't told Gray yet, because I want to be sure first."

Carlisle laughed and hugged her, delighted with the news. "That's wonderful! Gray will be thrilled!"

"Yes, your boys made him want his own. But wait, I've got a present for you." Tyler gestured to their driver, and Carlisle smiled as Johnny walked forward carrying Tyler's blue rocking horse.

"You might as well take it along. It's not fair for Esteban to have one when Enrico doesn't. With two, they won't fight over it."

"But you'll need it soon," Carlisle protested.

"Then you can send it back. We'll make it a family tradition, trading it back and forth each time we have a baby."

The women laughed and embraced affectionately. Then Carlisle went up on her tiptoes to hug her brother. "Take care of yourself and Tyler, and be sure and write if you hear anything else from Stone and his nun," she said, smiling. Then she grew more serious. "And thanks for being there when I needed you."

"I always will be," he answered simply. "You take care of those little boys. I've grown rather fond of them, you know."

As the train whistle sounded, shrill and impatient, Carlisle joined Chase on the outside rail platform of Gray's private Pullman coach. He'd already placed the children in the double wicker buggy, and as the train began to chug, Juana rolled the babies into the car.

Carlisle and Chase stood together, waving to Gray and Tyler until they could no longer see them, then walked inside to join their children. Juana was placing them in their matching bassinets in the guest bedroom.

Once satisfied that both boys were sleeping soundly, Chase took a firm grip on Carlisle's arm and led her purposely through the brown velvet portiere of the master bedroom. He turned her around and began unbuttoning the front of her gown.

"You're certainly wasting no time," she murmured as he impatiently tore at her bodice.

"It feels like ten years since I've been able to make love to you, and I've waited as long as I intend to. Damn these stays you wear. When we get to Mexico, I'm going to buy you some gypsy clothes. They're easier to rip off."

Giggling, Carlisle helped him with the offending garments, eager to join him beneath the bedcovers.

Naked, they lay close together, sliding their hands over each other's skin, reexploring the familiar, precious planes and hollows.

"I've missed this," Chase muttered. "God in heaven, you feel good."

Carlisle smiled and pressed closer, moaning as his touch began to inflame her.

"I thought I heard you say, the day the boys were born, that you weren't ever going to touch me again," she whispered weakly. "You swore it, if I remember right."

"I must have been out of my mind to say such a thing," he murmured breathlessly, as the train roared south toward Mexico and the Hacienda de los Toros.

The following is a selection from
DRAGON FIRE,
featuring Stone's story,
the third and final book
in Linda Ladd's "Fire" Trilogy
coming in January 1992
from Avon Books

Stone shoved back his chair. He was angrier than he had reason to be. Slokum was right—Stone had been thinking impure thoughts about the nun, probably worse ones than Slokum.

Feeling absurdly conscience-stricken, he gathered his winnings, pocketed them, then glanced out the nearest window. It had grown late; the black night was pressing like mourning bunting against the glass.

Several of the train's passengers were in the process of converting their day chairs into berths, but Sister Mary made no move to do so. She continued to sit motionlessly, her back ramrod-straight. He wondered if she were praying, and what about; then he wondered why the hell he cared.

Brows hunched down, his face took on an annoyed grimace. Maybe it was time he went outside and had a cigar. Maybe the cold night air would cool down his blood and get pretty little Sister Mary off his mind. Despite his resolve to ignore the nun, he found himself pausing beside her chair on his way down the aisle.

"Pardon me, Sister Mary, but if you'd like, I'll pull down your bed for you."

The nun opened her eyes. As their gazes met, Stone felt startled—as if she had grabbed the front of his shirt and pulled him close against her. The woman's effect on him was absolutely uncanny.

"You are very kind to think of me," she answered in her shy manner, casting her long lashes down over her magnificent sapphire eyes.

"Yeah," he muttered, one corner of his mouth quirking with a hint of irony. She wouldn't think him so kind if she knew the indecent thoughts he was entertaining. "I guess you'll have to stand up while I fix the bed, Sister."

She rose at once, demurely arranging her drab attire. Slokum was right. What a waste, a young woman as beautiful as she was garbed all in black, married for life to the Church. She should be in a man's bed, head thrown back, eyes half-closed with desire. His loins stirred as that mental image burned like a furnace blast through his veins.

Clenching his teeth, he arranged the seats to form the bottom bunk. Then he lowered the upper bed, which was suspended by chains from the car's ceiling. Finished, he stood back away from her, not offering to assist her. In his present, rather inflamed state of mind, touching her was not the thing to do. He waited silently as she placed her bamboo case on the top bunk. Then, despite her bulky dress and long veil, she stepped up lightly on the lower seat and swung herself with nimble grace onto the top berth.

From the beginning, she had brought out his protective instincts. He had considered her far too young and innocent to be traveling alone. He laughed inwardly, thinking what an unlikely guardian he would make for her. The Church would certainly frown on his cold-blooded vow to hunt down and kill Emerson Clan; and poor Sister Mary would undoubtedly wear out her rosary beads pleading for his soul.

"I hope you enjoy a restful night," he said politely. "These berths aren't too comfortable."

"Actually, this is a most luxurious bed for me. I am used to a simple pallet upon the floor."

Sister Mary smiled at him—a lovely, enchanting curve of soft, pink lips—and Stone caught himself staring at her in open-mouthed fascination, like some stricken swain. But, Lord help him, she had the most beautiful face he had ever seen. Their eyes locked with an intensity Stone understood all too well. Apparently, Sister Mary did not. Her friendly expression faded into vague uncertainty.

"Good night, Mr. Kincaid," she murmured, quickly drawing her privacy curtains together.

Apparently she had sensed his desire for her, he decided, and the realization had obviously frightened her. His passion had been aroused, all right. Stone still felt the heat warming his mind and body. Dammit, what the devil had gotten into him?

Since he had lowered himself to lusting so single-mindedly after a nun, he obviously was in need of a woman to share his bed. And there would be plenty of willing ladies around once he reached San Francisco. Meanwhile, he would do well to stay as far away from Sister Mary as he could get.

By now, most of the other passengers were abed; even Slokum had disappeared into his draped sleeper. One of the Negro porters was moving about the car, dimming the oil lamps that swung desultorily from the wall holders. Stone frowned, longing to stretch out and relax his tired muscles—but not in some closed-in, coffin-like bunk, one that was nowhere big enough to accommodate his long legs.

Since he had nearly been buried alive in the tunnel at Andersonville, he couldn't stand any kind of small, cramped place. He thrust his thoughts of the prison camp out of his mind as he settled into a nearby chair. It didn't matter where he spent the night, anyway. He wouldn't sleep much. He never did.

A while later, separating her curtains a mere fraction, Windsor discovered that Stone Kincaid had arisen from his chair and was on his way down the corridor toward the outside rear platform. At last, she thought, the chance she had been waiting for. Only livestock and purebred horses bound for the liveries of San Francisco traveled in the coach behind them. There would be no witnesses to her actions.

"Shhh, Jun-li," she whispered, her lips close to his bamboo cage. "It is time."

With great care, she hung the case across her body so that both her hands could remain free. Stone Kincaid was very strong, and much bigger than she. She could not underestimate him.

Briefly, with unwelcomed clarity, she remembered the moment he had bid her goodnight. His silvery blue eyes had radiated an intense, inner glow—a knowing, intimate look that made her uncomfortable even now.

She did not fully understand the significance of what had transpired between them in that moment, but she knew some unspoken communication had been sent to her. Unfortunately she knew little about men, especially the Americans. Hung-pin and the other disciples at the Temple of the Blue Mountain had been her friends. None of them had ever looked at her the way Stone Kincaid did.

Could it be that he had already suspected that she was not what she pretended to be? He appeared to be much more intelligent than the other westerners she had met, such as the loud-mouthed Slokum who was continually staring and grinning at her. But she could never let herself forget that Kincaid was a murderer, and very quick and dangerous if he had been able to capture Hung-pin. Her blood brother had been a master at martial arts, even better than she.

Pain touched her heart. Hung-pin had been bound hand and foot, rendered completely helpless to protect himself, while Kincaid and his friends tortured him to death. Only a coward would take another life in such a brutal, horrible way. Windsor's dainty chin angled upward, hardening with resolve. Stone Kincaid would not find her helpless.

Making sure the corridor was deserted, she slid from the bunk without a sound. Standing motionlessly, she listened. Then she pushed Jun-li's box around until it lay flat against her back where it would not trouble her if she had to use her fighting skills to subdue the big man. With the quiet tread she had mastered long ago, she glided down the aisle toward her victim.

She had nearly reached the rear door when suddenly, without warning, the train lurched to one side with such violence that Windsor was thrown backward down the aisle . . .